BlackHound

Evan M. Burgess

Book Three

For all those who gave me inspiration.
Family. Friends.
Couldn't have done it without you.

Prologue

Another wave, as big as the boat itself, pummelled against the large wooden craft. The boards moaned on its surface, its sails billowed angrily in the whipping wind and water ran down its various beams, ropes and boarded surfaces, making it seem as though the craft was in pain and bleeding. An unnatural orange light covered the surface of the main ship, the source of which was uncertain, originating from somewhere up in the tangle of ropes and crossbeams above the deck of the ship.

"Where is he?" a man drenched with seawater cried hoarsely. "By the Homeland, *where is he?*"

"I don't know, sir," his inferior called out to him, stumbling as another wave struck the massive boat. "Perhaps he still down below, sir!"

The first man's curt reply was drowned out by an even louder noise. Both men looked out to sea to watch in horror as a similar boat next to theirs was cracked in half by a giant, twisting body. The men on that boat were sent flying as the ship crumbled into nothing more than floating shrapnel. The finned, slimy body twisted back underwater, hardly a dent in its surface despite the arrows and spears the men on the ships hurled at it.

The creature reared back up out of the water, peering up out of the depths with feral eyes, sizing up each ship as if to decide which one it would destroy next. It flexed the fins running along its back, treading water with a pair of spiked flippers at the thickest part of its body. Blinking through two separate eyelids, it sank back into the depths.

Suddenly, all was still.

Not a word was shared as the deck-hands looked around at each other and across the black water to the other boats surrounding. The sergeant walked over to his inferior as quiet as he could, as if the slightest sound would cause the sea-serpent to strike again.

The sergeant seized the man and gave him a shake. "Where is he, where is the Commander?"

"Down below, sir, most likely! He could still be sleeping."

"Blast this all!" The sergeant turned to the sea, casting his eyes across the water. He let go of his inferior. "How can he still be sleeping? Fine, so be it. If he won't come up, I guess I'll have to take leadership. You there, man the ballista," he pointed at a baffled soldier standing on the deck of the ship. "And you—grab a spear and try to kill the beast as it emerges."

The man he had just ordered stood where he was, his eyes growing even wider. He shook his head, looking past the sergeant.

"What are you doing?" the sergeant demanded, the man still stood still. "What are you looking at—?"

The sergeant sensed somebody behind him and wheeled around to face a new man. He was dressed entirely in black, from his high-collared tunic to his large, metal-studded boots. His chest was thick, reinforced by his breastplate and hauberk underneath, despite the fact he wasn't in battle. He wore his sleeves only to his forearms, leaving dark brown skin exposed. Indeed, his face was the same colour as his arms: dark as molasses. Everybody's skin on the ship was the same hue.

The sergeant faltered and for a moment forgot about the sea-serpent.

"What exactly are you doing, Sergeant?" the Commander asked. "Could you possibly be taking action when no such orders were commanded of you?" He walked meticulously towards the sergeant, his eyes never leaving the other's for a moment. "Could you possibly be trying to act above my authority? Nothing permits you do to such a thing, not even in a situation such as this. This is treachery..."

To the right, a churning appeared in the depths. Bubbles appeared on the surface as a large area of the ocean began to froth. Suddenly, the sea-serpent reappeared, jutting up like a striking snake. It coiled its body, opened its great maw, showing teeth that were each as big as a man's arm. With a loud, hideous hiss, it flexed its smooth body and struck the boat next to the Commander and Sergeant's.

The serpent clamped its jaws around the ship's main mast and held tight, using its momentum to flip the boat over its starboard side. Then, it wrapped its coils around the ship and squeezed. The men standing on the deck were thrown into the churning depths of the sea while those inside were crushed between wooden beams and briny flesh. With half the vessel still in its vicelike grasp, the sea-serpent submerged itself back into the depths of the rolling waves.

The sergeant winced, less disturbed by what he had just witnessed than the Commander's unnervingly calm manner.

"Understand, Commander, I was only—only," the sergeant stuttered, "only doing what any man should do! You weren't there to command, so I had to do what was necessary."

The Commander cleared the distance between him and the sergeant in three graceful, decisive strides. "Let me make it *clear* to you, under *no* circumstances is anybody permitted to go against my orders, let alone direct *my* soldiers without first asking my consent. Your authority is nothing compared to mine. You insult me, your fellow soldiers and indeed the Homeland. Is this clear?"

"Yes, sir, I understand."

"Very good." The Leader turned away from him, his dark eyes narrowed to slits. "Now, what's the problem here? For what reason was I awoken from my rest?"

A ripple on the surface of the water next to the Commander's ship rippled unnaturally, betraying the sea-serpents presence before it arose from the depths once again. It glared down at the Commander and his crew, easily as tall as the mast of their very ship. It cocked its head at them, as if amused.

The Leader scrutinized it back. He pulled something out of his pocket, never breaking eye contact with the beast. It was an orb that fit perfectly in his palm, a sickly, pulsating green that echoed some sort of unnatural power.

The leader fingered the small ball in his hand for a moment, biting his lip. The sea-serpent reared back, opening its jaws wide once again as it prepared to attack. Its fins fanned out and its gills flared as it prepped to strike. The Leader hurled the orb at the creature, throwing it side-arm at a velocity and precision that was ordinarily impossible, uttering a small incantation as he did.

The orb, travelling as fast and straight as an arrow, hit the sea-serpent roughly in its chest. There was a flash of painful, brilliant green, a terrible crackling noise and the intense smell of burning flesh. An inhuman scream managed to escape through the tumultuous explosion caused by the little orb. A form writhed through a thick cloud and green flame clung to that crippled, mangled body and refused to let go.

Bone glinted through the choking smoke and when the sea-serpent careened towards the sea, it was evident it was dead. Half its head was missing and its innards were showing or otherwise protruding through a massive hole that took up half its chest. Pieces of it were sent flying several hundred feet over the ocean, the still-burning pieces illuminating hundreds of similar massive ships for a brief moment. The size of the convoy was daunting.

With many sickening *splooshing* sounds, the sea-monster and its separate pieces fell back into the ocean. There it stayed; floating on the surface, green flame dancing vehemently on its mangled corpse. Plumes of smoke wafted high into the air, causing every man on the ship to cover their face with their tunics to try and block out the smell of burning fish.

The leader glanced at a spike that had landed near him, a piece of its fin that had blown off. Sickly blood began to ooze out of it. Although the creature was dead, the screams of those still in the water—which was many—could still be heard over the sizzling of the sea-serpent's body, the rain doing little to calm the magic fires.

"That solves *that* problem," the Leader whispered to himself as the sergeant rushed over to congratulate or otherwise apologize. "And now for *this* problem." He picked up the spike near his feet in an instant and brought it up into the awaiting chin of his own sergeant, pointed end first.

He turned away as the sergeant fell over and onto the wooden planks of the ship. "You there—inform Arbom that he is now second in command." The one who had served the sergeant nodded, his face as pale as the moon above. "Oh, and also," he added, gesturing to the growing puddle of blood that surrounded the sergeant's corpse, "clean that up once you're done."

"Leader, what of those still in the water? If we keep our course, they will surely perish. Should we drop anchor and pluck them from the water?"

The Leader paused, sighing loudly. In a single, simple moment, he decided their fate. "No, leave them," he said coldly, turning towards the thick door that led to his quarters at the back of the ship. "We have more than enough troops and rescuing them will only slow us down."

"Yes, sir."

The Leader reflected what the purpose of this trip was for. He was anticipating the day when he would land upon the new continent's shore, this time with a full fleet, enough to conquer an awaiting world.

Chapter 1

Kael studied the landscape beneath them. They had left Vallenfend, Kael's home city, just over two days ago, and had been flying ever since. It would have been nice to stay in the city—or at least Shatterbreath's cave—for a while longer, but they needed to get back to their quest. They needed to recruit more cities to join their cause.

To defend against the BlackHound Empire.

And after flying for two days, he was expecting to recognize the landscape as they travelled eastward. He didn't.

"Shatterbreath," he yelled over her wing beats, "where are we? Aren't we going back to the Fallenfeld area?" He pulled out his water skin.

"In due time," she replied. "We're making a quick detour south, along the ocean."

"What for?"

"To visit an old friend." Kael choked on his gulp of water. Shatterbreath continued. "I've been reflecting on the prisoner's words. He said the BlackHound Empire would have a way to deal with me, one dragon. But what about two?"

Kael gritted his teeth. *A second dragon?* Although he had been surrounded by dragons in Shatterbreath's memories, the thought of being near another was extremely unnerving. Kael had grown used to Shatterbreath's presence and attitude but he had no idea what a new dragon would present. He began to worry, but he kept his peace.

It wasn't until the ocean lingered off in the distance ahead of them did Kael voice his concern.

"Do you think it's a good idea, visiting another dragon?" he said. "What if it's not...friendly."

"He's friendly," Shatterbreath replied.

"How can you be sure? When was the last time you saw him? What if he's changed?"

Shatterbreath snorted, sending a plume of smoke washing over Kael. He coughed. "Do not fret, Tiny," she said with a laugh, "I am an Elder Dragon! He will not dare harm me."

"You?" Kael's voice cracked. "I wouldn't expect a dragon to harm one of its own kind. It's me I'm worried about."

"There there, Tiny, be quiet. All will be fine."

The ground below gave way to a sheer cliff, with the ocean pounding at its base. Shatterbreath angled her wings and they dipped closer to the churning blue water. Kael studied his surroundings.

The cliffs were sharp and jagged. A fall from the top would mean certain death. The constant pounding of the water at the cliffs' feet permeated the air in a heavy mist and the rocky surface of the precipice glistened with moisture and green moss. Red crabs skittered along the cliff wall and the cries of gulls could be heard over the roar of the ocean.

Kael took a deep breath. He loved the ocean. Even under the circumstances of them being there, he had to pause to appreciate the beauty of the scene.

Shatterbreath roared and banked sharply, causing Kael to rock to one side. He cursed and tightened his grip as they raced towards the cliff wall where a gaping cave awaited.

She alighted in the cave and walked deeper into it with Kael still riding between her shoulders. Like the cliff walls, it was covered in sage moss and lichens. Coupled with the smoother stones and lack of stalagmites, the cave had a softer, damper feeling to it than Shatterbreaths. The smell was different as well. It smelled of sea and fish and a similar musk to Shatterbreath's but more...masculine.

"Silverstain?" Shatterbreath called out. "Silverstain? Where are you? I can smell you."

Though there were no glowing stones, the light of the fading sun pouring through the cave's entrance was more than enough to illuminate a large figure as it shuffled. Altogether, the other dragon became apparent.

It hefted itself up onto all fours and stretched briefly before turning its pine-green muzzle towards Shatterbreath. Overall, the dragon held the same build as Shatterbreath, if not thicker around the chest and lacking around his wings. But otherwise, the resemblance stopped there. Its wings had a more sparrow-like aspect to them and instead of spines it had a sail-like crest running the length of its back. As well, the dragon was nearly half the size of Shatterbreath, proving that he was also much younger as well.

The dragon cocked its head. It took a step forward and a patch of silver splayed across its chest shimmered in the harsh light—as if it had a stain of silver, true to its name. Kael noted that the dragon's pair of horns was smooth, white and shiny in contrast to Shatterbreath's, which were black and cracked.

"Shatterbreath," the dragon said. His voice was as gentle as a forest breeze. "It has been a long time since we have met. How long *has* it been?"

"Long indeed, Silverstain."

Silverstain's calm gaze washed over Shatterbreath. He stood with his chest puffed out and head held high, one foreleg placed carefully in front of the other. "Something is wrong, Shatterbreath. Something has happened to you." Silverstain glanced fleetingly at Kael. "Judging by that human on your back, something has gone *drastically* wrong."

"I'm going to be curt," Shatterbreath barked. "There is an empire coming from overseas—one which threatens to dominate this land."

"I know."

"You do?" Shatterbreath and Kael said in unison.

Silverstain squinted at Kael, his tail tracing small shapes in the air. "Yes. They came to me, you know." His voice grew softer as he talked. "They asked me to stay out of their way."

"And?" Shatterbreath growled.

Silverstain swayed his head. "I agreed, of course."

"Just like that?"

"No," Silverstain scoffed, matching Shatterbreath's firm tone. "I was reluctant to...fraternize with their human peacekeepers, but we settled on an agreement."

"What is that?"

Silverstain hunch his shoulders.

Shatterbreath growled. "What was your agreement?" she tried again.

"What about you?" Silverstain countered. "Why is that human on your back? Why are you so concerned about an empire? The humans will only kill each other, as is their nature. You aren't...worried for them, are you?"

"My motives are unimportant. The significance of this is obviously beyond your grasp, hatchling." Shatterbreath rose to her full height, horns grazing the ceiling. "Human the invaders may be, but they will kill anything that they consider a threat nevertheless— human or dragon alike. You will be slain. *We* will be slain, Silverstain. Our..." Shatterbreath hesitated and glanced backwards at Kael, jaw still open. "Our species is dying. Here we have a chance to prolong extinction or halt it entirely."

"Saving this land—saving the humans—won't save our kind," Silverstain said wearily. "Trying to stop the invasion is suicide. Your motifs *don't* matter to me, Shatterbreath. You may be willing to die for that morsel on your back, but I am not. I will not fight in *their* war."

Shatterbreath growled. "Yes, you will."

"No, I *won't,*" Silverstain hissed.

"As an Elder Dragon, I demand you to obey! You will fight along my side, until either victory or death."

Silverstain walked a few paces, turning so that he faced away from Shatterbreath. He pawed as something on the cave floor. "Look at you, Shatterbreath," he whispered, "you've let your horns grow black and cracked. By Darion's Crest, you're letting a *human ride you.* I don't even want to know what those things are in your wing. Shatterbreath, you're not the dragon you used to be. You're not the dragon you *should* be."

Shatterbreath winced. Kael felt her muscles relax beneath him. She considered herself, twisting her head and flexing her injured wing. For a heartbeat, it seemed as though she was going to accept Silverstain's comment. Instead, his observations made her angry.

Stone cracked under her tail as she slammed it down. She stood with her shoulders low, rear end high in a pouncing position. Kael caught his breath, at once realizing that being on her back was the *worst* place to be right then. In a matter of seconds, he managed to untie his pack from her shoulders. She released a bone-rattling snarl as he slid to the ground.

"My last warning, Silverstain," she hissed. "You *will* fight!"

Silverstain's calm disposition vanished in less than a second. "Make me!" he roared in reply.

Kael dove out of the way as Shatterbreath leapt at the other dragon. The whole cave shuddered as one massive body collided with the other. From the ceiling, a boulder the size of Kael's head was wrenched lose and he had to dodge out of the way to avoid it.

Unsure what to do, Kael crouched low, shield in one hand and pack in the other, watching the two fighting dragons. As they tumbled, Kael noticed that Shatterbreath had a hold of Silverstain's shoulder with her jaws. The smaller dragon writhed, trying everything to get free of her grasp.

Shatterbreath wrenched her head and with it, flung Silverstain across the room. He collided with the cave wall, sending more rocks hailing from the ceiling.

Wincing, Silverstain picked himself up, bleeding from the shoulder. Shatterbreath took a step towards him, thrashing her tail. Blood oozing from her mouth, she snarled. Eyes wide, pupils dilated, Silverstain stared at her, teeth bared. He glanced towards the cave entrance.

Kael hesitated. *Uh oh.*

Silverstain bolted for the entrance—right where Kael was standing. Unsure what else to do, Kael held his shield close to his body gritted his teeth, bracing for the impact.

Kael witnessed in altered time as the dragon bounded over him. He looked up to see a dark grey neck soaring overhead, closely followed by a heaving chest dappled with silver. One scaly foreleg passed by innocently, but the second clipped Kael, sending him reeling. A hind foot caught him completely. Kael's breath was ripped from his chest as Silverstain quite literally kicked him. The sense of weightlessness dominated all others as Kael soared through the air.

At first, Kael didn't know what was worse, the kick or the landing. He hit the floor square on his back, winding him further. His shield had bashed into his nose as well, so blood flowed freely from it, ruining his clean tunic.

Kael craned his neck to see Silverstain unfurl his wings at the mouth of the cave and take off into the sun. A shuffle and grunt alerted him of something coming at his feet. Before Kael could react, Shatterbreath jumped clear over him, giving him a fine view of her underbelly.

The ground shuddered as she landed. With two more bounds, she too was airborne and gone. Kael watched her go in disdain. *What about me?*

Carefully, he picked himself up and patted himself down. He ribs had been setting nicely, but once again, when he took a breath, he could feel things shifting around in his chest—which wasn't terribly comfortable. His shield was dented even more as well. So hard was the blow Silverstain had given that the outside surface had almost gone concave.

He sighed when he shook his pack, which he had been holding between his shield and himself. Sounded like something was broken in there too. *Splendid.*

Kael moved to the front of the cave and looked around outside, worried for Shatterbreath. He couldn't see her above the ocean, but he could hear her and Silverstain still somewhere overhead. They must have moved over land. Silverstain must have been hoping for a quick aerial getaway, but even with a bad wing, Shatterbreath would still be faster.

Kael needed to get to her.

The cliffs on either side were jagged and craggy—good for climbing, but also extremely dangerous. One slip or loose rock would mean a deadly vertical drop.

Kael threw his pack and shield over his back. He scooted closer to the ledge and reached out, grabbing hold of a protruding rock. After finding secure footings, Kael exhaled and looked up. There was a long way to go.

Trying not to think about the drop underneath him, Kael started to scale the cliff wall. Still the sounds of fighting dragons emanated over the ledge above. Roars, snarling and a *whooshing* Kael guessed was either dragon breathing fire.

Several feet above where he started, Kael's hand slipped on a loose rock. He lisped to one side, losing his grip with one of his feet as well, so that he hung sticking out from the cliff's face. He couldn't help but to look down. A huge sense of vertigo washed over Kael. The ocean stretched far, far below him, the waves slamming against the cliff's base, as if trying to rattle him off.

Kael gritted his teeth and got a better hold. He pressed himself close, head resting against some moss. *Why didn't I just wait in the cave?* Kael doubted he would be any help anyway. It probably would have been smarter to wait...

Somewhere nearby, a gull cried, as if to mock Kael. He hated seagulls. Summing up his courage, Kael reached up and caught hold of some scraggly branches and pulled himself up a few more feet.

Doubling his effort, Kael reached the top of the ledge within minutes. His hands bled from several cuts given by the sharp rocks and his entire upper body ached, but that was next to his main concern. Shatterbreath.

On cue, two shapes ripped by overhead, so close that the wind currents from them knocked Kael over. He picked himself up to watch Shatterbreath grab hold of Silverstain's tail in the air. They both crash-landed on the ground.

Dodging scorched earth, Kael sprinted to them. Evidence of their ongoing fight was spread across the grassy cliff-side plain. Gouges in the earth, burning grass and blood splotches. He wasn't sure how he could, but Kael had it set in his mind to assist Shatterbreath in some way.

The two dragons were closer now. Kael threw down his pack, brandished his shield and reached for his mace. It wasn't there. He cursed; it must have fallen off at some point. Thinking of no other solution, Kael unsheathed his sword—still broken from his skirmish with the bandits—and held it tight in his grip.

Dodging under Shatterbreath's tail, Kael circled them both, giving a wide berth to avoid wings and tails. He scanned Silverstain's armoured hide, looking for any opportunity to strike. Kael hesitated when his eyes resting on the dragon's thigh. Kael remembered how Vert has slashed Shatterbreath across the leg those many months ago. *That will do.*

Kael moved in. Clutching the handle with both hands, he plunged the half-foot of jagged metal into Silverstain's leg. The dragon howled in pain, blood gushing from the wound. Kael then remembered what happened *after* Vert had slashed Shatterbreath. She had kicked him.

Kael dove to the side just as Silverstain tried to do just that. The dragon then turned his attention away from Shatterbreath to Kael, snarling and flaring his wings. Silverstain took a deep breath, fire brimming at the back of his throat. Kael gasped and curled up behind his shield.

Fire erupted from the dragon's mouth, striking Kael's shield and spreading in all directions. Kael could feel the metal heat up behind his arm. It started to glow red hot. He gritted his teeth, doing his best to ignore the pain in his arm which was pressed flush against the inside of the shield.

The fire stopped abruptly. Shatterbreath had rammed into Silverstain, causing his fire to shoot into the air as opposed to at Kael. In response, Kael hurled his shield away, which sizzled in the grass. He rubbed his arm, which was burnt, but not too badly, then turned his attention to the two dragons.

Shatterbreath halted Silverstain's fire by pressing a paw to his neck. She sat on top of him, with her other foreleg resting on his chest. She had him pinned.

"This is your last chance!" Shatterbreath snarled. "Join us or die! I command you as an Elder Dragon!"

"I can't," he wheezed. "They promised me... If I leave them alone..."

Shatterbreath loosened the pressure on Silverstain's neck. Kael walked over to her, feeling quite flustered. "You will betray your species? For what?! What did they promise you?" she roared.

"I haven't betrayed anyone." Silverstain looked her in the eye. "*You* are the one who has betrayed our species. You are a broken dragon, Shatterbreath. You have submitted your authority through your grief."

Shatterbreath placed one of her hind paws on his stomach with a growl. Silverstain whimpered and coughed. "What did they promise you?" she tried again.

Silverstain shook his head. Shatterbreath curled her claws, digging them into his neck, chest and stomach. He winced.

"What did they promise you?!"

"If I complied to leave them alone," Silverstain said submissively, "they promised me safety. They promised to leave my family and me alone. Forever. You know how hard that is to get?"

She huffed and pulled away from him. He rolled onto his belly, coughing. She considered him from a distance. "You have no family, you naive hatchling."

The green dragon stopped his coughing. His crest went flat and he refused to meet Shatterbreath's eyes. It almost seemed like he was blushing. "I was hoping you'd be my family, Shatterbreath."

Kael thought her answer would be immediate, but she hesitated. Her tail went limp and she pulled her wings in tighter. For a moment, she considered what he said. Kael could read her thoughts on her muzzle. She was thinking about what it would be like to start a new life with Silverstain. No more strife, no more toil. *Safety.*

Worried, Kael placed a hand on her thigh. The muscles underneath his fingers tightened. Her wings twitched and her breath came shallow. Slowly, she turned her head towards him. Her expression softened and she curled her tail around him.

"I already have a family," she said with conviction.

Silverstain's tail, which had been tracing invisible shapes, stopped dead still. His expression, however, remained steady. "Then we are both standing our ground."

Shatterbreath frowned. "Indeed so." She gestured to Kael to climb aboard. He did so silently. "Consider yourself fortunate I am deciding to spare you."

"It was...a pleasure, Elder," he said unfazed.

Shatterbreath's eyes narrowed. "I hope we may see each other again one day." She turned away. *"Soon."*

"Don't worry," Silverstain replied. "We will."

Kael wondered at the dragon's words. If Shatterbreath was confused by his last comment, she didn't show it. With a grunt, she lifted off into the air and picked up Kael's pack and shield before flying away.

Silverstain watched them go.

Kael kept silent as he rode on Shatterbreath's back. He could feel the tension in her muscles beneath him. She was upset. It wouldn't take someone who had been around her as long as him to figure that out. Her wing strokes were heavy, her tail thrashed and whenever there was a bird nearby, she would veer off course to chase it down and eat it.

Then, altogether, she fell still as she caught a thermal. She soared like a hawk, wasting no energy. Kael reached out and put a hand to her neck.

"Shatterbreath?" She winced. "Are you okay?"

She didn't look back but began to tremble.

"D—do you want to talk about it?"

"No," she snapped. As she glanced back, Kael saw a tear fall from her eye, glistening in the light of the day. Kael lost track of it as it fell to the ground far below. Her eyes were painted with grief and regret.

"I understand." He paused to listen to her breathing. "Where to next?"

"I don't know," Shatterbreath sighed. "I'll head inland. We'll hit a big city eventually."

"Sounds good." Kael leaned back. He unsheathed his broken sword, which was now caked in blood. He beamed at it. Even broken, it was still useful to him.

Maybe one day, he could get it fixed. Somehow.

Chapter 2

Kael was in Shatterbreath's vision. In colours and clarity far superior to his own eyesight, he surveyed a large town as Shatterbreath soared towards it. It was set not too far from a lake, with its castle off-centered. From up in the air, Kael could see a sizeable part of the city reserved for military use. Just outside the low walls, battalions marched to and fro and practised their archery. On top of that, the gates were opened and caravans flooded through.

"This will do," Kael said, pulling out of Shatterbreath's vision. "Land on the far side of the lake; I'll walk from there."

In no time, Kael was walking along the main caravan route towards the front gate of the city. He paused as a battalion of mountain knights rode by, gleaming in their armour. He liked that. *This city would make a wonderful ally,* he thought to himself.

Kael walked through the front gates without a problem. The guards didn't even give him a second glance as he strolled through. With a city of its size, it would take far too long to ask each person who they were, even if they were visitors.

The streets were cluttered, despite how wide they were. The buildings held a more ostentatious feeling than any others Kael had seen elsewhere, with interesting designs—both aesthetically and architecturally—that seemed less about practicality and more about outside appearance. Indeed, the people reflected the style of the buildings, wearing flashy clothing that didn't seem all too comfortable. Some women, Kael noted, wore huge wigs that closely resembled white beehives. How they could move about with something so bulky on their head was a mystery to him.

To get a better feeling for the city, Kael took a detour to pass through the markets. Aside from more of the beehive wigs and flashy clothing, they seemed to put a lot of emphasis on scarves; more than half the market held stalls reserved for just that. Strange.

The castle itself seemed to spring out of nowhere. At first glance, it wasn't hard to tell the castle was far older than any other structure in the city. It was dull gray and built square, like a gigantic cinder

17

block. But it looked study. Evidently, every other building had either been destroyed by natural causes or torn down and rebuilt in the current ostentatious style except for the castle itself. It wasn't large either, being nestle in the two- to three-story buildings around it—almost like an afterthought if anything.

However, the tall, spike-covered brick wall surrounding it was hard to ignore. Indeed, all the windows of the castle were barred and closed, giving Kael the distinct impression the local king did not want any visitors.

Before he even reached elevated platform of gate, two guards detached from their posts to intercept him.

"Whatcha doing?" one of them asked. They were both clad in full sets of armour, each holding shields. The one who had spoken was carrying a hand axe, the other a flail.

These aren't guards, they're knights! Kael took a breath, trying to look impressive in his own dented set of armour. "I have an extremely important issue I must discuss with your king. Please, let me through so I may talk to him."

"Important business?" the guard holding the flail scoffed. "And *who* might you be?"

Kael hesitated. The plaza in front of the front gate had several people walking through it. Some of them stopped to glance at the commotion. Kael was conscious of one man at the bottom of the steps staring.

"Let me talk to your king," Kael demanded.

The knight detached his axe from his waist. "Listen, knave," he sneered, poking Kael with the top of the axe, "nobody sees the Holy King. Ever."

"His divine luminescence is too brilliant for your petty mind to comprehend anyway. Only the most sacred of sacred priests are allowed to commune in his basking aura."

"Yeh, besides, rats like you belong in the streets, not in the Holy Castle."

Kael clenched his fists. He remembered he had no weapon to fight with, so he bit his tongue. "Oh, that's okay," he said with a cheery smile. "I change my mind. I don't want to see your anti-social, megalomaniac king anyway."

"What did you say?" the guard snarled.

"Whoa, my friends," a man interrupted. It was the same person who had been staring from the bottom of the steps. He held two silver coins between his fingers. "No need to make a fuss on this fine day! Have a coin for your troubles, each of you."

The guards frowned at Kael a moment longer, but then took the coins. Wearing smirks, they resumed guarding their posts.

The man ushered Kael away. "What're you doing, making the guards angry? They could have turned you into paste!" He was a small man with wide eyes and greying hair mostly hidden by his travelling cloak.

"Psh, I would have liked to see them try. They would have been roasted before they landed a punch."

"Roasted?" The man hesitated, confused. "Wh—whatever. You don't know much about Uteral, do you?"

Kael shrugged. "It doesn't matter now. I'm leaving."

"Just like that?"

"Yeah." Kael considered the man. "What's it to you?"

The man considered him right back. "This place was established by a holy man. Ever since, he's passed his kingship to his heirs as well as—some believe—his *saintlihood.*"

"Is that a word?"

"Either way, you were right when you called him a megalomaniac. That man is *definitely* not a saint. I think any one of his dozen or so wives would agree."

"Thanks for helping me out," Kael said with a sigh, "but like I said, I'm leaving."

"Wait, you aren't Kael Rundown by any chance, are you?"

Kael stopped. He glanced around the plaza. Nobody else was paying attention to them. Kael shifted his weight uneasily, considering his options. "No," he lied, "but I'm a close associate—a messenger more like."

"Ah, well then, what a fortunate coincidence! I too am a messenger. I've been looking for your friend, Kael." The width of his smile was rivalled by the length of his nose. "Sire Respu, King of Rystville, wishes to speak with you—I mean, your master—in person."

Kael raised an eyebrow, intrigued. "About what?"

"Ah, beg forgiveness, but that is between Sire Respu and Kael Rundown."

"Kael is not so trusting," Kael countered. "He cannot simply be summoned without cause. His time is precious. And so is mine." Kael turned to leave.

The messenger faltered. "News of Kael's quest has stretched far," the small man explained, "many kingdoms know of his strife. What intrigues my king, however, is Kael's...transportation."

Kael chewed his lip. "Go on."

"They say your master travels with swift speed—that he can make a four-day journey by horse in a mere day! Without arriving with any beast either."

Kael frowned and shook his head. "I know not of what you speak of."

"Of course not..." The messenger narrowed his eyes. "Kael's transportation is not Sire Respu's only interest. It would benefit Kael greatly to visit our city."

Kael gave a humble bow. "Thank you, sir. I will pass your message onto my master at once. I think he will take your words into serious consideration."

The small man shook Kael's hand. "Thank you. I will ride at once to Rystville to deliver this news! Unless, of course, Kael beats me there..."

Kael gave him a nod and half-hearted smile and then turned away. He needed to discuss his news with Shatterbreath at once.

As he replayed his conversation with the Rystville messenger in his head, Kael exited the city without realizing it first. When a shuffle nearby broke his concentration, he was surprised to find himself well on his way to the far side of the lake. The sky was overcast now, with harsh thunderclouds churning from overhead. A boom of thunder sounded off. Definitely not Shatterbreath.

Altogether, Kael became aware of somebody trailing him from behind. Pretending to still be unaware, he continued on his way, focussing on whoever was behind him. His breath caught as he realized there was more than one person. Judging from the occasional *clink*, they were armoured and possibly carrying weapons. Kael stopped.

Schwing. The distinct sound of a sword being drawn. "Do not resist," a strong voice demanded. "Or you will not be granted a quick death."

Kael glanced to either side. Men wearing ramshackle outfits quickly surrounded him. Their faces were unshaven and their eyes cold and relentless. They were not local to Uteral or any other city Kael had visited. They resembled bandits more than anything.

"Who are you?" he breathed. "What do you want from me?"

The tip of a sword rested on Kael's shoulder. Kael batted it away and spun. The man who had spoken was hardened by nature. His face was wind-beaten and his lips chapped from the relentless sun. Through his wild hair which covered the majority of his face, he scrutinized Kael with slight amusement. He seemed unbothered by the fact Kael was nearly a foot taller than he.

"I am Jtoltly, and we are bounty hunters," he said in an unfamiliar accent. He rolled his tongue as he spoke. "You my friend, have a high bounty on your head. You will make us rrrich indeed."

Kael caught his breath. *Bounty hunters?* "From whom will you claim your prize?" Kael glanced at the sky, stalling.

Jtoltly grinned. His leather glove squeaked as he tightened his grip on his sword. "Numerous sources are interested in you, Kael Rundown." Kael flinched at the mention of his name. *Had the messenger in Uteral given him away?* "None quite as much as Vallenfend it seems."

Kael wracked his brain, trying to think of a solution. With only a broken blade as his weapon, there was no way he could fight his way out. He could only wonder where Shatterbreath was.

A light pressure to the back of his neck made him stiffen. Cold metal. Kael clenched his fist.

He glanced one more time up at the angry sky, then set his expression. "I'm a powerful wizard," he bluffed, "if you dare harm me, you will feel my power."

Jtoltly laughed, placing a hand on his hip. "Oh yes? I don't believe you."

"Leave now and I won't harm any of you. I don't hold grudges easily. We can pretend this never happened. Otherwise, I'll summon a demon from the depths of that storm."

A few of the bounty hunters looked up hesitantly. Jtoltly narrowed his eyes, unsure. "...I don't believe you."

A crack of thunder sounded from overhead. Several of the men jumped. "Do you want to take that risk?" Kael asked.

Before Jtoltly could answer, Kael spun around and batted the sword at his neck away with his gauntlet. Time slowed as Kael struck the bounty hunter twice in the face, sending him reeling. But before Kael could carry through, a spasm of pain exploded through his unhealed ribs, causing him to double over. The spasm cost him and a boot from behind knocked Kael to the ground. Two men grabbed him from either side.

Jtoltly knelt down Kael's level. "You're quick, I'll give you that... But if you're such a powerful wizard," he scoffed, "why didn't you use your magic to save you?"

"You don't understand how magic works, do you?" Kael scoffed. "This is your last warning. I will summon my demon if you don't let me go."

"Then do it!" Jtoltly yelled.

Kael scowled at him. The guards were holding him too tight; there was nothing he could do.

Jtoltly grinned like a fox. "I knew it. You're nothing but a liar! Now I understand why there's a bounty on your head. Any last requests?"

That gave Kael an idea. He hung his head, defeated. "Yes," he said sadly. "I wish to hold my beautiful sword in my grasp for one last time."

Jtoltly nodded. "Of course. It is indeed a nice blade." He leaned in and removed Kael's sword from his waist. "Let him go so he may have his honour."

The guards let him go and Jtoltly unsheathed Kael's sword to pass it to him. When he pulled out only to reveal that the blade was broken, pure bemusement overtook his features. Kael took the opportunity to put his fingers to his lips and whistle.

All the bounty hunters froze, confused by what Kael had just done. Kael threw his arms high in the air. "Behold my power!" he yelled.

A roar swept across the land. Every single bounty hunter flinched. Several of them pointed into the sky behind Kael.

"Look, Jtoltly! He wasn't lying! He is a wizard!"

Jtoltly's eyes were wide.

"By the gods, we're all going to die!"

"You fools!" Jtoltly cried. "Kill him! He is the source of the demon's power!"

Now Jtoltly believed him.

Kael stomped on the bounty hunter's foot next to him and then whipped around to catch the other square in the jaw. Kael finished the first man off with a kick to the temple.

Jtoltly rushed at Kael, who managed to defect all the slashes the man threw at him with his vambraces. Jtoltly tripped Kael with a low swing. Enraged, the bounty hunter moved in for the kill, but Kael pushed him away with both feet before rolling back upright.

Shatterbreath was on them. Kael raised an arm and a split-second later, was swept up by the dragon. He clambered up from the paw that had snatched him to sit between her shoulders.

"What's the verdict?" she growled.

Kael frowned. "Kill them all—except the short one with brown hair."

"Gladly."

Shatterbreath pulled up, tucked in her wings, spun around and then descended on the group of bounty hunters. With one swoop, she burned almost half of the group. As she turned around for another sweep, Kael watched the bounty hunters as they screamed and ran about. There was nothing they could do. He almost felt sorry for them. *Almost.*

With one more sweep, another large majority of the bounty hunters were dead. Then, Shatterbreath landed to finish the remaining men off with her teeth, claws and tail. When the carnage was over, the only one left standing was Jtoltly.

Kael dismounted. He walked over to Jtoltly, who had gone quite white in the face. At first, he only had eyes for Shatterbreath, but then altogether, Jtoltly realized Kael was approaching. Terrified, the bounty hunter tried to attack Kael, but to no avail. Kael dodged his blade with ease, using his ability to assist. He wrenched both his sword and Jtoltly's from the bounty hunter's grasp. Disarmed, the man fell to his knees, trembling violently.

Kael sheathed his broken blade and reattached it to his hip. He held Jtoltly's blade to its owner's neck. "What did I tell you?" Kael barked. "I am not to be reckoned with."

"Mercy!" the bounty hunter begged.

"Mercy?" Kael snapped. "Why should I give you mercy?" He pressed the tip of the sword harder into Jtoltly's neck, hard enough to break skin. The man grimaced. "Still, I will spare your life. Go tell your hirers what happened this day. Tell them the same fate as your partners awaits them unless they take the bounty off of my head. I am too busy to be disturbed by filthy bounty hunters like you." Kael pulled the sword away.

"Thank you, thank you!" Jtoltly cried. "I obey, oh powerful wizard!"

Kael smiled. "I think I like this." He climbed onto Shatterbreath's back and patted her side. "Away, demon. Let us leave this pitiful mortal."

Shatterbreath craned her neck to raise her brow at him, but didn't say a word. Stretching her wings wide, she gave one more roar, making Jtoltly flinch. In a matter of seconds, she was airborne and Uteral was shrinking into the distance behind them.

"What was that all about?" Shatterbreath asked, blowing smoke. *"Demon?"*

"Didn't you hear?" Kael scoffed, inspecting Jtoltly's sword. It was shoddy and unbalanced, practically useless. "I'm a powerful wizard. I told those men I would summon a demon from the sky if they didn't let me go." He cast the blade away.

"Clever."

"That's me."

Shatterbreath banked sharply, causing Kael to rock to one side. His ribs ached. "Why were they after you to begin with?" the dragon asked.

"I've a bounty on my head," Kael sighed. "That problem should resolve itself in time, thanks to our friend. That's not what concerns me though."

Shatterbreath snorted. "What does then?"

"There was a messenger inside the city looking for me. He said he was from a kingdom called Rystville, and that his king demanded an audience with me."

"That's a change of position."

"Indeed." Kael cradled his chin, deep in thought. "What's more, it sounded as though the Rystville king knows about us."

Shatterbreath glanced back at him. "Us?" she echoed.

"Yes. It seems he deduced that I'm using something more than a horse to travel with."

"Is this a concern?"

Kael hesitated. "Yes and no. The messenger hinted that his king is interested in my *mount*—not implying you're any old mule—but I can't help but to feel suspicious. He may want to see you."

"That could mean ill-will for us." Shatterbreath shook her head. "If they know about me, certainly they would prepare accordingly to kill us both if their true ambition is to do us harm. We'd be a nothing more than a deer and rabbit walking into a wolf's den."

"My thoughts exactly." Kael leaned back. "Do you know where Rystville is?"

Shatterbreath paused in thought. "Northeast of here."

"Should we go? The messenger did imply that my cooperation could mean the King of Rystville's as well."

"Hmm." Shatterbreath scoured the landscape, searching for something unknown.

"What lies between here and Rystville, do you know?"

Shatterbreath pointed her head. "Not much. A grove and..."

"What?"

"A cave."

Kael gritted his teeth. He could read her tone perfectly. *Cave.* Another cave meant another dragon. "What are we going to do? Should we go straight to Rystville, or ignore their invite?"

Shatterbreath still had her muzzle pointed to the side. "To fly straight there would confirm their suspicions. Does that truly matter though? I'm surprised it took anybody that long to figure out we're together—especially with your kingdom's knowledge of us."

"They have nobody to tell. That information is useless to King Morrindale."

"So then..." Shatterbreath snapped her teeth.

"A delay wouldn't hurt. It might throw their suspicions if we don't arrive right away. Either way, I think we should visit Rystville. If there's a chance to recruit another city to our cause, I don't want to miss it."

Shatterbreath angled her body so that it faced the direction her muzzle pointed.

"Then to the Grove," she announced, "of the Vigilant Five."

Chapter 3

With her supreme vision, Shatterbreath could see the grove far off in the distance before Kael could. A permanent haze seemed to surround it and on top of that, the forest encircling the Grove itself was thick, tangled and virtually inhospitable. As such, the Grove had remained untouched by humans for hundreds—if not thousands—of years.

"Where is this cave, anyway?" Kael asked from behind.

"Straight ahead is the Grove of the Vigilant Five." Shatterbreath studied the sky. "We will stay there tonight. Tomorrow we will visit my friend, who lives on the other side."

"The Grove of the Vigilant Five? Why is it named that?"

Shatterbreath considered putting Kael in her vision, but a gasp told her he had spotted them all the same. Beyond the tangled forest, five enormous willow trees stood towering over the rest of the landscape, easily taller than any human building ever constructed. The trees in the forest surrounding were pebbles compared mountain-sized weeping willows.

"These five trees have stood since the beginning of time," Shatterbreath explained. The trees were so huge, as she flew towards them, she seemed to gain no distance. "For aeons they have stood, ever-diligent, watching patiently as time unfurls. They weep for the pain and death of this world."

By then, Shatterbreath had reached the first tree. A wall of hanging branches met her; the leaves gently caressing her body as she flew threw them. At once, it seemed as though she was plunged into another world. The interior of the tree's was far darker and greener than outside, making it seem as though Shatterbreath was flying through a dense forest—*inside* a single tree. She flew between the branches, many of which were far thicker than her body.

"Wow," Kael remarked. "Amazing!"

Shatterbreath hummed. "Quite. The Favoured Ones attempted an attack on these trees you know."

"Why would they do such a thing?"

"These trees are sacred among my species, Tiny." Shatterbreath slowed down. "They are a symbol of the resilience of nature. Like us, time is no hindrance for them. The Favoured Ones—after they turned on my kind—wanted to deliver a blow straight to our hearts through these trees. They couldn't even knock down one, no matter how hard they tried." On cue, they passed by the trunk of the tree, which had an enormous black scar etched into the bark. "And try they did."

A cry echoed through the foliage. Kael winced. "What was that?"

Shatterbreath alighted on a branch as thick as a house, jutting out halfway up the massive tree's trunk. "Wyverns."

"Wyv—what?"

More cries echoed out. Over the lustrous sound of the waving branches, there came whipping noises. Fast wing beats. Kael dismounted and hugged close to her side as she laid down.

"Are they dangerous?"

Something purple zoomed by. Shatterbreath could see its details clearly. Sharp muzzle, strong wings propelled by muscle wrapped around the creature's chest... A fine specimen. Apparently Kael's eyes weren't quick enough to see it. He jumped.

"No, they're not dangerous." Shatterbreath said with a snort. "They're more like horses than anything—almost the same size, too."

More and more wyverns were darting around now. They were quick, like bats. One brave one landed right in front of them, its eyes wide in curiosity. Kael yelped, causing it to screech and take off again.

The colony of wyverns thrummed, invigorated by the sudden outburst.

"What was that for?" Shatterbreath barked at Kael. "You frightened it!"

"Frightened..." Kael hugged even tighter against her. "Are you kidding? It was going to attack! Did you see its teeth?"

"Yes."

"Are you sure they're not dangerous?"

Another wyvern landed on the branch in front of Shatterbreath, followed closely by another. Their hind legs were covered in ropey muscle and their feet equipped with long, sharp talons good for gripping prey. Unlike dragons, they only had wings for front limbs, so when they walked slowly towards Shatterbreath, they did so on the knuckles of their wings, which were reinforced with thicker scales. Their bodies were entirely purple, except for the pearl-white flash across their underbellies and the black scales highlighting more protrusive areas.

The closest wyvern cocked its head like a bird so that one amethyst eye faced Shatterbreath. They moved with twitches, always cautious, always aware of everything around them, like worried ravens.

The wyvern, chest low and rump raised, stretched its neck out towards Shatterbreath. She stirred, causing it to shrink back and hiss, exposing knife-like teeth.

"See?" Kael whispered. "They *are* dangerous! Let's get out of here."

Shatterbreath hummed. "You are so close-minded, Tiny. They're startled, that's all. They don't get visitors that often; you can't blame them for being so cautious! They're really kind-natured, watch."

She cooed, tucking in her wings to make herself less imposing. Gently, she craned her neck closer, sweeping her head in low to avoid frightening the beasts any further. She blew warm air at the wyverns, which closed their eyes, comforted. Shatterbreath stopped moving her head, but continued to hum. She let the wyvern come to her.

Hesitantly at first, the wyvern approached again, this time with more bravado. It leaned in a tail-tip's breadth from her snout and sniffed her a few times. Its body relaxed and the spines along its back went slack, telling Shatterbreath it accepted her presence.

Shatterbreath withdrew her muzzle. The wyvern chirped and then shrieked. Reacting to its call, the other wyverns relaxed as well. Several more landed on the branch and moved closer to Shatterbreath. Soon, they were climbing over each other to get closer to her. Kael made a sound that resembled a whimper and then clambered onto Shatterbreath's back.

With the wyverns no longer scared of her, they began to flock around her, chirping and screeching in delight. She hummed louder, enjoying their lively manner. They played together around her like young foxes, full of energy. Kael, however, seemed less thrilled.

Dragons and wyverns shared a friendly bond, but the creatures had likely never seen a human before. They started to climb up on Shatterbreath to study Kael, who was writhing on her back, trying to kick their pointed snouts away with little avail. Their claws tickled her hide and Shatterbreath shook, causing them to jump back.

Kael groaned. "Ugh, oof! Can you...get these things away?"

Shatterbreath snorted. "What? Don't you like them? Fine."

She stood up, stretched her wings and let out a roar that echoed through the canopy. At once, every wyvern's attention was on her. She leapt to the side of the branch and hesitated at the edge before diving from it. They all followed her.

The throng of wyverns soon surrounded her, their purple bodies all but blocking out the scenery around her. She followed the group of them as they wove in between the branches with deft speed and precision. She had to take a few banks wide or take another route together, wary of both her size and injured wing.

Nearing the end of their flight, Shatterbreath felt Kael leaned back. She hummed, content that Kael seemed to be enjoying the presence of the wyverns as much as she did.

It was almost night by the time Shatterbreath stopped.

As the last of day's light squeezed through the canopy, Shatterbreath found a suitable branch and alighted on it. From the spot she had chosen, she could see the middlemost tree, which was also the largest of the five. It was on that tree that the wyverns nested. She could see them sitting in the holes they dug into the tree's trunk, nestling down for the night.

A few wyverns slumped down next to her, curling up and cradling their heads underneath their wings. Kael hopped down from Shatterbreath's back and knelt next to one of the creatures to admire it.

"You were right," he said as he gently touched a wyvern's snout. "They are like horses." It snorted as if to agree. "Has anybody ever ridden one?"

Shatterbreath yawned. A couple wyverns followed suit, showing off their green tongues. "I don't believe so. I'm not sure if they could support a rider—I doubt they could."

"This is all so amazing!" Kael exclaimed, throwing his arms out wide. "I never knew such a place existed. I didn't even know *wyverns* existed. What do they eat?"

Shatterbreath dug her claws deep into the bark of the tree. "They eat—oh look, there's one now." Shatterbreath pointed with her muzzle to a small animal that was working its way along a branch. It looked like a marten, with a long, striped body and slanted eyes. It snatched a handful of leaves from a branch and started to munch on them.

Kael watched it. "What is it?"

"Who knows? These trees are their own thriving ecosystem! There are creatures here that live nowhere else on the world. This is another reason my race considers this place sacred. It's filled with life."

Kael pulled his bedroll free of his pack. He hesitated before unrolling it, looking for a spot among the wyverns. He found some space free close to Shatterbreath. "It's all wonderful." He yawned. "It's a shame we couldn't use the wyverns as mounts for battle."

31

"I wouldn't allow that," Shatterbreath said, shaking her head. "They are a peaceful species, almost untouched by human influence. I couldn't bear to see them harmed because of us. War is not a place for them."

"You're right," Kael agreed. "We can't drag them into this. Never mind what I said then..." He turned over. "Good night."

Shatterbreath listened to his heavy breathing as he fell asleep. The occasional screech resonated from the middle tree, but otherwise, all of the wyverns had fallen asleep. Only the night animals disturbed the quiet.

Shatterbreath rested her muzzle down between two wyverns. She had been telling the truth when she had told Kael that this colony wyverns had been untouched by mankind. However, others hadn't been so lucky.

She *had* been lying when she said no human had ever ridden one though. The wyverns that lived in the Grove of the Vigilant Five were the last of their species. Wyverns used to live elsewhere, but the human kind had all but eliminated them during their wars by using them as mounts. Wyverns weren't as easy to breed as horses.

If it wasn't for the Elder Dragons deciding to harbour a wyvern colony inside the Grove of the Vigilant Five, there would be no wyverns left at all. Kael's words echoed through her mind. *It's a shame we can't use the wyverns as mounts in battle.* The sad truth was, it was a shame they *could*.

A small voice pressed against Shatterbreath's consciousness. She tried to shake it off at first, but it was too small, too annoying to ignore. She opened her eyelids a crack. *Well no wonder.* Kael was pressing against her cheek, trying to wake her up.

She stirred and opened her mouth wide in a yawn, curling her tongue as she did. When she closed her mouth, she was too lazy to bring in her tongue all the way, so it hung out partway. Apparently, Kael thought this was funny.

"You should see yourself," he chuckled. "You look like a sleepy puppy! Aw...how c—"

She pressed her snout against his face, tasting the salt of his skin on the tip of her tongue. He yelled in disgust. "You shouldn't mock a dragon," she mused. "I think this is the first time I've slept longer than you."

"I don't know how you could sleep at all!" Kael wiped the saliva from his face. "Yuck! These creatures are so noisy! They scrape, they grunt in their sleep, they scream when they're awake. So noisy."

Shatterbreath stood up on all fours. Wyverns scattered as she did. Her stretch started in her tail, moving up to her hips, branching off at her shoulders and ending in an arch in her neck. "Are you ready to go?"

Kael's bedroll was already packed. He climbed up onto Shatterbreath's shoulders. "Let's be off. How far is the cave anyway?"

Shatterbreath sniffed at a wyvern. "Not very." She paused to think about it. "Just on the other side of the Grove, actually. We'll be there in no time." With that, she stretched her wings and lifted off. A few wyverns followed suit, flying lazily beside her.

The inside of the Vigilant Fives' canopy was dazzling. Rays of light burst through the curtain of branches in vertical slashes, painting everything in a tiger's coat. A sense of elation filled her chest and seemed to make its way out of her mouth in a roar. A chorus of shrieks met her in reply.

Shatterbreath was sad when they left the inside of the Vigilant Five. The thick forest bordering the grove gave way to a tall mountain range to the east. She pointed towards it.

"Do you really think this dragon will cooperate?" Kael piped up.

Shatterbreath took a deep breath, feeling the crisp air rush through her throat. It was much cooler so high up. So high, in fact, she spotted snow on a peak to her right. "I think he will be more *cooperative*. I have no idea if he'll actually help us."

"Dangerous?"

Shatterbreath chuckled. "You like to ask that, don't you?"

Kael shivered. "I'm sorry if I have no idea what to expect. I'm not used to your world. It's so much different. You have a lot of faith—or maybe audacity—to believe that things won't harm you."

"I know my world, Kael." She huffed. "Besides, what could *possibly* harm me?"

Shatterbreath flew in between two towering mountains, whose peaks were several kilometres apart. The mountains were wider than they were tall, covering more square feet of ground than any other mountain range Shatterbreath knew of. To any other dragon who didn't know their way around, it was a good place to get lost in. Thankfully, she had been forced to visit the range often during her time as an Elder so she knew where to go.

At last, she spotted what she was looking for. A vertical crevice was etched into a mountainside cliff not far away, looking as though some giant creature had scratched the mountain. The depths of that cave were inscrutable and dark, even with Shatterbreath's vision. Unlike when Shatterbreath had visited Silverstain, she couldn't smell the dragon's scent anywhere in the area surrounding, telling her that he had either moved to another spot or hadn't been out of his cave in a long time. He could even be...dead. Shatterbreath shook herself. Perish the thought.

"What's this dragon like?" Kael asked.

"I haven't seen him for..." Shatterbreath sighed. "He has a black hide and if memory serves, was an aggressive fighter back in his prime. He was easily the most savage of all the Elders, preferring to act rather than sit and discuss situations."

Kael choked. "He's an Elder? I thought you were the last!"

"No!" Shatterbreath scoffed. "How old do you think I am? There are still others—not many, mind you."

The cave wasn't far now. Shatterbreath hesitated in front of it, peering into the endless depths. A cold wind picked up, making Kael shiver on her back. Silverstain hadn't been happy to see a human riding her, would the Elder share the same displeasure? Reflecting on her words to Kael, she doubted he would be so accepting. Unfortunately, leaving Kael behind was not an option. It was cold up that high, and he would certainly freeze without her warmth.

She'd have to take the risk.

She angled her wings and soared into the cave, which was easily wide enough for her wingspan. The ground rose up to meet her feet and she landed, disturbing sharp gravel. The entire floor was covered in crushed shale. It didn't bother her tough paws, but it would ensure their presence would be well anticipated.

She crunched through the shale, peering around. Scratches lined the surface of the roof and walls, which had been evidently shaped by claws. At first, Shatterbreath truly believed the Elder was either dead or gone, but then she realized there were no creatures living in the cave. That was a good sign. Nothing else would move in if cave was still occupied.

The darkness of the cave became so thick, even Shatterbreath had trouble seeing. When she stumbled on something, she took a deep breath and then slowly let it out as fire, illuminating her mouth. The warmth glow revealed the inside of the cave and her heart sank; the only thing inside was a mound of stone covered with moss and craggy branches. Nothing more.

Shatterbreath closed her mouth, cutting off the light. She remained still, silent in the perfect dark. "He's not here," she mumbled to Kael. It was impossible to keep the disappointment out of her voice. "Let's go."

Something stirred. Shatterbreath brimmed the fire in her throat again, lighting up the cavern. A few rocks shifted on the mound, rolling to the bottom. Everything remained quiet for several heartbeats longer. Then, altogether, the mound shifted, uprooting the moss and causing it to spill to the ground. With a sliding sound that resembled leather being dragged over stone, the mound seemed to unfold. Two distinct shapes unfurled and stretched themselves out—wings.

35

From the base, a long, sinuous neck rose up and shook, revealing scales as black and shiny as hot tar. Muscles flexed and limbs protruded until at last, the Elder had freed himself of the disguise.

He was massive. Almost twice the age of Shatterbreath, his shoulders were easily a deer's height taller than hers. His aged body shook and his muscles didn't seem to hold the same strength they had since Shatterbreath had seen him, but by no means was he any less impressive. The spines on his back were long and sinister, shaped like sickle blades. Overall, his scales were also long and jagged, giving his body an imposing appearance.

His muzzle had more gray than Shatterbreath remembered. As well, his eyes had turned milky white—which grieved her to see. Otherwise, his face was the same as it had been for centuries. His teeth were oversized and jutted slightly forward from his skull, interlacing together so he had no need for lips. Though still covered by scales, his skin was tight around his muzzle, giving it a skull-like appearance.

His nostrils flared and he blinked, waving his head slowly to and fro. "Shatterbreath?" he called out in a voice that sounded like snake venom. "Ah, is that you, young Elder?"

"Young no more, Skullsnout. I'm sorry for disturbing you, were you...?"

"Busy?" Skullsnout barked. "Not at all. I'd been in that position for nearly sixty years! I'm glad I have an excuse to move."

"Sixty years?" Shatterbreath echoed. "Skullsnout, why would you remain still for so long? Your inactivity has taken a toll on your body."

Skullsnout closed his eyes. "Yes, I know. Dragons are meant to move. I—I suppose I gave up, brave Elder. Enough of me. What brings you here? I'm glad to see one of us is still in good health..."

Shatterbreath opened her mouth to speak, but Skullsnout sniffed and she held her breath. "What's that on your back?" the Elder asked. "A...*human?*"

Kael gasped and hugged close against Shatterbreath's back. Skullsnout merely chuckled.

"It may be beyond your comprehension, young mortal," he said, pointing his muzzle in Kael's direction. "But though I am blind, I can see you clearly."

Shatterbreath winced and bent her neck as to try and hide her cracked and blackened horns.

He took notice. "Be at peace, Shatterbreath. I can sense your spirit is not as neglected as your horns. Image means nothing nowadays."

Shatterbreath bowed her head. "Indeed. Thank you, Elder."

"To you, young human, be of no worry. Any friend of Shatterbreath's is a friend of mine. A sense you two share a strong bond. Please tell me, what has brought this to fruition? Certainly, you wouldn't befriend a human under ordinary circumstances."

"Too true," Shatterbreath said. "There is an empire, Skullsnout."

The dragon grimaced. His tail stopped dead still, hovering inches above the ground. "Go on."

Shatterbreath described to him how Vallenfend had sent soldiers to try and kill her for three decades. With Kael's help (he was reluctant to speak at first), she described how they had met and the events leading up to their visit to the Grove of the Vigilant Five.

Once they had told their story, Skullsnout remained silent, his blind eyes staring at the ground. He turned his unseeing gaze to Kael.

"A descendant of the Favoured Ones..." he muttered.

Shatterbreath could feel Kael squirm on her back.

"A fine spirit he has. Amazing. I thought the Favoured Ones would be forever evil, their souls tarnished by the blood of our kind." He leaned in close, his snout nearly touching Kael's chest. "How wrong I was... I will talk with you later."

Shatterbreath swayed her tail. "We—I should say Kael, has collected together several kingdoms to assist fending off the invading BlackHound Empire. Unfortunately, I don't know if it will be enough."

Skullsnout closed his eyes.

"Time is of the essence," Shatterbreath added.

"So you want my help?" The Elder's eyes shot back open. "You want me to assist you in battle?"

Shatterbreath cringed back. She worked her jaw, unable to answer. She shouldn't have come. He was too old. There was no way he would agree. It was Silverstain all over again. She began to worry about her and Kael's safety. If Skullsnout became violent...

"What's your standing in this, Shatterbreath?" the Elder Dragon asked.

The question caught her by surprise. "I stay by Kael's side. Always. I will fight."

Skullsnout nodded. "You are a strong dragon. One of the strongest I've ever seen. Your conviction is absolute. From the first day I met you, the day you became the first and only female Elder, I was impressed by your conviction. You've always stayed with what you believe. I commend you, Shatterbreath."

"Thank you," Shatterbreath said humbly, moved by his words.

"If you will fight, then so will I."

Shatterbreath hesitated. "It will be no easy task. They will have ways to deal with dragons—even us. You could very well be slain. That wouldn't do. *I'd* be the oldest dragon on the continent!"

"I suppose that was a compliment," Skullsnout chuckled. His expression went stern. "I've seen my golden years drag past. No, I will rise up and join the battle. If I die, so be it. The fury of two Elder Dragons fighting together will be legendary."

"We will crush them."

"Shatterbreath, Kael Rundown, you are both free to spend the night," Skullsnout declared. "I want to discuss this further. Right now, however, I wish to speak to the Favoured One alone. If you'd be so kind...?"

Shatterbreath frowned. *Why did he want to talk with Kael?* She considered it for a moment, giving Kael a look. He only shrugged and climbed down off of her. If Kael was worried, he didn't show it. After Skullsnout gave her a nod, Shatterbreath reluctantly turned around and proceeded to fly out of the cave. She could only wonder what they would discuss.

Kael was extremely unnerved to be alone with the gigantic black dragon, but he wouldn't let Shatterbreath know. He watched her leave the cave, almost wishing he had left with her.

The black dragon huffed, bringing Kael's attention from Shatterbreath to him. Skullsnout took a step, muscle rippling underneath his tight armoured skin. Neck arched, he brought his head in close to Kael. Kael held his breath. Skullsnout—as impossible as it seemed—was even more intimidating than Shatterbreath, despite his mild manner. Shatterbreath had been correct about his appearance, but it seemed his personality had changed with time.

"I assume you know the history of the Favoured Ones?" he huffed.

Kael nodded. "Shatterbreath informed me."

"What do you think of them?"

The question caught Kael by surprise. "Um... I'm not sure. I'm angry, I suppose. Disgusted that they would be so quick to turn on the ones who gave them their power. It's not right, what they did to your kind. I wish I could repay you in some way—all of you."

Skullsnout back away. With a sigh, he slumped to the ground, body shaking as he did. "The death of my kind can never be undone." His expression was unreadable. His emotion was more spread across his body than his muzzle and right then, he was sitting dead still. "However, you may be able to secure us a better future."

Kael clenched his jaw. "How?"

"You stand for hope, you stand for freedom. No doubt people look up to you and see a hero. I'd bet my horns you've given Shatterbreath a new reputation as well. You've changed how people see her, young Favoured One. You could very well do the same for all of us.

"Did Shatterbreath ever tell you about the leader of the Favoured Ones? Before they were evil?"

"No."

"He was the cleanest spirit I'd ever known. His soul was incorruptible. He stood as a symbol for our belief in mankind... A truly miraculous human being."

"What happened to him?"

"Time took a hold of him, as it does to all of your species. He died an old man—but no less a hero. With him, I'm sorry to say, my faith in humanity died as well. I'd given up on your kind, Favoured One. Until Shatterbreath flew in here with you on her back. As soon as I saw you two, I knew the times had changed. She had more reason to hate you than any of us, yet..."

Kael remained silent. He studied Skullsnout's milky eyes until the dragon faced his muzzle towards him.

"You are the beacon we lost when the first Favoured One died. You hold the same pure spirit he did. The same potential. I shouldn't wonder why, either... Considering," the dragon gave him a sly look, "you are his direct descendant."

Kael winced. "What?"

"It is clear to me now. I knew the moment you entered my cave that I had felt your presence before. My speculations were corroborated by the sword that you carry."

Kael frowned and detached the sword and sheath from his hip. Gripping it with both hands, he shook his head. "No, this is nothing special. It's just a regular sword I fished out of Shatterbreath's cave. Besides," he said, unsheathing it, "it's broken."

"A minor inconvenience. Not all broken things can be fixed. Your sword, however, is an exception." Kael perked up. Skullsnout's tail danced; the equivalent of a smile. "That blade, without a doubt, is the first Favoured One's legendary sword, *Vintrave*. The lion was his crest. The words etched into its surface were carved by dragon claws. After all, it was given to him by us as a gift."

"It was? B—but how did it get in Shatterbreath's cave?"

"Who knows? Maybe she had a subconscious attachment to it and decided to bring it along with her as she moved from cave to cave. Maybe fate alone decided to reunite blade with master. Either way, it is yours to wield now. Wield it with strength. Wield it noble, strong and proud."

Kael twisted the broken blade in his grip, admiring the lustrous details adorning the hilt. He had always felt it belonged to him, but had been shamed to carry it knowing it *wasn't*. Hearing the Elder Dragon's words changed everything. It *was* his blade. It *was* meant for him. It was his to wield, and his alone. He *was* the descendant of the hero Skullsnout mentioned. Which brought up a problem...

"I wish I could," Kael said as he sheathed it, "but it's no use to me now."

"Don't be so sure. Like I said, some things can be fixed."

The Elder Dragon exhaled, sending warm, ashy air flowing over Kael. He stretched out his neck and stopped inches away from Kael. His nostrils flared as he inhaled, ruffling Kael's tunic. Then, over so gently, Skullsnout closed the distance and touched Kael's sword with the tip of his muzzle.

Kael gasped as a flash of white magic erupted from the sword.

Shatterbreath sat at the entrance to Skullsnout's cave, scouring the gentle mountain slopes around her. *He was going to fight alongside her.* The very concept was almost hard to grasp. Especially after visiting Silverstain. A new sense of accomplishment washed over her. *She had done this.* She had assisted. She felt successful, but more than that, relieved that she would have somebody to back her up in battle.

A shuffle behind alerted her of Kael's presence.

"Did you hunt well?" he asked.

Shatterbreath hummed. "There is good prey on these mountains." She turned to him and nuzzled him. He laughed and hugged her snout. "What did Skullsnout say to you?"

Kael sighed. "Oh...things." He climbed over her paw and sat down between her two forelegs. "Secrets."

"Swell."

The sun was setting by then. West. Any day, the BlackHound Empire would arrive from the west. When they did, everything would change.

Kael stirred. He pulled out something with a *schwing*. Curious, Shatterbreath cocked her head. He was admiring his gleaming sword, which was now back together in one piece. It shined brighter than dragon scales.

"A gift?" she asked.

Kael stared at the sword, mesmerised. "One of many, yes. Shatterbreath... We can do this."

Shatterbreath turned her gaze back to the sun set. It had disappeared behind the mountains before them. "Yes, Tiny. We can. We will."

Chapter 4

Kael slashed *Vintrave* through the air at the entrance of Skullsnout's cave, then blocked an invisible attack with his shield. He followed through with a lunge. The pain in his ribs was gone, leaving him in fit fighting condition. In fact, he hadn't felt so good in months! It felt as though he had just woken up from a week-long sleep feeling rejuvenated and ready for anything. He owned his healthy condition to Skullsnout, who had bestowed many blessings, one of which he couldn't tell Shatterbreath yet.

The sun had risen long ago, but hadn't been visible over the mountain range until that very moment. The fresh sunlight refracted off of Shatterbreath's scales as she watched him, sending small beams of light everywhere. She raised a brow when Kael turned to look at her. "Someone's happy," she said. "Glad to have your sword back?"

Kael beamed. "Quite so. Not only did I get my sword back, Skullsnout healed my wounds as well. I haven't felt this good in...a long time."

"He healed your wounds?" Shatterbreath echoed. "He did that for you? That was...nice of him. I didn't know he held such power. He mentioned before that he could see as well... Curious."

"Curious indeed." Skullsnout's muzzle appeared through the darkness. The shine on his scales could be seen before the outline of his body. "Though I may be lacking in physique, my understanding of magic has greatly increased, Shatterbreath." He sat down near her with a sigh. "I wield it with greater control than even Darion."

Shatterbreath considered him. "Is that possible? What has lent you such understanding?"

"Time. Time and time alone. I have had *very* long to consider such things by myself." He swished his tail. "I may not have been moving, but my mind has been ever-active, studying the magic inside me.

"Would you like an example?"

Shatterbreath frowned. "What are you going to do?"

"I see your wing was damaged, Elder." Skullsnout took a breath. "That could be detrimental in the future."

"You can fix it?" Shatterbreath asked, breathless.

Kael walked over to Skullsnout. "Of course I can. Stay still." Skullsnout wrapped his tail around Kael's body. He reached over behind Shatterbreath's neck and lightly touched his muzzle to the shoulder of her folded wing.

A surge of energy rushed from Skullsnout into Shatterbreath. Slowly at first, a golden light appeared at the beginning of the tear in her wing. It ran along the tear until the wound was completely submerged by golden energy. As the light subsided, Kael noticed that the wound was gone, vanished, as if had never existed. The clips he had put in her wing were still there, but not a second later, they fell to the ground, sheared off as if cut by a flaming blade.

Kael frowned. He was glad that Shatterbreath's wing was healed, but he had worked hard to put those clips in.

Skullsnout released Kael.

Shatterbreath opened her eyes and flexed her wing tentatively, as if disbelieving such a feat could be accomplished. The membrane stretched perfectly. Tears formed in Shatterbreath's eyes.

"Thank you," she mumbled. She stood up and braced against herself against Skullsnout, almost as if she was hugging him. He placed his muzzle against her shoulder.

"Anything for you, proud Elder. Fly well."

Shatterbreath nodded and backed away. "We will," she said, tears streaming over her cheeks. "Words cannot express my thanks, Elder."

Kael strode over to Shatterbreath. "It was a pleasure to meet you, Elder Dragon," he said with a bow, addressing Skullsnout.

The Elder beamed. "To you as well, Favoured One. Keep safe and make sure Shatterbreath stays out of trouble. Keep *Vintrave* close, it will protect you."

Kael nodded and climbed onto Shatterbreath's back. "Of course."

"And Favoured One..."

Kael hesitated. "Yes?"

"Be wary of my gift. Use it well."

Kael blushed as Shatterbreath craned her neck to give him a confused look. "I will," he said to Skullsnout. "Shatterbreath, let's be off."

"Farewell, Elder," Shatterbreath said as she took off. She roared as they glided away from him. A heavy roar met them as a reply, echoing in the mountains long after.

"Let's get to Rystville," Kael announced. "They'll be waiting."

"Indeed. What a joy to be able to fly unconstrained once again!"

Kael frowned, knowing what would come next. He grabbed on tight to the spine behind him just as Shatterbreath pulled into a deadly nosedive.

Their flight through the mountains took longer than Kael would have liked. Shatterbreath was so elated to have her full flight back, she started to do aerial tricks. For a good two hours, she dipped, spun, and wove through the mountains with frightening speed and bravado. The ride had been so twisting and jarring, Kael had even gotten sick partway through a backwards loop. He wasn't even sure which way his breakfast fell as Shatterbreath zoomed on, unheeding Kael's discomfort.

When Shatterbreath finally calmed down and flied straight, she was taking deep, hoarse breaths. Kael almost was too.

"Are you done?" he asked, smacking her back.

She wiggled in excitement. "No. I need a break and besides, you don't seem to have a great degree of tolerance."

Kael leaned out over her shoulder. Down below, the mountains had given away to forest, and beyond that to the northeast, what looked like rolling fields. They passed effortlessly over a small farming city. Now that Shatterbreath's wing was better, she was flying far faster than they had before. Kael would have suggested slowing down, but he doubted she'd listen anyway.

"What do you know of Rystville?" he asked.

"The location." Shatterbreath paused. "Oh, the city has a nickname too, used by its inhabitants. You could probably use it to try and fit in."

45

"What is it?"

Shatterbreath glanced back at him, her eyes gleaming. "Slugcity."

"That's not funny."

Over the next hour, Shatterbreath slowly descended, preparing to drop Kael off. Once the city was in view, she flared her wings to land. Kael jumped off her shoulders before she had even folded her wings.

"We may have thrown them off by taking our time to get here," Kael told her, "but arriving with no mount may prove their suspicions."

"What are you going to do?" Shatterbreath asked, blowing smoke into the air. "Steal one?"

Kael sighed. "I'll have to take my chances I suppose. I'm going to mostly check the city out, see what their true intentions are."

Shatterbreath frowned. "What if they want to kill you?"

Kael fixed his vambrace. "I'll whistle once if I'm in trouble. With my renewed health and your fixed wing, it should be easy for us both to escape. I'll whistle twice if..."

"If what?" Shatterbreath considered him. "No. I don't want to be gawked at again."

"I'm sorry for doing that to you," Kael said, arms outstretched, "but can't you just...make a small sacrifice? Having someone look at you for a minute or so can't be that painful. If it means recruiting another city to our aid, I think it's quite worth it."

Shatterbreath snarled. She thrashed her tail, smashing a pile of rocks behind her. Nevertheless, she agreed. "You're right. Whistle twice and I'll come down for you, *peacefully.*"

"Thanks." Kael turned to leave. "I'll only call if it's absolutely necessary. I'll try to avoid it as best as I can."

"Sure," Shatterbreath snorted. "Just hurry."

Kael set off in a light jog, eager to get the Rystville. As he made it over the gentle hill, the city rolled into view. It was a medium-sized city, slightly smaller than Vallenfend, but judging from the sizes and shapes of the building, more spread out. A wall cut through the city, but only partway, with houses on both sides. Kael had the impression that the wall used to surround the city, but had been mostly torn down. Consequently, there were no front gates and Kael was able to walk straight into the heart of the city.

However, although there was no central entrance, there were armed guards patrolling the main streets. Kael strolled straight up to a small group of guards.

"I am Kael Rundown," he declared. Several people walking on the street stopped and turned towards him. An oxcart even stopped nearby, its driver leaning over curiously. Kael faltered. "I...I heard King Respu wants a word with me."

The guards were all dumbstruck. An older man found his voice. "Wh—why of course, Mr. Rundown. Welcome to Rystville! King Respu has been eagerly awaiting your arrival. He has freed up his entire schedule just for you. We will...take you to him."

The older man started forward, motioning for Kael to follow. The other two guards circled behind and marched behind Kael. They passed through the city, receiving interested expressions from the populace. After crossing a wide bridge over a river that cut through the centre of the city, a great castle loomed into view. To Kael's surprise, its precipices and spires were decorated with green brick. As he approached, however, Kael realized that it wasn't the colour of the brick, but a thick layer of ivy that seemed to only cover the upper half of the castle. How a plant would grow in such a way was beyond him.

They stopped in front of the castle, which had a low spiked gate and a moat bordering it. The guard leading Kael put out his hand.

"Excuse me, but you must wait here, Rundown. Protocol. I will return shortly with King Respu."

The guard rushed over the lowered drawbridge and disappeared into the gaping entrance to the castle itself. Kael shifted his weight. They were friendly enough, but he had been fooled once before. The memory of Fallenfeld came to mind. They had pretended to have faith in him, but in the end had tried to murder him. He was not so willing to let it happen again. He kept his hand on *Vintrave's* hilt, ready for anything.

Several minutes passed by. The sun was beating down on Kael, making him conscious of how hot a suit of armour could get. If the guards on either side of him felt the heat, they didn't show it.

Finally, a man appeared in the entrance of the castle. As he approached, Kael studied him, trying to deduce what kind of a person he was. He wore a long robe with wide sleeves, so that he had to keep his arms elevated as to not trip on the hems. His attire was almost all one colour, an interesting mixture of yellow and lime green. A modest silver crown adorned his head, semi-hidden by his nest of curly black hair. A small patch of hair dotted his chin, just under his lower lip. Out of all the kings Kael had met, he seemed the youngest and most energetic.

The king paused at the end of the drawbridge, hardly a bowshot away from Kael. A huge smile engulfed his cheery face. "Rundown!" he shouted, throwing his arms out wide. "I've heard so much about you! What a pleasure it is!"

Kael returned his smile, confused. King Respu talked as though he and Kael had once been great friends that had been separated and then reunited. "King Respu... Uh, hi."

The king laughed and in three spry strides, he was almost face-to-face with Kael. He scooped up Kael's hand and shook it with a vigour Kael found somewhat disconcerting. "What a pleasure indeed! But please, please, come inside! Before you sizzle in this atrocious heat. Wow, it is a hot day, isn't it? Come, inside, come!"

Before Kael could react, King Respu had already spun on his heel to head back inside. Caught off guard, Kael merely remained where he was, trying to digest what was happening. The king seemed trustworthy enough, so Kael followed him inside, the guards still in tow.

King Respu briskly led Kael through the inside of his castle. He chatted almost the whole time, telling Kael stories of the castle—which were all quite redundant and somewhat similar. They moved so quickly Kael couldn't even appreciate the inside before they burst through the backdoor, submitting themselves to the blinding glare of the hot sun once again.

"Ah here we are!" he cried at last. "The courtyard! Please, sit down, make yourself at home. I've prepared a small feast for you— I'm sure you're terribly famished from your travels."

The courtyard of the castle was massive, probably taking up more square feet of land than the building itself. Peacocks roamed the gardens, strutting in between the flowers and breaking the calm silence of the courtyard with their resonating cries. A cobblestone path wove through the gardens, periodically covered by pergolas. In the middle of the courtyard there were chairs and a large table covered by all sorts of bowls containing fruit and other food.

Kael grinned and headed over to the table of food. He spied a big juicy apple and snatched it up, all at once realizing how hungry he was. King Respu sat across from where Kael stood, clutching his own apple.

"And...speaking of travels..." King Respu leaned forward in his chair, raising an eyebrow.

Kael pursed his lips. Jaw working, he carefully placed the apple back in the bowl he had retrieved it from. Face grave, he sank into the closest chair.

King Respu frowned. "I hope I didn't...offend you in any way. Please, eat."

"Why have you summoned me here?" Kael asked, voice stern. "What do you want from me?"

King Respu waved his hand. The two guards that had entered with them left, leaving Kael alone with the bubbly king. "I've heard about your exploits, Rundown. I know about your quest. I've heard about the so-called empire that is coming. We'll get to that, don't worry. What I'm concerned about right now is your means of transportation."

Kael snorted. He leaned forward and snatched the apple back up, taking a big bite. "That's all?" he said through chews. "Your messenger told me something similar. You people have heard of *horses* before, right?"

"Horses cannot travel between cities in a mere day." He scowled. "Not the cities you've visited anyway. Where is your animal, then? Assuming, of course, you did in fact come here by horse."

Kael savoured the taste of the apple in his mouth. He hadn't had one in what seemed like forever. King Respu's cheery manner had disappeared. Kael took a breath. "I don't bring my horse into cities. I don't want him stolen."

"That seems like a great inconvenience."

Kael took another bite. "When you have a horse as fast as mine..."

King Respu sat back in his chair and rubbed his face with his hand. "A horse, eh? Hmm. That's a shame." He stood up and paced around Kael, hands clasped behind his back. "For you see, I have a deep interest in extraordinary creatures, whether mythical, magical or extinct. I've seen my fair share of them too. Have you ever seen a wyvern? I didn't think so."

Kael raised a brow. However, he let King Respu continue.

"What interests me the most, however, are *dragons*." Kael nearly choked on his apple. King Respu placed both hands on the backrest of Kael's chair. "They used to be abundant on this land, you know. Something happened a long time ago, though, something unwritten in our scrolls. Ever since, their numbers have been dangerously low, and decreasing. As they grow rarer and rarer, men seem to want to make a name for themselves by slaying them."

"What does this have to do with me again?" Kael asked.

"They are said to be strong, fast, cunning, stealthy and extremely intelligent. They wield magic like no other creature!" He made a fist. "They are truly a magnificent species. It would make me a very happy man to see one in person."

Kael placed his half-eaten apple down on the table, contemplating King Respu's words. "A dragon used to live by my home city. They're not what you think. They're vicious, ruthless and greedy. That one dragon alone is responsible for most of the men's deaths in my city. Are you sure you'd still want to meet one?"

King Respu sat back down and shook his head. "It would be a pleasure to die by a dragon. Even if I only saw it for a fraction of a second."

Kael narrowed his eyes. "That's a little extreme."

"You can understand then," King Respu said with a sigh, "how excited I was when I heard about you, Rundown. When I heard the stories about you, I thought for sure you were using a dragon as transportation. It seemed like the only solution. Well, that or something more than a mere *horse.*"

"I'm sorry to disappoint you then," Kael said. "Now, about the BlackHound Empire."

"The invading force?" The king slumped lower in his chair. "Oh yes, that. Uh, go on, I suppose."

Kael put a finger to his temple. He could tell that he had lost King Respu. Only one thing would convince him to join Kael's campaign now. "Tell me, King Respu, can I trust you?"

The king perked up. "Hmm?"

"Can I trust you? You aren't planning any tricks, are you? You wouldn't do anything like that, right?"

King Respu frowned. "No. It was never my intention to harm you. We are a peaceful city, we have never meant anybody harm. If we fight, we do so to defend, never to destroy."

That's all Kael needed to hear. "I hope you trust me too. For your sake, I hope you're telling the truth. If not, this city will burn. Come with me."

The king stood up as well. "What? Why? Where are you taking me? What do you mean, burn?"

Kael shook his head. "Just come with me," he said. "I want to show you my horse. It's a very nice horse. You could ever say it's *extraordinary.*"

The king seemed to get the message. Without another word, as if he was afraid if he spoke, he'd dissuade Kael, King Respu allowed Kael to lead him back outside the castle. Kael hustled through the city, doing his best to remember the way out. Of course, the sight of the king grabbed attention and within minutes of leaving the castle, they already had a large crowd of city people at their heels. Kael let them come too.

Kael exited the boundary of Rystville. He walked far enough from the outermost building that the majority of the bystanders they had collected were standing in the crisp wheat field.

"I lied. You were right," he announced, loud enough for everybody to here, "I don't ride a horse. King, people!" He paused. "Meet Shatterbreath."

He put his fingers to his lips and whistled. Twice.

A clap of thunder echoed overhead. The crowd chattered amongst themselves, some pointing at the sky, others standing frightened, mouths open, unsure what to expect. Kael stood wary as well. If she hadn't appeared already, chances were, she was going to do something unexpected, like...

Suddenly, Shatterbreath swooped in from behind, announcing her presence with a mighty roar. She cupped her wings just as she came over the crowd, coming in close and fast, so that every single person had to duck to avoid her hind claws. And, to further expand the grandeur of her entrance, she released a huge breath of fire as she landed beside Kael.

Kael buried his face in his palm. *Dragons.*

For several minutes, the crowd cowered before her as she sat proudly, staring back at them slyly. She didn't say anything, she didn't even move besides breathing in and out. Just the tip of her tail twitched.

It was King Respu who overcame his initial fright. He separated from the crowd, which had been slowly going back into the city, as if they thought any sudden movements would cause Shatterbreath to attack. King Respu, keeping his eyes on her, inched forward, step by humble step. His face was wide with awe and his hands were both open as wide as his mouth. It seemed as though he wasn't sure what to do with his own body.

Once he was within a bowshot away, Shatterbreath seemed to take notice of him. She shot her emerald gaze towards him, a puff of ash-laced spoke escaping her nostrils. Kael could see her jaw clench and she uncurled her tail from around her body so that it thrashed freely.

"Back, morsel," she growled.

King Respu didn't listen. Lost in his infatuation, he took another step. Shatterbreath bent her head to the king's level and hissed viciously. King Respu broke free of his trance and stopped, putting out one hand as if it offered some sort of protection.

Kael leaned placed a hand against Shatterbreath's foreleg. She glanced at him from the corner of her eye, muzzle still facing the king. Kael needed King Respu's cooperation. It was obvious he wanted to touch her. Letting him do so might just gain that cooperation.

Shatterbreath understood the message. She sighed, closed her eyes and lowered her muzzle even more, so that it was nearly grazing the grass, and tucked in her chin. King Respu smiled and after Kael gave him a nod of permission, moved closer to Shatterbreath.

He reached out. Shatterbreath opened her eyes when he was within a foot of touching her and rumbled, sending a rush of air that ruffled the king's trousers. Ever so gently, King Respu placed his palm against the top of her muzzle, above her nostrils. He smiled.

Shatterbreath growled and nudged him away. She huffed, scorching the ground in front of her, then bounded off in the opposite direction. She shook her body and began rubbing her head on the ground like a wet dog would.

"Very dignified," Kael muttered. He turned to King Respu. "I'm sorry she's so rude. She...doesn't care for humans very much."

"Oh no, I don't mind in the least." King Respu giggled, elated. The crowd had significantly calmed down as well. Some people were even laughing as Shatterbreath flipped onto her back to roll even more. "I thought that I'd see a dragon once in my life at best. But touch? *Touch!* You have made me a happy man, Kael." He clapped his hands together. "My, my. She's truly wonderful."

"It depends how you look at it," Kael said sarcastically. Vallenfend was so close to Shatterbreath's lair, he had never even thought that dragons were so special. To him, she had just been an *unfortunate* part of his life, and for the longest time, something to dread and fear. Kael would have never imagined that somebody would actually like dragons, let alone want to touch one.

"I suppose it does," King Respu laughed. "I guarantee you, Kael, the story of what happened today will be passed on for generations. People will say to their grandchildren, 'I saw a dragon once. Why,

King Respu even got to touch one!' The people of Rystville will know your name well."

Kael shrugged. "Huh, I—I guess so."

"Wow, what a magnificent creature. Kael, on us you can rely. We will stay by your side to protect this land."

"Really? Just like that?"

"Of course. I believe your story, about the invading empire. I believe it completely. After all, how can such a noble beast be wrong about something as this?"

Kael tried his best to hold his smile. *Enough of Shatterbreath!*

"I will send our military force to the east at once, to join forces with your cause." King Respu put out his hand.

Kael took it. "I appreciate it, King Respu. With Rystville fighting at our side, we stand a greater chance than ever. But we're stripped for time, I hope you don't mind if we..."

"Leave?" King Respu mused. "Of course not! I understand, Rundown. I wouldn't want to hold you back not a moment longer. Leave, so you may return to your quest, I insist."

Kael grinned. "Thank you so much, King Respu. I greatly appreciate it." He took the king's hand and shook it rigorously. "Listen, the faster you can get to Vallenfend, the better. The BlackHound Empire may be arriving any day now."

"Unfortunately, not all of us have dragons to ride." King Respu laughed. "We will move as fast as we can."

Kael nodded. "Farewell, King Respu. It was a pleasure." Kael waved at Shatterbreath. She stopped rolling and strutted over. Kael clambered onto her back. "Farewell, Rystville. I will see you again."

"Stay safe!" King Respu called out. "To you, mighty Shatterbreath, fly well."

Shatterbreath gave an awkward bow, more of a nod than anything. "Always. Good-bye."

Without further hesitation, she took off and started flying away as fast as she could.

"Well, that was fun," she commented once Rystville was out of sight. "I rather enjoyed that king actually. Why aren't you more like him, Tiny?"

Kael snorted. "What, obsessive, eccentric and patronizing?"

Shatterbreath shook her body, nearly bucking Kael off. "No! Sweet of voice and appreciative of my beauty."

Kael gagged.

"Well," Shatterbreath mumbled. "Maybe he was a little extreme..."

"There we go." Kael stretched. "Where to next?"

Shatterbreath thought for a moment. "There's a massive city north of here with an even larger army. They would make an excellent ally; however, I doubt you will have an easy time convincing them of your cause."

"Might as well try," Kael said with a shrug. "Are there any other cities near it?"

"Yes."

"If I fail at the one city, I can always try the other." Kael put his arms behind his head and leaned back, closing his eyes. "Set sail for that city. Wake me when we get there."

"Set sail?" Shatterbreath scoffed. "I am not a boat. Foolish *human*. Get your sleep. I'll let you know when we arrive."

Kael smiled. He drifted off to Shatterbreath's muscles working underneath him and the comforting experience of flight surrounding him.

Chapter 5

Kael floated back into consciousness, aware of something warm and moist pressed against his face. He tried to ignore it, enjoying his rest. It was probably just Shatterbreath breathing on him or something. Trying to find his dream, he let sleep overcome him once again.

The warm thing came back again. This time, it covered his whole face, nearly suffocating him. It had strange little barbs covering its surface except for the backside when Kael grabbed at it, trying to remove it.

Fully awake, he pulled whatever it was away from his face. He nearly heaved when he realized what it was. Shatterbreath had licked him.

"Ptu! Aw, gross! Shatterbreath, you donkey, what was that for?"

Shatterbreath let her tongue hang out. "You are impossible to wake up! At least I've found something that works now. That's what you get for sleeping in, you lazy bear."

"I asked you to wake—oh, never mind." Kael wiped his face on his arm. A long line of saliva stuck between his sleeve and face. "Ugh, gross. Where's the city? Tell me about it."

Shatterbreath craned her neck. Kael stood up and leaned against her. With a rush, he was in her vision, gazing across the land. A massive city stood several miles away, placed close to a decent-sized lake. At once, Kael was both surprised and impressed by the protection of the city itself. Its black walls rivalled Arnoth's, both tall and thick. Even as Shatterbreath surveyed it, he could see large scratches and gouges where the wall had obviously succeeded in fending off attack. Indeed, the city seemed prepped for war, with ballistae lining the top of the wall as well as large cauldrons used for dropping hot pitch.

The city's wars in were evident in the land surrounding as well. As far as the eye could see towards a northwest direction, the land was barren and empty except for the occasional bunch of crabgrass sticking up on the bland horizon.

"Any advice?" Kael said as he came out of Shatterbreath's vision.

"I don't know much about this city, Tiny," she replied. "I don't come this far east often."

"Wish me luck." Kael set off towards the city. Shatterbreath had landed far away because the land was so flat surrounding it. He had a long walk ahead of him. Shatterbreath took off behind him, flying high into the sky until she was nothing more than a speck against the hot midday sun.

After an hour or so, Kael strolled up to the large front gate, putting a hand on *Vintrave's* hilt. There were two sets of guards. One group of three on the left, another group of three to the right. Kael walked up to the closest group.

"Oi, what's your business here?" one of the guards asked through a heavy accent. "I don't think I recognize you. You Tehpuu or Sansan?"

"I beg your pardon?" Kael said. The other group of guards had turned their attention to him as well. The only difference Kael could spot between the groups was a coloured dash underneath the crest emblazoned on their breastplates. The young men Kael were talking to had green dashes, while the others had yellow.

The guard talking to Kael turned to his friends and chuckled. "This guy's a knot! Listen, chum, I asked you a simple question. Is there something wrong with you?"

Kael frowned. "I—I'm sorry, I'm not from here. I...don't understand what you're getting at."

The guard laughed harder. "Aye, look boys, we've got ourselves a genuine knot here! Don't even know what a Tehpuu is! Wah hah, you *are* a great knotter!"

Kael glanced across the way at the other set of guards. They too, were laughing. Kael cleared his throat and started again. "I'm not from here... What's a Tehpuu?"

The guard leaned over, using his halberd to balance. He wrapped an arm around Kael, pointing his fingers at the other guard squad. He smelled faintly of whisky. "See those, chum? *Those* are Sansan. What a great bunch of *knots* they are too. We be Tehpuu."

The other group glared at them. They shifted their weight fiddle with their weapons.

Kael struggled to wrap his mind around what was happening. He couldn't quite. "Uh, okay... May I enter? I have important business to attend to."

"Oh, like being a knot?" the guard laughed. "You're doing a good job so far, I'd say."

"What a knotter."

"Double bowline if you tell me," another guard whispered.

Kael removed himself from the guard's arm, thoroughly confused. He couldn't understand their obsession with knots. *Tehpuu, Sansan.* What was happening?

"Well, uh... I have to be on my way. May I...?"

The guards nodded. "Yeah, whatever. Get your knottin' behind in there. I'm done wiff you." He knocked on the gate twice with the end of his hauberk. "Eh, Gurt?"

"Name's not Gurt!" a voice replied. "I've told you that before."

"Knottin' Sansan," Kael's guard muttered. "Yeah, knot you too. Just open the gate for this knotter, alright?"

There came a low *chunk* from the other side of the gate. A second later, the massive wooden door swung inwards to let Kael inside. Once he was, several soldiers pushed it back closed and slid a massive beam into place to lock it.

Kael gasped once he was inside the city. Just like the outside, the inside of the city was geared for war. The buildings closest to the wall had tall, sturdy fronts, with small rectangular windows for firing arrows through. The entire city seemed to be built upwards, like a rounded shield, so as to inhibit the advance of soldiers to the castle. Every building was tight and secure, with barred windows and metal-reinforced doors.

As Kael wove through the streets, huge battalions of soldiers passed by, girded in heavy armour and carrying powerful weapons. Archers lined the rooftops and never was a guard out of sight. Everywhere Kael went, there seemed to be the whisper of war.

Kael switched onto a random street. He decided to explore a while longer before going to the castle itself. As he hit another major street, he frowned. There was something...odd. It took him some time, but at last, he realized what it was. The architecture was different. Just from crossing the street, the style of the buildings had gone from straight, bold edges to smoother and more delicate. The bricks were a slightly lighter colour as well.

Kael stood in the middle of the street, looking back and forth and comparing the two sides. He noticed that the doors on the darker buildings had the corners highlighted by green paint whereas the houses across the street were highlighted with yellow.

It made sense now. There were two factions living inside one city. Kael had been wondering why everybody in the city walked in groups. Evidently, the two factions weren't friendly. He guessed that if somebody was walking somewhere alone, they were sure to be attacked by the other faction.

That realization made him worried. If either faction mistook him for the other... He oriented himself, finding the castle that loomed off in the distance, and headed straight for it.

On his way, he witnessed as a woman dropped a crate of apples she was carrying. The crate broke when it hit the ground, sending the apples everywhere. With an angry voice, she cried out, "Knot!"

With that came another realization, one which made Kael scowl. Knot was their swearword. He didn't like this city very much so far. Hopefully, the king would make him think otherwise.

Before he knew it, Kael was standing outside the castle. There was a large area in front of it, packed with people, like Vallenfend's often was. There were people screaming up at the castle, which was separated from them by a heavy iron gate. Kael caught only bits and pieces of whatever it was they were so worked up about.

"Finish off those knotters once and for all!"

"Let's get them now!"

"Death to Nestoff."

This city was one question after another. Who was Nestoff? Why did they want him dead so bad? Was he the king, or the ruler of one of the factions? Kael stood at the edge of the thronging crowd, wishing to stay out of their way.

Somebody yelled something. Without explanation, he turned and struck the person next to him. "Get out of my face, you knottin' Sansan!"

59

"Hey, you don't touch him!"

"Oh yeah? Knot you!" The angry Tehpuu jumped at the other Sansan and before Kael fully realized what had happened, the entire crowd had broken out in a brawl. Kael inched along the wall he was beside, trying to keep out of the fight as best as he could. He was going to just leave the city, before any more madness began!

Somebody appeared on the castle's balcony. Judging by his crown and shining armour, he was the king. He was laughing with a woman beside him, but when he spotted the crowd, he became angry. "Hey, down there, stop this at once! Surcease!"

The crowd continued fighting.

The king took a deep breath, leaned over the railing and shouted. "Hey, you great pile of knots! Stop it!" The people stopped fighting. The crowd quickly separated and turned their attention to the king. "That's better," he said with a smile. "What are you people doing? Tehpuu, Sansan, what does it matter? We're brothers living under the same roof here! We shouldn't be enemies with each other! Nestoff is the true enemy. They must be destroyed, before they destroy us."

"Aye! Let's kill them now!"

"Death to Nestoff!"

It sounded as if Nestoff was a city. Kael backed away from the crowd even further. They were once again shouting curses at Nestoff. Which probably meant another brawl would start again...

"Yes, yes, Nestoff will fall" the king said, waving his hands. "But only in time. For now, keep your peace, my brethren. We will reign yet. Well, have a nice day." With that simple remark, the king retreated back inside his castle, wrapping his arm around the woman that was with him.

Kael cradled his chin idly, brooding on the king's words. He needed to speak to the man personally before he left. It sounded as though the city had quite the army at its disposal. If Kael could redirect their focus, the city could prove to be a very formidable ally.

As the crowd slowly dispersed, Kael made his way to the castle gates. There were two knights standing guard. They eyed him as Kael approached.

"No entry," one of them said.

"I need to see the king."

The guard raised a brow and shoved Kael away. "No *entry.*"

Kael frowned at the guard, but nevertheless turned away. He would not be denied so easily. Acting casual, he walked a fair distance around the castle gate, and glanced back at the two guards. Kael started to climb the iron fence. There wasn't much to grip onto and coupled with his smooth gauntlets, the task proved to be impossible. Climbing over wasn't Kael's true intention though.

"Hey, what the knot? S—stop that!" A guard rushed over and pulled Kael away from the fence. "What do you think you're doing? You stupid knot." He shoved Kael back over to the main gate.

"We told you!" the other guard spat, "no entry!" He cuffed Kael over the head.

In response, Kael lashed out and struck him square in the face. Blood gushed from the man's nose as he fell to the ground, unconscious. Kael made his move.

He pressed against the gate. One moment it was locked, but after a surge of power from deep within Kael's chest, it clicked open. Kael flung the doors open and rushed inside. *Thank you, Skullsnout.* With a cry, the other guard rushed after him.

Kael threw open the door to the castle and slammed it closed behind him then pressed his ear against the sturdy wood. He could hear the guard approaching. Before the man full reached the door, Kael threw it open, smashing the guard in the face and knocking him unconscious. Kael grinned and then wheeled around, trying to focus his eyes in the semi-darkness of the castle's interior.

He pressed against a wall, deciding which way to go first. There were two yawning hallways, one to his left and the other to his right. Finding the king was one of his main objectives, but he figured he should learn his way around first, in case his intrusion was welcomed with...little enthusiasm. He played a quick game in his mind to decide which hallway to venture down first, then set off.

For the next half-hour, he worked his way through the castle. It was actually far smaller than he had first thought. He found out why when he looked out of a window. Just outside, he could see soldiers marching around an area enclosed by the castle walls. The castle had only looked large because it shared the same land as the city's training grounds, much like Vallenfend—except this city's was several times larger, with at least a hundred barracks that Kael could spot. The size of their army was truly daunting.

Enough exploring, Kael needed to find the king.

The castle itself was only comprised of three levels. Most of the rooms were on the outside side of the curved hallways, telling Kael that there must have been something occupying most of the space in the middle—a throne or dinner room most likely.

Back on the ground level, Kael realized that he was also at the front door. Two hallways stretched to either side, but a third continued straight ahead. Somehow, Kael had missed it to begin with. He ran through the hallway, which led to a set of thick double doors. He placed his head against it, listened for three heartbeats, then shoved it open.

Kael was expecting a large room, but what met him was breathtaking. He had guessed that there would be a main room, but had underestimated how big the castle truly was. The room's roof stretched far above, so high that even Shatterbreath wouldn't be able to touch the ceiling with her snout. Kael wouldn't have doubted that at least two Shatterbreaths could have fit into the room.

The walls were painted in a consistent shade of sky-blue, giving the illusion that Kael was not actually indoors. The illusion faded, however, lower down on the walls, where gold stencilling crawled up from the floors, as if to reach for the heaven of the ceiling far above.

The room was tiered, with each level containing different sets of furniture until finally, at the largest and tallest plateau, a richly lavished throne sat alone and omnipotent. Contrasting to the colour of the ceiling, all the furniture was a deep, magenta red.

Kael gasped as he realized there were *people* filling the furniture. The king himself was sitting in his throne, leaning to one side. His frown was piercing.

"Oi, what are you doing in here, chum? This is a private meeting!" He waved his hand. "How dare you disturb the dukes and me!"

Kael was suddenly conscious of all the men's eyes. They were all scowling at him, not a kind or understanding face among them. Kael noticed the furniture of the bottommost tier had yellow legs while the two tiers above—including the king's throne—had green. Fascinating.

"I'm sorry to disturb you, King," Kael exclaimed, giving a humble bow. "I need to speak with you at once concerning urgent business."

The king considered Kael. Kael considered him right back. Now that he was relatively closer, Kael could see his features better. His hair was long and somewhat greasy, slicked back behind his ears, but falling ahead of his shoulders. His eyebrows were both thick and slanted, giving him a nerve-racking scowl. An earring accented his right ear, matching the many gold rings he twisted on his fingers.

"I don't usually allow visitors. Especially ones that *intrude* like you, but you seem innocent enough. I'll let you speak. What do you want?"

Kael thought for a moment. "I'd like to know who Nestoff is."

The king reached over and picked up a goblet. He took a long swig out of it before answering. "Ah, wonderful ale. Nestoff is the city to the northwest. We have been at war for centuries. For years, the city's opposing clans, the Tehpuu and Sansan have been fighting against each other, allowing Nestoff to grow and prosper, like an ignored weed. Because of their squabble with each other, we were never allowed to reach our full potential. That is no longer! They have learned to—well, more or less—settle their differences. I have taught them who the real enemy is. Nestoff will fall."

"You are Tehpuu?" Kael asked.

The king put down his goblet. "That doesn't matter now. I have all but united Tehpuu and Sansan. The people don't see me as Tehpuu; they see me as the mediator. I don't serve one faction, but both equally. As a king should."

"We've had problems with that before," an elderly man added.

"You've done a lot for you city," Kael said, "you're timing couldn't be better. For you see, there is an empire coming from overseas, one which—"

"An empire?" the king exclaimed. "Overseas?"

Kael hesitated. "Yes. They're an incredible threat. I've been gathering forces to help fight against them before they have a chance to—"

"Where'd you say you were from?"

Kael bit his tongue. He hated being interrupted. "Vallenfend, but I was exiled."

The king threw his head back and laughed. The other twenty or so men chuckled as well. Kael shifted his weight, remembering Vallenfend's reputation. He had been in trouble once before just because of where he came from.

"Ha, ho! I was wrong about you, stranger!" The king slapped his knee. "You're a greater chum than I thought! What the knot are you doing here? Are you crazy?"

Kael worked his jaw. "I—I'm sorry, I don't follow. Did I say something...offensive to you?"

"No!" the king scoffed. "Just stupid! Why, you have no idea where you are, do you?"

Kael made a fist. "What are you talking about?"

"Listen, chum." The king got up from his throne and leisurely strolled down the tiers. "Before you go around, preaching your bowline nonsense, you should do your research first. You don't know what a Tehpuu is; you don't know what a Sansan is." He counted on his fingers. "You don't know what Nestoff is. Knot, I bet you don't even know the name of our city."

"Uh..."

"That's what I thought." The king grabbed his thumb and wiggled it. "Oh, here's the big one." He was right in front of Kael now. "We know what BlackHound is."

Kael grimaced. "Wha?" he gasped. "Y—you do?"

"You great knot. We *support* BlackHound."

Kael's head was spinning. He nearly stumbled. "No, that can't be! Why would you ever...?"

"The BlackHound Empire helped to calm the storm between the Tehpuu and Sansan. They redirected our rage towards each other and helped organize the wonderful government system you see before you right now. In fact, we're supposed to assist them with their landing in..." He spun around. "What? Six days? Yeah. In six days, we will help the BlackHound destroy your sad, poor little Vallenfend. You don't think they'd rely on their forces alone, did you? A great knot indeed."

Kael took a step back, aghast. Suddenly, the room seemed to be stained black. He was dazed, stunned. The king's twisted smirk was all too evident.

The two main doors behind Kael burst open. A squad of soldiers entered, headed by two men with bloody noses. "There's the knot now!"

"Oh," the king chirped. "Just in time! Kill him."

The soldiers drew their swords. Kael did the same. All at once, they bull-rushed Kael. Had he been in the same predicament a week later, before Skullsnout had blessed him, he surely would have been slain right then and there.

As it was, Kael was in perfect fighting condition. Time slowed to an absolute crawl, giving Kael plenty of time to react. He ducked under a blade, turned his body and twisted his wrist, bringing his blade to a guard's chest in a powerful diagonal backslash.

The soldier was wearing a breastplate and tunic underneath. He might as well have been wearing just the tunic. Kael's sword, both sharpened to a razor's edge and hardened by magic, sliced straight through the breastplate, cutting deep into the man's chest.

Kael blocked a mace with his shield while at the same time deflecting a blow with *Vintrave*. He carried through with a kick to the guard to the right, spun around, dodging another flailing weapon, and slashed two men across their bellies. He smashed his shield into the face of one last guard until an attack made it through his defences.

The sword of a guard stuck partway into Kael's shoulder. It didn't hit bone, but the blade definitely made it to flesh. Kael kicked the man, then ran him through. With a wince, Kael quickly yanked the blade from his pauldron. He could feel blood trickle from the wound, but it wouldn't inhibit him much.

Kael faked an attack, but instead jumped to the side and then sprinted around the remaining five or six soldiers. Kael didn't even look back at the throne room. His only interest now was escaping alive. The BlackHound Empire's influence was heavy—the city was a lost cause. It was the enemy.

Kael burst through the front doors of the castle, stumbling as he did. He tripped on the three steps just in front of the castle and tumbled, but quickly rolled back into his feet, straight into a mounted knight. Kael put up his shield just in time as the knight swung what looked like a claymore at him. The sword glanced off Kael's shield, going wide. Taking advantage, Kael lunged up at the man, aiming between the plates of his armour. The sword found flesh in the knight's belly and the man went limp. Kael backed off and seized the knight's leg and yanked him off the horse, which brayed in protest.

Pulling his sword free, Kael clambered up onto the horse. With some difficulty, Kael steered the startled horse away from the castle and flicked the reigns. He should have payed attention to what was waiting for him first. A collection of cavalry was waiting in the plaza just outside of the castle. Kael gritted his teeth and hugged closer to the horse's back. The ballistae lining the city's wall ensured that Shatterbreath couldn't swoop in for a quick escape. There was only one way out—through them.

Kael flicked the reigns, starting his stolen horse forward. Several of the mounted knights spurred their horses as well, charging towards Kael. The first soldier swung his mace at Kael, who leaned as far as he could over to the right. The mace smashed into Kael's shield, which was protecting the majority of his body, nearly knocking him from his horse.

Keeping a hold of the saddle, Kael was able to pull himself back upright. What he saw made his heart sink. He was in the thick of the group of cavalry now. Kael dodged a lunge from a halberd by leaning over again, but couldn't recover fast enough to steer his horse away from the next attack. One of the knights rammed the end of his spear straight into the horse's chest. Kael's horse screeched and its legs buckled. Thinking fast, Kael stood up and leapt from its back towards the man who had just stabbed it. Kael collided with the man, knocking him from the saddle and tipping the horse over.

The horse landed on its rider as Kael hit the ground hard. The soldier screamed, but was silenced a second later by Kael's sword. Kael waited as patiently as he could while the horse got back up on its feet, then clambered onto its back not a second later. Blocking several blows with his shield, he pulled on the reigns, turning the horse toward the exit of the city. Then he slapped it as hard as he could on the rump, spurring it to run.

Kael sheathed his sword and snatched the reigns with both hands, standing up in the stirrups to coax the horse to go faster. He had lost many of the soldiers because they had stayed behind with their injured comrades, but there was still an uncomfortable amount chasing at his heels.

Kael sped through the streets on his horse, coming close to running down several civilians as he did. He wasn't terribly concerned for their safety anyway. He turned a sharp corner in an attempt to lose his pursuers and was nearly bucked off as his horse jumped over a knee-height wall. From behind, he could hear as one or more of the soldiers' horses tripped on the same wall.

He patted his horse's neck and whispered a compliment. After another sharp turn, the front gate loomed into view. It was open too! A caravan of some kind was making its way through the gates, probably carrying supplies for the army. Kael nudged the horse's sides, willing it to go faster. The guards Kael had met earlier at the gate noticed as Kael raced towards the entrance, but it was already too late. The horse barrelled through them like they were nothing more than corn stalks.

Kael made it through the gate. However, as he did, he had the misfortune of looking up—only to fleetingly see a dozen or so archers taking aim from the top of the wall.

Time slowed as the archers released their arrows. Kael watched them in horror as they moved sluggishly through the air. His horse continued on unaware of the impending peril, muscles taut and mouth foaming. Kael turned around in the saddle and braced his shield close against his body. There was nothing else he could do.

Several arrows bounced off his sword or armour. The horse wasn't nearly as lucky. At least six arrows pierced into its backside. With a shriek, it faltered for a moment before tumbling, sending Kael soaring from its back. He smacked into the ground and slid for what seemed forever, kicking up clods of dirt and a shroud of choking dust.

His whole body ached and he was winded. As hard as he tried, he couldn't bring his body move. As the cloud of dust dissipated, he could clearly see the archer positioned atop the wall, taking aim once again. Out in front of him, Kael could see his horse writhing on the ground, and beyond it, the mounted soldiers catching up at last.

Before the arrows or knights could reach him, however, Kael heard a mighty roar. Shatterbreath swooped in close to the gate, releasing a breath of fire that consumed a huge section of its southwestern wall, taking at least five ballistae with it. With another breath, the front gate was sent ablaze, incinerating the entire battalion of archers. The cavalry she didn't even bother with, the burning gate kept them from exiting the city.

She swooped in and snatched up Kael in her front talons, heading away from the city before its remaining ballistae could aim towards her.

Still short of breath, Kael went limp in her paws.

"Well," she snorted, "how'd it go?"

Kael sighed and placed a hand against his forehead.

Chapter 6

Kael held on tight as Shatterbreath performed a barrel roll. Once she was upright once again, she hummed, sending low vibrations through Kael's body.

"If that city back there is working for the BlackHound Empire," she said, "why don't I just burn it to the ground?" Kael had filled Shatterbreath in on everything that had happened inside the city overnight.

"That's too risky. That city is armed to the teeth. I can't have you struck by a ballista again. Even if you did eliminate all their ballistae, I'm sure the sheer amount of archers would take you down eventually." Kael scratched his chin, looking off into the distance. "Then how would I get home?"

Shatterbreath huffed.

The faint outline of a city appeared on the horizon. Within minutes, Shatterbreath had touched down in a grove relatively close by.

"Tiny, don't take any chances with this city," Shatterbreath advised. "You said yourself; the BlackHound Empire will arrive in six days. Your friends will need you in fighting condition."

"I'll be careful," Kael reassured her, "and I'll be quick."

"You better be."

Kael patted her snout and then started on his way to the city. At once, it was obvious that the city was indeed Nestoff. It was as battle-scarred as the last city. Unlike the last city (which Kael had nicknamed Knot-Town), the front gates were wide open, permitting Kael to enter without any hassle.

The inside of Nestoff was not as tight as Knot-Town, and neither was it constructed as tactical. The buildings were designed in no specific order, giving Kael the impression that Nestoff worked on the offensive more than Knot-Town. Kael could spot no castle rising up from the city anywhere, though he did see a large, circular building. An amphitheatre of sorts. He wondered about it, but put it to the back of his mind.

Also unlike Knot-Town, there were less guards walking around the city. When Kael did find one, however, he was startled. The man was a bear! He was tall and lumbering, wearing a thick set of armour that would otherwise incapacitate any ordinary man. He carried both a tower shield over his back and a thick lance which was supported by a metal hook built right into his heavy breastplate. Most of his face was covered by a smooth plate attached to the front of his breastplate, off centered to his right side. In his idle hand, he carried a frogmouth-helmet. Kael thought at first that the man must have been dressed up for a different reason, so he walked past him. He was wrong. Another person wearing a similar set of armour lumbered past, just as hulking. Indeed, everybody in Nestoff seemed to have a powerful build. Kael noticed that even the women meandering on the streets were heavy with muscle.

Kael hesitantly approached one of the armoured guards after several minutes of avoiding them. "Excuse me," he muttered tentatively.

The man turned to face Kael, scowling at him from over the plate guarding his chest. "What?" he grumbled.

"I was hoping you could direct me to you castle... I wish to have an audience with your king."

The man scrutinized him. "What for?"

"Matters considering grave peril. Your city—indeed every city on this continent—is in serious jeopardy."

The guard shifted his weight. "You speak big. King may have audience with you. I bring you to castle so you may talk with him. Follow."

Kael hesitated, caught off guard by the man's broken speech. Nevertheless, he followed after him. It didn't take long for Kael to realize the entire city spoke in an incomplete dialect as they strolled through a market. He could catch fragments of conversations here and there. He chewed his lip. Having to adapt to their strange way of speaking would be slightly difficult.

On their way, Kael and the thick guard passed by the amphitheatre. "What's that structure?" Kael asked. "What is it for?"

"Games," was the guard's reply. "Is big stadium. Every soldier plays games to prove himself—also for public entertainment. We have jousting, fighting, and many other battles. Only...only strongest warriors fight in military. Losers either killed or...guard duty."

"Oh." Kael went silent. Obviously enough, the guard hadn't won his battle. Kael had a hard time believing he was one of the *losers*. *What did Nestoff's military even look like?*

Instead of veering away from the amphitheatre, as Kael was expecting, they continued walking around it until they had come to a few archways set in its side. Men, women and children were exiting from the many archways, chattering excitedly. Many of them stopped outside to swap money before either skipping or stomping off. The guard pushed his way through the crowd, which wasn't hard for him to do considering his size. The pointed lance at his side probably helped.

Light poured in through more archways leading into the centre of the amphitheatre itself. Kael couldn't see into the amphitheatre itself for the steady throng of people blocked it from view. Instead of taking the same route the civilians were, the guard took Kael to a smaller, gated entrance to the side. He protruded a key from the depths of his breastplate and stuck it into a lock.

"King Goar waits inside." The guard opened the door for Kael. "Good luck."

"Thanks," Kael said. "You were very helpful."

"Forget. Oh, stranger..."

Kael hesitated. "Yes?"

"I hope you good at games."

Kael gave him a strange look. The guard only smiled and clomped away without any further explanation. Confused by his last statement, Kael climbed a set of stairs made of marble. He stepped out of a hallway and gasped.

There was a huge stadium before him. Countless tiers of seats surrounded a central area, almost an equal size to the Vallenfend's castle grounds. People were still exiting the building, looking like nothing more than dots on the far side of the amphitheatre, giving Kael a perspective to how truly vast the structure was.

"Ahoy, who are you?"

Kael whipped around. Just up another flight of stairs, a giant of a man stood, peering down at Kael with deep-set eyes. Through his light beard, Kael could see his lip curl in a hint of disdain. From the duel-feathered crown adorning his short-haired head and the rings on his meaty fingers, Kael quickly deduced that he was the king or leader of Nestoff.

"Uh, hello," Kael stammered, thrusting out his hand. "My name is Kael Rundown."

The man stared at Kael's hand. "Yes, and?"

"And..." Kael paused, frowning. "I'm from another city, seeking your help. Your kingdom is in grave danger."

King Goar sniffed, amused. "That so?" He waved his hand at a woman occupying his booth with him. "Gerlinda, leave. I be with you shortly."

A thin woman wearing very little clothing walked up to Kael, reaching out to stroke his chin with a long fingernail, puckering her lips as she did. Kael stiffened.

"Woman, I said leave!" The king's frown was venomous. Wearing a pout, the woman slipped out of sight. Kael released his breath. The king sat down in an ebony armchair overlooking the arena. "What were you saying?"

Kael flinched. "Oh yes. Uh, I've come a long way to plead for your help. Please, I ask you to just listen to what I have to say for a moment. If it's not too much trouble."

The king shrugged. "Is fine. Please, sit, relax."

Kael rested on the cushioned chair next to the king, leaning forward to lace his fingers together. "There is an empire coming from overseas." Kael stopped, wondering for a split second whether Nestoff was working with the BlackHound Empire as well. "They...are coming to conquer this land, starting with my city. Once they have established themselves in this land, they will stop at nothing until they rule dominant."

The king started out at the empty arena. He took a lasting breath. "We are strong. We will endure."

"No you won't." Kael cringed at the king's scowl. "But together, we can stop this empire's advance before it begins. I have collected a force several kingdoms strong to try and defeat them. I'm afraid it won't be enough. With Nestoff's help, though, this continent will stand a far greater chance."

The king thought for a moment. "I know what you speak. Empire came to Nestoff. They were weak, speak of many promises. Many nice things."

"Did you believe them?"

The king shook his head.

"But you believe me, right? Will you help us? I can offer protection."

The king laughed. "Protection? What you speak? Nestoff doesn't need protection. We are most powerful city—none can defeat us. What we possibly need protection from?"

"Knot-Town," Kael mumbled.

"What?" The king shook his head. "Protection not needed, but I believe young Kael."

Kael bowed his head. "Thank you."

The king raised a ringed finger. "However, King Goar only trust warrior. Nestoff's military needed...elsewhere. Cannot surrender military so willingly."

"I offered protection. What else do you wish? Do you want go—" Kael stopped himself, remembering he had already promised Vallenfend's gold to somebody else.

"I want know if you are strong warrior. You must prove self." The king gave a slow nod, smiling like a thief. "You must play game." He threw his arms out and leaned back. "You win? I consider what you say—probably even agree. You lose?" He shrugged. "Well, no guard duty for foreigners. Only one other option."

Kael blinked slowly. *Death.* "Games, eh?" He chewed his lip. "What kind of game? I will only play if I can have you *word* you will help in my cause if I win."

The king cracked his fingers. Kael could feel his muscles tighten with each *pop*. "Game of strength. Game of speed and cunning. I'm

73

think a fight. Yes, fight good test of warrior. You will fight my champion. Unless problem...arises, if you win, Rundown has my— and Nestoff's—support. Agree?"

Kael ran a hand through his hair. He could feel his heart quickening its pace. For a time, he struggled to find any words. "How soon can I fight?"

The king smirked and cocked his head. "I will call people back at once. They get special treat today!" he exclaimed, clapping his hands together. "Two games, one day."

Kael gritted his teeth. "Lucky for them..."

Before Kael knew it, he was standing in the middle of the arena. The stadium was nearly filled and the roar of the crowd closed in on Kael from all directions. He played with one of his leather gloves, doing his best to try and ignore them.

He was wearing traditional Nestoff armour designed for hand-to-hand combat. A shoddy leather breastplate was all he wore across his chest (they had trouble finding a size that would fit his frame), strikingly similar to the standard-issue Vallenfend armour. As well, he had been given greaves, vambraces and soft leather gauntlets. Underneath his armour, he wore a brown tunic, also given to him by King Goar.

Standing a bowshot away was the king's champion. If Kael had been imposed by the first guard he had met, he was terrified now. The man stood a good foot taller than he, rippling with muscle and glistening with sweat from just walking out into the sun. Wrapped around his meaty head was a cloth circlet with two silver pegs attached to the front. Kael eyed the glinting metal, aware that the circlet was a trophy, a sign he was indeed the city's best fighter.

Kael gulped.

A horned blared from the side. The two men assisting the champion quickly scurried off and out of sight, leaving Kael alone with the giant. They approached each other. The champion smirked, giving his right eye a severe squint. Kael noticed that the same eye was off-centered and cloudy. He made a mental note of that. *He's vulnerable from that side.*

They shook hands, the champion's paw engulfing Kael's. "You luck."

Kael nodded. "Good luck. Hope I don't beat you too bad."

The champion laughed heartily and spun around. "Little man want death. I give, I give!"

Kael stood on his starting spot, hopping up and down. He kinked his neck to either side, rolling his shoulders. The champion waved to the crowd, which roared in response.

A horn blew. Three more to go. On the third, it would be time to fight.

The champion sobered up, planting his feet on the ground and adopting his fighting pose. One hand posed down below, the other hovering close to his chest, fingers curled. He glowered at Kael over the top of his glove.

Another blast of the horn, followed closely by a crack of thunder. Kael glanced at the sky. No doubt Shatterbreath was not happy with what he was doing. He hoped she wouldn't try to intervene. More importantly, he hoped she'd forgive him.

A blow of the horn. One more to go. Kael bent low, coiling up like a spring. His heart was beating faster and faster, sending adrenaline coursing through his body. Anticipation itched at his muscles, tightening his throat and forcing the massive crowd to melt away.

The last horn blew.

With a booming war-cry, the champion charged towards Kael, rearing back his left fist. Kael stayed motionless, letting the scene slipped into altered time. He breathed in every detail before he made his move; the strands of muscle which were evident in the champion's arms, his teeth that were bared, the cracking of his knuckles as he tightened his fist, bracing for the instant knockout he was no doubt planning for.

He was within a broadsword's length away before Kael finally moved. Still in altered time, he spun to avoid the incoming fist and then jumped towards the man. His face twisted into ugly surprise as Kael planted a leg on the champion's outstretched thigh. Releasing his coiled strength, Kael brought his fist up with explosive strength, assisted by a power deep within his chest. His blow struck the champion straight in the side of his face, narrowly missing his temple.

Time, quite rudely, returned to normal. The man was sent reeling before he eventually slumped to the ground. Kael landed on his side, but rolled over and sprang to his feet.

The crowd went silent.

The champion writhed on the ground for a moment, clutching his face. Kael had struck him on his bad side, making it even worse. Already, a nasty bruise was forming as well as a lump.

"Little man...punish for this!" The champion slowly rose to his feet. "I will crush like wicker reed! Bones will be powder!"

Kael folded his arms. "Give me your best."

The champion howled in rage. Once again, he charged Kael, only this time, faster. Kael dodged his fist blow, ducked underneath a second and delivered a series of sharp jabs to the champion's gut. It was like punching a door. Bad idea.

Out of nowhere, a fist that seemed the size of a pumpkin struck Kael. Instantly, his face was engulfed in raw, stinging pain. He was rocked to the side, hardly able to stand due to the stars spinning across his vision. Not a moment later, a foot collided into Kael's upper back, forcing him halfway to the sandy ground.

Doing his best to ignore the pain, Kael whipped around in time to haphazardly block another kick with his forearms. *That* one hurt. He scrambled away, putting a comfortable amount of distance between him and the champion to gain his breath.

"Lucky first hit," the champion rumbled. "Not again. You catch me off-guard no more. I ready now. You give up now? Let walk away...mostly intact. If walk at all."

Kael shook his head rigorously, also trying to rid himself of his dizziness. His head was still churning from that first hit.

The champion shrugged, assuming his stance once again. "Fine. Cleaners have to scoop up with shovel when I done with you."

The champion charged again. This time, Kael was more prepared. He dodged to the champion's right. The man missed his punch and Kael was able to avoid his second, but it was kick that caught him off guard. Kael practically caught the champion's foot, absorbing most of the blow with his hands. It was still enough to knock him flat on his back. Kael blinked, slightly dazed.

Again, his ability to slow time saved his life. A fist reared down, but Kael rolled out of the way, causing it to slam into the ground instead. The champion whistled, shaking his glove free of sand.

"You fast, little man," he said, grinning. "Fast good for nothing. Only able to run. Never win battle with run. That is why Nestoff always win. Nestoff is strong. Nestoff never run."

This time, it was Kael who charged him. However, unlike the champion, Kael didn't try to punch. He didn't attack at all. Instead, he dove underneath a fist and between the champion's legs, sliding completely underneath. Before the champion could turn around, Kael was already up. He sprang up onto the champion's back and began kneeing him repetitively in the ribs from behind.

The champion cried out and reached behind his back. Not only was he faster than Kael had expected, but more flexible too. Kael was beginning to understand why he was Nestoff's champion. He wasn't inhibited by his size and muscle mass.

He snatched Kael's arm with one hand and a fistful of tunic with the other. He pried Kael free of his back and tried to throw him. As Kael went forward over the champion's shoulder, he grabbed onto man's hair. Using the momentum he had already gained, he swung towards the champion knee first. Kael's knee struck the man's face. Hard.

That made the champion let go, but before Kael could gain any distance, the man fell forward on top of him. Face pressed into the arena sand he thrashed underneath the huge weight of the champion's body to no avail. Somehow, Kael managed to squeeze an arm between his neck and the thick man's keeping the champion from choking him out. Kael twisted enough to free his left arm. He struck the champion in the side of the face several times, trying to get the brute off of him.

The champion shoved Kael's face even deeper into the sand, making Kael gasp for breath. Kael continued to thrash, still to no avail. He faltered for a split second—enough to let the champion tightened the grip around his neck. Kael could breath, but just barely. He wheezed and gasped, more concerned with precious oxygen than anything else. Stars bordered his vision. On the verge of collapse, Kael's body involuntarily relaxed.

He was vaguely aware of a great weight lifting itself off of him. Then, Kael seemed to be airborne. A pressure at his back lifted him upright, where he hovered above the sandy ground for a moment or so.

Thwack. Pain pierced into his dazed body. Kael slumped over backwards on the ground. He could feel something warm flowing over his face. Gingerly, he touched his cheek. Scarlet glistened on his fingers.

More pain erupted on his scalp, shaking the haze from his mind further. Once again, he was hefted upright, this time to stand on the ground. Through a puffy eye, he could see the champion winding up for another shot. This would be the finisher.

Kael wasn't quite done yet.

Once again, time slowed to a crawl. The fist was coming towards him, slow as a snail. Kael cringed, waiting for the inevitable. Even with his time-warping ability, there was nothing he could do to stop it. He was worn out, done. Beaten.

Skullsnout's words suddenly resounded through his mind. *Be wary of my gift. Use it well.* That's it. *Gift.*

Kael reached deep down inside himself, summoning a strength buried deep within his chest. One that hadn't been there before his visit with Skullsnout.

Inches in front of Kael's face, the champion's fist stopped. His wrist buckled and bones cracked in his hand, as if he had just hit a solid brick wall. Kael remained motionless. He didn't even flinch.

The champion howled and clutched his broken hand. His knuckles had split open, oozing blood and revealing tendon. The crowd gasped, shocked by what just happened.

Trying to control Skullsnout's gift, Kael brought back his fist. Summoning all his strength, he punched the champion as hard as he could in the chest.

He didn't know what he was expecting, maybe for the champion to light on fire, maybe for him to go soaring across the arena. He would have been ecstatic if he was knocked unconscious. Kael would have happy even if the man was knocked over.

As it was, nothing happened. Kael blushed, fist flat against the champion's leather breastplate. The man, still clutching his fist, gave Kael a strange look.

"Uh..."

The champion drove his knee into Kael's gut. Kael doubled over, just in time to receive an uppercut. This time, the world went dark.

Chapter 7

Kael awoke with a start, bolting upright in his bed. Not a second later, pain lanced through his body as a reward. He screamed, unsure which part of his body hurt more.

"Ah, he wakes!" a familiar voice mused. Kael glanced sideways to spot King Goar sitting on a cot nearby, fingers laced together.

Kael put a hand to his throbbing temple. "Where am I? How long was I out for?"

The king smiled. "In warrior barracks. You be unconscious for no more than day, relax. No more games for you. If you are wonder, you...lost."

Flinching, Kael rubbed a sore arm. "Thanks, I think I realize that now."

The king stood up to begin pacing. "You should be dead, Kael Rundown. Be thankful I am such generous king. Champion should have killed you."

Kael flinched again, but not from the pain. *Shatterbreath was going to be furious.* "Why didn't you kill me? I failed your game."

The king stopped pacing. "You good fighter, Kael Rundown. Better than I expect. Honourable, too. You would have never accept game if not believe in what strive for. Your ambition great."

"Thanks," Kael mumbled, "but ambition isn't everything. I don't suppose you'd agree to assist me in my cause anyway...?"

The king sniffed. "No. Understand, is kingdom policy if foreign warrior lose, he is exile. Just for record, Kael, you are banish from Nestoff."

Kael sighed and rubbed his stomach. *That made two cities.* "I know about your squabble with Knot-Town," Kael said suddenly.

"Bah, is old news. We've been enemies for centuries."

"They plan to attack. You will be outnumbered."

King Goar retorted quickly. "Nothing we can't handle. We will destroy." He waved his hand with a soft chuckle.

Kael lowered his head, nursing his cut lip. He tasted blood on his tongue. "No. You won't." Kael leaned forward. "Listen, I can help with your plight. You need my help. Their forces are vast. Unless something is done, you could very well be overrun. Even if you manage to fend them off, there will be great loss."

King Goar scrutinized him for a moment.

Kael leaned in even closer. "And...*off* the record, I can help you. I know things. I've been inside their town, *and* their castle. With my help, you can finally settle this feud. With my help, you can ensure safety and peace for Nestoff."

King Goar cocked his head. "Why would you help Nestoff? What can benefit from this? You will still be banish."

"I know." Kael shifted his weight on the cot. "I like your city better than theirs. Mostly, I want Knot-Town out of the way. They are working for the invading empire. As far as I'm concerned, they are the enemy too. We have something in common then."

King Goar scratched his beard. "I'm listen."

"They have two factions within the city which don't cope well together. The king they have now has united them in a common cause. To destroy Nestoff. I believe all it would take to make them hate each other once again is one small *tip* of the scales."

"...That make them fight." The king narrowed his eyes. "While they busy killing each other, Nestoff march in and take advantage of chaos." He beamed. "I like plan! I was right, you are formidable warrior. How are you make them fight, though? We try sending Nestoff spies. They always spot! What is plan?"

"Your people are big and strong, and well, very easy to spot. I'm a smaller guy. In fact, I stopped by there a day or so ago. The people there thought I was one of them. I should have no problem getting in." Kael rubbed his chin. "As for upsetting the two groups... I know a way.

"There is one thing though," Kael added.

"What?"

"What are you going to do with the city?"

The king frowned. "Destroy it, or maybe enslave. Depend on resistance."

Kael shook his head. "That won't do. I am practically fighting to avoid the very same thing! No, I cannot help you with that, even if it is against Knot-Town."

King Goar stomped his foot. "Foolish! Why think wars are waged? It is either their destruction, or Nestoff's."

Kael snapped his fingers. "Then don't completely destroy them! Just their military! Without an army, there is no threat against you. You don't have to kill the innocent civilians; they serve no threat against you. You could just...stop by once and a while to make sure Knot-Town is harmless in the future instead of completely decimating them. I'm sure the people will eventually realize that *anything's* better than extermination. Hey, maybe you could even form a friendly relationship with Knot-Town."

"Friendship?" King Goar wrinkled his nose. "Your proposition is... Is..." He thought for a moment longer. "I suppose you right. Maybe better to be friend than enemy. Maybe benefit from each other. If Knutton slips out of line, though, we destroy."

Knutton? Was that the real name of Knot-Town? Kael's nickname had been more accurate than he thought. He shrugged in reply. "Sure."

"If your battle wages for long and ours doesn't, we assist you."

"Really?"

The king pounded his chest. "If you break stalemate between Knutton and Nestoff, we be in your debt. It would be honour...to aid you in cause."

Kael nodded, feeling comforted. He may have been beaten to a pulp as well as banished, but he counted this trip as a success.

After swapping the arena armour for his personal set, Kael discreetly exited the city. Once outside, he scanned the skies for Shatterbreath. He even whistled several times to no avail.

Suddenly, there was a *whoosh* behind him. Shatterbreath clipped Kael with her hind paws, sending him several feet. When he had stood back up, she was in front of him, teeth bared, wings outstretched, tail thrashing. Kael shied away, genuinely scared for his life.

"How dare you!" she roared. Kael tried to speak, but she cut him off with a snarl. "I told you to stay *out* of trouble! Why did you deliberately disobey me? Why would you do such a thing? You could have died! You idiot!" Shatterbreath smacked him with her tail. "Did you even pause to think what ramifications your actions would have? What if they *had* killed you, Kael? What then?"

"Please, Shatterbreath..."

"No! Enough of you!" She flared her wings and rose up on her hind legs. "Do you know how close I came to incinerating that city? I was going to burn it down because of you. A whole city would have died. A whole city filled of innocent people, Kael. Thousands of people nearly died because of *you!*"

The blood drained from Kael's face. "I—I'm sorry I made you so worried, Shatterbreath, but..."

"Sorry!" she roared. She began trembling in rage. Her eyes had reduced to slits. "Sorry doesn't *begin* to satisfy what you did! Your recklessness is...is..." She reared back and hit Kael with her muzzle, sending him sprawling. She slammed either paw down on either side of him, glaring at him with one eye from a hand's breadth away. "I told you to be careful, to *stay out of trouble!* Almost as soon as you set foot in the city, you were making a bargain for your life! Why would you do such a thing?"

"I had a good reason!" Kael exclaimed. "The king was willing to help me if I agreed."

Shatterbreath slammed her tail down, literally cracking the ground. "That's *not* a good reason!" she hollered. For a moment, Kael feared he would break an eardrum. "If you'd have *died,* Kael, everything you worked for would be undone. Vallenfend would crumble; your precious friends would *die.* Was the gamble worth it? What did you accomplish?"

Kael tried to shove her snout away. She snapped at him, missing his hands by mere centimetres. "I have a way to eliminate Knot-Town!"

"What?" she hissed.

Kael scooted out from under her, putting out his hands defensively. "Th—the town working for BlackHound." He pointed

83

to the horizon. "It's too dangerous for you to try and burn it down— they'd shoot you out of the sky! But I think I've found a way to get them out of the way."

Shatterbreath scrutinized him, lip still curled. "What exactly does that entail? No, we only have so many days left, Kael. We can't waste any more time with that place. If anything, we should be heading back home."

"That's why we have to be quick." Kael moved towards her. "We have to go at once."

"Then *you,*" Shatterbreath hissed as she reared away, "better borrow a horse." With a powerful leap and a whoosh of air, she took off, leaving Kael behind.

He watched her go, anger boiling deep in his veins. *What?!* She was leaving him behind? He picked up a huge rock and hurled it from over his head. It landed three yards away, hitting the soft ground with a barely-audible *thump.*

Fuming, Kael started back to Nestoff. On his way, he kicked the same rock. With a surge of power, it literally exploded, sending shrapnel flying several yards.

Chapter 8

Kael hadn't really appreciated how far away Knot-Town was from Nestoff. He left as soon as he could after Shatterbreath stormed off, stealing a pale-brown horse from Nestoff first. He would have borrowed one from King Goar, but with Kael banished, he doubted the man would be so accommodating. Even though he pushed the animal until it was frothing from the mouth, it was dusk by the time he reached Knot-Town's outer wall.

Kael dismounted his horse, removed his pack—again generously donated by King Goar—then slapped the beast over the rump. With a grunt, it charged away, leaving Kael alone in the increasing darkness.

He reached inside his pack and pulled out an anchor that resembled a three-pronged fishing hook attached to a long line of thick rope. The memory of when Kael scaled Vallenfend's wall flashed through his mind as he started to swing the hook. That was to escape. This was to *enter*. The hook sailed flawlessly upwards, disappearing over the lip of the wall. Kael waited a heartbeat before tugging on the rope. It was secure.

Just in case, Kael pulled out his knife and gripped it with his teeth. He started to scale the wall, at once conscious to how much weight his armour, sword and shield added. But in only a minute or so, he had climbed the wall. He rounded the edge and landed softly on top, crouching low and darting his gaze up and down either end. His heart skipped a beat as he spotted a guard meandering in the other direction. Somehow, he had walked past Kael's hook without seeing it. If the man had spotted him, Kael's mission would have been over before it even began. Snatching his knife from his teeth, Kael sprinted over to the man and silently dispatched him.

Wiping the blood from the blade, Kael returned to where his climbing rope was still hanging. He removed the hook and stuck it into the guardrail on the either side, wrapping his hand around the rope. Take a breath, he swung over the side of the wall and repelled down to the ground. Kael left the rope hanging there and darted into the cover of the houses. He would have to find a better means of escape later. He doubted he could even find his way back to that particular spot anyway.

It was a lot of work to avoid the main gate, but Kael was positive it would be worth it. He wasn't going to take the chance; if the same guards as before were there, they would undoubtedly recognize him. That would only spell trouble.

Kael slipped in between a row of houses. He studied the architecture for a moment. Tehpuu. Avoiding the streets, he made his way his target, reviewing what he knew about Knot-Town in his mind. The Tehpuu and Sansan hated each other, but were united under their current king, who himself was Tehpuu. That was unusual considering what Kael knew. The Tehpuu seemed like the more aggressive group.

As such, Kael was guessing the Tehpuu wouldn't be too happy to find their king murdered by the hands of a Sansan. If things went according to plan, the Tehpuu would be outraged enough to start brawling with the Sansan. The Sansan were milder, that was for certain, but when it came to fighting, they didn't hold any reserve. The incident in front of the castle proved that.

The plan was foolproof. Except for one thing. Kael wasn't Sansan. He stopped where he was to think about it. He considered for a moment whether he could simply hire a Sansan to assassinate the king for him, but decide such a thing would be impossible. The Sansan didn't seem like a group that would have hired killers easy at hand. Plus, he doubted any sum of gold would convince a Sansan to overturn the semi-peaceful state the city was in.

So it was up to him. If he was going to go through with his plan, he was going to have to become Sansan. But how?

From between the houses he was hiding behind, Kael spotted a group of young men stroll by, laughing raucously and yelling all sorts of variations of the word "knot." These boys were Tehpuu, but their presence gave Kael an idea.

Kael shifted his route away from the castle, darting in and out of the Tehpuu streets. At last, he reached what he was looking for. The road that separated the Tehpuu houses from the Sansan. Again, he dipped into the cover of the close houses. It was almost as if stepping into a different city altogether. The shift of architecture within one city was still startling.

Kael kept moving until he thought he was a satisfactory distance away from the Tehpuu/Sansan border. Not too far, not too close. There, he slumped against the side of a house, waiting for the opportune moment. It didn't take long for it to arise.

Kael perked up. A group of young men were approaching. Like the Tehpuu Kael had seen, they were using "knot" all too frequently, although with less vigour. It was a group of guards and judging by the yellow stripe emblazoned below the city crest, they were all Sansan.

Throwing himself out of cover, Kael threw out a few curse words, stumbling like a drunk. With a twinge, he realized that his swears were incorrect, so he changed them accordingly.

"Oi, you great pile of knots," he bellowed. "What in the blitty are you doing?" He hesitated, realizing he had used a bandit curse by accident. "Knottin' knotters never know when to knotting...knot."

The guards stiffened. One of them, an older boy with a scraggly goatee brandished his spear. "You stay away now. We don't want no trouble."

"Trouble?" Kael roared. "You Sansan are always looking for trouble! Aw, knot you, knot you all! Why, I should knock some sense into you right now! Teach you knots a lesson!"

"How many ales you think this chum's had?" one of the guards whispered.

Kael frowned. They seemed more amused than anything else.

The guard with the goatee moved towards Kael. "What are you doing on our side, Tehpuu? You best be going before some real trouble arises."

Kael grabbed hold of his spear. "You saying I'm not good enough to be here? You Sansan think you're all special. I'll bet you're not so good at fighting."

"Please, sir," the guard said, trying to pull his spear free, "we don't want any trouble."

"Trouble," Kael hissed, "I'll show you trouble."

He pulled on the guard's spear, pulling him closer to the Sansan. Without further warning, he struck the man across the face, snatched him by the shoulders and grounded his knee into the guard's gut.

"Hey!"

A second guard unsheathed his sword and thrashed at Kael, who spun to deflect the blade with his shield which was still strapped to his back. Carrying through, Kael knocked him out as well. The third guard got even less as far as his partner and before he could draw his weapon, Kael's boot collided with his ribs.

Kael seized the spear the guard with the goatee had dropped. He used it to knock each guard out, then threw it to the side. Kael hesitated, standing in the middle of the exposed street with three unconscious men around him. He judged which man was his size, then dragged him off to the side. Acting quickly, Kael removed the guard's armour and then his own. He slipped the breastplate over his shoulders. Perfect fit. Kael also detached a knife from the guard's thigh to strap it to his own. Unsure what to do with his own armour, Kael placed it on the ground. It was truly a nice set, but there was nothing more he could do with now. He couldn't take it, it would only burden him. If fortune permitted, maybe he could find it again on his way out. That possibility, however, was very low.

Saying a silent goodbye to his faithful set of armour, Kael set his sights on his goal. He had Sansan armour, and he had a Sansan knife. He was ready to cripple Knot-Town. He turned to face the middle of the city and set off in a direct route to the castle.

It was time to kill the king.

After a few minutes, Kael was lurking on the outskirts of the plaza in front of the castle gate. He studied the spiked fence keeping people like him from entering the building. At that time of night, the plaza was empty. The only sign of life came from the two guards standing at the gate as always, though they hardly seemed alive at all. The nightshift must have been boring.

Kael wracked his brain, trying to think of a way to get past them. He probably wasn't going to at all without some sort of confrontation. He needed to stay *out* of sight. So instead, Kael wound around the front gate. He knew what was to the left, so instead, he went right. The plaza narrowed until it was nothing more than an alleyway. The fence itself ended at the edge of the castle's wall.

Halting, Kael looked up at the castle's wall. There was a small window, maybe large enough for him to squeeze through. Better yet, there were no bars on it. Just a glass window. But it was high up, certainly too high to jump.

Kael scratched his chin. The gap between the castle wall and the wall of the house next to him wasn't too great. If he could find a way on top, he could just jump across...

Running a hand along the building's wall, he rounded a corner, coming to the edge of a small street. The houses were large and hubris in this area, obviously belonging to Tehpuu noblemen. Trims of gold made the doors and windows stand out in the waning light of the mid-night moon.

Cautious at first, Kael crept up to the front of the house closest to his target window. There were no torches burning inside, and indeed, no signs of activity anywhere on the street. Somewhere, an alley cat screeched, but otherwise, all was still. Taking a stifled breath, Kael pressed himself up against the wall, near the front door. Pausing for listen, he jumped up and grappled onto the overhanging ledge.

His legs flailed for a moment until he found a foothold. The window had thick wooden borders around the glass, which helped significantly as Kael hoisted himself up. This was one of the houses with a balcony. Resisting the urge to peer inside the house, Kael stood up on the railing and lifted himself up one more ledge, this time onto the roof.

The roof was slanted sharply to a square point, with only a foot or two of leeway along the edge to walk on. Straining on balance, Kael made his way around the roof until he was facing the castle wall.

Perfect. The window was across from him, a few feet lower than the ledge he was standing on. From way up high, Kael realized how far the jump really was. He swallowed, trying to think of any other solution.

Before he could second guess himself any further, Kael took a step back—as far as the roof would allow—then hurtled himself at the small window.

Kael became painfully aware of the situation as he soared towards the small window. The night wind, bringing the smell of the city along with it, whistled in his ear and ruffled his hair. Kael focussed on the glass window, pleading that he would make it. He was too low, no too high! He was going to hit his head, or his arm, or his feet. What if he hit the wall instead? What if he didn't jump far enough? The ground was awfully far away. He scrunched up as he neared it, folding his arm over his head. He wasn't going to make it!

The glass was harder than Kael was expecting. He struck against it, and for a dreadful moment, he thought the window wasn't going to break. Altogether, it shattered inwards. Showered in shards of glass, Kael tumbled into the castle, rolling several times before coming to a stop on his belly.

Kael picked himself up from the glass-covered carpet and shook himself, sending more fragments scattering about the room. Pausing to picking out glass out of his hands, Kael glanced around. He was in a medium sized room with a curtain dividing it through the middle. Just behind him, directly under the window he had just crashed through, was an enormous iron tub slightly filled with gray water. He was in the bathing room. Pulling the curtain aside corroborated Kael's guess. Several towels and two housecoats hung along a brass bar along one side of the room. On his left, there was a shoulder-width square door. Curious, Kael tugged on the knob, opening it up.

A small wheel met him, hanging from the top of the chamber. Running over the wheel was a vertical-hanging rope, the other end of which stretched down the chute and out of sight. A hook was attached to the rope. Kael pulled it downwards and the wheel turned in reply. Fascinating. It looked to be some sort of way to ferry water from the lower level to the upper. He wondered if the chute would be big enough to fit a human... It

Kael closed the door and turned away. He needed to focus on his task. He leaned against the door leading into the hallway. He knew he was on the second floor, that much for certain. He also knew—or as common sense would dictate—that the king's bedroom would be on a higher level.

Right, he would start on the upper levels and make his way down.

He opened the door and strolled into the hallways. Across the way, the poster of the hairiest man Kael had ever seen adorned the wall. Kael hesitated to gawk at it. What's more, it was a *woman*. Shaking his head, he continued on his way.

After climbing the nearest staircase, Kael found himself on the upper level. He was surprised to find no guards inside the castle whatsoever. The outside of the structure must have been impenetrable. Apparently, they hadn't been counting on anybody breaking in through the small window Kael had found.

Making his way through the castle was simple work. He'd slowly open a door, peer inside, close it and move along. He tried five rooms before he opened the one he was looking for.

As soon as he had stuck his head inside, he knew had the right room. It was decorated in the same lavished style as the downstairs meeting room Kael had been in before, with gold glinting in the moonlight pouring through an open window at the back. Though the darkness of the light faded the colour of the room, Kael could still distinguish that it was a dark magenta, again, same as the meeting room.

Aside from the various pieces of furniture, the largest bed Kael had ever seen took up the majority of the room. Poles stuck up from each corner, supporting a frilly canopy that practically smothered out the ceiling. Lying in that bed were two shapes. A crown hung on a hook above one side, telling Kael which shape was the king. He hoped.

Taking a risk, Kael slunk over to the crown side, knife in hand. He tested its edge with his finger. The blade wasn't very sharp, but for what he needed it for, it would do.

With a moan, the shape turned over to face Kael. It was indeed the king. Kael held his breath as the man groaned some more. So slightly, his eyes cracked open and he mumbled something. Kael raised his dagger.

The king's eyes shot open. "Who, what?" He bolted upright in his bed. "What are you—?"

Kael buried the dagger hilt-deep into the king's gut. The man gurgled. "For the Sansan!" Kael roared, jabbing the knife twice more into his lower chest, one between his ribs. Blood splattered over his arm and pooled on the sheets.

The other shape in the bed thrashed. A woman sat upright as well, pulling the sheets over her body. The moment she spotted what had happened to the king, she opened her lips and screamed. That was Kael's cue to leave. He rammed the knife into the king's chest, piercing the man's heart.

Over the woman's sobbing, Kael could hear startled yells from outside.

"Please, don't kill me!" the woman pleaded. Kael glared at her. *Should* her kill her? She was crying hysterically now, and trembling so hard the entire bed shook. Her lifeless lover's eyes gazed sightlessly towards the ceiling, his arms sprawled out on the bed.

"I don't want to kill you," Kael mumbled. "My issue was with *him.*"

"But why?" she wept.

There were noises outside the door, bumps and clinking armour. Guards were almost upon him. Kael turned to the woman. "Because he was Tehpuu."

The door shot open. Kael jumped sword-first at the guard who attempted to enter, tackling him back into the hall. He removed *Vintrave* from the guard's throat and held it high over his head. "Long live Sansan!" he hollered.

Shield raised, Kael barrelled through the small squad of guards. He sprinted down the hallway towards the stairs.

"The king!" Kael heard from behind. "He's killed the king. Murderer! Alert the troops! Catch that Sansan!"

Kael gave the guards a mock salute before darting down the stairs. His smile was real. They believed he was Sansan.

Kael exploded into the second-floor hallway before he even knew what was awaiting him. It happened to be another squad of guards. He slammed into the first man, coming face-to-face with the crest emblazoned on his breastplate—as well as the yellow dash underneath. *Sansan.*

"Hurry!" Kael pleaded, giving the man a haggard shake. "The king's been murdered by the hands of a Tehpuu! They—they tried to kill me too. Tried to eliminate the witness..."

Their faces all displayed the same expression. Horror mixed with anger.

"The Tehpuu will pay for this!"

"Go!" Kael yelled. "Kill the murderers! They are trying to blame us for their terrible deed! The king's guards used a Sansan knife! I saw it with my own eyes! It...it was too late to stop them."

By that point, however, they guards were barely listening. The majority of them had already rushed up the stairs. Kael let them pass, joining in with their enraged shouting. Up the staircase, he could already hear loud voices and the clash of swords.

Kael hesitated a moment to listen to the brawl. Things were about to get messy in Knot-Town. He needed to escape at once and leave. He set off at a sprint, leaving *Vintrave* unsheathe in case he needed it.

He did.

Before he could make it to the next staircase, a group of soldiers rounded the corner. These were more than ordinary guards. Their armour was thicker and every man carried a tower shield with them. They were also Tehpuu. Kael had been lucky to slip past the last group of guards. There would be no wordplay that would save him from these men.

The leader of the pack, a brawny man with a flat nose pointed a sword at Kael. Kael couldn't quite catch every word he said. "Knot... Sansan... Kill..." The message was still quite clear.

Kael took a few steps back as they began to charge. He spotted something familiar from the corner of his eye. It was the same hairy portrait he had seen before, just outside the...*bathroom!*

He threw open the door, jumped inside and slammed the door closed. He didn't have much time. At once, his attention was turned to the window. It was high, but he figured he'd make the fall without any injury. However, there was a chance some of the soldiers would follow. That wouldn't do.

Instead, Kael opened the door to the chute and peered into the depths. Nothing but darkness. Sighing, he placed his lower body into the vertical shaft, leaving his chest and shoulders still exposed. He waited a few more seconds.

The door burst open. Kael gasped as the flat-nosed man charged in, then threw the rest of his body into the chute. Kael screamed, letting his voice echo as he fell. Before he got very far, however, he stopped himself by stretching out his legs and snatching onto the rope.

He could hear the soldier cry out in alarm.

"The knotter's gone down the chute! Quickly, we'll catch him at the bottom. Go, go!"

The heavy footsteps of the soldiers faded away, leaving Kael to listen only to the strain of his own body. The chute was small, almost too small. An overwhelming sense of claustrophobia overwhelmed him. He needed to get out!

Trying his best to stifle that immediate fear, he haphazardly scuttled back to the top of the chute. Glancing into the room first to make sure all was safe, Kael crawled out of the chute and sprawled onto the glass-covered carpet. He had never thought of himself to be claustrophobic. He was beginning to reconsider that.

With the guards chasing a false trail, Kael was safe to climb out the window. Broken glass lined the edges of the window, so Kael first snatched a nearby towel to place down. With a hop, he swung over the window and fell the remaining distance to the streets below.

Kael landed on all fours with a *whump*. Pain throbbed in one of his ankles, but it seemed neither broken nor fractured. Perhaps a bit strained. Kael could tolerate strained.

The city had been sleeping soundly hours earlier. Now it was fully awake. News of the king's sudden demise had spread far faster than he had anticipated. Screams and shouts pieced the night, echoing over the city and sending chills up Kael's spine. Over the rooftops, he could see the faint glow of a house that had caught fire nearby.

It was then the gravity of what he had just done truly sunk in. He had killed a king and crippled a city. Kael had to stop and put a hand to his chest, trying to reassure himself that what he did *had* to be done. For his sake. For Vallenfend's sake.

The streets were dangerous. Kael had to make his way carefully through the city as to avoid the many riots and fires that had broken out. People everywhere were fighting one with the other. The deep hatred between both clans was now let loose. On more than one occasion, Kael had witnessed as *soldiers* joined in the brawls, bringing their weapons with them. Also more than once, he saw those soldiers hack down unarmed men and women that were of the opposite clan. It wasn't just the aggressive Tehpuu that were on full assault either. The Sansan were fighting right back.

Kael walked into the middle of the street when he thought it was clear.

"Oi, Sansan!" an angry voice yelled at him.

Maybe not so empty.

Kael turned to face them. A mob of six Tehpuu men stood a few feet away, brandishing makeshift weapons—pieces of wood, bricks, a metal bar, even a clay pot.

"Get him!" the same voice roared. The man leading the mob threw his brick at Kael, who only sidestepped it.

The mob overwhelmed Kael—or tried to. Even with their numbers, they were no match. Kael was wearing armour, and he was armed. They were only enraged civilians. Kael let the first angry Tehpuu's piece of wood clang against his armour. He shook his head and kicked the man down. The next rioter posed even less of a threat. Kael spun and smacked him with the flat of his blade, doing the same to the next. He knocked two more away before deciding the mob was no longer a threat. The last man he left alone, instead choosing to sprint past. As he left them moaning and writhing on the ground, he heard the last Tehpuu call after him.

"Yeah, that's right!" he screamed, voice cracking, "you better run!"

Kael could only laugh.

Shield and sword at the ready, Kael rushed through the city, going down the gentle slope that led to the walls. The question of how he was going to get over was soon answered for him. He spotted a great cylindrical shape attached to the inside of the wall. A guard tower! That would lead him straight to the top. He'd figure out what to do from there.

Taking a chance, Kael sprinted into a plaza. He wished he hadn't. The largest battle of all raged directly in the middle, comprised only of the city's military. Men-at-arms, knights and cavalry were all fighting amongst each other. Before Kael quite knew what he had stepped into, he was in the heat of battle as well.

A mace glanced off Kael's shield. He flinched and bent low in a fighting stance as a line of Tehpuu approached. There were several Sansan soldiers to either side of him, keeping the line. At first, Kael was hesitant, but he joined their ranks once he realized only the Tehpuu would be after him.

With the other Sansan men at his side, Kael fought against the Tehpuu, slowly making his way across the plaza. He cut down soldier after soldier with only one thought in mind. Escape. His ability to slow time proved infallible.

Halfway across the plaza, a Tehpuu knight managed to make close enough to Kael to make contact. With a cry, he swung his mace at Kael, which struck him hard in the chest. Kael's stolen breastplate saved his life. Something snapped in Kael.

Not a second later, the Tehpuu knight burst into flames. Kael yelped and backed away from the man, who screamed in pain. After only a few seconds, the Tehpuu slumped to the ground, dead.

Kael closed his jaw and glanced around. The fighting around him had stopped, giving the burning body a wide berth. They stared at his singed body as the flames licked out of existence. Kael was the first to move. After taking a single step, a familiar man pushed his way through the Tehpuu crowd to point a finger at Kael.

"You!" he shouted. "I know you! You're the one who broke me nose! You're the chum who broke into the castle!" He frowned. His nose was indeed crooked. "You're a Sansan? Oi, he's the one who killed the king! Get that knotter!"

That was all Kael needed to hear. He shoved his way into the Sansan crowd, conscious that a large group of Tehpuu soldiers were now chasing after him. It wasn't easy making his way through the battle. Everybody was moving and everybody was wielding a weapon of some kind. The group chasing him was faring better. They were just cutting down any Sansan who got in their way. Any Tehpuu they met joined the group. Still, Kael managed to keep ahead of them.

By the time Kael made it to the far end of the plaza, the group chasing him had nearly doubled.

Once he hit the streets, he broke out into a sprint, weaving in and out of alleyways. Every so often, he glanced back at his pursuers. He was losing some of them, but not enough for comfort. By the time he finally hit the wall, there must have been two dozen Tehpuu soldiers still at his heels.

Stairs wound up the side of the cylindrical guard tower, double back on itself twice before reaching the top. It gave the tower a tapered look, as the base of it was thicker than the top. Halfway up the stairs, there was an open doorway set into the wall.

Kael hit the base of the stairs at a sprint. He stumbled and fell onto his belly, rolling over onto his back just in time as the first of his pursuers reached him. Kael kicked the man in the chest, sending him back to the bottom of the steps. He clambered back to his feet and started to ascend.

It wasn't long before another soldier caught up though. Kael turned to face his attacker. They locked blades. Kael was the first to break the lock. He batted the soldier's sword to the side, caught the man under the chin with the edge of his shield and ran him through the gut.

The soldier, clutching his ruined stomach, fell over backwards, bowling into his comrades waiting on the stairs below. It was more difficult to fight on the stairs, but there was only room enough for one or two soldiers to attack at a time.

Kael reached the middle of the stairs, where the doorway was. He peered inside for a split second. Moonlight cascaded through a small slit in the wall, illuminating a small room inside the tower. Kael jumped inside.

He waited just inside the doorway for a soldier to come in. As the man rounded the corner, Kael tackled into him, shoving him off the staircase. Kael turned to strike down yet more soldiers. But no matter what he did, somebody else replaced whoever he cut down. There was too many of them.

Kael fought his way up the staircase, doing his best to both defend against his attackers and climb at the same time. It was a difficult task and proved to be very fatiguing. Once he finally reached the top, he was horrified by what he saw.

More soldiers.

Soldier after soldier lined the top of the wall. Further along, Kael could see some Sansan fighting against Tehpuu, but nearest to him, there were only green dashes highlighting the soldier's armour. The majority of them were manning the ballistae, pointing them towards the *inside* of the city. Even as he watched, they fired a projectile, which soared to knock down a Sansan building.

When they spotted Kael, however, most of the Tehpuu soldiers topped what they were doing to face him. Altogether, Kael became painfully aware of the yellow dash on his own chest.

"Get that knot!" one of the soldiers cried from behind.

A familiar noise disrupted the angry shouts of the men suddenly charging toward him. One which Kael never found more relieving. One which he wasn't sure he'd ever hear again. A roar that sounded like thunder.

A plume of fire from a hundred yards down caught the soldiers' attention and Kael sprinted for the edge of the wall. Planting both feet Kael on the ledge, he jumped as far as he could. To his left, he could see a shadow rushing at him through the air, belching fire along the wall as it did. The fire consumed at least a hundred men; whether Sansan or Tehpuu, the inferno didn't discriminate.

Kael slammed into Shatterbreath's shoulder. Hard.

She continued on her way, burning a long section of the wall before banking away. She nudged Kael with her paw, shoving him fully onto her back, where he lay trying to catch his breath. With three strong beats, they were a safe distance away from the city.

"Let me see," Kael said.

He was rushed into Shatterbreath's vision. She was looking at Knot-Town, now consumed with civil war. Fire raged over a good portion of the city and almost everywhere, Kael could see people fighting. Even from where he was, he could hear the screams of people and animals alike.

"What have I done?" Kael whispered.

Shatterbreath huffed. "It would have been worse if *I'd* burnt it down. You did what you had to do."

Kael came out of her vision and rubbed his eyes. "You're right. Thanks for saving me."

"Again," Shatterbreath added. "I hope you know how upset I am with you."

Kael smiled. If getting in a one-on-one fist fight made her angry, what he had just done must have made her furious. He chose his tone delicately. "I know. I am sorry."

Shatterbreath took a lingering breath. "I'm just glad you're alright."

Chapter 9

Usually, it took some time to get used to the flexing of Shatterbreath's shoulders beneath him before Kael settled down on her back. As soon as they were a safe distance away from the city though, Kael nodded off. His adventured had more than tired him out.

When he drifted back awake, he was alarmed to see the sun in the middle of the sky above them.

"Huh?" he exclaimed. "What time is it? How long did I sleep?"

Shatterbreath yawned. "The rest of the night and the majority of today. It's just past noon."

"That means there's only..." Kael counted on his fingers. "Four days left! What's the plan? Are we going straight home or to another..."

Kael rubbed his eyes and looked around. At once, he recognized Skullsnout's mountain range to the west.

"Where are we? Are we visiting Skullsnout first?"

Shatterbreath exhaled sharply, sending a plume of smoke washing over Kael. "No. I've been thinking about our visit to Rystville. I may have been...wrong about humans. Not all of them are interested in harming our kind. That king—silly though he may have been— proved it for me. I know a city... It was once known for its kindness towards dragons. They worshipped us like gods and provided us with temporary shelter if we needed it. In fact, most of the Favoured Ones were chosen from there."

"Hmm. Are you sure they're still friendly? It sounds like you haven't visited this place for a thousand years. People change, Shatterbreath."

"I've never actually been there," Shatterbreath countered. "My...mate had been though. I can't remember how long ago— probably three centuries or longer—but he said they had been friendly to him. Your species can't change that much, three hundred years is a wink!"

Kael raised his eyebrows. He couldn't tell if she was joking or not. "Let's go for it then."

Shatterbreath hummed. "It's coming into view now."

Kael stood up and stretched. "Let me see." He was rushed into her vision.

Wyrmguard. The name sounded friendly enough. Friendly for dragons anyway, which was good enough for Kael. The name alone was a good sign, being close Skullsnout's lair helped as well.

The buildings of the city weren't elaborate. They were simple even. No more than two buildings were more than a story tall, one of which looked like a makeshift castle. The roofs were thatched and the windows as well as doors seemed to be constructed out of nothing more than reeds. Overall, the city appeared to be nothing more than an oversized village, with a plaza and adjacent amphitheatre taking up most of that space.

The city seemed to hold no regular shape. Only two streets were actually roads, the rest being more like muddy paths than anything. Perhaps it was the fluid simplicity that further attracted Shatterbreath to the city. Either way, she had must have been more impressed with Rystville than Kael had thought, for she headed towards the middle of the modest city without the faintest hesitation.

To Kael, however, there was something wrong. He could see the people below now without the aid of Shatterbreath's vision. Indeed, their reaction reflected Shatterbreath's words. They were excited, jumping and waving their hands. Still, something was just...wrong. The amphitheatre for one looked almost abandoned. It was massive, with several buildings branching off from the many rows of seating, each building the size of a barn. Kael couldn't even imagine what any of it could be for. His first thought was that it was used for games, like the ones held in Nestoff, but the amphitheatre didn't look designed for that. Far from. It seemed accommodated for...larger contestants.

"Look at how they welcome us! They are waving. See, Tiny, I told you this city was friendly towards dragons."

"Uh huh."

Kael turned his attention back to the people. Their clothing was tattered and dirty, matching the style and cleanliness of their city. Their voices were cheerful, yet still hold a hint of something unfamiliar. Something...sadistic.

"Where should we land?" Shatterbreath said. She sounded cheery, as though she was looking forward to their visit. Kael sighed. Maybe letting King Respu praise her had been a bad idea. Sure, he had recruited an ally, but he had also inflated Shatterbreath's ego.

Kael leaned over her shoulder, studying the city. The amphitheatre seemed like the most obvious choice. The plaza next to it wasn't quite large enough. "There," Kael declared, pointing.

The feeling of uneasiness intensified as Shatterbreath was hovered above the amphitheatre, preparing to land. The inhabitants of the city came rushing into the arena to surround her as she landed in the arena, body shuddering as she hit the muddy ground. The people were overwhelmed by her presence, as if she alone was the single greatest thing in the world. They were almost beside themselves, dancing and cheery madly. Kael tried to focus on a single person to try and hear what they were even screaming, but found he couldn't. The mob was too active. Any person he focussed on soon disappeared behind other bodies.

Shatterbreath beamed, craning her head as if to bless each person with her gaze for but just a moment.

"I take it back," Shatterbreath said to Kael. "Maybe I was wrong about humans! Look at how delightful these people are! Your kind isn't so bad after all."

The uneasy feeling spiked. Kael spotted something out of the corner of his eye. "Shatterbreath," he gasped, "take off! Now! FLY!"

The dragon grimaced as something was flung into the air. Kael looked up to watch as the object arced directly overhead to descend upon them. A massive iron net fell onto Shatterbreath. It was thick and heavy, weighed down by several metal balls attached to the edges.

It wrapped over her shoulders, shoving Kael off of her back. He landed beside her and had to roll away to avoid her thrashing talons. The dragon roared and shook, trying to free herself of the metal net. She flared her wings, but only succeeded in getting tangled further. The net must have been extremely heavy, for even with her great strength, it took everything she had to move towards the crowd.

But before she could move any closer, another net was fired upon her. It snatched her rear end, sending her tail and hind legs crashing back down to the ground. The rest of her followed and soon, Shatterbreath pressed tight against the ground.

Kael was spurred into action. "Let her go at once!" he screamed.

The people of the town rushed over to Shatterbreath once they knew she was down for good. With practised efficiency, they produced several long spikes which they used to secure wires around her snout. In a matter of seconds, they had immobilized her head, keeping her from incinerating them all. Then, they nail the edges of the net into the ground, further anchoring Shatterbreath.

"Let her go!" Kael yelled again. His and Shatterbreath's roars went unheeded.

Kael jumped into the crowd, charging the ones nailing down the spikes. He slashed a man across the chest and smashed another with his shield. Without hesitation, unarmed and men and women replaced them. It was then Kael realized. They weren't ordinary people. They were savages.

They gnashed their rotten teeth and clawed at Kael with no worry for the safety of themselves. Kael cut down one after the other. There were just too many. They were overwhelming him, digging their fingernails into any exposed flesh. Kael curled up into a ball, trying to keep their hands away from his face.

Their filthy bodies pressed down on him from all angles, compressing him, suffocating him. Kael struggled against them with no avail. Then, something snapped inside him.

Most of the people smothering Kael burst into flames. The ones that weren't were sent reeling away from Kael, stunned. He soon dealt with them. Time slowed, allowing Kael leeway to move in between their clawing fingers. He slashed, hacked and cut them down without them so much as laying a finger on him.

He lost count of how many he killed. They came wave after wave. Relentless. *Bloodthirsty*. Kael stayed near the one spike, determined to keep them from nailing it down.

All at once, the people backed off. They must have realized that they were making no progress with him. They stayed just out of the reach of *Vintrave* as Kael swung it furiously.

"Back!" he shouted. "Back you monsters! Release her now! I swear, I'll kill you all if I have—"

Kael didn't get to finish his threat. Something struck him from behind. He spun to fall on his back, staring up at a savage who had hit him from behind with one of the hammers used to nail down the spikes.

Dazed, Kael was helpless as the savages bound his upper body with cords. Roughly, they hefted him up and threw him down beside Shatterbreath's pinned head. She was thrashing wildly, but to no avail. They had secured the two nets over her too tight.

Kael's wits returned to him. The savages had started dancing. They whipped their limbs about and writhed on the ground, all the while humming a deathly tune. Their eyes rolled to the back of their heads. Kael watched them, transfixed with disgust.

The crowd suddenly split to reveal something that absolutely terrified Kael. It was huge man, standing naked, painted from head to toe in blood and dirt, carrying a ghastly blade. His head was hidden by a gleaming white mask with bright feathers. Not a mask, Kael realized. A *skull*. Unlike any other skull Kael had ever seen. Its teeth were pointed and its eyes shaped more like tapered ovals.

Shatterbreath stopped moving and gasped. "Wyverns?" She snarled. "That's a wyvern skull! Murderers!" She released a huge jet of flame. Kael cringed from the heat. But the masked giant, who the flame was aimed at, didn't even flinch. The flame came up short. Shatterbreath couldn't breathe properly with her head in such a way.

The masked giant took a step forward. Kael's eyes were glued to his weapon. He held it with both arms, muscles bulging from the weight. The blade itself was the length of Kael's body, sickly dark and with a jagged, chipped edge. It looked sharp.

The man held the weapon up over his head. "Esh krim na guul!" he cried. It took Kael the second time he spoke to realize he was speaking a different language entirely. "Jor man kem, laga!" The crowd cried out in unison. It sounded feral, inhuman. "An sacrafaso." He held up his index finger. "Na doo sacrafaso!" He raised a second finger.

Flames suddenly ignited on the arena wall behind the giant. Kael's mind was racing. Sacrafaso... Did that mean *sacrifice?*

Unfortunately, Kael received his answer a moment later. Between the two largest torches sat a strange looking idol. It must have been at least ten feet tall. It resembled a man, standing with one hand clutching a mace. Its head, however, was far from human. It had the head of a beast. A hound. It perfectly resembled the hound described on Kael's shield. The BlackHound Empire... They had been here.

Shatterbreath saw the idol too. She stopped moving, jaw taunt, to stare up at it. Fright filled her emerald eyes. Kael couldn't recall ever seeing her actually scared. Kael had come close to death more times than he could count, but seeing Shatterbreath's expression frightened beyond anything else he had experienced.

The masked man yelled something, but Kael's attention was drawn somewhere else. What he saw next was and would continue to be the most horrific sight he had ever seen.

To the side, one of the doors to the barn-like structures swung open. Kael gasped. A gargantuan corpse filled the majority of the barn. He knew at once what it was. The size alone gave it away.

It was Skullsnout.

They had disembowelled him.

Kael tore his eyes away, unable to stomach the white of his exposed ribcage and the soft pink of his innards. His body lay in a heap, limbs sprawled and bent at irregular shapes. Parts of his body were missing, looking like he had been partially eaten. His neck rested on the ground, hardly even attached to his body anymore because of the multiple gauges. Of his head, only his lower jaw remained, forever gaping.

Kael could feel Shatterbreath tense beside him. Every muscle in her body flared, etching deep lines across her body. Her eyes were wide and every scale stood on end. Unlike Kael, she couldn't take her eyes away from the mangled remains of the once proud Elder.

The shouting of the crowd escalated. Kael heard the sound of chains and looked reluctantly back towards Skullsnout's corpse. At least two dozen of the savages were pulling on chains connected to a massive skull. Skullsnout's skull. It gleamed pure white in the undying sun. It was the whitest thing Kael had ever seen.

Shatterbreath began to tremble.

The savages slowly dragged the skull to where the masked giant was standing. The crowd was going ballistic. The masked giant pointed his blade from the skull to Shatterbreath and shouted something.

Kael was breathless. He turned to Shatterbreath, who's head was lying in the mud beside him. Still trembling, her eyes shot wide. Even as he watched, her pupils dilated and her lips curled to reveal her full set of teeth.

Then, she thrashed even harder than before. Kael thought for sure the violence of her writhing would break free for sure, but somehow, the nails kept the net tight over her.

She roared. She roared so hard and for so long, her voice cracked and fizzled out at the end, sounding coarse and haggard. Kael placed his hands over his ears, but it did little to help.

The masked man with the blade started to approach.

Shatterbreath roared again. "I'll kill you all!"

Step after step, he was getting closer.

"You will all burn for what you've done today!"

He raised the blade, flanking Shatterbreath to her right. He was heading for the base of her neck.

"You will all suff..." Her threat turned into a wordless shriek. The masked giant hesitated.

Shatterbreath's entire body seized. She snarled, pushing as hard as she could against the restraints. They held tight. Then, reality

106

itself seemed to shift. A strange pulse emanated from Shatterbreath, distorting Kael's vision and sucking the breath from his lungs. He lost her eyes in her fury.

The shockwave—or whatever exactly it was—hit the crowd, knocking every single person off of their feet. To Kael's right, he heard a *ping*. The nail holding down the net nearest to him exploded into the air.

Several more *pings* resonated as all the nails suddenly unearthed themselves. Kael registered what was happening. Shatterbreath was using her magic.

Shatterbreath lifted her head, and with it, the rest of her body rose as well. The weight of the two nets didn't seem to hinder her at all. An unnatural fire burned in her eyes.

The masked giant let out a cry and ran towards her, holding the blade above his head. Shatterbreath jumped back from his attack and slashed at him with her paw. The blade was knocked from his grip. Shatterbreath lashed out and snapped him up in her jaws. And chewed.

The crowd, crazed with bloodlust only a moment later, exploded in fright. They started screaming, running in every which direction.

Shatterbreath leapt towards the mob and began tearing it apart. Kael rolled onto his back and then propped himself up with his feet. He ducked underneath Shatterbreath's swinging tail. He needed to get on her back, before she inadvertently harmed him. She was in a blind rage and he had no intention of stopping her.

Giving her a wide berth as she slowly killed the savages, Kael struggled to free himself of the cords. They were too tight, forcing his arms behind his body. He glanced around, feeling helpless. Something caught his eyes nearby. *Vintrave!* He had dropped it when he had been hit by the hammer.

It was sticking up out of the mud, sharp edge pointing upwards. Perfect. Carefully, Kael knelt down beside his sword. With some trouble, he managed to cut the cord. He then picked up his weapon and turned his focus back to Shatterbreath. She was going wild. Blood was splattered across the front of her body. Even as he watched, she released a jet of flame, killing a vast amount of the

107

savages with one breath. But they were escaping, flooding out of the main entrance and back into the city.

Swhoop. Kael spun around. A net whipped through the air towards Shatterbreath. She noticed it last second and dove to the side, rolling back onto her feet.

She growled and charged towards the source of the net, a pair of ballistae designed to launch nets instead of arrows. This was Kael's chance. He ran towards her and leapt, slamming into her side. He was on her shoulder, being rocked back and forth as she continued sprinting.

She slammed into the ballista, smashing it to pieces. The sudden stop gave Kael a chance to climb aboard. The nets on her back were gone, stuck in the mud from when she had rolled. Shatterbreath realized this as well, for not a second after Kael was on her back, she spread her wings.

They rocketed into the sky, hovering a few storied above the amphitheatre.

"Suffer!" Shatterbreath roared down below to the city. "Burn! DIE!"

She released a jet of flame. Kael watched over her shoulder as section by section, she burned the city to the ground. The fire spewed relentlessly from her mouth, eager to consume the fragile buildings which burned so perfectly.

Men, women and children disappeared in the onslaught, turning into nothing more than char. It took several hours before the entire city was reduced to a flaming pile of ash and cinders. Everything was black. The only resemblances to what used to be a city were brick walls scattered here and there. The only reason Shatterbreath stopped is when she had run out of fire.

It seemed to take even longer for Shatterbreath to calm down. She circled above cinders for what seemed forever, fuming and breathing out smoke. Her muscles were tense underneath Kael. He left her alone. She needed to grieve, and so did he.

At last, she broke down. Her head bowed and the tempo of her wing beats faltered. Still without a word muttered between either of them, Shatterbreath angled sharply towards a patch of grass far outside the burnt city.

She made no attempt to land. Her chest hit the ground hard, causing her head to dip as well. She bounced once before sliding to a stop. She let her wings fall where they were outstretched, her limbs she left limp, trailing at her sides.

Then, she wept.

Kael tried to hold back his emotion, but he ended up sobbing as well

Chapter 10

Kael sat on Shatterbreath's back, feeling absolutely numb. They were flying due west, back to Vallenfend. He was through, he couldn't take anymore. He was finished. He was sick of visiting strange places, sick of trying to convince people of his cause. Sick of killing. Sick of death. He was sick, sick, sick.

Soon, there was only going to be more killing. More death.

Shatterbreath was silent. She hadn't said a single word since Wyrmguard. She was through as well, it wasn't hard to tell. Something in her died with Skullsnout and something else had died with that city.

Kael rubbed his swollen eyes. She was grieving. He jaws kept clenching and unclenching. He supposed he should try and talk to her.

"Shatterbreath?" he ventured.

She winced.

"How are you feeling?"

Pain spread across her muzzle. Tears brimmed in her eyes. Still, she said nothing.

Kael rubbed her back, pushing some mud away. "I—I'm sorry," he said softly.

She kept her head forward. Kael was at a loss for words. He rubbed her back more, trying to think of something to say.

"They killed him."

Kael sighed. "Yeah."

"Your kind killed him."

"No, Shatterbreath. The BlackHound Empire killed him. You saw that idol. The Empire must have twisted that city into worshipping that thing."

"Humans," she spat. "I hate them. *All* of them."

"Even me?" Kael furrowed his brow.

Shatterbreath glanced back at him. "Of course not. You haven't done anything bad, Kael."

Kael shrugged. "I wouldn't say so."

Shatterbreath caught his tone. "What do you mean?"

Kael winced. He knew this conversation would arise eventually. He only wished it was under more...pleasant circumstances. "Skullsnout gave me his magic," Kael blurted out. "It's my fault he died."

Shatterbreath rumbled. "*Excuse* me?" Her tone was deadly.

"When Skullsnout talked to me alone, he gave me three blessings. He fixed my sword, healed my wounds and then...lent me his magic." Kael hesitated to hold back a sob. "He said it would assist me. I—I tried not to take it, but he insisted, saying that he'd take it back when we met later."

"Kael..."

"I know," Kael cried. "I shouldn't have borrowed his magic! If—if he still would have had it, maybe there was a chance he could have escaped like you! I'm sorry, so sorry. It's my fault one of your kind is dead! I killed an Elder!" Kael buried his face in his hands.

Shatterbreath stayed silent. Through teary eyes, Kael looked to her. Her muzzle was pointing vaguely in his direction, but here eyes were distant. A scowl was affixed upon her face. Kael watched the muscles of her jaw tighten. She glanced at him once, unreadable, then turned away. Kael's grief only intensified. He stared at her back, fearing she would never forgive him.

After over an hour of flying in tense silence, Shatterbreath huffed. "Giving you his magic," Shatterbreath breathed, "was an incredible honour. It proved he had faith in us, faith in you. Never has *any* human been given such a gift. The power of a dragon."

Kael sniffed and slowly looked up. "You're not upset with me?"

"I am extremely upset," Shatterbreath said with a growl, "But look at you; you are as distraught as I. You feel Skullsnout's loss. You *care* for our species, Kael. Skullsnout saw that in you. He wouldn't have lent you his power if he didn't. Maybe he knew he was going to die. Maybe he had foreseen that you would need it. Either way, it was his last blessing. Cherish it."

Kael nodded. "I will."

They fell silent once again.

Shatterbreath was the first to break it this time. "Tiny? This... This is really it, isn't it? This is what it's all been about. Every obstacle, every triumph and failure all lead to this."

Kael sighed. "Yes. It does. Are you ready?"

Shatterbreath shook her head. "No. Are you?"

He sighed again. "Not even close. Still, I will stand and fight. We will rise against the BlackHound Empire."

She hummed in agreement. "Together."

"To the last breath."

Shatterbreath craned her neck to rest those wise eyes on him. "To the death."

Chapter 11

The trip home wasn't a happy one. Skullsnout's death weighed heavily on Kael and Shatterbreath both. And when Kael tried to pry his mind away from the memory of the proud dragon, he found himself contemplating the horror to come. He knew Shatterbreath thought the same. With every passing hour, her muscles stiffened and her breaths became shallower and shallower. It got to the point where they had to land because Shatterbreath couldn't handle flying.

Kael jumped down from her back, taking several steps away. She was trembling. Physically trembling. She had been relatively calm about the incoming war during their adventures. It never occurred to Kael how worried she really was.

Putting his hands on his hips, Kael gazed out at the land before him. They had landed at the edge of a desert, with the Arnoth mountains just in sight to the east. He knew the land to the far east, beyond the mountains, but he and Shatterbreath hadn't actually gone in this direction from Vallenfend, so they had skirted around the entire stretch of land between Shatterbreath's mountains and Arnoth's. There wasn't much to miss.

The desert stretched for what seemed forever, the curve of the land hiding Shatterbreath's mountains. He doubted he would have been able to see that far anyway. Kael marvelled at the scene, remembering Vert's tale of how he had traversed the same desert. The land was filled with history. Would the desert, sea or sky echo the tale to occur? Better question, would it be of hope, or tragedy?

Shatterbreath sat down on her haunches beside Kael, basking in the warm sunlight. Her scales shimmered slightly, as if wishing to shine like her eyes. Kael admired her.

"Your scales are different," he commented. "They're brighter than before."

Shatterbreath looked herself over, a ripple running over her hide. "I suppose you're right. I don't think I've ever spent so much time out of my cave before I started living there."

"You're beautiful."

Shatterbreath beamed. "You know how to charm a dragon. Thank you." She snorted. "As a human I suppose you're..."

Kael smiled. "What? The mighty Shatterbreath isn't actually going to *praise* her loyal servant, is she? Heaven forbid. That would mean there's a heart somewhere in that scaly chest."

She raised a brow. "Hardly," she mused. "I was going to say tolerable. You're tolerable. I'll give you that. Nothing more."

Kael chuckled. "Thanks?"

The dragon nodded, flexing her wings. "I'm more relaxed now. We should get on our way."

Kael frowned. He didn't want to. He was happy right then, alone with her. He never wanted the moment to pass. He didn't want to trade his content world for one filled with fury, war and pain. He didn't want the storm that was coming. Unfortunately, he had no choice.

With a sigh, he said, "alright, let's go."

They took to the air once again.

The heat of the sun was extreme, but bearable. Kael simply held his shield over his head for a while, blocking out the sun. He had taken off his armour a while ago, content to leave it resting behind him on Shatterbreath's back. The shield grew heavy, so Kael reached back for his pack. With a frown, he realized it had been torn from Shatterbreath's back in Wyrmguard. So not only had he lost his gleaming set of armour in Knot-Town, now he had lost all of his things as well. He shrugged. It was a small price to pay. All he had was basic survival gear anyway. A piece of flint, spices and medical supplies. All expendable.

So, instead, he simply turned his back to the sun. His hair had grown long over his travels. It would do well to protect his neck from sunburn.

Over the blue of Shatterbreath's body, Kael watched the scenery behind him stretch away, giving away to the endless desert. He wondered how the armies he had convinced would cross it. Probably without a problem. Vert had done it alone, with hardly any supplies. Surely an entire army would bring enough food and water to last a war, let alone a trip across the desert.

Kael lost himself in his thoughts, letting his mind carry with the wind.

Eventually, he registered that Shatterbreath wasn't flying as fast anymore.

He was about to turn around to ask why, but quickly got his answer.

Shatterbreath's mountains were in view. They were close too. Seeing those mountains sent a wave of emotions and memories flooding over Kael. He had never even been to the eastern side of the mountains, but the effect was all the same.

He remembered those harsh words spoken by King Morrindale. *Banished.* Banished from his own home. He remembered the sights, smells and sounds of the wild forest which used to be a terrifying thing. The memory of the first time he met Shatterbreath still burned bright in his mind's eye. The day he had lost his friends. The day he had lost his former life.

His former life...

He could recall that fateful day when he had received that white letter on his doorstep, white as an angel's gown, yet ink as black as the deepest night. Everything before that seemed so distance, so foreign. It was like looking back on a life, a time, that didn't even belong to him. As if he was only recollecting a tale he had once heard from a friend around a campfire. That life working in the fields and blacksmithing with Korjan had been so simple it seemed unreal. Yet, it had been everything to him.

How the times had changed. How *he* had changed. It was all so...stifling.

Kael could only imagine the things Shatterbreath was thinking about. Was she as nostalgic as Kael? Was she reliving the life she once used to have too? A time before Kael was a regular part of her life? She had so much to look back on... Kael almost felt ashamed dwelling on a past that was so young.

She pumped her wings harder as they approached the mountain, sending them up and into the eternal fog that smothered the peaks. It was like flying into a dream. The gently mist caressing his skin, moistening his cracked lips only proved to strengthen Kael's nostalgia.

For whatever reason, the appearance of the ground beneath them was like a wakeup call. At once, Kael's thoughts turned to the BlackHound Empire. The tranquility that had befallen him not a moment earlier was entirely replaced by anxiousness and fear.

"Do you wish to land here?" Shatterbreath asked, referring to the mountaintop lake, "or fly directly into my cave? Your friends are probably waiting."

Kael took a sharp breath. "They can wait a bit longer. Fly down to Vallenfend. I need to see it."

Shatterbreath nodded and obeyed, angling her wings earthward. The fog that overwhelmed them subsided, giving way to a dazzling view of Vallenfend and the area surrounding. It was just as Kael remembered it.

The entire city held an elliptical shape, resembling a round egg. In the middle the Royal Castle spiked up, standing like a tainted obelisk. Even from he and Shatterbreath hovered, he could see one of the seven courtyards in full bloom. Summer was almost over.

The workers in the fields continued their work, oblivious to the danger that awaited them, soon to arrive on the beach far to the west. They had almost cleared the fields. Soon, they would start burning to pave way for next year's crops. Would their work be in vain? Or would Vallenfend survive to see the springtime?

"Alright," Kael declared, "let's head back to your cave."

Shatterbreath nodded and banked back towards her mountain. "Look, over there." She flicked her head towards the base and pointed a paw.

Kael flooded into her vision. A few miles south of Vallenfend, there were several hundred tents set up with small fires burning here and there. Shatterbreath scanned the camp, revealing thousands of soldiers either practising or eating stew. Every man wore familiar gold and green outfits.

Kael gasped. "Arnoth," he proclaimed. "Fly down there."

Shatterbreath sneered. "At once."

She swooped in fast, flaring her wings as she approached the outskirts of their camp. The soldiers in the vicinity screamed and their horses ran away. Kael slipped off Shatterbreath's back as her paws hit the ground and strode into the camp.

"We're friendly!" Kael declared. "I am Kael Rundown. Where is Vert Bowman?"

"I was wondering when you'd arrive!" a familiar voice cried.

Kael smiled as Vert emerged from behind a row of tents. He snatched the reins of a horse, forcing the animal to stay still.

"Well excuse me! It's not my fault it took so long to get here. Blame Shatterbreath." Kael glanced back at the dragon, who wore a disapproving scowl. Glaring, she backed away.

"Ah well, I'll forgive her I suppose." Vert handed the reins of the horse to a soldier. He strode over to Kael. Kael offered his hand. Vert considered it for a moment before embracing Kael in a tight hug. Shatterbreath growled.

"It's good to see you too, Vert." Kael looked past his friend at the several-dozen soldiers calming the horses behind. "How was the trip over here?"

Vert let go of Kael and laughed. "It was a lot easier coming home than leaving."

"It usually is."

Vert's expression went serious. "It's time, isn't it, Kael?"

Solemnly, Kael nodded. "We only have days."

"Then let's annihilate them." Vert clasped Kael's shoulder. "Arnoth is by your side, Kael. Until the end."

Kael nodded, moved. "Thank you, Vert. Thanks to all of you."

Vert leaned in. "So, how many other cities were you able to convince?"

"Uh..." Kael hesitated. How many indeed? "Let's see... Rystville for sure, and maybe Nestoff. Depends how quick they deal with Knot-Town. Probably *not* Fallenfeld."

Vert raised a brow. "That's it."

"Yeah. Oh, and a colony of bandits."

Vert sighed. "Bandits? Okay... Well, I suppose it all depends on BlackHound's numbers. I guess we'll see once they arrive. I hope your other armies are skilled. I know Arnoth is. We've been here a while, training. I've hatched up a few strategies too."

Kael chuckled. "I'd be happy to hear them later. First, I have to visit my friends up in the mountain. I'll come back down later. We have much to discuss. I'm considering you the overall director here, Vert, not me. I'm sure nobody else is more capable than you."

Vert beamed. "Probably not. Hey, whatever happened to Rooster? I see that carrion isn't with you."

Kael shrugged. "You and Shatterbreath were right about him. I should have listened. Anyway, I'll see you later, alright?" He turned around and waved goodbye, then hopped aboard Shatterbreath.

Without so much as an acknowledgement, she took off, leaving Arnoth's army behind.

Shatterbreath huffed halfway up the mountain. "You're friend isn't my favourite human out there." Kael tried to interject, but Shatterbreath cut him off. "But he's a good person."

Kael nodded. Vert really was a good friend. At once, Kael's thoughts were turned to Laura. He had once thought that she would have been his friend forever. Maybe even something more than that. Like his old life, that was just a dream.

Laura. He was apprehensive to see her. She had not been so welcoming last time he visited. Kael doubted this time would be any different. He wondered what it would take to convince her that he was telling the truth.

He sighed.

The sight of Shatterbreath's cave spurred so many memories. For just a moment, it was like stepping back into the past. He was removed completely from Shatterbreath's back, instead placed on the smooth granite of the mountainside, peering into the inscrutable depths. His troupe surrounding him, their faces personifying the fear Kael felt heavy in his own chest. Despite their numbers, he felt no more secure. He had never been so alone. A heavy breath echoed from inside the cave and with it, a rush of warm, rancid air.

Shatterbreath landed, jolting Kael back into reality. He shuddered, realizing it had only been a memory. He clutched the spine in front of him as Shatterbreath started forwards. He stared at it, unable to tear his gasp away. It reminded him of the stalagmites in the cave.

Once again, he was back with his doomed troupe as they shuffled through the cave. Somewhere in the blackness, the monster loomed, waiting to kill them all. Whatever light would have been shining in the cave was choked out by a dense fog—Kael could swear he smelled smoke.

Ernik cried out. *"There it is!"* The words echoed through Kael's consciousness.

"Is there something wrong?"

Kael flinched and blinked several times. Shatterbreath's eyes were fixed on him, slanted in concern. "You look pale. And you were shivering."

There was a lump in Kael's throat. He struggled to speak past it. "Being back just reminds me..."

Shatterbreath inhaled slowly.

"Do you remember that day as clearly as I do? For the longest time, that's all I could think about. I—I almost forgot about it, actually." He gave an awkward laugh. "How could someone forget such a thing?" He looked up at her, receiving a mixture of feelings. "I almost forgot what you *are.*"

It was Shatterbreath's turn to flinch. She exhaled over Kael, warming him and filling his nostrils with the chalky scent of ash.

"Kael..." she started.

"Kael?" a voice called out. "Is—is that you?"

"Yeah, it's me! I'm back!" Sliding down Shatterbreath's side, Kael was met by Faerd. Kael had replayed his return several times in his head on his journey back. He thought his friends would surround him, cheering and asking him where he had been. He was expecting at least a smile as he was greeted.

Perhaps it had been a selfish to think like that.

Faerd's expression was far from cheerful or even relieved. He looked pained and tears streamed down his good eye. He was on the verge of crying.

Kael's grin was wiped from his face. His heart jumped. "Faerd? Wh—what's wrong?"

119

"Kael's it's...it's Malaricus."

Shatterbreath took a step forward, her jaw taut. "What about him?"

Faerd glanced fleetingly up at her, but his eye rested on Kael. "He took ill. There wasn't anything we could... He—he..."

"No," Kael said. "Don't tell me..." He pushed past Faerd.

The rest of the refugees were at the very back of the cave. The group had grown larger. A few women were sitting away from the others, hugging their children, while the majority stood surrounding something. Kael was terrified by what he would discover. Still, he pushed through the crowd, ignoring the few familiar faces he caught glimpses of.

Finally, Kael reached the middle of the crowd. What he saw made his knees go weak. Like the middlemost ring of people—his closest friends—he slumped to the ground.

"Malaricus?" Kael whimpered. He reached out to the cold, lifeless cheek of the wise scholar, but stopped himself. Mouth agape, eyes closed, Malaricus the Wise lay there, bundled up in thick blankets. He didn't move. He didn't breath.

He was dead.

"How long?" was all Kael could muster.

Korjan was nearby. The blacksmith bowed his head. "No more than three hours. You just missed him, Kael."

Kael began trembling. He glanced up at Shatterbreath, whose muzzle hovered directly above him. Her eyes were so wide. Aside from him, Kael had deduced that Malaricus was the only other human she cared for.

"What happened?" the dragon asked, voice monotone.

Helena spoke first, leaning against Korjan. Under ordinary circumstances, Kael would have been overjoyed to see them both, especially together. Now, he simply felt hollow.

"He became sick. We're not sure what from. He was old, older than anybody truly realized. He..." She let out a sob. "He couldn't fight it off."

"Didn't you try to heal him?" Shatterbreath asked too loudly. "Wh—what, you just sat here and watched him die?"

"We tried everything!" Helena countered, voice rising as well. "We tried everything... If we had been in town with proper supplies, he may have pulled through. But being up here with nothing but wild herbs..."

Shatterbreath huffed, her face growing dark. She stared at Malaricus's body for the longest time before suddenly whipping around to bolt for the cave's entrance. With a booming roar, she was gone.

"He kept asking for you," Korjan whispered to Kael. "He wondered where you were, if you were okay, what you were doing. He wanted to say good bye to you, Kael. He wanted to give something to you."

Kael stroked one of the blankets covering the scholar. It felt as though grief was choking him, constricting his throat and inhibiting him to breathe.

Korjan shuffled over to Kael. There was a rustling as he reached into his pocket, but Kael didn't watch. He couldn't tear his eyes away from the limp form buried in blankets.

Without a word, Korjan handed Kael a white piece of paper. It was neatly folded into three sections and had Kael's name handwritten on the top front. Kael took it, hardly registering the smooth feel of the paper between his fingers.

"Read it when you're ready." Korjan's voice had never seemed so deep.

Kael nodded. Right then, however, he couldn't pull away. He couldn't leave his friend. Not yet.

Kael only left once they picked up the body to move it. How long he had waited by the scholar's side, he knew not. Time seemed irrelevant at that point. Kael tore himself away from the others and exited the cave. He couldn't take the dank smell of the cavern. He needed to be outside in the fresh air.

Finding a quiet place, Kael settled down. He placed both hands on the surface of the massive boulder he had found, feeling the mossy rock under his fingertips. The length of parchment was sitting on his lap half-unopened, waiting. It took all Kael could muster to scoop it up and unfold it.

He had to force down a sob as he realized what it was.

This is a record of military exemption, in and for the behalf of Kael Rundown. Under no circumstances may this person—of age or otherwise—be forced to obey the law of conscription so set by Basal Morrindale, current ruling monarch of the city of Vallenfend. Hereby...

Kael looked away and instead focussed on the swirling fog. He couldn't read any more. His swollen eyes wouldn't let him. He took a moment to himself, swallowing deep, and then looked back down to the bottom of the document.

> *Signed,*
> *Malaricus and Zeptus*

Malaricus had been right. Kael *had* been exempt. All this wasn't supposed to have happened. None of it. He was never supposed to climb that mountain. He was never supposed to meet Shatterbreath. It all could have been avoided. Every event that lead up to that point.

As he paused to contemplate it, though, Kael found he couldn't even imagine the life he would have had. He would have just grown up as a regular person, ignorant to the looming danger. And, like everybody else, he would have been slaughtered when the BlackHound Empire arrived.

So, despite all the trouble that arose because of him being drafted, it turned out all for the better. *But why?* Kael wondered. *If I was indeed protected, why was I still drafted?*

Brooding, Kael flipped over the parchment and discovered more writing on the back. The letters on the front were written straight and clear, as was the custom for legal documents. The writing on the back was more elegant, with beautiful swirls adorning the tips of every word and a style that flowed like honey. In Malaricus's calligraphy was written:

Kael,

I never meant for any of this. Please, think whatever you want about me, but know that I tried everything—everything, Kael—to get you out of the training grounds. But...I failed. I guess I am just a rickety old man. I've seen my end coming for a long time, Kael. I knew that death would take me up eventually. So, I managed to sneak into town one last time. I'm afraid that journey might have been what made me sick. It was cold, and I ill-prepared. Alas, I managed an audience with Zeptus one last time. I only asked one question. There was only one question. Why? Why was this document ignored? Why were you sent to fight against Shatterbreath? Why, why why?! I've lost many nights wondering the very question—as I'm sure you have as well. The answer is clear and simple. The BlackHound Empire. It all comes down to them. This is how Zeptus explained it to me. Most of the men protected from the enlistment are very strong individuals. Look at Korjan, for example. The BlackHound Empire ordered King Morrindale to start sending these people off to die, to further ensure the downfall of Vallenfend in preparation for their arrival. They were worried that somebody would discover their plot eventually and would try to do something about it. Who would be most likely to do such a thing? The ones protected of course. I suppose their theory was correct, judging by what you have accomplished. You weren't the only boy sent that shouldn't have been, though you were one of the first. In fact, Zeptus showed me a list of recruitments. Korjan was in fact on that list, despite his protection as well. I don't know if you've come to terms with all that's happened to you, but please, please, know that I am sorry. Terribly sorry. And proud. You've become such a strong, smart boy. You are the embodiment of hope, Kael. You alone have the key to saving this land. You are doing a fantastic job. I doubt anybody else could have accomplished what you have in such a short time. For the longest time, it was a mystery to me why Shatterbreath spared you. At last I see. She must have sensed the good in you, Kael. She must have been attracted by your pure spirit. I could go on, my boy, but I feel myself growing faint. By the time

123

you read this message, I may have already passed away. Don't grieve for me long. I've dwelled on the past enough for the both of us. Keep strong, and never lose sight of what you fight for. Above all else, win this war, Kael. For me. For us. For everybody.

And know, I loved you like a son.

Malaricus.

Kael folded the letter back up, feeling a weight lifting off his shoulders. As he read, his emotions had fluctuated. It had made him grievous, then curious. Then, it was a relief. He finally knew why he had been drafted. But the solution only made him angry. No, furious. Malaricus had said it himself, it all came down to the BlackHound Empire. The core to all Kael's problems, strife and pain. It was all, *all*, because of them.

Something shuffled. Kael gritted his teeth, willing who or whatever it was to go away. He wanted to be alone. He needed to vent his anger.

Kael's anger vanished as he saw who it was. Laura stopped, giving a slight gasp and putting a hand to her chest. She met his eyes for just a moment, but quickly looked away.

"I—I'm, sorry," she said. "This is where I go to think. B—but I'll leave."

Kael was on his feet. "Wait," he cried. She stopped. "Don't go, please. I need some company." He needed *her* company.

Laura walked up around the rock, then stepped out onto its wide surface. She sat close to Kael—but not close enough to touch.

They sat in silence. Kael watched the fog swirl.

"Where have you been?" she asked, breathless.

Kael bowed his head. "Everywhere, it seems. I've wanted nothing more than to come back."

"Why didn't you?"

"You know why."

"No, I don't." Kael craned his neck. Her gaze was penetrating.

"Not this again," Kael grumbled. "I'm not going to argue with you anymore, Laura. The BlackHound Empire should be arriving in a few days. We'll see who's right then. But now, I just want to mourn my friend."

She nodded. "Okay." She hugged her knees. "He was a good man, Kael."

Kael sighed. "I know."

"He never stopped complaining, right until his last breath." Laura chuckled.

Kael laughed as well. "That's our Malaricus. The smartest man I knew, but not so tolerant."

Again, they sat in silence. Memories of Malaricus flitted through Kael's mind. Both good and bad. He remembered a time when the scholar had given him a special gold coin. Kael had cherished the coin and had nearly cried when he had traded it for food. He could still recall the visit they had shared before Kael had been sent off.

Smothered in memories and lacking the sun as his guide, Kael lost track of time. He could have been sitting there, pondering for days for all he knew. All at once, he realized that he couldn't sit there forever. Despite the huge loss, he had already set a commitment for that night.

Kael rose to his feet and stretched. He suddenly felt so tired. "I should go," he stated.

Laura stayed where she was.

"Thank you, Laura," Kael said to her, "for spending some time with me. I... You may hate me for everything that's happened to you—that's alright. I'm sure I deserve it. Somewhere deep down, though, I hope you haven't given up on me. I hope we can be friends once again when we're through all this."

"We'll see," was her only reply.

Kael frowned and whistled. A roar came in reply. A few moments later, Shatterbreath came swooping in. Her jaws were bloody, telling Kael she had killed something. Whether or not she actually ate it, he was unsure. By the way it was dribbling down the front of her chest and splattered over her forearms, he was guessing she had mauled something—brutally.

"Come on, it's time to see Vert."

Shatterbreath licked her chops. "Are you sure?" she asked gently. "Kael, are you alright? I'm sure your friend can wait. You need more time than this to mourn."

Kael closed his eyes, forcing back tears. "No. No, I'm fine. I— I've had enough time. What about you? Are you okay?"

Shatterbreath glanced back at Laura fleetingly and huffed. "I liked that scribe. He was one of the few I did like. He helped me when you were ill. He saved your life."

Kael nodded. "He was a great man. Bless his soul. Have a good night, Laura."

She didn't say anything. Shatterbreath nudged Kael and he clambered onto her back. Shatterbreath flared her wings, testing the air. "Is there anything you need first?"

"Tooran. I think he should be part of this. Head down to the cave."

Shatterbreath crouched low and then pounced. With only a single beat of her wings, she soared down a section of the mountain and swooped into her cave. Kael watched Laura until she was out of sight.

They only stayed in the very front of the cave. Malaricus's body was still in there. He didn't want to see it. It was just a corpse. The scholar's spirit was...elsewhere. Looking at that body would just summon more pain.

"Tooran?" Kael shouted into the depths. He could see the faint shimmer of the glowing stones far back. "Are you in there?"

"Which one is Tooran again?" Shatterbreath asked.

"Korjan's son."

She snorted. "And who's she?"

Kael shook his head. *"He's* the blacksmith."

The dragon sat down, jarring Kael. "You humans have all the same names. What does it matter? Kael, Smert, Laida, what's the difference? You should all have simple names, like dragons. We never mix up who's who."

"Uh huh." Kael wasn't in the mood to joke around. He knew Shatterbreath was only trying to cheer him up, but it wasn't working. He still felt numb. She recognized this and stopped talking.

After a short wait, Tooran emerged, squinting because of the change of light

"Sorry I took so long. What is it, Kael? We're going to bury Malaricus soon."

Kael's stomach clenched. "I have a meeting with Vert Bowman, the leader of Arnoth." Tooran raised a brow. "The army that's camped out south of Vallenfend."

"Oh, them. I figured they were with you. You want me to come?"

Kael nodded, leaning forward. "Can you spare a moment?"

Tooran glanced at Shatterbreath. "Are you sure tonight is a good night to have this? You haven't had a proper reunion yet. Everybody will want to see you. There are many who have joined us since you last came."

"I told my friend I'd return tonight. He's very...punctual."

"I suppose the others can handle the burial. How are we getting down? We're not taking the dragon are we?"

"No, a donkey," Kael scoffed. "Of course we're riding Shatterbreath. Come on, he's probably waiting."

Tooran looked pained. He stared at Shatterbreath for a long time. "Do you have room for one more?"

Kael cocked his head. "Why? Who else would be coming?"

"The prisoner."

"Go get him, quickly." Kael's heart leapt. The BlackHound prisoner. When Kael had seen him last, he had been on the verge of death. When Tooran returned a short while later, it gave Kael some consolidation to see that he was doing very well.

He was no longer the thin, emaciated shell he was once been. His body had regained most of its muscle and his face had more colour than before. He leaned on a stick for support, proving that he was far from fully recovered, but well on his way.

"Hail, Kael Rundown!" the prisoner called out. "Hail, mighty dragon."

Shatterbreath rumbled and gave a short bow.

"Hello," Kael replied. "I don't think I caught your name from our last conversation."

127

The dark-skinned man bowed. "Sal'braan, at your service."

Kael sized him up. "You've made quite a recovery."

"Yes. Your army has been more than accommodating; I owe my life to them. I wish I could repay them is some way..."

"You could begin by lending me your knowledge," Kael answered quickly, "concerning the BlackHound Empire. Are you up to it?"

A shadow fell over the man's face, as if he was recollecting a nightmare. "Yes. I will tell you everything I know."

Kael clapped his hands together. "Great. We should be leaving at once then." He clambered up Shatterbreath's side. Once he was sitting in his usual spot between her shoulders, he leaned over and offered a hand to the prisoner.

The dark-skinned man instead moved further along her body to climb up her hind leg, using her knee as a step. Kael watched in disbelief. Despite his obvious condition, he was still very spry.

Kael turned around but was surprised to find Tooran was gone. He heard a shuffle from behind. Tooran was already on her back, just behind Kael.

"How do you do that?" he asked.

Tooran squinted, clutching one of Shatterbreath's spines gingerly. "Do what?"

Shatterbreath huffed. "You're smooth, rebellious soldier, I'll admit. But I could still teach you a few things on stealth."

Tooran clenched his jaw and only nodded. With Kael and the other two men on her back, Shatterbreath stood up, jarring her three riders. As she edged towards the place where she always took off from, Kael glanced back at Tooran. Despite how brave he usually was, it wasn't hard to see he was anxious. Perhaps heights scared him.

That, or he wasn't comfortable with the fact that his life was in Shatterbreath's grasp now. Shatterbreath roared as she took off, buffeting Kael with generous amounts of sound and wind.

In a matter of minutes, Shatterbreath was alighting just outside Arnoth's camp. Vert was eagerly waiting for them.

Chapter 12

"Alright," Vert sighed, placing both palms down on the improvised table they had set up—a tower shield propped between two logs. "Where to begin..?"

They had swiftly set up a meeting place outside of Arnoth's camp, to both keep the meeting exclusive and to keep Shatterbreath from frightening horses or troops. Currently, everybody except for Shatterbreath was sitting on logs within a dell wide enough to comfortably contain all of them. Two fires burned heartily on either side of the glade, illuminating the area.

They had already acquainted themselves, which had taken a considerable amount of time alone. Vert had been interested to learn more about Tooran's previous *employment,* and especially interested in Sal'braan's. Though Kael understood the necessity of their meeting, he couldn't help but wonder what time he would be going to sleep that night.

"First off, I'll need to know numbers. Mr. Sal'braan, what are we up against?"

The dark-skinned man leaned forward, holding his cane with both hands. His face screwed up in concentration. "A vast amount. A moment, please." He closed his eyes, lips twitching, fingers counting invisible numbers. "The BlackHound Empire's numbers are impossible to determine—they are just too vast."

"Gee, that's helpful," Vert growled.

"But their invasion force is a different story. To effectively take root as well as to support their conquest, anywhere from twenty- to sixty-thousand would be feasible."

A rare anomaly followed; Vert was speechless.

"Though sixty would be a tad generous," the prisoner added gingerly.

Vert put a finger to his temple. "Okay, so we're looking at a possibility of, say forty-thousand? What do we have? I know for a fact Arnoth has around six-thousand here and available. Kael?"

"I managed to recruit one more city for sure. Two others...not so sure."

"Numbers?"

Kael shrugged. "I don't know. Not the size of the force you've brought, Vert. It's hard to say, I'm sorry."

"Twelve-thousand—if that," Vert thought aloud. "And *that's* being generous. Anything else?"

Shatterbreath grunted. "There are also the smelly bandits."

"That's not going to help much," Vert retorted.

The dragon growled.

"Tooran," Kael cut in, "what about Vallenfend? You mentioned there were more of you than the last time I visited."

Tooran folded his arms across his brawny chest. "Yeah. The message we delivered when you saved my father stuck better with the people than I thought. Zeptus has played a part as well."

"Zeptus?" Vert scoffed. "I hate that scrawny guy."

"That's what King Morrindale was planning on." Tooran paused to swat at a fly. "We can explain why later, but ever since we gave Zeptus back, things have been looking better for Vallenfend. He controls a great portion of the King's Elite, and as such, there hasn't been a single person unjustly thrown into jail. Also, it seems Zeptus is subtly convincing the people of King Morrindale's tyranny. All in all, we have almost doubled in size. Last time I counted, our numbers were just shy of two-hundred. That was last week."

"I'm glad to see that Vallenfend is doing better," Vert said, "but two-hundred still won't affect much. It seems we're going to have to rely heavily on tactics for this battle, gentlemen."

Shatterbreath hissed.

"And gentle...dragon."

Sal'braan, Tooran and Shatterbreath all stared at Vert blankly. Kael caught the bait. "Tactics, eh? Hmm, who better to think up a batch full of tactics—?"

"Than yours truly?" Vert beamed. "I've been working hard to conjure up a whole plethora of tricks and traps. Ten-thousand or eighty-thousand, they're still going to feel it when we strike."

Tooran shuffled. "Forgive me for asking, but how can we trust the battle plans of one as young as you? You don't seem battle-hardened. I doubt you have seen any *true* war."

"Oh, and you have? I didn't become the General of Arnoth for no particular reason you know."

"Silence, both of you!" Shatterbreath snarled. "Who cares how young he is? Who cares what he's done? You, stop being so prejudice, and you, stop being so sarcastic. The fate of this *continent* is in your hands and you'd prefer to argue with each other like irked squirrels? I would have thought by now we'd all be able to put our preconceptions to the side."

"Indeed," Sal'braan concurred. Tooran glanced at the man, touched more by his single word than any of Shatterbreath's.

"Please," Kael said as if the moment might burst like a bubble if he spoke too loudly. "Calm down, all of you. Vert, we'll just stick with the basics tonight. We'll get to the more advanced things tomorrow. We still have some time."

Vert sighed. "How much time exactly? You said they should be here within a few days. The more we can get done, the better. I guess we *should* start simple though. The first step is the most obvious."

"What's that?" Kael asked.

"We take Vallenfend."

Only Kael winced. Was he the only one who didn't see that coming? "Take Vallenfend?" he echoed. "Why?"

"For the very reason why you were sent to me, Tiny," Shatterbreath said.

"Taking Vallenfend is vital," Tooran elaborated. "In it lies our most powerful tactical advantage. Anybody can see that. It will be easy to defend and extremely hard to take under full defence."

"They will try to defend!" Kael shouted. "People might get hurt or killed."

"Ha, King Morrindale's actions will be beneficial to us, and detrimental to BlackHound. Don't worry, Kael," Vert exclaimed with a wave of his hand, "we will be swift in taking Vallenfend to minimize casualties. It shouldn't take long at all."

131

Kael slumped on his log. Vert and Tooran were right, taking Vallenfend was the most important task at the moment. With correct defences, the city could become a giant fortress. Having it under their control would prove to be crucial. Still, it didn't seem right. Knowing that King Morrindale's plan would succeed, whether in his favour or not, still felt like a huge loss.

Shatterbreath perked up, raising her head above all of them. "Someone is approaching."

Before she could elaborate, one of Arnoth's soldiers came bursting through the bushes, red in the face and short of breath. Kael recognized the man as Clodde, Vert's second-in-command.

"General!" he cried. "General!"

"I told you not to interrupt! We are to be left alone. What we are doing here is of—"

"They're here!" Clodde interjected. "They're here, General! The BlackHound Empire...th—they've arrived!"

Kael was stunned. Contrarily, Vert was spurred into action. He sprung to his feet. "I suppose we're going to have to take Vallenfend sooner than I thought."

Perhaps the meeting wasn't going to take all night after all.

Chapter 13

"What's the situation?" Kael asked.

Vert squinted, squeezing the reigns of his horse. He was leading Arnoth, which was marching towards Vallenfend. After Clodde had interrupted their meeting, Shatterbreath had dropped Tooran and Sal'braan off at her cave so that they could prepare the refugees to leave as well. It was time for them to go home. Kael and Shatterbreath had then returned to find that Arnoth was already heading out. Now, Shatterbreath walked beside Vert as he clopped along on his faithful horse.

"Our spies at the coast missed their morning report. We thought nothing of it until our evening spies missed their report as well. When one of our men did come back, he was in a dire state." Vert's brow furrowed. "He had been lunged through the chest with a spear. He woke up only a few hours ago to tell us of the news. BlackHound has arrived."

"So that's how it is," Shatterbreath mumbled.

Kael nodded. "They're early."

"So far, Kael, Arnoth is the only city to come to your aid." Vert gave him a serious look. "I hope the others stay true to their word."

"They'll get here."

"Let's hope so." Vert shifted his breastplate. "The whole of BlackHound won't siege us tonight. They can't cover that much ground in one day, but that doesn't necessarily mean they won't still *attack*. Chances are they will have at least scouting parties heading our way. We need eyes. Tell me what they're up to."

Shatterbreath nodded. "We'll return shortly. Hold on, Tiny." With a hop then a bound, she was airborne and rising over Arnoth. As individuals blended into the moving throng, Kael set his eyes towards the darkened horizon.

The BlackHound Empire had arrived. It seemed as though the day would never come. It seemed for a time that Kael was only preparing for a nightmare, an intangible enemy. But Clodde's announcement snapped something inside Kael. They were real, and

133

they were coming. It gave him some consolidation know he had been right, and Laura wrong.

The sound of Shatterbreath's wings came as no comfort. Kael's heart was beating too fast and his throat was constricting. A heavy knot was forming in his stomach as he pictured over and over in his mind what they would see when they reached the coast. Time and time again, the memories Shatterbreath had shared with him flitted through his mind.

They never reached the coast. After almost an hour, Shatterbreath twitched and gazed downwards. Without explanation, Kael was thrust into her vision. Far below, a large group of cavalry was charging across the rolling landscape. At least five-hundred knights garbed in black spurred their horses faster and faster while a massive plume of dust followed them. The insignia of the flags they carried was unmistakable. It was the same that was inscribed on Kael's shield.

BlackHound.

"Have they seen you yet?" Kael asked as he pulled out of her vision.

"No. We're too high and the night sky protects us."

"Good. Let's get back to Vallenfend as fast as possible."

Without a word, Shatterbreath banked sharply, nearly throwing Kael off her back. She set off a breakneck speed, quickly leaving the group of knights behind.

Shatterbreath flew straight to Vallenfend. To Kael's relief, no ballistae were fired in their direction. The city was illuminated by thousands of torches, making it easy for Kael to see movement within the streets. As Shatterbreath approached, he registered that Arnoth's soldiers were already spread throughout the city. In fact, it looked as though they had taken it already, in the mere two hours that Kael had been gone.

Shatterbreath circled above the city and together, she and Kael watched as Arnoth soldiers surrounded the castle. Kael was surprised to find that the King's Elite were only congregated in one spot—the castle training grounds. What's more, they weren't fighting. They were just standing there, as if waiting for orders.

Shatterbreath cocked her head. "Zeptus," she stated.

"What?"

Without explanation, she swooped in towards the group of trained assassins, who all cringed. She landed with a shudder to the side of the group. If they were frightened by her sudden appearance, their initial cringe was the only sign they gave. Otherwise, their eyes were all fixated on one thing. Kael traced their gaze.

Zeptus.

Zeptus stood just outside the castle's back doors, with his arms folded behind his back. He began strolling over just as Kael spotted him.

"Hail, Grand Shatterbreath," he called out.

"Purple Eyes..." The dragon regarded him carefully "What is happening here?"

Zeptus stopped just in front of Shatterbreath, peering up calmly at her. "Your friend is in charge of Vallenfend now. He broke into the castle only a few minutes ago. To guarantee as little conflict as possible, I've gathered my soldiers together to keep them out of the way."

"That's very noble of you, Zeptus," Kael said, sliding off Shatterbreath's back to face him. "But what of King Morrindale and everybody else inside?"

"Your friends are dealing with them now."

Kael raised his eyebrows. "Dealing?" he repeated. "How so?"

"I believe the castle guards are being forced out here." On cue, the door to the castle burst open, and several young men wearing blue tunics stumbled out. They glanced around, unsure, then tentatively began meandering towards the barracks, giving the group of King's Elite a wide berth. "Same with the servants. The king himself was thrown in the dungeons, I believe."

Kael sighed in relief. "Good. I want him alive for now. I haven't had my way with him yet... Where's Vert?"

The purple-eyed man cocked his head and frowned. "Who?"

"Never mind. Shatterbreath, could you c—"

"Vert!" Shatterbreath hollered. Kael clapped his hands over his ears. "Vert!"

"What, what?" A head poked out of one of the castle's windows. It was Vert Bowman. He smiled when he spotted Kael and Shatterbreath. "Hey! Come up here!"

Before Kael could do anything, Shatterbreath picked him up by the back of his breastplate with her teeth. She jumped up with help from her wings and clung to the side of the castle, roughly placing Kael down in the windowsill.

Jarred, Kael stumbled into the room and collapsed on the carpet. Vert chuckled as he picked himself up.

"Warning would be nice," Kael grumbled at Shatterbreath. "You were quick, Vert. I didn't believe overtaking an entire city would take so little time."

"Vallenfend is big, but its population isn't. Everybody is pretty much just staying in their houses. There wasn't much to overtake."

"Listen, Vert, there's a group of mounted knights coming our way. Not a small number either. I'd say... Shatterbreath?"

The dragon snuck her nose in the window—which almost didn't fit. "More than five hundred for sure, maybe even a thousand. They'll be here very soon; they were on horses."

Vert scratched his chin. For no particular reason, he snatched a vase that was resting on a pedestal nearby and hurled it at the wall. Everything else was smashed in the room as well, which seemed to be dedicated to holding pieces of art at one time.

"Horses? How in the world did they get horses...? Bah, not now. Let's give them a great welcome then, eh? Kael?"

Kael snapped to attention. He was reeling. Everything was happening so fast. He couldn't register it all. "Oh, yes. Of course. What do you want us to do?"

"Spread the word," Vert chimed. "Tell everybody to hide. Doubtless, this vanguard will charge straight to the castle. My troops are centralized around the castle already. We'll strike here and cut them off. Hopefully, we'll keep the element of surprise."

"Of course. Shatterbreath, let's go."

"No," Vert barked. "Kael, I need you here. Shatterbreath, I'm sorry to say, but once you've delivered your message, I need you to fly away."

She made a strange growl, unamused by his statement.

"They're going to see you otherwise," Vert explained with a shrug. "We can't hide you here."

Kael hugged her snout. "He's right. Watch from above, make sure nothing goes awry."

The dragon nuzzled him. "Fine. I'll listen to Smert. Stay safe." With that, she pulled her snout of the room and pulled away from the castle, banking out of sight. He could hear her voice as she ordered Vert's troops to conceal themselves. Already, he missed her. After all his adventuring inside strange cities, he felt as though there was no further reason to be apart from her anymore.

"Smert?" Vert scoffed from behind.

Kael whipped around. "Alright, Vert. You've quickly taken charge here, what's the plan?"

"Right now," Vert grunted, draping himself over a tipped cabinet. "We wait."

Kael tried to run the numbers through in his head. The soldiers had been going very fast, but still, there was a fair distance between the sea and Vallenfend. When he and Shatterbreath had stumbled upon them, they must have been...three quarters of the way to the coast. The way they were pushing their animals, they could have arrived within an hour. Kael had been sitting in that room for an hour already. Obviously, their animals couldn't take that much strain.

"I can't get over it," Vert whispered.

Kael blinked, forced away from his calculations. "Hmm? What?"

"Horses." He leaned back in his chair, digging his fingers into the mauve material. "How did they get horses? They couldn't have brought them over, could they?"

Kael shrugged. "They have use of rudimentary magic."

"How could that help?"

"Not sure. We'll have to ask Sal'braan later. Maybe he'll know."

"Either way, this interrupts with my plans. I didn't account for horses, Kael."

137

Kael rubbed his chin. "What are you going to do?"

"Carry through I suppose. Things will have to change, but I'm sure it won't be significant."

Something interrupted their conversation, a strange sound. An explosion? Exchanging glances, Kael and Vert moved to the window and peered outside. Torches still illuminated Vallenfend, but not to the same degree as before. Even in the fainter light, Kael could see smoke rising from a section of the south-eastern wall. The vanguard had arrived.

To Kael's amazement, the gate in the wall had been blow free, leaving a gaping hole in which the vanguard flooded through. As he watched, the soldiers clopped into town, dispersing among the streets.

Screaming ensued.

"Vert," Kael said lowly.

His face was stern. "Steady now."

"What are they doing?"

He frowned and closed his eyes. "They think the city is theirs. They're looting, Kael. Stay calm, we have to maintain our element of surprise. We...have to let them continue. They'll make their way to us eventually."

Kael gritted his teeth, only able to imagine the things the men were doing down below. He was just glad none of his immediate friends were down there. The trek down the mountain was at least a day's journey.

As much as he detested just standing there, listening to the terror, Kael knew Vert was right. If the vanguard discovered the army hiding within Vallenfend, the war would start early. And with that many civilians caught in the middle, innocent lives would undoubtedly be taken—which would be worse than whatever was happening down below.

"What if they discover your army?" Kael said, voicing his concerns.

"Let's hope they don't."

They both fell silent, listening to the city as it fell prey to the vanguard. Slowly but surely, the screaming and sinister laughter grew louder, signifying the majority of the vanguard force was making its way to the castle. Once again, Vert was correct; their main task was to take the castle. Though they had taken their time doing so.

"Here they come," Vert remarked. "Let's go. Kael, are you ready?"

Kael unsheathed *Vintrave* and fitted his shield onto his left arm. He inspected both. His sword gleamed like new in the warm glow of the torch nearby. His shield, though worse for wear, was sturdy and strong. His stolen armour, though not as dazzling as his last set, was secured firmly about his body. He was ready. He nodded to Vert.

"Let's do this."

Chapter 14

Laura hadn't believed them at first. Tooran and Sal'braan came rushing into the cave, saying it was time to go. *Go?* Go where? Why, when, how?

She was even more sceptical when those questions were answered. They were going back to Vallenfend to *take it over.* They were going home. Because the BlackHound Empire had arrived.

As alluring as the prospect to go back home was, she couldn't swallow the idea of *how* they were going to do it. They were going to march down to Vallenfend and just *take* it. As if such a thing would be easy. As Tooran prompted them to hurry, he mentioned something about an army assisting or leading. Something similar.

Huh. As if a city could be taken with such ease. Even Vallenfend, with its missing men.

"What do you think of this?" she asked Faerd, who was bundling up his few belongings beside her.

His eye lit up. "Home, Laura! We're finally going home! You should be relieved."

"Why am I not?"

He frowned. "I think it's the reason why. We're going back because the Empire is here. We have to take Vallenfend before they do. We have to defend out city. I don't think you're okay with that because it means Kael's right."

She stared at him, aghast. "I see no evidence telling me Kael is correct, do you?"

"I don't see too well anyway." He stuck his tongue out at her. "Now come on. I don't care if you're angry or not, I'm sure you don't want to be left behind now, do you? Let me help you with that."

He hefted Laura's pack over his shoulder and joined the throng as they excitedly poured towards the cave's entrance. Laura stayed rooted to where she was kneeling. Despite everything that led her to take shelter in the cave to begin with, she would miss it. During their many months staying within its depths, she begun to regard it at home.

Then what will I be returning to?

She picked herself up to join Faerd as they left the cave. Forever.

They hiked down the mountain with swift speed—which wasn't the easiest thing to do. Their numbers didn't help any. Still, Tooran was relentless. As they descended, Laura found Bunda among the refugees.

"What do *you* think of all this?" she asked, looking for somebody to join her side.

"I'm wondering what has become of my shop," Bunda grumbled. "Ooo, I bet it's full of rats now." She gasped. "Or even worse, *cats.*" She shuddered.

"What about the silly empire? You don't actually think..."

"What?"

"That they're...here, do you?"

"I know how you've blamed all this on Kael, Laura. We all know how you don't believe him either. But the evidence is staggering, my dear. What other reason would the king have for sending so many men to the dragon to die? What other explanation is there for everything that's happened to us?"

Laura twisted her lips in a sneer. "Well..." She tried to find a suitable retort, but none came. Truth was, there was no other feasible solution. Anything else would be even more absurd.

"You have to promise me, girl," Bunda said, catching her hesitation, "when the times comes to face the truth, you'll forgive Kael."

Laura stumbled on the path. Faerd caught her before she fell. He had been listening to their conversation. She pulled away from him and folded her arms. "I—I don't know. Even if he *is* correct, is that an excuse for deserting us so many times? For his lies?"

Bunda shrugged. "I would think so."

The butcher's words lanced through Laura.

Bunda's face screwed up. "Ah, my aching feet! How much longer do we have to hike? How am I supposed to see in the dark anyway? Why—"

Laura pulled away from the butcher, who had begun one of her fits of complaining. She was so conflicted. It was getting harder and harder to deny the fact that Kael might have been right the entire time. She suddenly felt so callous, so shameful for being harsh to him. He only meant well all along.

No. He wasn't correct yet. She wouldn't believe him until she saw them herself. She wouldn't even consider forgiving him until she could see the whites of their eyes.

Faerd wrapped an arm around her shoulder. "Look," he said, pointing through the trees. "There it is! Vallenfend. We're making excellent time. We're going to be there before you can know it! Won't it be great to be home?"

She wasn't sure.

Despite the eager pace they travelled at, it took longer than Laura thought to finally get down to Vallenfend. She had forgotten just how high up on the mountain they had been, or how long it had taken to get there to begin with.

The sun was beginning to peek through the trees as they finally neared the base of the mountain. After being stuck up so long in the cave, where pure, natural sunlight was an oddity, seeing the golden light was a relief. It was a refreshing contrast to the permanent blue they had been suffocating in.

Overall, their trip had been extremely dangerous, especially when they had walked past the waterfalls, but this time, nobody was harmed. One lady—Laura still hadn't learned her name—twisted her angle when she slipped, but aside from the constant complaining, that was the worst of it.

As they stepped out of the forests and into the fields, Laura was startled to see a great quantity of smoke rising up out of Vallenfend. She couldn't see the flames over the wall, but it was evident a part of the city was burning. It seemed to be coming from the south-western wall.

A murmur ran through the group of refugees, halting them. Laura retrieved the bow from her back and pushed her way through the crowd until she was at the front with Tooran, who was frozen to the spot.

"Tooran, what is it? What's happening?"

The man's brow furrowed. "Quiet. Listen."

Laura closed her lips, straining her ears. Nothing.

"Swords... Screams... Battle!" Tooran produced a sword from the depths of his cloak. "They are under attack! To Vallenfend's aid! Hurry!"

With that, he broke out in a run, closely followed by his father. It took a moment, but the rest of the refugees followed, brandishing whatever weapons they were carrying. Women carrying bows, spears, swords and maces rushed past Laura, towards the city under apparent danger. Laura stayed where she was, dumbstruck.

Under attack? No, it couldn't be...

It wasn't until Faerd seized her by the hand did she move. Joining the group, they rushed towards the city. As they approached, the sounds Tooran had mentioned became evident. Over the wall, sounding distorted and detached, Laura could clearly make out the sounds of battle. Metal striking metal, screams of pain and howls of animals caught in between.

The gates closest were shut tight, so the group was forced to run around Vallenfend until they reached the smouldering section of the wall, which seemed to have been blown open. The gate was left in shambles, ripped from its hinges and with parts littering the area surrounding. The large beam used to lock the doors was split in two, pointing inwards, signifying the door was blown inwards by a force from the outside.

As they rushed through the destroyed gate, Laura's greatest fears were realized. Vallenfend had fallen prey to chaos. As she watched, she could see a house burning nearby, with the occupants leaning out the windows, screaming and choking on the smoke. She could see soldiers moving through the streets, yelling commands to each other. They seemed to be rallying together, getting ready to fight. Who, though, Laura wasn't sure yet.

Tooran yelled something and a soldier nearby turned to look their way. The relief on his face was clearly visible. He waved Tooran over. Laura ran up to the two of them.

"...Been fighting all night. They're scattered throughout the city, but most of them are congregated near the castle. We need all the help we can get. Can you spare—?"

"What do you want us to do? Where do you want us?" Tooran demanded.

"We have to push whatever stragglers we can find to the castle. We'll be able to finish them off faster there. We can't afford to let any escape."

Tooran nodded. "Of course."

Laura gasped, trying to find her voice. "Tooran, what's happening?"

He paused a moment to frown at her. His eyes seemed so hard, so disapproving. "The BlackHound is here. Kael was right."

The words held so much gravity. Tooran could have struck her with the back of his hand and it wouldn't have hit as hard.

Tooran waved his sword over his head. "To the castle!" He roared. "Kill any soldiers wearing black armour! Come, for Vallenfend!"

Kael stood next to Vert, staring in iron concentration at the castle's front door. He had never been to the front of the castle; his previous intrusions had never required him to go that way.

The area he stood in was open, wide enough to fit the hundred-or-so Arnoth soldiers that accompanied him. The lobby was nearly as large as the castle's treasury. Kael had almost forgotten how truly massive the castle was.

In other entrances to the castle—namely, the training grounds gate—more forces were waiting to repel. The BlackHound vanguard wasn't taking the castle without a fight.

Kael stiffened as he heard the tromping of the vanguard just outside the door. Their voices were loud and tone jocular, signifying that what would come next would be a total surprise for them.

There came a rattle on the door, then a pause, as if whoever was leading was confused. Kael could understand them expecting little resistance, but did they really think the doors would just be unlocked? Would King Morrindale be so accepting?

The pause persisted for a good minute or two. Kael glanced sideways at Vert, who only gave him a staying look. As if to prove the silent warning he had given, something hard smashed against the door, causing it to bend inward, creaking on the hinges. Kael took a few steps back. They were breaking their way through the door.

Vert waved his hand and crouched low. Kael and the majority of the men followed suit. Two lines of archers notched their arrows at the back, aiming at the door. *Slam, slam.* The bracket holding the door shut was cracking. Sweat had begun to bead on Kael's neck. Any second, they would be through. He didn't know what to expect. How many would the archers be able to take out? How many had decided to take this door? How many were there in total? Worst of all, how many casualties on his side would there be?

Slam, slam. The next hit to the door seemed to take forever. Kael thought for a moment that they had simply stopped, but then the door began to heave slowly inwards and he registered that time was slowing for him. His gift made the breach happen painfully slow. The door smashed open, sending splinters floating through the air and dust expand out towards them.

Time returned to normal as BlackHound soldiers rushed through.

Few had the chance to register surprise before Vert gave the order.

"Fire!"

A hail of arrows soared overhead, skewering the front line of the vanguard force. The soldiers carrying the battering ram—which seemed to be comprised out of a beam from a house—were the first to fall. Kael set his jaw grimly as he watched the arrows pierce into the bodies of the soldiers. Every man in the front line of the vanguard fell with only a few behind receiving wounds. The bodies of their doomed comrades saved them.

Once the front line of the archers released their arrows, they took a step back, letting the second line fire. More BlackHound soldiers fell, but considerable less than the first wave. With both lines of archers now reloading, Vert yelled another command, ordering his men to attack.

With a cry, Kael rushed towards the throng of soldiers. He was the first to strike. He smashed shield-first into the nearest soldier, knocking the dark-skinned man to the ground. Kael followed through with a diagonal slash to the next soldier, effectively killing him. He was able to take out three more soldiers.

Then, altogether, the BlackHound vanguard recovered from their initial shock. Kael soon found it harder and harder to land a finishing strike. These were no ordinary guards. These were neither bandits nor bounty hunters. These men were trained killers. And chosen to lead the BlackHound Empires first strike, they were the elite.

The numbers against Kael and Vert's soldiers was staggering. With every BlackHound soldiers they killed, three seemed to take his place. It wasn't an easy task to fight in the confines of the room either. As the stench of spilled blood and sweat permeated around him, Kael struggled to find his breath. The room had been small to begin with, but now filled with battle and even more soldiers, it was choking. More often than he would have liked, Kael found himself shoulder-to-shoulder with one of his allies.

As they sheer numbers of their enemies seemed to finally be getting the better of them, relief came. The Arnoth soldiers that had been hiding in the city came to their aid. The general attention of the BlackHound soldiers was turned away from the relatively small group inside the castle's lobby and instead to the swarm of soldiers approaching from all angles outside.

Doubling their efforts, Kael, Vert and his chosen soldiers were able to push the vanguard force outside of the castle lobby and into the awaiting blades of the rest of Arnoth's army. Even heavily outnumbered, the BlackHound men didn't give up, taking the battle into the streets. But despite their ferocious efforts, Arnoth's numbers overwhelmed them. Instead of killing the handful of BlackHound men pinched in between Arnoth's soldiers, they were incapacitated or knocked unconscious. How long it took, Kael was unsure. Time never seemed so irrelevant.

Vert didn't miss a beat as the BlackHound soldiers were dragged back into the castle to be placed into the dungeons. "Captain, report!"

A knight wearing prestigious armour and bearing a flag with Arnoth's crest strode up to Vert and saluted. "It's hard to say, General, but it looks like four hundred of BlackHound is dead. They caught wind of our ambush at the back, so many of them managed to get away. They're spread throughout the city right now."

Vert cursed wildly. "How many?"

The captain coughed up blood. Kael just noticed the dagger sticking out of the notch in his armour between his breastplate and pauldron. "Again, it's hard to say. A good portion. Probably as many as we killed just now."

Again, Vert cursed and then turned to Kael. "We need to find those men, now. Before they manage to escape or retaliate. If we don't hurry, they may find somewhere easy to defend."

"I'll call Shatterbreath," Kael said with a nod. "We'll survey from above. If anybody escapes, we'll get them before they—"

Bright light and enormous sound. Kael was flung off his feet by an unknown force. He hit the ground hard. The world swooned around him and his ears rang. Blinking and working his jaw, Kael rolled onto his side, trying to make sense of what had just happened. Two identical streams of smoke plumed to his left. Not two, he realized, but one. As his vision corrected itself, Kael worked his way back onto his feet. He traced the plume of smoke to its base, where a crater glowed an unearthly green colour. Surrounding it were blackened bodies, many of them dismembered. Not a single one moved.

People were screaming all around him, but he couldn't hear any noise. Kael was struck with panic. Had he gone deaf? Kael recognized Vert in the din yelling noiseless orders which people seemed to understand. Kael clutched his chest, suddenly aware of how much it throbbed

As Kael moved towards Vert, there came ringing in his ear. That was a good sign. He had lost his hearing temporarily before when Shatterbreath roared. Ringing always preceded the recovery itself. This was nothing like Shatterbreath's roar though.

"Vert, Vert!" Kael yelled. At least, he thought he was yelling. He could just barely hear himself.

Vert turned to him. "Kael, what happened?"

Kael put a hand to his temple as another wave of dizziness befell him. "I'm not sure. Probably the same thing that happened to the gates. Are you okay?"

Vert nodded. "I'm fine, but several of my men aren't. Whatever we were hit with, I hope they don't do it again. We need to find them, Kael. Get in the air at once."

Kael nodded and put his fingers to his lips to whistle. Before he could even blow, he was buffeted by a strong wind. At first, he was terrified that another mysterious explosion had occurred, but then he realized it was only Shatterbreath.

The dragon's eyes were wide. "Kael, are you alright? Something strange happened. It was like a ball of green fire erupted beside you. I was worried it had devoured you."

Kael's hearing still hadn't quite returned, but he could clearly hear the building behind Shatterbreath crumble as she hit it with her tail. He winced as the roof caved in, hoping nobody was inside. She didn't even notice what she had done. It reminded Kael that Vallenfend was no place for a dragon.

"I'm fine. We have to get airborne. We can't let any BlackHound soldiers escape."

"Hop on," she exclaimed. Instead, she scooped him up and placed him on her shoulders. With two strong beats, they were already a fair distance above Vallenfend.

From up high, Kael could see the sun's rays glowing over Shatterbreath's mountain. It hadn't seemed like it, but he had been fighting all night. With that realization came a wave of fatigue. Doing his best to ignore it, he leaned over Shatterbreath's back.

"See anything?" he asked.

"Everything. BlackHound soldiers are still fighting against our allies in some places. There's a great deal of them near the middle-western part of the city. It looks as though they're trying to escape."

"Let me see." Kael was submerged in Shatterbreath's vision. True to her word, there were a collection soldiers in dark armour working their way slowly west, weaving in between the houses.

Their interest in plundering and terrorizing had vanished now. He came out of her vision. "Can you get them?"

"No. Unless you want your city burned to the ground."

"Should we wait until they jump out in the open, or land and tell Vert where they are?"

Shatterbreath thought for a moment. Instead of answering, she flicked her head, something on the ground catching her attention. "Look," she said.

He followed her gaze. Down below, a group of people were sprinting through the fields. Kael recognized them at once. They were his friends, his family.

"Wait," Kael blurted out. "Fly lower, keep watch on them. I don't want any of them harmed, understand? How quickly could you get to them if you had to?"

Shatterbreath shook her neck. "Three seconds, without you."

"Then drop me off. I need to be there with them and I need you ready to help. Hurry."

Without question, Shatterbreath banked sharply and pulled into a nosedive, heading towards the nearest courtyard. She was acting very calm towards his ordering her around. Kael figured she realized that from now, she would have no choice but to follow orders.

Kael jumped off her back before she even hit ground. He rolled and popped back onto his feet, just as she took off again, buffeting him with air. With a slight pause first to orient himself, Kael took off westward, using the spire of Saint Briggon's Monastery as a guide. After a while, the clanging of metal against metal led him as well. It didn't take long to find his family.

Kael emerged from an alleyway into an open street. Fighting amongst the shops and houses were BlackHound soldiers and past them, he could spot tarnished armour. Undoubtedly the same that the refugees had borrowed from Shatterbreath's cave. Kael watched his family fight for a while before intervening himself.

Tooran had trained them well. The majority of the refugees were women, but fought with as much strength and skill as any male soldier. The ladies wielded their weapons with confidence as they fought and refused to back down. Reinforced with what little of

Vert's troops there were that far outside the centre of the city, they were doing a fantastic job keeping the retreating vanguard at bay. They were faltering though. Even as Kael watched, the BlackHound soldiers managed to take another house, pushing the refugees further away. Without reinforcements from Arnoth, the BlackHound vanguard would be able to push past them and escape—which in itself wasn't alarming. It was the fact to do so would probably mean the death of all if not most of the refugees.

There was no telling when friendly reinforcements would arrive. Vert's army was spread throughout the city, searching the BlackHound soldiers down. Apparently, they hadn't reached this far yet and there was no telling when they would. If not soon, it would be too late.

Fine then. Kael would have to be the reinforcements. And, if necessary, Shatterbreath.

Kael ran the first soldier through before the BlackHound soldiers even realized he was there. He snuck across the road to the cover and pressed up against a house before eliminating a second one as well. It was the third BlackHound soldier that heard the choking gasp of his dying comrade and whipped around, his dark eyes burning with fury.

"Brother!" he screamed, alerting the others of Kael's presence, "I'll avenge you!"

He charged Kael, wielding a terrifying double-handed mace. The thing seemed impossibly huge, dotted with heavy studs and intricate carvings of hounds. As he raised the weapon as if it weighed no more than a wooden club, Kael had a vague thought. *There was no way he was going to block this.*

A door flung open, smacking into the BlackHound soldier. The soldier reeled to the side, knocking into a column supporting the building's overhang. A woman stepped out of the door, looking flustered but feisty. In one hand, she held a knife, the other, a pan. Before the soldier could recover, the woman smacked him across the face with the pan, sending him crashing to the ground.

The great mace *thudded* when it struck the dirt.

The woman tossed the pan to the side and gripped the knife with both hands. She hesitated, so Kael moved it and gently pried it from her grip. She frowned at him. "Rundown?" she gasped.

Kael didn't know the woman, but it wasn't a surprise that she knew about him. It gave him satisfaction to know people knew his name. He cast the knife to the side and stabbed the soldier through the heart with his sword.

"Thanks for the help," Kael said to her. "Now, stay inside. We're here for you."

The woman nodded and retreated back into her house, looking quite pale.

The soldier's cry had not gone unnoticed. Almost as soon as the door closed, a soldier rushed at Kael, who brought up his shield to block the axe. Kael took him down with relative ease, moving on to the next man. More soldiers came at him, quickly identifying him as the greatest threat.

Kael fought them back as best as he could. His ability to slow time kept him from being skewered or smashed from their weapons, but even still, he could not avoid injury. A bruise against his arm from a hammer, a cut across his thigh and the worst, a slash above his brow which sent blood flowing into his eye.

Kael slowly retreated, being overwhelmed by soldiers. He was having a hard time keeping up against the four enemies bearing down on him. There was no room for attack; he was too busy trying to defend.

Kael focused on a particular soldier—one wielding a crooked halberd. This man was causing him the most trouble. He needed to kill him first if he was to improve his situation. As he was about to attack, Kael noticed something reach out from behind the soldier. Two hands garbed in smooth black material snatched the man's head around his chin and near his opposite temple. With a twist and snap, the soldier crumpled to the ground, revealing someone Kael had never been more relieved to see.

Blade glistening with blood, Tooran stepped over the body and hacked off the arm of the next soldier. A broadsword lodged itself into the base of another soldier's neck. After kicking the dying man

151

to the ground, Korjan also appeared.   Then Faerd, Bunda and Sal'braan.

The soldiers that had outnumbered Kael were now the ones *being* outnumbered.   Realizing this, they tried to retreat, but were only caught in the backs by arrows.   Laura and Helena reloaded their bows.

Kael managed a smile, despite how fatigued he was. "Hey guys," he wheezed. "We never had a formal reunion, did we?"

"Kael..." Before he knew it, Bunda had her arms wrapped around him and was crying.

"Look what they did to our city!" Helena cried. She was in tears as well.

Laura seemed to be holding hers back.

"We saw you fighting," Tooran declared, business as usual, "and came rushing to help you. I'm afraid we had to break the line to do so. They've escaped."

Kael glanced past him and saw a sizeable chunk of the refugees standing behind his friends. Many of them were crying. All but a few were staring at the damaged buildings in sorrow. Blood soaked the street.

"Escaped," Kael muttered, still registering exactly what Tooran had said. "That's fine. That problem should fix itself right..." He snapped his fingers and pointed in the direction the vanguard had fled. "Now."

On cue, a blue shape raged overhead. Shatterbreath released a jet of flame that scored across the land. Undoubtedly, most of the vanguard force had just died with one breath.

Kael turned back to his friends. "It's good to be home."

Chapter 15

A few hours later, Kael, his friends and Vert went to the castle as Arnoth's soldiers continued to hunt down whatever remained of the BlackHound vanguard. Shatterbreath was patrolling the borders as well. There was no way any of them were going to escape.

Kael could feel the fatigue of the battle he had just been through, as well as his day and a half lack of rest, but he did his best to ignore it. There was no time to rest.

Something dawned on Kael as they neared the castle's gleaming white walls.

"Vert," he said, "how thorough were you when you took the castle?"

Vert shrugged. "Thorough enough. Why?"

"To the top level thorough?"

Frowning, Vert paused to look at him. "No. That's Zeptus's level. As we went up, he came down, ordering people to follow him. "Why?"

"That level is mine, understand?" The top level held the treasury room. "You may do what you wish with the castle and prisoners, but that entire floor belongs to me."

Vert opened his mouth, but Kael interrupted him.

"Please, respect my wishes, alright? That floor is to be left alone by *everybody*. Unless I say so."

Vert considered him for a long time. "Fine," he said at last. "It's all yours." He waved his hand in dismissal.

Kael sighed in relief. He promised all that gold to the bandits. Vert wouldn't likely be interested in the hoard, but it was better to keep it a secret.

Kael felt a tap to his shoulder. He slowed as Faerd leaned in close. "Why do you want that level?" he asked. "What's up there?"

Kael caught the rest of his friends looking at him for an answer. The refugees had been directed to the castle's training grounds. They were to be trained by the King's Elite. Kael's closer friends, such as

153

Bunda, Helena, Faerd, Korjan, Tooran, Laura and her mother would be living in the castle. Kael needed them closer.

He hesitated, but decided it would be safe to tell them. "You remember the pile of gold I told you about? The treasure the BlackHound Empire gave to Murderdale as payment?"

His friends' eyes lit up as they realized what he was talking about. Tooran's expression remained steady. "You mean...?" Bunda gasped.

Kael gave a stern nod, glancing at Vert. The butcher clapped her hands over her mouth.

"Wh—what are you going to do with it?" Faerd whispered.

The group stopped at the front doors of the castle, which were now in shambles thanks to the BlackHound's battering ram.

"I have a plan," Kael muttered, cutting off that conversation. Talking about the treasure reminded Kael of something though. King Murderdale. The greedy king was in their custody. He was the reason for all this. He needed to be punished. Kael turned to Vert. "I want to see the king. Now."

"No. Rest up first," Vert mumbled, looking tired himself. "You've been going too long. Once you've recovered some energy, he's all yours. Get me first before you do it. I want to be there."

Kael didn't argue. He and Vert climbed the first flight of stairs before separating; he and his closest generals were occupying the first floor. Motioning for them to follow, Kael proceeded through the rest of the castle. Or at least tried to. They only managed to climb one more set of stairs before Kael became completely lost. It was a good thing Tooran was there to guide them the rest of the way. Kael had forgotten that he used to be a King's Elite. Tooran knew this structure probably better than the king.

Once at the top, Tooran found them several large rooms to sleep in. The women went in one, and the men in the other. Only furniture occupied the room, no beds. Kael was more than happy though. After sleeping in the wilderness for so long—on the ground, on Shatterbreath's back or on a giant tree limb—the bumpy, dusty armchair was more than welcoming.

Thoughts flew through his mind, doing their best to keep him from falling asleep, but eventually, his fatigue won over.

He awoke from his dreams with a start, panting and sweating. Frustrated, he tore off his armour which he had forgotten to take off before curling up on the armchair. A window was open at the far end of the room and he walked towards it. In his dreams, he had been walking through a forest, much like the one west of Arnoth. But instead of bloodwolves jumping out at him, there were hounds as black as tar.

Pulling his thoughts away from his nightmares, Kael placed both hands on the window sill. Vallenfend stretched before him. It seemed so much different than he once remembered it. Had it changed, or had he? From behind, he could hear the gentle snoring of Faerd as well as Korjan's heavy breathing.

"Troubled?" a deep voice asked. Kael whipped around. Tooran was leaning against a bookshelf, a small book cradled in his hand. "I thought you were wrestling a bear, by the way you thrashed in your sleep."

Kael rubbed his neck. "Yeah. Nightmares. What time is it?"

"Nearly time to meet your friend. I have news too."

"Oh?"

"It seems most if not all of the vanguard has been eliminated. Also, some of your allies arrived today."

Kael was fully awake now. "Really? Who?"

"Messy folk. They don't have banners, so I'm not sure where from." Tooran turned a page in his book. "They were thought to be thieves at first until Shatterbreath swooped down to greet them."

"Bandits," Kael declared. Tooran eyed him over his book. "Ha, she greeted them? She doesn't even like them. I'm glad they've arrived. Where are they now?"

"Not sure. Shatterbreath informed us of another large group heading across the desert as well. Their crest bares a predatory bird of sorts."

"Fallenfeld?" Kael couldn't believe it. His meeting with Yseph worked better than he expected. "Wow, that's amazing! I didn't think they would come through. I'll have to check for sure. Still, that's fantastic news. Any word from the BlackHound Empire?"

"You'll have to ask your friend. I heard no news." Tooran placed his book down. "Kael, I have a question for you. Concerning...the war."

Kael hesitated. "Go ahead."

"With so many arriving, you're going to need generals to keep your allies in line. You're going to need somebody to lead the forces into battle."

Kael knew where he was going at once. "No, Tooran," he said, shaking his head.

"You need me, Kael. I have experience. I will not fail you. Give me forces to lead. A section of Arnoth and Fallenfeld. We can't have Vert running everything."

"No," Kael said again, firmer this time. "You're right, I do need you. But your place is here, with your family. With your father. I am assigning you to take charge of whatever forces Vallenfend can rally—and the bandits too."

Tooran pushed away from the cabinet, clenching his fists. "Kael..."

"It's not open for discussion, Tooran." Kael sighed and put a hand to his temple. "I care for these people more than anything else. Everything I've done is for my family. I wouldn't allow anybody I didn't have absolute confidence in to lead them. I trust you above all else, Tooran. Having you to protect my family is the greatest honour I can bestow."

Tooran's frown persisted. At long last, however, he softened. "Thank you, Kael. I understand. My place is with my people. I will protect them well."

"As I believe you will." There was a shuffle and Kael glanced to the side. Korjan was awake. How long he had been listening, Kael knew not. He beamed at his son. No words were exchanged.

"Come on now," Kael said with a stretch. "I have a long-overdue meeting with the king."

After waking the others, Kael led the group through the castle. At least he tried to. It didn't take long until Tooran took over once again.

As they walked, Bunda fumed.

"Oh, this is more like it. At last, we'll going to get back at that loathsome, greedy maggot! What are we going to do to him? Whip him? Let people throw vegetables at him?" She rubbed her hands together. "I think we should behead him. Ooo, or let the dragon devour him. Wouldn't that be irony for you? I bet he'd make good sausage. Let me at him, Kael!"

Kael laughed. "We'll figure out something." Truth was, he had no idea was they were going to do with him. The obvious choice was to kill him, but Kael wanted his suffering to last. Not just physically either. It sickened him to think such dark thoughts, but then he remembered what he had been put through because of that one man.

Mrs. Stockwin stayed silent. She had suffered even greater than Bunda, but she didn't say a word. If anything, she was pale, as if in disbelief that their revenge was finally going to be carried through with.

"Tooran, could you get Vert and tell him to meet us atop the back wall? I think I can find my way from here. Everybody else spread the news. I want the city to see what we're going to do."

In a matter of minutes, Kael was left alone, standing at the steps to the dungeons. He stared down into the depths, a mephitic stench rising up, despite the fact that most of the prisoners were gone. That smell would probably never leave.

One step at a time, he descended. The horror of being trapped down there echoed through his mind. The inhuman screams, the unnatural stench, the sinking feeling of hopelessness and despair... All he wanted was to get in and out as fast as he could.

He found Morrindale at the very back cells—where he himself had been imprisoned.

King Morrindale's frame was thinner than Kael remembered. The rings on his fingers didn't seem so tight-fitting and his cheeks had taken on a sunken appearance. His skin had lost its healthy hue and the drunken rosiness in his cheeks had been replaced by a sour yellow. He hardly looked like the same person anymore. Kael almost pitied him.

Almost.

The king, before Kael even spoke, twitched, as if realizing who the person was.

"Oh, how the tides have turned, Rundown." His voice was delicate, void of his usual surliness. He sounded defeated, hopeless.

"Your grand scheme failed, Murderdale. Did you really think you could get away with it?"

The broken king looked up. Something stirred inside Kael gazing into his sullen, defeated eyes. "It was you. I never should have underestimated you. I should have killed you that day, instead of letting you walk back off to your pet dragon. What a fool I am."

Kael wrapped a hand around a bar. "Your greed got the better of you, murderer. Why? Why King Morrindale? Why did you do all this? Be honest with me, man to man. Why didn't you just find other means to acquire something as common and petty as gold? Why did so many have to die? I think I deserve an answer."

The king considered him for the longest time. "You really want to know? The gold was only a bonus. The BlackHound Empire has no short supply of the stuff. It never was my main interest. Heh, the very thought..."

Kael shook the bars. "Then what?! What did they have that was so tantalizing, you greedy..."

There was a glimmer in Morrindale's eyes. "Eternal life."

Kael went still.

"They offered me my youth again. Eternally. To live forever in a perfect body. And for my daughter the same. I love her so much—I'd do anything for her safety."

"Is that it then?"

The king bowed his head. "And my wife. They promised me my wife back."

Kael was struck by his last statement. He was struck hard. The Queen had died during childbirth. What he himself wouldn't give to see his mother again. King Morrindale's love for his daughter was obvious, but Kael had never known he cared so much for his wife.

So much that he'd destroy his own people to get her back. Morrindale must have truly loved her.

"You really think they could do that?" Kael asked. He tried to keep his voice stern, but desperation managed to creep in.

Morrindale remained still. So still. "I could only hope. Any chance at all was worth the risk. If it wasn't for your meddling, I might have actually seen her once again..."

Kael heard enough. He now knew Morrindale's motives. He had all the answers to every question that had plagued him since recruitment. "Come now. Your people await."

Kael had forgotten the key to the cell, but that didn't deter him. With a slash from *Vintrave,* the door swung free. Kael pushed it aside and entered, standing tall before Morrindale's thinning shape.

"Where's my daughter?" Morrindale asked before standing up.

Kael took him by the shoulder. "I don't know." He pushed him roughly out the door.

But Kael didn't have to guide King Morrindale. The man clearly knew he had no chance of escape. On their way back, Kael noticed several limp forms garbed in black armour. BlackHound soldiers. He hadn't noticed them on his way in. Their arms were chained to the back of their cell and they remained still. He could hear their breathing, so they were still alive. Kael pushed the king onward, wondering what they would do with the men.

"Where is my daughter?" King Morrindale repeated halfway up the steps.

"I really don't know. I'm telling the truth. I have no idea. She's probably out in the barracks with the rest of the castle's workers."

King Morrindale whipped around at the top of the stairs. He grabbed Kael's free hand. With his other, Kael pressed *Vintrave's* tip against the king's chest.

"Promise me, Kael. *Promise* me you'll let me see her again. Just once."

Kael gritted his teeth but relaxed his blade. "Sure. Bring me to the wall—the spot where you used to give your public displays."

Some fire returned in King Morrindale's eyes. Perhaps knowing he would see his daughter again had sparked some hope in him.

159

Without further argument, Morrindale did as he was ordered. In no time, they stood at a door. From behind its splintered surface, Kael could hear people yelling. The voices of disgruntled Vallenfend.

"Without Zeptus as your mouthpiece, your scapegoat, what will you do now?" Kael hissed.

The king frowned. "Zeptus... You changed him. You fixed him. How?"

"Out," Kael prodded him forward. "Go out. Meet your people."

Morrindale opened the door and sunlight cut in, blinding Kael. He walked out, holding a hand over his face to block the light. As his eyes adjusted, he was met with a startling view. The entire populace of Vallenfend stood before him. Whenever Kael had been to the king's public displays, there had always been large crowds. But nothing like this. It wasn't just the women most distraught by the king's conscription, but *every single* member of Vallenfend.

The sheer amount of people easily filled the area before the wall and flooded into the streets. Between the houses, Kael could just barely see the end of the crowd far away. The bandits were there as well, off to the side, looking somewhat out of place, but yelling along with the rest of them. Out of their faces, he found Tomn's. The king of bandits gave him a solute.

Thunder boomed overhead and not long after, Shatterbreath appeared from above. Kael was relieved to see her. It had been a long time since he had. Too long. She scanned the crowd as they flinched from her presence. Wearing a fierce scowl, she landed along the wall, three legs straddled on it, one resting on the ground behind.

She lowered her head to let Kael touch her fleetingly. "Be strong," she whispered.

Kael nodded and turned back to the crowd. Slow at first, they grew silent until the dogs in the background could be heard barking. It was so quiet. Every eye was on him, waiting for an explanation. They all knew who he was, yet he only knew a fraction of them.

"People of Vallenfend!" Kael yelled as loud as he could.

Somehow, it went even quieter. From the side, Kael was suddenly aware of several people. Zeptus was there, watching him, flanked by two King's Elite. He nodded at Kael, who turned his attention downwards.

Kael surveyed the crowd for a long time. "The time has come. The empire I tried to warn you about has arrived. You've witnessed first-hand what they are capable of. The vanguard that attacked last night belonged to them. The BlackHound Empire is here."

Kael spotted Laura down below among the refugees. She looked up at him with such anticipation, hanging on to his every word. Did she finally believe him? He couldn't read her expression.

"You all knew this day was coming, didn't you? I gave you all plenty of warning! Who believed me?" So many faces dropped until it seemed only the refugees and the bandits were still focussed on him.

"Shame on you!" Shatterbreath roared. "The evidence was staggering, yet you chose ignorance. Only when the BlackHound soldiers arrived in the flesh did you truly believe us. You had to see them to believe them. Are you of such little faith?"

Kael put up a hand to stop her. She would go on if he let her. "They are here. They will come soon to destroy us. They would have too, without incident. Your king here has ensured this."

A few yells of anger broke out. King Morrindale's expression remained steady—blank.

"For thirty years, he's been sending your men and boys off to die. For thirty years, he's been preparing Vallenfend to be destroyed."

The crowd was growing in intensity. There wasn't a face to be seen that wasn't yelling or cursing up at King Morrindale. The king stood there, arms at his side, taking it all. His blank expression kept for a time, but slowly, started to twist. Kael was sure the regret was getting to him. To his surprise though, Morrindale slapped his palms down on the edge of the wall. He wasn't upset. He was *angry*.

He shouted something down at the people, but they were too loud.

"Silence!" Shatterbreath snarled. "All of you! Let the liar speak."

King Morrindale's face was beat red with anger. It hadn't taken long for his colour to return.

161

"They will kill you all!" he roared. The crowd went deathly silent. "Every last one of you. And you know what? You deserve it. You deserve it! You think your pitiful resistance will stop them? No. Nothing can stop them now. Thirty years they've been planning this invasion. *Thirty years.* They aren't about to be stopped by your...your...*pitiful* resistance. You. Are. All. Doomed."

Kael stepped, silencing Morrindale. The king took a haggard breath and placing a hand to his hollow chest, winded. "He is wrong. Our resistance is not pitiful. Arnoth is here by our side and soon, others will follow. The BlackHound Empire may be strong, but our spirits are stronger." The crowd was no longer silent by then. A dull roar fought against Kael, forcing him to raise his voice. "We are not like you, *Murderdale.* We are not afraid. We will stand, and we will fight. And we will survive."

"I'm done here," King Morrindale announced. Kael could barely hear him over the roar of the crowd. "Punish me how you wish, Kael. I'm through."

"I made you a promise," Kael said, "that I intend to keep. You can't see your daughter if you're dead."

"What punishment is worse than death?"

Kael nodded at Shatterbreath, who roared to silence the crowd.

"*My* punishment."

"King Morrindale," Shatterbreath declared, "you have betrayed your own people—killed thousands of innocents in the name of greed. You have used countless as pawns in your tyrannical campaign." She paused. "Therefore, I hereby banish you, with an authority even greater than your own."

"What?!" the king exploded. "This is an outrage! You cannot exile me from my own country, forbid me to walk on my own land! This is still *my* city."

Shatterbreath roared, easily drowning out the king's laments. Almost every person in the crowd slapped their hands over their ears, but as Kael did it himself, he found it didn't help whatsoever. The king shut his mouth, turning deathly pale.

"You have no choice in the matter, frail human!" Shatterbreath hissed. "I suggest if you want to continue to live with all your limbs intact and attached to your body, that you take my advice and leave at once."

The king contemplated something for a moment. "An authority higher than my own...? That's how you did it! By the gods, that's how you fixed Zeptus. But how does a dragon have higher authority than—?"

"No more," Kael hollered. "No more of your lies! No more of your plotting. Take him away. Get him out of Vallenfend."

The soldiers on either side of Zeptus stepped forward to apprehend King Morrindale. The king wriggled for a second, but quickly realized how futile it would be. As they carried him away, Kael clasped one of their shoulders.

"Take him to his daughter first. I made a promise that I must keep."

The soldier nodded and continued. In a matter of seconds, King Morrindale was gone. Forever. Would Kael ever see him again? If so, in what possible circumstance? The crowd cheered as he was carried off.

Kael tried to quiet the crowd, but he couldn't. They were still cheering over King Morrindale's banishment. It took another crackling roar from Shatterbreath to silence them.

Kael raised his hands. "With King Morrindale gone, Vallenfend may stand a chance yet. The BlackHound has arrived. Let us stand up against them. Please, greet our allies with vigour. They may be your only chance. And...thank you. Thank you for believing in me at last. Stay strong."

More cheering. It was a sight that warmed Kael's heart. The city he so loved was finally on his side. It was frustrating what it took for that to happen, but he was more relieved and thankful than anything. Satisfied, he turned to the door he had exited from, but stopped himself.

Under Shatterbreath's watchful gaze, he strode across the gates to where Zeptus was standing. "Are you with me?" he asked.

Zeptus gave him a strange look. "Of course. My sole purpose is to assist now, Kael Rundown. As I wanted to from the beginning."

"Good. I'm in need of your...skills. Meet me at the stairs to the dungeons in five minutes."

The man nodded complacently and glided off. Waving to Vallenfend, Kael mounted Shatterbreath.

The dragon snorted once he was in between her shoulders. "Where are we going?"

"Just find Vert. I've been thinking about our prisoners."

"Oh?"

"I know how to make them...useful. Come on."

In little time at all, Shatterbreath had found Vert. He was among his men, the majority of which had taken shelter in the training grounds. With the refugees, bandits and castle attendants also taking up space, the grounds had become quite crowded. The barracks had long since been filled and many tents had been erected to house more people. Vert walked among the wounded, checking to see how they were doing.

With some difficulty, they managed to pry him away from his army and a few minutes later, Kael, Vert and Zeptus stood at the top of the steps. Shatterbreath had to wait outside as Kael proposed his idea.

"Can it be done?" Kael asked once he had finished.

Zeptus stroked his chin. "In theory, yes. It will be nearly impossible to convince them against what they have been through."

Vert chuckled. "I'd imagine so. You don't forget something like that. Having your comrades die around you and getting captured can't be an easy thing to forget."

Zeptus sneered. "Indeed so."

Kael pondered for a moment. "What do you need," he asked, "to convince them?"

"Time." The purple-eyed man shrugged. "And information. I'd have to formulate a feasible solution to explain what had just happened. What you are suggesting is very, *very* different than what happened in reality, Kael. I might be able to find a subtle connection between your idea and the truth and border the gap—"

"We don't have time."

The trio fell silent. Kael wished Shatterbreath could be there discussing it with them. The stairs stretched out to Kael's left, occupied solely by the captured soldiers of the BlackHound vanguard.

"How about strength?" Kael suggested. "I mean, if you had more power, could you..."

Zeptus frowned. "Power? How so?"

"Your gift is fuelled by dragon magic, right? Just like mine. Well, I so happen to have a bit of *extra* magic. Given by a...friend."

"What are you talking about?" Vert asked.

"Long story. Ask Shatterbreath sometime. Think it will work?"

Zeptus shook his head. "I'm not sure."

"It's worth a shot, right?" Kael clapped his hands together. "Let's try. Vert, go prepare an escort and several horses."

Vert nodded. "They'll be waiting out in the training grounds."

Once Vert was gone, Zeptus cleared his throat. "Follow me."

Kael waited for Zeptus to lead, but the man hesitated.

"I heard what happened to Malaricus," he whispered.

The memory of the scholar lying there came flooding back. Kael blinked back tears. "He was a good man."

Zeptus sighed. "Better than any of us. He saved my life, I owe everything to him. He was the only one who ever believed me. The only one that could see past my... The only one that never tried to use me."

Kael set his jaw. "I'm sorry if—"

"No, don't be. If there's a chance to right the wrongs I've made, I'm willing to take it."

Kael studied him closely. He still didn't trust Zeptus. Then again, if Malaricus did whole-heartedly, what was there to worry about?

"Are you ready?"

Kael nodded. "Yeah, lead on."

With a flourish, Zeptus descended the stairs with Kael in tow. He stopped in front of the cells holding the BlackHound soldiers. There were seven in total, scattered among several cells. Judging by the pool of blood at their feet though, Kael had to guess two of them had died from their wounds.

Unsure at first, Kael placed his hands on Zeptus's shoulders. They were shockingly thin. He focussed on the energy deep within his chest, trying to summon it up to the surface. He tried to pull it up, will it to do his bidding. Zeptus. He needed it to be on Zeptus.

He felt something shift within him. Zeptus twitched as well.

"I think that's it," Kael mumbled. "Give it a try to make sure it'll work."

Zeptus nodded. "BlackHound soldiers, stand up and give your attention to me. I am now your master." The two injured men remained limp, proving them to be dead, while every other stood and focussed on Zeptus. It was progress, but still a long shot from success.

"Do something else," Kael suggested. "We need to make sure."

Swallowing, Zeptus tried again. "You there, sit down. Good. Now back up. All of you, touch your nose." Sure enough, they all obeyed. It was frightening, actually, how obediently they listened. Like they were no longer themselves, but puppets. This was Zeptus's power perfected. It reminded Kael of the time Shatterbreath had controlled the former advisor.

"Very good," Kael heard Zeptus mutter. He couldn't see the man's face, but he could imagine the sly smile on his face. Whether an ally now or not, Zeptus was still very unnerving. "Soldiers, listen closely. We are letting you free." Not even a reaction. "You will return to you comrades at once. Once you leave this city, you will forget everything that happened here. Instead, you will tell your leaders that Vallenfend has been overrun by bandits. Their forces are not significant, but obviously enough to overcome your vanguard. You are the sole survivors. The remaining bandit force is small— less than two thousand. It will be an easy task to take the city with your full force."

Zeptus put Kael's plan into perfect words. Kael nodded as he spoke. *This was going to work.*

"Now," Zeptus said, producing a set of keys, "off you go. You will be escorted out of Vallenfend. Horses will be waiting for you.

Fly back to the BlackHound Empire and report this news." He unlocked the first cell. "Follow me, please."

Kael removed his hands, gasping as he did. He hadn't realized it, but the flow of power between him and Zeptus had been powerful indeed. Once he had stopped, he could feel the jolt as it returned to him, and then a wave of dizziness. Zeptus felt it too and stumbled, but Kael caught him.

Uttering thanks, Zeptus proceeded to unlock the other cell doors.

Forty five minutes later, Kael watched from Vallenfend's western wall as the four soldiers rode away on their horses. Every so often, they glanced back, as if they had indeed just escaped from a fresh battle.

After they disappeared from sight, Shatterbreath swooped down to land in front of the wall. She muzzled Kael. "What happened? Why did you let those four go?"

Kael quickly filled her in. Shatterbreath, once had finished, frowned.

"That was very clever. Did you think of that?"

"Yup," Kael said, beaming.

"Do you think it was wise to lend Skullsnout's magic to Zeptus like that?"

The question caught Kael by surprise. "Why, of course." He patted her snout. "Zeptus is on our side now, remember?"

Shatterbreath bowed her head and scraped her black horns against the wall's stone surface. "Never make assumptions," she said when she came back to his level. "Zeptus is a very good actor. I'm sure he has good intentions, but I think some caution towards him is well-deserved."

"You're right. As always," he added, beating her to it. "Fallenfeld is going to arrive soon, correct?"

Shatterbreath stood straight, her neck raised high above. "Yes. They should be coming through the northern pass soon."

"Let's be here to greet them, eh?" Kael climbed over her shoulder onto her back.

She roared once and then pounced into the air.

167

It was short flight to the pass. The pass itself was a river that cut through the mountain ranges as it worked its way to the ocean. It was a bit of a tight squeeze—another reason why Vallenfend's position was so ideal. Any hostile force caught within the pass wouldn't stand a chance.

As Kael and Shatterbreath approached, the front of the Fallenfeld army was just emerging from the pass. When they spotted her, horns blared in alarm and arrows soared towards Shatterbreath. Kael wondered at their reaction at first, then remembered he hadn't told them about her.

Luckily, any arrows that reached Shatterbreath through the air currents of her wings only glanced off her hard scales. She snarled and banked away.

"Let me down," Kael yelled to her. "I'll just walk over to them."

Shatterbreath huffed as she hit the ground. She shook her neck, dislodging a lone arrow that had penetrated her scales—barely. Kael picked it up started walking towards the Fallenfeld army, twirling the shaft in his palms.

Of course, Fallenfeld's attention was primarily focussed on Shatterbreath, but it didn't take long for them to notice Kael. All at once, the soldiers at the front started yelling at him, brandishing their poleaxes and shields. Putting up his hands, Kael tried to shout back. Nobody listened.

"Stop!" Kael caught that one word clearly. He recognized that voice. King Henedral pushed through the front line. "Kael? Is that you? By the gods, it is. Hail! What in the world are you doing with that dragon?"

Kael considering the king. He was wearing heavy platemail with a long flowing cape. The chest of his tunic displayed a dazzling rendition of Fallenfeld's crest, described in wonderful detail and highlighted in gold stencilling. At his hip, his ancestral sword rested.

"Hail, King Henedral! It's okay, it's alright. She is friendly."

The king walked over, eyeing Shatterbreath from a distance. "Are you sure?"

"Most of the time." Kael laughed. King Henedral did not. "Seriously, she's not a threat. Do you want to meet her? Shatterbreath!" Kael waved her over.

As she sauntered over, King Henedral put up a hand to calm his soldiers. "Easy! Easy," he yelled to them. Still, every archer had their bow raised. The king himself grew very pale.

Shatterbreath stopped right in front of him, leaning over so that her head hovered directly above his. The dragon curled her lips and the tip of her tail flickered ominously. Kael watched closely.

"You," Shatterbreath rumbled.

King Henedral tried to stand straight, but couldn't keep himself from trembling. "H—hello."

"You tried to kill Kael. You tried to kill me."

King Henedral fell to his knees. Kael moved in, waving her off. "That doesn't matter now, Shatterbreath. That's behind us."

The dragon flicked her head away and shook her upper body. At once, Kael knew she was only joking. He gave her a very sour look as she pulled away to sit on her haunches. Over her muzzle, she wore a snarl, but it wasn't hard for Kael to detect the smile in her eyes.

When Kael turned back to King Henedral, he was getting back up, though the colour hadn't quite returned to his face. Kael helped him stand.

"I'm sorry I didn't tell you about her before, King Henedral."

"Don't be," the king breathed. "It is I who has to apologize for what we did to you Kael. You and..."

"My name is Shatterbreath," the dragon hissed. Her expression softened. "It is a pleasure to meet you, King of Fallenfeld."

The king nodded awkwardly. "As to you. S—Shatterbreath." He turned back to Kael. "I'm sorry. I wanted to trust you, but what you suggested seemed so..."

Kael waved his hand. "Ah, don't worry. I know what you mean. I'm just glad to see you here. What made you decide to come?"

"Yseph," the king replied. There was a twinkle in his eyes. "He was...very convincing. As was the sign you delivered to us. There hasn't been a bandit raid since you left."

169

Kael laughed. "How can there be—with all the bandits *here* instead?"

King Henedral's smile vanished. "What?"

Shatterbreath rumbled, amused. "Welcome," she declared, loud enough so Fallenfeld's army could hear, "to Vallenfend."

Chapter 16

Kael placed both arms against the windowsill, first taking off his gauntlets. He rubbed the wood, feeling the smooth grain under his fingertips. Out before him, Vallenfend stretched forth. No longer did the city seem so vulnerable. The walls had been greatly reinforced over the last three days and several more ballistae constructed. Behind the walls themselves, the pens reserved for pigs and chickens had been cleared, instead replaced by catapults. The houses closest to the western walls had been evacuated, instead converted into archery posts.

Fallenfeld and Arnoth were camped behind Vallenfend, pushing up into the forest itself. Within several minutes, either army would be able to move up in between the trees and disappear. The bandits were staying in the castle grounds, being trained alongside the able-bodied citizens of Vallenfend by the King's Elite. At any time of the day, Tooran was down among them, overseeing the whole operation.

The stash of weapons and armour had proved beneficial for the refugees before, and still continued to. Kael and Shatterbreath had made trips between Vallenfend and her mountain until all the supplies had been fished out of her cave and distributed between the militia and the bandits. Though some of the weapons were dull and the armour rusted, it saved them from having to forge new gear.

The combined allied force Kael had rallied together had tried to keep the refugee's name, *Kael's Army*. He didn't like that and had protested greatly against it. Not only was it vain to have his army named after himself, he thought the name was terribly ill-suited. He didn't see it as *his* army. Sure, he had brought them together, but ultimately, they were fighting for their land, and not him. Besides, he could bring himself to actually say the name.

So, after some deliberation, they had settled on calling themselves the Allegiance. Much better.

A blue shape passed by the portal, jarring Kael's thoughts. He reached out to try and touch it as he swung back. Shatterbreath's tail twitched as Kael's fingers grazed it. She was sitting on top of the spire Kael was in. Kael wasn't sure it was the greatest idea, putting strain on the castle's structure, but he was glad to have her nearby. It wasn't easy to spend time with her anymore. Any time he had was focussed on preparing Vallenfend and it was hard to fit her inside the city.

A *click* resonated from the back of the room. Kael turned around. The room was filled with dusty things; dented sets of decorative armour and paintings the king apparently didn't want anymore. A plate bearing the original king's crest sat off to the side, looking very forlorn. The door opened to reveal somebody Kael wasn't expecting.

Laura.

Kael's shoulders relaxed, causing his armour to scrape together. He had traded in his borrowed set of Knot-town armour for a heavier, sturdier set. He still wasn't quite used to it.

"There you are," Laura said softly. "I've been looking everywhere for you. So...has your friend, Tomn."

Kael studied her, drinking in the familiar sight of her silky blonde hair and pale eyes, as well as the unfamiliar bulk of her armour which emphasized the contours of her body.

"Hey. I just needed some time to myself, sorry."

"I understand." She stayed where she was, looking conflicted. Kael placed a hand back on his windowsill. She noticed and walked across the room, weaving in between the forgotten decorations. She too, then placed her hands on the window's edge.

Kael smiled and leaned against it.

They stayed like that for a while, simply admiring Vallenfend.

"Laura," Kael said gently, "what do you see?"

She squinted. "Vallenfend. The once-innocent city we grew up in."

"Yes. What else?"

"I'm not sure."

"Do you want to know what I see?" She didn't say anything. "I see misjudged people fighting for a worthy cause. I see men and women who are ready to fight for their people. I see warriors who will die to save their country. I see brave souls who will fight until the end to save their forefather's land. I see many kingdoms, strong alone in their endeavours, but unbreakable as a nation united as one against a common enemy. *I see hope.*"

Her lips were pursed. "You see all that? Down there?"

Kael laughed softly. "Well... You might have to walk around a bit to see all of it. What about out there—beyond Vallenfend?"

Laura averted her gaze. "Nothing, Kael."

"I see a threat to all. I see a dark cloud looming out on the horizon, ready to destroy everything. I see what we fight to overcome. I see opposition. I see the BlackHound Empire."

This time, she did look. "I still see nothing."

Kael took her hand. "Then let me open your eyes." With his free hand, he reached out and grabbed hold of Shatterbreath's tail. Instantly, he and Laura were both thrust into the dragon's vision.

Shatterbreath's supreme eyesight stretched far across the land, well beyond the scope of human eyes. A dreadful sight presented itself to them. Kael heard Laura gasp beside him.

The BlackHound Empire. Wave upon wave of soldiers marched across the land in perfect square formations. The numbers were truly daunting. Horses pulled wagons of supplies and wheeled along ballistae, or otherwise carried riders with long spears and halberds. Throughout the massive procession, flags bearing the BlackHound insignia could be clearly seen, as well as each shining crest emblazoned on every soldier's breastplate. Shatterbreath and Kael had tried to count their numbers earlier. All in all, they had reached a number roughly close to thirty-thousand.

Kael and Laura were both removed from Shatterbreath's vision. Laura slumped to her knees, breathless. Tears streaked down her face. Kael sighed and knelt beside her.

"I—I'm sorry, so sorry," she sobbed. "I should have never had doubted you. Can you forgive me?"

Kael set his jaw. *Could* he forgive her? After she had been so reluctant to forgive him? Only a week before, she had hated him. They had been the best of friends, but yet she still denied everything he had said and done. Like so many others.

173

"If we make it through this war," Kael said, "then yes, I will. For now, I'm not sure if I'm ready to forgive you, Laura. I thought we had trusted each other. I guess I was wrong."

"Kael..."

Angry voices echoed from outside. Kael only caught bits and pieces. "...Is he? We've looked all over. Wher in the blitty...? Have you checked this door?"

Tomn entered the room, looking quite flustered. "Oi, ther he is! Wha' the lerk are yeh doing in her? Ah, foo, nevermend." He strutted across the room and leaned out the window. "What yeh two lookin' at?"

Kael pointed out. "The BlackHound Empire is down there."

Tomn raised his eyebrows. "Uh, yeah, I know. We're scramblin' to gert ready! What are yeh doing, Kael? Come on, come on, let's go! Unless yer just going ter watch?"

The reality of what they were up against had hit Tomn harder than Kael was expecting. The man was ordinarily so calm, now he was a wreck. Worried and anxious. Of course, Kael didn't blame him. It was just strange to see how he changed under stressful circumstances. "Of course. Give me a moment. Shatterbreath? We need you on the mountain, out of sight."

"Of course," came the faceless reply. With a whoosh of wings, she was gone, heading towards the forest behind Vallenfend.

"Alright. Let's go," Kael said. With that, Tomn shot out of the room, hurrying through the halls of the castle. Once Kael had told the bandit where the gold was, he had stressed on getting to know his way through the labyrinthine halls. Kael had spent just as many—if not more—nights in the castle as Tomn, but he still barely knew his way around.

Kael, Tomn and Laura made their way through the castle, which had been modified since it had been taken over. The outside rooms had been gutted of their useless furniture which was replaced instead by spare bows and a lifetime's worth of arrows. The doors on the ground floor, which were open to let them pass, had been entirely replaced. Comprised of solid beams, the new doors were reinforced with metal bars and as thick as trees. There was no way anybody was going to get through easily.

Anxious faces met Kael and Tomn as they exited the castle. Laura was disappeared into the crowd. She knew where she was supposed to be. She had probably snuck off just to be with Kael that short while. She might have been punished for it too.

"Assemble!" Tomn ordered. Some of the bandits ran off, towards Vallenfend's western wall. The rest that remained were Tomn's closest, as well as a squad of refugees to watch Kael's back. Among them was Korjan.

Korjan handed Kael a bow and quiver or arrows. Kael nodded at him, taking the weapon and strapping the quiver to his back. Korjan looked quite imposing, garbed in the suit of armour he had made himself. It was thick about the chest, shoulders and thighs, but looser everywhere else. Over his back was slung a broadsword, two smaller swords and two axes. Kael couldn't believe that he could—and would—use all of them, but he had heard the stories.

"Are you ready?" Korjan asked.

Kael shrugged, giving him a fake smile. "As I'll ever be."

"Move out!" Tomn yelled. He was in charge. Not because Kael didn't want to be, but because the BlackHound Empire believed the city had been overrun with bandits. The greater the illusion, the better.

On his mark, the rest of crowd started walking to the wall. The streets were empty. Any citizens that could fight had already been given weapons, armour and rudimentary training, then sent to the wall to defend. The rest had been evacuated to the eastern part of the city, as to avoid conflict.

The wall loomed into sight, lined with bandits and militia. The inside had been reinforced with earth, so now all one had to do was climb up the slop to get to the top. Shatterbreath had played a key part collecting all the earth to line the wall. She had been given the two largest bathtubs to be found and ferried earth back and forth from a stretch of land to the west. Not only was the almost impenetrable now, but the divot carved into the land would serve a purpose to deter the army's advance. Many other people had

175

contributed to building up the wall of course, but without Shatterbreath, the whole process would have taken much longer than a day.

Indeed, she had been an invaluable help during their fortifications. She brought trees from the mountains and stripped them of their limbs and bark so they could be used for various purposes, like strengthening the outside of the wall and building ballistae and the accompanying bolts.

Kael climbed the earthy slope, which still hadn't fully dried, to stand atop the wall. Even in the time Kael had taken to go from the top of the castle to the wall, the BlackHound Empire had come considerably closer. Close enough to see out on the horizon.

Kael's heart skipped a beat and he put a hand to his chest. In no time at all, everything he had once known would be destroyed. His life would become focussed around war. Nothing would *ever* be the same. His mouth went dry contemplating the fact that many of the people who he knew wouldn't survive the battle. The friends he had made during the fortifications, during his travels abroad, during his *lifetime*. He looked left and right across the wall. Suddenly, their numbers seemed so little.

"Wher'd they get those?" Tomn muttered beside Kael. Kael had to squint to see what he was talking about. Siege equipment.

"From their boats," Kael explained. "Shatterbreath and I flew over their camp. They had been disassembling their boats to construct those. It's not like they'll be needing ships anymore."

"Blitty then. How many boats did they bring?"

Kael shrugged. "Couldn't count. Around...two hundred and fifty, give or take. Big ones too."

"That sounds about right." Sal'braan hiked up the mound to join Kael and Tomn.

Kael scowled at him. "You're supposed to be waiting in the castle." Sal'braan had wanted to help defend, but there was a very high chance he could be slain in battle. If one of Kael's allies mistook him for the enemy... "You're no good to me dead, you know."

"They'll be a while yet," Sal'braan grumbled. "I can stay here until they get closer. The BlackHound Empire would have required more ships, but they put their soldiers into a kind of coma for the long journey."

"Really?"

"Yes. We have a type of herb that can do that. They put horses asleep too. Otherwise, it would be impossible to bring the beasts."

"Vert had been wondering about that," Kael chirped. "Very interesting. But bad news for us."

They fells silent to watch the BlackHound Empire march closer and closer. Once the empire had halved their distance, Sal'braan retreated back to the castle. Any other soldier wandering returned to their post. The tension was tangible up on the wall. The sound of their marching, thousands upon thousands, was deafening.

Then, altogether, the BlackHound Empire halted its advance. Kael gulped and glanced sideways at Tomn, who had gone quite pale. Their plan suddenly seemed quite foolish—suicidal even. How long would they be able to hold those masses off for?

"Remember," Kael muttered. "On Tomn's mark. Fight as long as you can. I'll call for backup only when we *absolutely* need it. Tell the others."

As the message spread either direction, a lone man stepped out from the masses of the BlackHound Empire. He was dressed entirely in black, from his high-collared tunic to his large, metal-studded boots. His chest was thick, reinforced by his breastplate and hauberk underneath. He wore his sleeves only to his forearms, leaving dark brown skin exposed. His voice reminded Kael of cold stone and it was louder than physically possible. He strode up on a natural point that jutted up a ways.

"We are the BlackHound Empire. We are here to take this city." His tone was selected, careful, perfect. It almost sounded as if this was just another drill. "Surrender at once, filthy bandit scum, and we will promise you quick executions."

Kael caught his breath. Their leader thought the city was indeed under the control of just bandits. They're plan worked. So far.

Tomn stood up on the castle's stone railing. "Oi, you lerks! Never! We took this city fair and square. You can't take it ferm us! Git yer own!"

Kael studied the man down below. Was this Commander Coar'saliz, the leader Sal'braan had warned him about? It was hard to see, but the man's expression seemed to remain steady. He made a gesture over his head with his hand. "Prepare," he ordered. "We're taking the city. By force, it seems."

Tomn stepped down from the ledge. "This is it, Kael," he gasped.

Kael nodded. "Yes it is."

"Prepare to defend!" Tomn yelled. "Arm ther ballisters. Arm ther catapults. Keep the wall!"

Thunk. "What was that?" Kael turned around just in time. He ducked as a massive arrow rocketed by. *Thunk, thunk.* The sounds of ballistae.

They were already attacking.

Tomn yelped. "Argh! Retaliert, retaliert! Fire, fire, fire!"

Thunk, whoosh. And just like that, the war had begun.

Kael remained ducking. It was a good thing too, because a wave of arrows came flooding at the wall. Several people on either side of him tumbled down the slope, hit by the projectiles. The wall did well to protect against arrows, only if one ducked behind the safety of the three-foot-high guardrail,

Kael notched his own bow and hesitated to read the hail of arrows. There seemed to be no relent. When he considered the amount of soldiers out there, it made sense. They would have to stop soon though, wouldn't they?

A catapult from within the city launched a massive rock that had been dipped in oil and set aflame. It soared overhead and out of sight, into the awaiting BlackHound soldiers. From where he was, Kael could hear the crunch as it struck. The hail of arrows faltered.

More and more boulders were sent flying over. Shatterbreath had fetched more than enough stones to throw. The hail of arrows stopped altogether, giving Kael a chance to peek over the wall.

The BlackHound Empire must have realized that the catapults were the greatest threat, for they had stopped their archery assault to instead charge the city. Catching his breath, Kael pulled his bowstring back and let an arrow fly. It struck a soldier in the neck.

He released arrow after arrow into the incoming swarm, aiming to discharge as many as he could before they would have to repel the borders. Ladders could be seen here and there, dotting the army. As some soldiers approached, they swung grapple hooks up the wall as well.

A hook latched onto the guardrail only a foot away from Kael. He leaned over and shot the soldier with an arrow before cutting the rope with his knife.

More and more men were making to the wall now. The bandits and refugees were doing their best to halt the progress, but it just wasn't enough. The BlackHound archers had begun firing once again with no apparent concern for their own men.

Kael dropped behind the guardrail, narrowly dodging an arrow. He gasped, trying to catch his breath. Something next to his caught his attention. A soldier had successfully climbed to the top of the wall. Before the soldier had plant both his feet, Kael drew *Vintrave* and ran him through, pushing his body and ladder back down.

Along the wall, Kael could see more soldiers climbing over. "Tomn!" he cried. "Behind you!"

The bandit king took notice and swung his bow at the approaching BlackHound soldier, but missed. The soldier leapt at Tomn. Kael tried to run and help him, but soldiers popped up onto the wall in front of him before he could make more than three steps.

Kael knocked a helmet off with a strike from his sword and deftly killed the man right after. He smashed another man with his shield, knocking him off the wall, and dispatched yet another. When he was finished, he saw with relief that Frebbor, Tomn's second-in-command, was already by the bandit king's side. Even as Kael watched, Frebbor killed two soldiers with one swing of his hammer. He caught Kael's eye and gave a mock solute, assuring Kael that Tomn was safe with him.

A gurgle caught Kael's attention from behind. He whipped around, face-to-face with a BlackHound soldier. The man's face was strangely relaxed. Shuddering, the soldier slumped to the ground. Korjan removed his broadsword from the soldier's back.

"I got you, Kael," the blacksmith rumbled.

Kael flashed him a smile, then turned his attention back to defending. Two more arrows found their targets before he had to use his sword again. Then, there was no more opportunity to use his bow. There were too many soldiers up on the wall.

"Kael?" Tomn's voice rose over the din.

A massive bolt *whooshed* by. "Not yet!" Kael hollered. He threw a hook off the wall. "Phase two, phase two!"

Tomn nodded. "Yeh got ert. Archers, back ter second line!"

With his command, about half of the friendly forces on the wall slipped back into the city. In the time it took the archers to fall back, the BlackHound took a serious step. They nearly completely overwhelmed the wall. Kael and those remaining fought hard to stay alive, let alone keep them at bay.

Once the archers had reached the buildings, they started firing. More and more soldiers fell to the combined effort of those fighting up on the wall and shooting from the windows of nearby buildings. Despite the BlackHound losses, though, the bandits and refugees were losing.

Something whizzed by overhead. Kael only caught a glimpse of it before it smashed into a building. Looking like two massive iron balls chained together, the projectile tore into the building, destroying the entire front wall.

Kael gasped as he watched another one of objects whirl by overhead. It was so close, he could feel the buffet of air as it passed by. He turned his head as that one too, smashed into a building filled with archers. He spotted Tomn nearby. The bandit was crouched low as Frebbor smashed his way through soldier after soldier.

"Kael!" he screamed. "We have ter fall back! We—we can't hold ther line much longer!"

Frebbor cried out in rage as he smashed a soldier's skull in.

"No! Just a bit longer! We need them..." His voice was drowned out by the sound of another projectile. "Closer. We need them closer.

"But—arg! But Kael!"

"No!"

"Come on, you lerks!" Frebbor was in a fury. His face was flushed and his limbs were literally shaking from adrenaline. "Come and gert it! I'll kill yer all!"

Kael took a breath, awed by the man's mettle. Something caught Frebbor's attention and the man turned around with a gasp. Time slowed as Kael realized what it was.

An arrow the thickness of a horse's head rushed towards Frebbor. Kael yelled out, but it was already too late. Sickeningly slow, Kael witnessed as the arrow struck Frebbor in the chest. It tore through his armour as if it was nothing more than tissue, and ripped out the other side, painted in blood. The force of the impact was enough to launch the burly man from his feet, sending him careening down the slope.

"Frebbor, no!" Tomn's voice brought Kael back into normal time.

It was enough. "Fall back, fall back!" Kael screamed. He put his fingers to his lips and whistled. Three long, shrill notes.

Before retreating, Kael stood tall to see where the majority of the BlackHound Empire was. His heart sank. He was expecting the most of the army to be storming the city. In reality, only a fraction to their overall force was actually attacking.

The bandits and refugees abandoned the walls. Korjan was close behind Kael as they sprinted down the banks and into the streets. The archers still in the buildings were firing away as fast as they could, but at that point, it didn't matter. There were too many to take down.

A loud thunderclap echoed over the land. Kael paused at the side of a building to stare skyward. He smiled. Reinforcements.

He couldn't see, but he knew exactly what was happening outside the city. He, Vert and the others had planned it well. The bandit defence was only a stage, to lure as many BlackHound soldiers to the front as possible. Then, Arnoth and Fallenfeld would come sweeping in from the north and south of the city, decimating as many as they could.

Judging from the cries and reactions of the enemy soldiers still up on the wall, their plan was coming to fruition. Kael could imagine it now; the full force of both Arnoth and Fallenfeld charging to meet the BlackHound Empire. Arnoth's army would be headed by cavalry—they would dominate until the BlackHound pushed their pikemen forward. Fallenfeld had cavalry as well, but weren't using all of them quite yet.

The flow of BlackHound soldiers coming over the wall had halted with their attention turned elsewhere, but there was still a fair amount of soldiers waiting within the city. They needed to be dealt with.

"Tomn?" Kael called out. He turned to Korjan, but the blacksmith only shrugged. "Tomn, where are you?"

"Right here, Kael." Tomn stumbled out from a corner, clutching his shoulder.

"Rally the men. Push them back to the wall. We need the soldiers *out* of the city."

Tomn nodded with a wince. "Aye, captain. Ert once."

As he stepped forward, Kael registered the arrow protruding from the back of his shoulder. Before the bandit could carry through with his order, Kael stopped him.

"You've done a good job, Tomn. I think the surprise is over. Go get some medical attention."

The bandit bowed. "Yeah. I'll let yeh do yer thing then." He started to shuffle away.

"Tomn."

"Yeah?"

"You did well. The bandits have proved themselves today. You are more than just petty thieves. You are proud warriors. I'll ensure generations to come will know of your bravery."

Tomn beamed. "Thank yer, Kael. It means a lot ter me."

"Of you go." He watched the bandit leave. "Ready, men! Push to the wall! Get them out of Vallenfend."

There were war-cries to his left and right. A moment later, the bandits and refugees burst from their places, waving their weapons over their heads. Kael was right with them as they engaged with the

BlackHound soldiers, who seemed conflicted whether to take the city or rush back to assist their comrades against the surprise attack.

The battle was gruelling. The soldiers were well-trained and well-armed. It took every ounce of energy to finish off each one. But at last, the refugees and bandits managed to push the soldiers back to the top of the wall. Kael and Korjan worked efficiently together, defending each other's blind spots. They were the first two to stand back on top and witness the battle raging below.

As planned, Fallenfeld and Arnoth had caught the attacking force off-guard, swiftly surrounding them. As Kael watched, the two armies were squeezing together, forcing a large chunk of the BlackHound into a tight circle. To Kael's disappointment, the portion of the army they had surrounded was much smaller than he was expecting. The majority of the BlackHound had retreated back to a safe distance outside the range of ballistae and catapults.

At a glance, there appeared to be ten-thousand soldiers caught in the ambush. That was being generous. It wasn't as many as Kael would have liked, but if the allies managed to kill them all, it would still count as a victory on their part.

Korjan jumped to the side, skewering a soldier and reminding Kael that the battle was far from over. He sprung into action as well, notching an arrow and letting it fly.

The rest of the bandits and refugees caught up. With renewed vigour, they managed to push the line of soldiers right back to the wall. Soon, Vallenfend was free of BlackHound soldiers once again.

As Kael dodged an arrow, he heard a consoling sound. The crack of thunder. Shatterbreath came swooping in from the east, snarling ferociously. She swept over Vallenfend's wall, brushing any remaining soldiers free. Slipping past arrows, she flew to the southernmost end of the battle raging in front of Vallenfend. Kael stopped to watch her.

Rising, she twisted in the air, aligning herself north to south.

"Kael, look out!"

Korjan tackled Kael to the ground. As he did, another ball-and-chain projectile whirled overhead. As Kael picked himself back up, he realized it wasn't Korjan who had saved him, but Tooran.

"You better keep an eye out," Tooran panted. "You might catch one of those with your teeth if you gawk so much."

Kael's voice was drowned out before he could finish his retort.

Shatterbreath raced over the battle, releasing a massive jet of flame as she did. The fire washed over a huge section of BlackHound soldiers killing hundreds in one go.

If the BlackHound soldiers fighting within the circle of Kael's allies had been calm about their situation, they weren't anymore. They started to panic, pushing against those on the outside battling, making their situation only worse. Many people were flailed around as they were burned alive, only striking further fear amongst the men. As they spotted Shatterbreath turning around for another go, their panic only spiked higher.

Despite Tooran's warning, Kael stopped to watch Shatterbreath again.

She raced towards the crowd of soldiers, releasing a breath of fire. Before she made it halfway though, something lunged out at her. A large net wrapped around her body, catching around her wings.

"Shatterbreath!" Kael screamed, taking an involuntary step forward.

With a roar, she spun helplessly through the air, rocketing south. Before she even hit the ground, Kael leapt off the wall. He was vaguely aware of somebody yelling his name. Korjan maybe. He sprinted towards where Shatterbreath had crash-landed, ignoring everything. The soldiers around him, the pain in his ankle, his burning pulse throbbing in his forehead; none of it mattered.

The first soldier Kael ran into didn't know what hit him. Without even so much as raising his shield, Kael barrelled through the man. Skullsnout's magic pulsed as they collided and a moment later, where a soldier had once stood, there was nothing but char.

Without missing a step, Kael continued his dash, slashing several more soldiers down without the slightest hesitations. Kael gripped the blade with white knuckles as *Vintrave* effortlessly cut through armour, flesh and bone. In his wake he left nothing but mangled corpses and trails of blood.

Something tripped Kael and he sprawled out, scattering dirt. A dark-skinned soldier raised his spear. Kael tried to deflect the tip with his shield as it lunged down at his face. It missed impaling his eye, only to lodge in his breastplate instead. He felt the spearhead sink into muscle.

With a groan, Kael rolled to the side, wrenching the weapon out of the soldier's hand and the tip out of his chest. He threw it to the side and glowered at the man, who drew a falchion of some kind.

They locked blades. The man glowered at Kael as they struggled to overpower each other. With every accelerated heartbeat, Kael could feel blood flow from the fresh wound; it was deep and he was losing strength from it.

With a shove, the BlackHound soldier won over. *Vintrave* was thrown from Kael's grip. The soldier threw several attacks at Kael, who managed to block them all with his shield. He needed to find *Vintrave*. Without it, he could only defend. He needed to get to Shatterbreath!

Kael dove to the ground to dodge a zealous attack. His free hand brushed up against a shaft of some kind. With a gasp, he snatched the spear that had stabbed him.

Rolling once, Kael sprang to his feet, ducked underneath a horizontal slice and with both hands, rammed the spear into the soldier's stomach. The spearhead dented deep into the soldier's armour, but didn't penetrate. Clutching the haft with both hands, the soldier took several steps back, trying desperately to keep it from piercing through. With a flourish, Kael removed the spear, whipped around and cracked it over the soldier's head.

He fell to a knee as the soldier slumped over before him. Another sword finished decapitated the man.

An unfamiliar person bobbed up and down, waving his now-bloodied sword. He wore Fallenfeld's crest. He yelled something which Kael couldn't understand. It registered in Kael's mind that time was moving slowly—very slowly.

"We've got your back," the Fallenfeld soldier assured. There was a group of them, fighting BlackHound soldiers at bay. They must have broken off their own front lines to assist Kael. There were even a few bandits among them.

A strong hand hefted Kael to his feet and *Vintrave* was thrust into his hands. Tooran gave Kael a shove towards Shatterbreath.

"Go, go!" was all he said.

Kael nodded and sprinted off. With time moving at a surreal pace, he wove in between the battle as it raged on. Confusion was everywhere; it was ambiguous now. It was everything. Swords clashed, horses shrieked and everywhere, men were in agony. More than once, Kael had to jump over severed body parts. It didn't take long for the horrors to numb his mind. All he felt, all he registered was the immediate need to help Shatterbreath.

He could see the dragon's wings above banners, weapons and cavalry. Pausing, he stretched up on his toes to see there was a mass of people working their way towards her. Whether they were BlackHound or ally, he couldn't tell.

As he rushed ever towards her, more and more Allegiance men joined him until he had a huge force in his wake. It was just as well, for as they neared the edge of the battle and the throng of people thinned, Kael could see that the mass of people he had spotted were indeed BlackHound soldiers. They had obviously watched Shatterbreath crash.

Shatterbreath was lying in a field, at least half a kilometre away from the outer edge of the battle. She was writhing furiously and breathing jets of flame, but to no avail against the net. Whoever reached her first would determine her fate.

"Hey!" An armoured horse rushed up beside Kael. A mounted knight bearing Fallenfeld's crest reached out a hand. Kael snatched it and even as the horse kept running, swung up onto its back. "General Grodem at your service!" the knight declared from up front with a solute.

"We have to get there first!" The words didn't need to be said.

There were several horses already running towards Shatterbreath, but General Grodem's outran them all. It was the strongest horse Kael had ever seen. Its flanks rippled with muscle with every step and despite the weight of the general, Kael and the chainmail it was wearing, it didn't tire.

It was a good thing too, because the BlackHound horses were outrunning the rest of the Allegiance cavalry as well.

Shatterbreath was very close now. Her position reminded Kael of the time in Wyrmguard. The more she thrashed, the more tangled she became. The net was sturdy, constructed out of some kind of thick, flexible rope. Kael wished she had stayed still instead of thrashing about. He might have been able to just pull it off of her. But with it snagged on her spines, wings, tail and horns, the only option he had left was to cut it.

Just as they reached the dragon, an arrow struck General Grodem's horse in the shoulder. The horse shuddered and then whinnied. Altogether, its front end buckled which launched Kael and the general from its back.

Kael hit the ground shoulder-first and was able to more or less roll back up onto his feet. The general was not as lucky when the BlackHound cavalry arrived shortly after. Kael deflected a poleaxe with his shield, creating sparks. Kael looked away just as the swinging halberd decapitated General Grodem.

Shatterbreath belched a stream of flame, which consumed three mounted knights to Kael's left. The other two posed more of a problem. They were all carrying long weapons and with his short sword, Kael was ill-suited to deal with them.

The best he could do was to dodge or block the attacks the BlackHound knights threw at him in an attempt to keep them away from the incapacitated dragon. It wasn't good enough. More soldiers were arriving and the line of Fallenfeld soldiers was still a ways off. Out of the corner of his eye, Kael could see a knight notching his bow on the back of a horse nearby. He aimed it at Shatterbreath and let it fly.

Kael jumped into the path of the projectile, aiming to stop it with his outstretched shield. He missed. The arrow pierced his armour, sinking into his upper arm. It was enough to make his shield arm go limp.

Despite the handicap, when more BlackHound soldiers arrived, Kael was thrown into a fury. He blocked or dodged every attack the soldiers threw at him, all the while trying to lead them towards Shatterbreath's maw. He succeeded and in one fiery breath, she killed two soldiers and their horses.

As Kael's energy began to fade, the Fallenfeld cavalry arrived. They easily outnumbered the BlackHound cavalry and soon, there was nobody left to fight.

Kael realized this was his chance to free Shatterbreath.

"Shatterbreath, I've got you, don't worry. Stay still."

"Hurry, Kael!"

He climbed up onto her back and snatched up a handful of the rope. Confused by her words, he glanced back. BlackHound soldiers and Fallenfeld soldiers were deep in combat just in front of them. The cavalry had set up a perimeter around Shatterbreath, doing their best to keep the enemy soldiers at bay.

The BlackHound archers, however, we free to shoot.

Pain shot lanced up his leg. His armour had taken most of the force. The tip must have just penetrated flesh. Ignoring the arrow protruding from his thigh, Kael slashed and cut a large section of the net free.

Another handful of rope freed Shatterbreath's left wing. She flared it and lifted her body. Kael had cut away enough to allow her to stand up. He stumbled on her back from the movement, dropped to his hands and knees.

Shatterbreath's chest rumbled as she yelled something. "Kael, look out! Duck!"

A hard object hard caught him across the cheek. The last thing he registered before he blacked out was the massive gauge it carved in his face, then movement.

Chapter 17

Kael flitted in and out of consciousness. His dreams were filled with chaos and darkness and when he was wake, it was only the same. The two became impossible to differentiate so he soon gave up on trying to interpret what anything meant or where he was.

Everything seemed to shift in such slow motion. Kael thought that maybe his gift had backfired, fuelled by the magic in his chest, so that it had become permanent. The concept terrified him—mostly because the possibility was very real. Zeptus was living proof.

As things began to clear up, it became obvious that that wasn't the case. He still had control over his gift, and the magic stayed dormant in his chest. The real situation, though, was even direr.

For the few hours at a time he could stay awake, he was aware of moaning around him, as well as the fetid stench of rot and disease. Gray cloth surrounded him at all angles, blotting out all sights or explanations. He was in a tent, laying on nothing more than a bed of grass covered by a blanket. His armour had been stripped away, leaving him with only a thin tunic.

After what he guessed was several days, he realized that he was in a makeshift hospital, though separated from the general throng of the ill. It wasn't hard to see the thick wooden planks sealing him in his small room or the silhouettes of guards standing just outside the cloth door. All this brought him to the next conclusion: he had been captured by the BlackHound Empire.

The knowledge of this dragged him into despair. It wasn't his own life that worried him but those he had been separated from. Korjan, Faerd, Laura. Were they okay? Were they functioning properly without him? Was the war still raging, as he lay there, disoriented and disheartened? Most of all, he was worried about Shatterbreath. The very last thing he could remember was being struck in the head while on her back. He could only hope and pray that she was alright.

He supposed he was being looked after. He never saw anybody, but the wounds on his chest, arm and leg were healing nicely and always seemed to have fresh bandages. He tried to discern when the bandages were changed and would spend hours staring at them. There'd come a strange smell not unlike perfume, and then he'd always wake up, not even realizing he had fallen asleep, and find them already changed. Kael came to the deduction that they were putting something in the water that appeared by his bed every time this happened. So he decided not to drink it anymore. It still happened.

He tried escaping more than once. Either by trying to break down the walls or run past the guards. All his attempts failed. The walls were sturdy and the guards were quick. He never got further than four feet outside his room. The images of the wounded he saw were enough to stop his attempts. He settled instead to shout curses at the guards.

Every day was the same. He lost track so quickly. He couldn't stand not knowing what was happening. The war was on, he could tell by the screams of the injured they brought in almost hourly. He found himself slipping closer and closer to madness.

Until finally, somebody entered his room.

Kael sprang to his feet and at once his hands started shaking. The man scrutinized Kael, a disciplined smirk spreading across his face. He unclasped his hands from behind his back to put a hand to his mouth.

He cleared his throat. "What's your name?"

Kael pursed his lips.

"Listen, I want you to understand that we mean you no harm. In fact, we're willing to let you go, if only you tell us about your allies. Numbers, strategies, weapons, supplies. I want to know it all. You will tell me."

"And if I don't?"

There was a gleam in the man's eyes. "We will take the information by force."

Kael sized up the man, top to bottom. It was the same man who had addressed Vallenfend for the initial attack. The leader. *Commander Coar'saliz.* Up close, Kael could see his features clearer. Like everyone else of his kind, his skin was dark, but his eyes even darker. The darkest eyes Kael had ever seen. His hair was short and extremely curly, sitting on his head like black moss. Lastly, he spotted the sword at the Commander's hip. He quickly averted his gaze. The Commander didn't notice.

The man sighed and walked around Kael. "I don't know why your people are fighting us. Your defeat is inevitable. You might as well give up."

"Never," Kael spat. "We will never stand down to you! We would rather die proudly in battle than let your kind enslave us."

Commander Coar'saliz rubbed his face. "I'll give you one last chance. We will torture you. Let's start with your name."

"Fine." Kael shook his head. "I'll tell you everything. My name is Don Huntson. I am an infantryman in Fallenfeld's second leading squad."

The Commander's expression remained steady. If anything, a frown crept across his brow. "I'd appreciate it if you didn't lie to me. I thought we had a mutual agreement."

Kael exhaled slowly. "Who says I'm lying?"

The cloth door was cast aside, revealing a person Kael never thought he'd see again. "I do," Rooster said with a smirk.

Suddenly, the room seemed so much more crowded.

Kael tried to leap at him, but Commander Coar'saliz grabbed him across the chest and threw Kael to the ground. Rooster placed a boot on Kael's stomach.

"Hey there, buddy," he chirped, "I haven't seen you in a while."

Gritting his teeth, Kael snatched Rooster's boot and twisted it. Rooster fell to the ground with a yelp. Kael scrambled over to him and landed a punch to the boy's jaw before the Commander pulled him off.

A strike to the back of the head made Kael slacken. His vision swooned; he was far from recovered from his concussion. He was vaguely aware strong hands holding him upright.

Then, a hot breath wafted in his face, smelling of mint. "You're a tough one, but I've broken tougher. This is your final chance." The Commander slapped him across the face.

"He'll never tell you want you want," Rooster snarled, wiping blood from his mouth. "Skip the formalities."

"I swear, Cleaud, I'll kill you for this," Kael hissed. "You betrayed me once and I let you go. This time, you die. That is a promise."

The boy clicked his tongue. "You're in no position to be making threats." He rubbed his jaw. "I'll leave you to him, Commander."

With a grunt, Kael shoved Commander Coar'saliz into Rooster. As they both reeled, he reached out and snatched the Commander's sword from his hip. He swung at an angle. But instead of striking the man against the chest, the blade stopped inches before.

Confused, Kael brought it back. This time, a lunge. The same thing. The tip halted just before his breastplate.

"Fool!" the Commander yelled. "You presume to kill me with my own blade?" He grabbed Kael's wrist and twisted it, releasing the blade from his grasp. Commander Coar'saliz pressed the tip into the middle of Kael's chest, which halted as it struck bone. Panicking, Kael held onto the blade with both hands to keep it from sinking in further, which only succeeded in cutting both his palms deeply. "We cannot be hurt by our own weapons. Our enchantments ensure this.

"But enough of you." The Commander snapped his fingers three times. "I've tried to offer you grace, but obviously you wish to choose suffering instead. So be it."

Rooster's grin was utterly detestable. He gave Kael a mock solute. "Have fun, mate."

Kael hated that boy.

As the Commander left, he paused to mutter something to the guards. "Start with the splinter-snake venom for now. I'll oversee the rest."

The two guards nodded and turned around. One of them held up a strange vial, the other cracked his knuckles. "This should be fun," the knuckle-cracker said.

Chapter 18

The moon shone down on Shatterbreath. It bounced off the armour that covered her body. Korjan had made it for her. It had taken him an entire week to piece together enough breastplates and other sheets of metal. It had taken even longer to reshape them and attach them together to fit them over her entire body. Overall, the set of armour clinked, itched, caught on her scales and made it harder to fly. But she was grateful all the same. If having to carry half her weight worth of metal over her body meant keeping a bolt out of her side, she would take it. Plus, she knew how much work the blacksmith had done. He had spent all the time making the armour for her instead of fighting in the war. And for what she was about to do, she needed all the protection she could get.

For rescuing Kael would be no small task.

He had selflessly come to rescue her from that net. She had lost him when she stood up to run away and had made it back to the safety of the mountainside before she even realized he wasn't with her. With the net still wrapped around one of her wings, there was no chance of going back to save him. A grounded dragon was just a big target against an entire army. There had been nothing she could do.

At first, she had fallen into a state of depression. She was positive that he had been killed. So she hid up in her cave, sobbing and hating herself. It was the first time she had lost the will to survive since her family had died those centuries ago. He was her everything and it was her fault he had died.

She lay there for several days, occasionally peering out to see who was winning the war. Numbly, she recalled seeing Rystville arrive to help. The same day, some of Kael's friends made it up to her cave. The dark-skinned one, the traitor to the BlackHound Empire, had assured Shatterbreath that Kael was alive—that they had witnesses report they carried him away alive. If they discovered his importance, they would keep him alive to torture him.

She closed her eyes, listening to the beating of her wings and the scuffling of her armour. *Still alive.* If there was a chance, any chance at all, that he could be saved, Shatterbreath was going to take it. Even if it meant her life.

It had taken two weeks before Shatterbreath had convinced the Allegiance to lead an attack force to rescue Kael. Well, convinced wasn't the right word.

She snorted, sending a plume of smoke trailing behind her. Why did it take her threatening to burn down the city to spur them into action?

Sal'braan had laid down the formation of their camp for Shatterbreath. He told her where any prisoners would be held, the location of their hospital, where the horses were and further on. She didn't care for any of. She just wanted to know where Kael was.

The BlackHound Empire was in her view now. She scanned their camp, searching for the tents Sal'braan had described. The darkness of the night was doing well to protect her from their sight so far, but the moon was betraying her. It was full tonight. She recalled how that silly Vert Bowman had suggested another night, but she wouldn't hear of it. They were torturing him. She couldn't bear the knowledge of that, especially considering the fact that it was her fault.

There! There were the tents. Just near the hospital section. Sal'braan had told her the BlackHound wanted their prisoners fully healed before they tortured them. That way, they'd feel everything they...

She didn't want to think about it.

She began her descent. She reviewed the plan in her mind as she inhaled deeply. Then, as she reached the border of the camp, as the sentries finally caught notice of her, she released the flame.

She beat her wings harder, trying to gain more speed. Things exploded behind her—what they were exactly, she wasn't sure. Her breath ran out and she dipped skyward. What she had thought to be a long sweep of fire turned out to not even be a quarter of the length of the camp. They were spread out far, with huge gaps in between their tents. Perhaps for this very reason alone.

That didn't matter.

Her primary focus was not to burn their men. She angled her wings, aiming for the north end of their camp, where she knew the majority of their animals were. She could hear the *thunks* of ballistae, shooting either bolts or nets at her. She changed her direction often, avoiding the projectiles. She had quickly learned to do so over the length of the war, but still, flying amid the thick of the army was a dangerous thing. At least three bolts ricocheted off of her armour.

Thank you, Tooran, She thought to herself. Or was it Korjan who made the armour?

She took a breath, preparing to burn their animals. The horses saw her coming and began to panic. Some jumped out of their stables, while others simply kicked the doors down. It didn't matter what they did. For in one sweep, she had killed a fifth of their horses.

She pulled into a tight loop, preparing for another sweep when something penetrated the air. The smell of the ocean, both salty and fishy. No. They were too close to the ocean. There was only one possibility.

She heard the *whoosh* of his wings before she heard his snarl. Despite the warning, Shatterbreath was ill-prepared as Silverstain rammed into her side. They twisted through the air, coming close to the ground before they broke off. Without any words shared, they charged each other. Shatterbreath didn't have to ask why he was attacking her. She already knew. His bargain with the BlackHound Empire had been more than he suggested.

He was assisting them.

He dodged her claws and whipped around to her backside to plant his jaws deep into her shoulder. In turn, she slashed his exposed side. Blood rained down below.

Despite the raw instinct that overwhelmed her mind, she was aware of one tangible thought. *Hurry, Kael's friends. Save him.*

Korjan followed Tooran as he led the charge. Faerd, Laura and the majority of the King's Elite were among their ranks as well. Shatterbreath had refused to let Bruce, Sal'braan or Vert come, because of their inexperience or importance respectively. Faerd and Laura, however, had been insistent.

The party, three hundred strong, left Vallenfend in the middle of the night. They rode southwest of the city for several miles before pointing due west, along the south border of the BlackHound camp. According to Sal'braan, the best place to strike would be from the south. That is why Shatterbreath would direct the army to the north, to distract them.

About a mile away from the camp, Korjan dismounted his horse with some trouble. He wasn't used to riding the beasts. Until the war, he had never had any experience with horses. It showed.

"Here, let me help you." Tooran pulled Korjan's boot free of the stirrup.

Korjan cleared his throat. "Thanks."

They tied their horses to a scraggly tree nearby. They wouldn't need them to escape—if they were even able to. From that point, they crouched and crept through the grasses. Only a few King's Elite followed, the rest remained there, waiting for Tooran's signal. Korjan marvelled at the assassins as they crept along. They moved along without as much as a soft rustle. Korjan was not nearly as graceful. Even Faerd and Laura were faring better.

Suddenly, Tooran put a hand to Korjan's chest. Without a word, he perked up his head, which was wrapped in a dark cloth. He raised his hand just above the grasses and made a motion.

"What is it?" Korjan whispered.

"We're here," his son replied. "The grasses end soon; we will have no cover. There are sentries patrolling the perimeter. We'll have to take them out."

Laura sidled closer to Tooran, drawing her bow and quickly stringing it. "Do you need...?"

"No, we'll take care of it. Stay here." Tooran whistled softly and three King's Elite shuffled forward. Tooran pointed over the grasses. "Target one, there. Target two, target three. That one's mine. Two of you, stay back." He clasped one of the assassin's shoulders. "Perkan, you're with me. Let's go."

With practiced precision, the four men snuck through the bushes. Korjan straightened his back to watch. He could see four BlackHound guards standing near torches, alert. One of them was smoking a pipe of some kind. Even from their distance, he could smell the sour smoke.

He was the first to fall. Tooran and the other assassin, Perka, flew out of the bushes like living shadows. They covered the distance with surprising speed. The man smoking cursed and drew his blade. With a flash of metal, Tooran deflected the blade and slit his throat. Not a moment later, the next guard fell to Perkan's blade.

One of the remaining guards was only able to take two steps before an arrow pierced his neck, fired from the King's Elite hiding in the bushes. The guard on the other side fell down as well, but Korjan couldn't tell where the arrow hit him.

Still crouched, Tooran waved them over.

The group rushed over. Tooran removed the blade from the fallen guard and wiped it on the dead man's tunic. "Listen, this has to be quick. Our primary focus is to save Kael. Don't lag behind, because we're not stopping. There's no turning back from here." He made put his hands together and whistled through them, making a call that resembled a loon. On his mark, the King's Elite waiting at the tree charged the BlackHound camp. Dozens of the assassins rushed past where Tooran, Faerd, Laura and Korjan stood. But despite their numbers, their advance only sounded like a rustle of wind through the grasses. "Spread out," Tooran whispered to them as they flew past. "Kill as many as you can; buy us time."

Korjan realized what his son was asking was suicidal. They were going into the heart of the enemy's territory. Their numbers would surely overwhelm them. None of this, however, needed to be said. The King's Elite fully understood. They only nodded. Korjan was impressed beyond words.

Just then, a roar echoed across the land. A moment later, the sky was lit up by a jet of flame.

"Are you ready? Let's go." Without waiting for an answer, Tooran rushed forwards. Korjan and the others followed him closely, weaving in between the BlackHound tents. The King's Elite killed many without as much as a yelp from any of their victims. Detection, however, was inevitable.

Korjan heard a horn blare in alarm. They were in the thick of the BlackHound camp by then. There was no turning back. He doubled his efforts, pumping his arms and legs harder. They were getting close...

Kael wasn't sure what was real anymore. The BlackHound torturers gave him a herb or something that caused hallucinations. When they first whipped him, he had thought it was Malaricus holding the whip. Then, it was Bunda cutting his forearms with an obsidian dagger—which reminded him of a giant man painted in blood, with a skull for a face. Laura would burn his ear with a red-hot poke and every third day Faerd would come and break the same finger with his bare hands.

Still, Kael refused to tell his enemies—or friends?—anything. The pain was intense, but he kept his mouth shut. If it was too much, he would instead tell them lies. Rooster was there watching every moment. He would inform the torturers that Kael was lying. Kael could have sworn he even noticed King Morrindale watching the torture one day. But...but that was impossible, wasn't it? The king was... He was... Kael didn't even know.

He tried recalling happier times at night, but he found when he did, they were doused in pain and fright. His mind was under constant stress as he tried to differentiate between what was real and what was a product of the terrible hallucinations. He couldn't. Everything seemed so surreal.

There had come a time when it had been too much for him. He told them the truth. They hadn't believed him and only beat him harder. It made Kael realize there was no hope for him. He was going to die by their hands, no matter what he did. So, he kept his mouth shut entirely. They had to force his mouth open as to get food and water down his throat.

He never heard of anything considering the war—if there even was a war going on. He was dragged through the hospital each day on the way to the torture tent, but he only supposed that those injured men were recovering from their own torturing.

His friends would visit him at night. In his dreams, they were dying over and over in every worse way. Sometimes, they would appear to him in his room one at a time, where they would then mock and scorn him, calling him useless, pathetic and stupid. He believed them.

He lay on his bed, shivering. A strange sound caught his attention. It sounded like a clap of thunder. Careful of the cuts across his back, he sat upright, trying to remember where he knew that sound. It was more than just the weather.

Screaming. There was screaming outside. As well as the clanging of swords. Kael tucked himself in tighter, terrified. Whatever was causing the commotion, it was heading in his direction. Was it a monster, a demon, coming to tear him to pieces? It had happened before, and every time, he had woken up. This time was different though. He was awake, wasn't he? It was hard to tell anymore.

Several silhouettes passed by his cloth door. Kael held his breath. He could hear people pause outside, breathing heavily. The shadow of a sword stretched across the door.

"Where is he?"

"Check here."

The door was flung open. He could count four of his friends. Four. He knew at once why they were there. They were finished with mocking him. Now, they were going to kill him at last.

199

Korjan shoved the cloth aside, and then ripped it down. His heart leapt as he spotted a curled-up figure lying against a low pile of blankets. It was Kael Rundown. Or at least Korjan thought he was. His eyes were sunken and his hair cut short and caked with blood. Sores seemed to cover his entire shirtless torso and he favoured his back in a certain way, giving Korjan the impression he had been whipped more than once. The ring finger on his right hand was blue and bent at an irregular angle, bulging from broken bone.

Worst of all was the absolute terror spread across his face.

He wasn't excited to see them. No. The opposite. The very sight of Korjan terrified him. As the blacksmith approached, Kael shuffled back and grimaced.

"Let me see him!" Laura brushed past Korjan. "Kael! K— Kael?" She crouched low, reaching out towards him. Kael crossed his arms out in front of himself as if to block an incoming attack. "We're here to save you, Kael!" Laura said softly. "We've come to rescue you."

"No," he wailed. "Get back! All of you. Leave me alone! You've tormented me enough today. No!"

Tooran had his back to Kael, wary of attackers. He glanced back and frowned. "He's been tortured. Viciously. We have to get him out of here. We have to get him to safety."

"Kael, relax. We're not here to hurt you." Korjan stooped over and grabbed hold of his wrist. There was no time for gentleness.

In turn, Kael thrashed. He may have been the BlackHound's prisoner for over a month, but he was still strong. But Korjan was stronger. He roughly hefted Kael over his shoulders and turned to leave. Laura gasped.

"His back."

Korjan glanced over his shoulder. They had whipped him. Recently. The blood from the open wounds was already oozing onto Korjan's shoulders.

"Let's go," Korjan grunted. His hands were shaking.

As Korjan and the others started making their way through the camp, they ran into far more soldiers than they had anticipated.

Shatterbreath's distraction wasn't work well enough. Something must have gone wrong. He hoped she hadn't been shot down again. She was the main reason they had gone on this mission.

Luckily, any members of the King's Elite that saw them joined their ranks and soon, they had a sizeable group to defend them. But it simply wasn't enough. They lost more of the assassins with every battalion of BlackHound soldiers they met than they gained.

Kael was screaming hoarsely too, which only alerted more soldiers. After a particularly bloody skirmish between the King's Elite and a group of soldiers, Tooran knocked him across the head with the hilt of his blade. Kael fell silent and limp.

"Come on," Tooran hissed, ignoring the group's shocked expressions. "We're cutting it close. We can't take another fight like that."

Korjan glanced about. Sure enough, the numbers of King's Elite surrounding them was far less than they once were. It didn't help that the majority of their forces were now scattered throughout the camp, trying to draw attention elsewhere.

A burst of fire lit up the sky. To Korjan's horror, he saw *two* dragons race by overhead.

"There's the prisoner!" a BlackHound soldier cried. In response, Faerd unsheathed a sword from Korjan's back and ran the soldier through before he could utter another word. It was too late.

The cries of more men could be heard through the tents.

"Come on, we're almost there!" The group didn't need any more convincing.

With all efforts for stealth gone, they sprinted through the tents, with the King's Elite doing their best to slash down anybody who got in their way.

Through the torchlight of the tents, Korjan spotted something irregular. Blackness! They were nearing the edge of the camp. They were so close!

A line of soldiers seemed to appear out of nowhere. Some of them were holding swords, most had bows aimed towards the Korjan and the rest. "Halt!"

Korjan took a slow breath, his brow furrowing. *So close.*

"Look out!" one of the King's Elite shouted.

Korjan spun around in time to see two massive shapes heading towards them. The armour lining Shatterbreath's body glinted in the moonlight as she came careening at them. Korjan threw Kael down and dove to his stomach.

Shatterbreath crashed into the camp, crushing several tents as she tumbled along with another green dragon. Pieces of wood were sent flying everywhere, from splinters to beams the size of Korjan's thigh. Weapons and armour were also flung into the air, crashing all around. A mace landed unnervingly close Korjan's head.

For a time, everything was still.

Then, there was a snarling. One of the dragons—Korjan couldn't tell which through the haze—picked itself up. With a flap of its wings, it cleared the dust away. Shatterbreath reared up on her hind legs and released a powerful roar. Dropping back down on four paws, fire burst from her maw, killing the BlackHound soldiers that hadn't been crushed by the dragons' crash.

"Kael!" she gasped. "Blacksmith, I am indebted to you. Quickly, gather your men. The whole camp is headed this way. We must leave at once."

Korjan picked himself up, brushing away debris. Laura and a few other King's Elite soldiers did the same. They picked up Kael and, with the dragon's help, placed him upon her back.

"Now your turn, hurry."

Laura clambered up her armour and sat in the middle of her back. Many of the King's Elite found places along her side and clung there. Korjan, however, hesitated. "Where's Tooran?"

"Over here, father..."

Korjan traced the voice, buried under a thick beam. He knelt down and cleared away a pile of splinters, uncovering Tooran's head. His cloth mask had fallen off. Blood rimmed his lips and his eyes were strangely distant. He reached out a gloved hand and touched Korjan's face.

"Tooran..." Korjan muttered. "Wh—what...? Are you alright, my son?"

He coughed in reply and pointed to the beam lying over his stomach. Korjan tried to move it. It was too heavy. "Shatterbreath," he pleaded.

The dragon wrapped her tail around the wooden beam and lifted it up. As she did, a huge spike came free of Tooran's stomach, covered in crimson.

Korjan stared at it, horrified. He threw his gauntlets off and placed both hands against Tooran's face, which had gone very pale. "By the gods, Tooran... Stay with me, stay with me!"

Tooran blinked slowly and gave a fleeting smile. "Father, it was an honour to fight beside you in battle. I—I'm sorry."

"No, son. Don't...don't..."

"I did so many evil things. Killed so many innocent people..." Tooran's hands found the gaping wound in his belly. "J—justice...has finally found me."

"To hell with justice!" Korjan cried, socking his fist against a beam. "This is not justice. Son, I just got you back. I can't lose you again. *Not again.* Don't leave me, please. Please, Tooran. I... You..."

Tooran's lips barely moved. His eyes fluttered. Korjan had to lean in to hear what he said next. "Win this war. I'll give your regards...to my mother..."

His body went slack.

"Blacksmith?" Korjan ignored Shatterbreath's voice. "We must leave. There will be time to grieve later."

He closed his son's eyes. "Grieve." He tasted the word. "Grieve? He wouldn't be dead if it wasn't for you! This was all your idea! His death is *your* fault!"

Shatterbreath knocked him to the ground with her snout. "*Don't* you dare. I will leave you here to die. I wouldn't feel an ounce of remorse."

Something stirred behind Shatterbreath. It was the second dragon. It must have been knocked unconscious from the fall and now it was waking up.

Shatterbreath glanced back at it and hissed. She opened her wings wide and reached her paw out at Korjan. For a moment, he thought she was going to kill him with her claws right then. Instead, she scooped him up. Korjan clung to her scales tight, feeling his throat sink into his stomach. The second before she was airborne, he saw her pick up Tooran's body with her other front paw.

He couldn't tear his eyes away from his son's limp form as they flew out of the BlackHound camp. He could hear arrows and other objects swishing past close by, but he didn't care.

Tooran.

Chapter 19

Kael's nightmares were even worse that night. He thrashed in his sleep, but couldn't wake himself of the terrible dreams. Monsters with sharp claws and teeth, ridged with jagged spikes and blistering flesh lashed out at him. Their bodies seemed to mould into each other, making it impossible to pick out any individual creature. They all wore human faces. Familiar faces.

When he finally woke up, some of those faces were there to greet him.

He gasped and tried to fight back, but couldn't. Something held him down to the bed. He scanned the room, trying to figure out where he was. The walls were a charming mahogany and rich furniture garbed the large room. A window allowed pure light to flow in, illuminating a carpet stretched across the floor like a lazy cat.

"I hate cats," Kael murmured.

"Kael!" a voice proclaimed. "You hate what? Never mind. You're back! How are you, my boy?"

He stared at the person who had just spoken, a roundish lady with bright orange hair. Bunda, the butcher that slashed his forearms. There were others in the room as well. Faerd who broke his finger, Laura who burned his ear, Korjan who beat him, Helena who would dunk his head underwater until he nearly drowned.

"Get away from me," he stuttered. "All of you. Please, don't cut me anymore. Don't...don't cut me. I..."

"K—Kael, I'd never cut you."

"Liar!" he shouted. "I have the scars on my arms to prove it! You cut me, you cut me." He broke into a sob, repeating those words.

Then, before he knew it, the people were gone. He was left alone. As glad as he was to have them away, he missed them as well.

"They hurt you so much," he growled at himself, "why do you miss them?" He blinked a few times. "They...they were my friends, weren't they? Friends don't hurt you though. Never."

205

Several hours passed where he lay there still, staying at the mosaic in the ceiling, comprised of tiny pieces of varying marble. It was the most interesting thing he had ever seen. When some more people entered the room to try and talk to him, he found himself focussed on the mosaic instead, stifling out their words, praying they wouldn't hurt him again.

Fatigue would strike him at any moment in the day. One moment, he'd be wide awake, the next, he would find himself waking up screaming. The line between reality and his dreams was beginning to appear, though. Not like before. Before, everything was one great nightmare. At least now he could tell that he was indeed awake. Pain was no longer as apparent in the waking world. A finger on his right hand still hurt, as well as his back, but otherwise, his body felt all tingly, as if it itself had fallen asleep.

Every so often, various people would come and tend to him. For the most part, it was his friends trying to comfort him, which only made him scared. Other times, somebody would check the sores healing all over his body, to make sure they weren't becoming infected. He didn't know the man. Kael did know one person that came regularly to check on him though.

He looked forward to seeing her. A girl with hair the colour of fresh corn. Janus Morrindale. He would look at her long and hard every day, trying to remember where he had met her from. He couldn't recall if she was actually a friend, but she had never hurt him before. That's all he needed to trust her.

Over the next few days, Kael could feel his mind returning to him. It was like a fog was slowly dissipating around him. When he friends came to see him and feed him, he no longer yelled at them. They even released his restrains, faithful he wouldn't try to run away. He still didn't trust them though. When they tried to convince him to eat, he would tell them of all the things they had done to him and then show them the wounds to prove it.

Except for Faerd. When Kael tried to show him the finger he would break every third day, he was shocked to find it gone. Just like that. Right down to the first knuckle. He held it up to the sunlight, far more interested in his hand than anything else.

"The medic took it off," Faerd explained. Laura grimaced. "The BlackHound torturers broke it too many times. It was useless, Kael."

"BlackHound torturers?" Kael repeated.

Faerd nodded. "You were tortured, Kael. We've been telling you that for the last week. Sal'braan told us you were drugged too. I think that means they gave you something that made you hallucinate. It made it appear as though it was us hurting you."

Kael pondered his words for the longest time, debating whether or not it was true. He didn't say anything, but instead went back to studying his hand.

"I'm so sorry, Kael," Laura sobbed. "I can't even imagine what you went through. What it was like..."

She was interrupted by two stern voices echoing through the halls. The door had been left open, so Kael could hear every word. "Yeah, yeah, I know. But she's *insistent.* She won't leave me alone. I have over a thousand mouths to feed. Do you know how hard it is to cook with her pestering me all day? I reckon it'll do him good anyway."

"I don't care," Korjan's voice replied. "Let the impatient beast wait. He is in no condition to see her. You've seen how Kael reacts to us. He's terrified. He's barely keeping it together, Bunda. How are you expecting him to react to—?"

"Shut up," Bunda barked. "The door's open."

The two of them entered. Kael placed a hand over his face as if he was having a bad migraine. He didn't want to see either of them. Their argument had caused him to tremble.

He listened as Bunda sat down nearby with a sigh. "I'm sorry, Kael."

"I want to see her."

"No." Korjan shook his head. "Not an option. You're not well, Kael. You must realize this. Maybe in a week or two..."

"Let me see her." Kael lowered his hands. Korjan had his arms folded, standing there by the doorway. "Now." He wasn't even quite sure who *she* was.

Korjan cocked his head. "Now there's a bit of the old Kael. Stubborn as always. I guess they couldn't snuff the fire inside you after all, boy." He walked across the room and placed his palms on the windowsill. "Fine. We can take you to her right now if you want."

"I want her here," Kael said. He still didn't know what was happening. He was worried that Korjan might change his mind, so he added, "If that's alright."

"Somebody else call her," Korjan grumbled. "I don't want to deal with her." With that, he turned and left the room.

"I'll get her then," Faerd said. He leaned out the window and whistled. Kael put his fingers to his own lips, recalling a similar whistle that he once knew. He would try later.

Thunder boomed in reply. Kael bolted upright in his bed, recognizing the sound. That wasn't normal thunder. A massive blue shape flashed past the window, sending a current of air buffeting into the room. A tremor ran through the walls and there was a loud scratching against the outside of the wall. Kael's heart thrummed in his chest.

As she peered into the room with her thick blue muzzle, memories came flooding back into his mind. Of their times together, soaring on currents high above the ground, bathing in the sun, laying against her scales and enjoying the immense warmth of her body.

The sound of her powerful voice was so comforting. He could feel the tension flowing out of his body. The heavy musk of her body was familiar, and he welcomed it, breathing deep.

Those emerald eyes focussed on him, brow furrowed in concern.

Tears streamed down his face and he let out a sob. *Shatterbreath.*

He ran to her and threw his arms around the end of her snout that was protruding into the window. Pearly tears rolled down the contours of her muzzle, either dripping off near her canines or catching in his gray robe.

He drank in the feeling of her scales against his fingertips and the warmth flowing from her body into his. He kept repeating her name between sobs. He hadn't realized until then how much he had missed her. He had never seen her face during the time he was being tortured. It was always his friends who hurt him, but never her. She would never hurt him. She was more than a friend.

They could have stayed like that for hours, with Kael's arms wrapped tightly around her muzzle and her straddled against the side of the castle, with one paw gripping the window's edge. She was the first to speak.

"You smell."

Kael backed off, tasting the salt from his tears. "What?"

"How long has it been since you've bathed?" She considered him with one eye, a sly grin spread across her features. "And what are you wearing? Get dressed and I'll take you to my lake to wash off. I have a lot to tell you. We have a lot to mend in you."

Kael glanced at his missing finger. Could he be mended? Nevertheless, he nodded.

Laura and Bunda left the room to let Kael change into a brown tunic. Faerd talked quietly to Shatterbreath as he slipped into the clothing. Kael could only guess at what words they shared.

Once he was finished, he stood in front of her. She raised a brow, leaned forward and licked him. He laughed, trying to push her away. "Aw, gross!"

She snapped her jaws. "Hmm, you still taste like Tiny. I'm convinced."

Kael's grin faltered. "Why wouldn't you be?"

"Never mind," she said quickly with a flinch. "Hop on. The rest of the day belongs to just us."

"Bring him back before sunset," Faerd said as Kael clambered onto her paw.

She snorted at him, filling the room with ashy smoke. Faerd coughed and swore at her, which only made her rumble in amusement.

Once Kael was sitting comfortably in between her shoulders—where he belonged—she launched off the castle's surface and was airborne. From that height, Kael had a clear view of Vallenfend and the surrounding area. Soldiers wearing black armour were fighting against other soldiers wearing assorted colours.

"The BlackHound Empire," Kael mumbled. "They did this to me?"

209

Shatterbreath turned her head back to look at him. "Yes, Kael. They caught you when you saved me. I'm sorry; there was nothing I could do. I th—thought I had you, thought you were on my back. By Darion's crest, what if they had decided to just kill you instead?"

Kael didn't say anything. Fleetingly, he thought, *I wished they had.* He shook himself. Though he wasn't sure of everything yet, he was alive and safe. And with Shatterbreath.

"How has the war been going?" he asked her.

She only shook her head. "We're not going to talk about that yet. You're in no condition. I'll let Vert fill you in later. Until sunset, this time belongs to us."

"I do have so many questions." Kael rubbed his bruised cheek gingerly. "I'm not sure of anything anymore, Shatterbreath. Except you."

She hummed. "Isn't that all that matters?"

He knew she was making a joke, but he didn't smile. She winced and turned her head back around, resuming her flying. After a brief trip through the fog, the top of the mountain came into view. Shatterbreath flew past the mouth of her cave. Slowly, the memories came trickling back to him.

She alighted near the lake on the top of her mountain. Kael clambered off her back and shuffled to the water's edge. She placed her forelegs in the water and grumbled as she lowered herself until just the lower part of her chest was submerged. Folding her wings, she set her wise gaze on him.

Kael considered stripping down to bathe. He stopped himself, remembering the lashes across his back. He didn't want Shatterbreath seeing. So, tunic still on, he waded into the water. Waist-deep, he stopped to inspect his reflection.

A man Kael didn't recognize stared back at him. His face was pale and thinning, with fresh scars lining his cheeks and jaw. A formidable layer of stubble had overtaken his chin, slightly lighter in colour than his hair, which the BlackHound torturers had cut short. He hated his hair short. He turned his head to find half of his left ear missing. Burned off by Laura. *Not Laura,* he corrected himself, *the BlackHound torturers.* His eyes were the same colour as ever, but they seemed so much more different than he could remember. They were darker and fear shone within them. He rubbed his face, holding back tears.

"Kael." Shatterbreath's voice made him flinch.

"Water's cold," Kael said quickly. "Give me a moment."

He dunked himself under the water and scrubbed himself off rigorously, trying his best not to expose or reopen his gashes. The coldness of the water was refreshing. It stung his limbs and made his senses come alive. He tried to rub the experience of his torture away, but once he stepped out of the lake, it was still with him.

Shatterbreath took him to her cave, where she lit a fire at the back using her breath. With the stones glowing in the ceiling to add a comforting glow, Kael curled up beside her to dry off. She wrapped her tail around him loosely.

"How do you feel?" she asked.

Kael shifted. "Confused, scared. I can only remember bits and pieces. I remember the pain of them torturing me. Remember the screams and the nightmares. It was all so surreal. It *was* real, wasn't it?"

"Yes, Tiny."

"That's what I thought." He frowned. "What scares me the most are my friends. I'm not sure what to think of them anymore. I mean..." He took a breath, searching for the right words. "I only still call them my friends because I don't know what else to call them. Are they still my friends?"

"Why wouldn't they be? They are very concerned about you, Tiny. Can't you see that?"

Kael stood up abruptly. "They're nursing me back to health, that's all I know. They might just be doing so to torture me again, to make sure I don't die."

"That's not what they're doing. What motives would your friends have to do something like that to you? Kael, you were poisoned. It was supposed to seem like it was your friends torturing you. They weren't." She snapped her jaws, silencing his retort. "The sooner you realize this, the quicker your recovery will be. They were *not* your friends. Your friends care for you. They're here for you now. I'm here for you."

He scowled at her for a long time, conflicted. He shook his head, putting hand to his temple. Was the poison still working on him, muddling his thoughts? "You're right—as always."

"There you go."

He slumped back up against her and she stretched her wing over part of his body. He felt the leathery membrane, recalling the time he had driven spikes through her wing to keep it together. "Shatterbreath?"

"Yes, Tiny?"

"What did you mean when you said you were convinced that I'm still me?" When he turned to look at up at her, her jaw muscles were taut.

"Some people think that they did something to you, Kael. Something to your mind. They think the BlackHound changed you, made you a different person. Like you were torn down something new grew in your place. They think you might be loyal to the BlackHound Empire, and that you are their spy. They don't think they can trust you, and are prepared to keep you locked away."

Her words hurt. "Who thinks these things?"

"That doesn't matter." Her scales scraped against the stone floor as she stretched her hind legs. "I know damage has been done to you, Kael. I can see it across your body, in your eyes. But you are no traitor. No matter what happened in the enemy's camp, don't ever think otherwise."

"Thank you." He rubbed Shatterbreath's side, feeling the coarseness of her interlocking scales. He shifted, sending pain shooting through his back. He tried his best to digest what Shatterbreath had told him. It was the BlackHound Empire that had tortured him, not his friends. Not his friends. Kael tasted the name on his lips; "BlackHound Empire..."

Shatterbreath nuzzled him gently with her snout. "You will have your revenge, Kael," she purred. "I promise."

They sat there in silence for the rest of the day. Kael stared at the fire, thinking of all the ways he was going to kill those who had

212

tortured him. By the time the sun was beginning to set, he was ready to take action. As much as it upset him that his and Shatterbreath's time alone together was over, he was looking forward to wielding a blade once more.

He was ready to face the BlackHound Empire again.

Chapter 20

Shatterbreath delivered Kael back to the kingdom before sunrise, as she promised. As soon as they touched down just outside the training ground wall, a messenger whom Kael didn't recognize came gingerly up to them.

"Master Rundown," she said with a bow, "if your health permits, King Henedral requests your admittance to an important meeting taking place immediately."

"Shatterbreath?"

"Go. You'll be fine," the dragon reassured. "Just remember that you can trust everybody here. You're safe. I'll be close if you need me."

"Okay." Kael turned back to the messenger. "Where is it?"

"I'll lead you there. Follow me, please."

Kael hesitated. He wasn't comfortable leaving Shatterbreath's presence yet. There was still so much he was unsure about. Still, he followed the woman. She walked along brusquely with Kael in tow, passing through the gate and then the thriving training grounds immediately after. The grounds had undergone a radical change since Kael had seen it last. The right side, where the archers used to train, was now filled with white hospital tents whereas the right left supported what seemed to be a huge, open kitchen. His initial thoughts were confirmed as they passed by. Soldiers were lined up holding bowls or plates, waiting to get their lunch of stew and bread. Among the many cooks—all of which seemed to be Vallenfend volunteers—he spotted Helena and Bunda fleetingly.

They left the business of the training grounds and entered the castle. Once inside, they didn't have to go very far. The leaders of the Allegiance had converted King Morrindale's dining hall into their war-room. The messenger opened one of the thick doors and ushered him in.

"Ah, Kael!" a familiar voice cried. He looked much different wearing a full suit of armour instead of his robe with the huge sleeves, but it was hard to mistake King Respu and his cheery manner. He strode up to Kael and threw out his hand. "How are you doing? I heard you had quite the rough time."

Kael considered his hand, but did not shake it. "I'm better, thank you. I am very glad to see you arrived in safety, King Respu. I take it the journey wasn't too hard on you?"

The king withdrew his hand awkwardly and shook his head. "No, no. The desert gave us some trouble, but as you can see, we pulled through. We're here to back you up, every step of the way."

Kael nodded. "Very good."

"Kael!" another voice proclaimed. He barely had time to register who it belonged to before Vert Bowman came rushing up, arms out wide to give him a bear hug. Kael put out a hand to stop him, but Vert seized him tight, crunching his arm in between them. Kael shuddered. "Finally, you're back! I was beginning to worry about you." His grin was so huge, Kael was wondering if his face was going to split in half. "You're too strong for them though. I guess hanging around a dragon has made you a tough nut to crack, eh?"

Kael wriggled out of his hug and gave him a weak smile. "Yeah. They couldn't beat me. How's the war going, Vert?"

"Ah, not so great right now, Kael. Come over here and I'll tell you everything. If you can guess, a lot has happened since your... Um..."

"Capture."

"About that." Vert turned to him, wearing a grave expression. "You didn't tell them anything, did you? Anything at all?"

Kael paused. Several images of his torture flashed through his mind, so vivid that he truly believed he was reliving them. Once they subsided, he swooned and King Respu gave him a hand to support him.

"I'm sorry," Kael said, rubbing his forehead. "I tried my best not to talk, Vert. It was...too much. I broke down once or twice, but they didn't seem to believe me anyway."

He placed a hand on Kael's shoulder. Kael squirmed. Why couldn't Vert realize he *didn't* want to be touched? "That's alright, Kael. Nobody's going to judge you for what happened. Even the best of us have our weak moments."

215

Vert brought Kael to the middle of the room, where a large round table held an equally large map of Vallenfend and the surrounding area. King Henedral, Korjan, Tomn and a few generals whom Kael didn't know surrounded the table. Korjan waved at Kael whereas King Henedral gave him a mere nod. Spread across the map were chess pieces, placed together in black or white clumps.

"Those pieces are the BlackHound Empire," Vert explained, pointing to the black chess pieces outside of the city walls. "These are ours. Each piece represents five hundred men. As you can see, we've whittled down their numbers quite significantly over the last month and a half."

"A month and a half?" Kael gasped. "Was I gone for that long?"

"We were all worried you had been killed, but Sal'braan assured us you were alive. Shatterbreath pestered us every day to make an attempt to rescue you." He laughed.

"Why didn't you?" Kael yelled. "Why did it take you so long?"

Vert frowned. "I'm sorry, but saving you wasn't a very high priority."

Kael's shoulders slumped. *Count on Vert for brutal honesty.*

Vert continued. "A mission like that—spearheading straight into the heart of the enemy base to retrieve one person—is very costly."

"I'm the one who brought you all together. You wouldn't even know about the Empire if it wasn't for—"

"Yeah, we know," Korjan interrupted. "We've had enough chastisement from that dragon. Can we continue, please?"

"When Shatterbreath went down," Vert said, "a good portion of Fallenfeld backed off to help her. The BlackHound soldiers we had surrounded made a push to her, as well as a squad of cavalry from the main group. With Fallenfeld's numbers spread thin, they were able to break through. A lot of BlackHound men escaped. Still, that was our most successful day. We killed over five-thousand men, with minimal losses.

"After a lot of convincing from Shatterbreath, the King's Elite, under Tooran's leadership, volunteered to bring you back, Kael. As I said, a mission like that is costly. Out of the hundred or so men that left, only about ten returned, half of them riding on Shatterbreath's back."

"Tooran," Korjan said tonelessly, "didn't...make it."

Kael quickly turned his attention back to the table, dodging Korjan's eyes. He blinked several times, willing tears to come. None did. *Tooran was dead because of him.* Kael was disturbed how casually he took the news.

He counted the pieces resting on the map. Twenty-four for the BlackHound Empire, seventeen for the Allegiance. That made twelve-thousand men for the enemy, eight-thousand five-hundred for the allies.

"As you can see," King Henedral said, placing a hand down on the table. "Their numbers are no longer double that of ours. The arrival of Rystville helped, of course. They have been losing men at a far quicker rate than we have—almost double at one point. It seems Vert's tactics have been working well."

Vert reached across the table and plucked a white piece from the table. He sighed and rolled the piece in his fingers before casting it to the side. "But they're catching on. Their rate of loss is decreasing, while ours is increasing. Unless something is done, *they* will be winning. Take in mind, we're going to wait a few days— maybe even a week—before trying anything radical. So until then, try and think of something that could turn the tides. For now, we will continue to fight."

Kael studied the map for a long time. "Send me out."

"Excuse me?"

"I want to fight. I need to fight."

"No," King Henedral snapped. "You are in no shape we can't risk your capture again."

"I agree Kael." Korjan crossed his arms. "You are no condition to battle."

"Not to the front lines," Kael replied. "But somewhere where I can help. I need blood for what they did to me."

"Very well," Vert said.

"You can't be serious!" King Henedral cried.

"If ther man wants ter fight, let him," Tomn stated. It was the first thing he had said the entire time. Overall, he seemed out of place, standing there awkwardly, glancing frequently between the leaders. "This is Kael's war. I think he can make his ern decisions."

"Besides," King Respu said with a grin, "I'm sure Shatterbreath will stay close to him. She'll protect him."

"She's the reason Kael was captured in the first place!" Korjan yelled.

"And I'm sure," Kael breathed, "that she won't let that happen again. I'm going to fight. That's that."

Korjan scowled at Kael for a long time. Kael shivered. "Fine," he said at last. "Fine. But I'm fighting with you." He rubbed his temple. "You're going to need more than a dragon to watch your back. At the break of dawn, go to the armoury, suit up. I'll meet you there."

Kael had won the argument, but he didn't feel like the victor. With no further comment, he slipped out of the room and into the halls of the castle. It suddenly dawned on him that his faithful shield and—more importantly—his sword were gone. It grieved him to know that he had lost *Vintrave*. What happened to it? Would he ever get to see it again?

He headed up to the room he had been staying in for the last week. When he arrived, he found it empty. With much difficulty, he managed to fall asleep, though his dreams were wrought with monsters and pain. He didn't sleep well.

The next morning, being careful to avoid the bustling of the soldiers in the training grounds, Kael made his way to the armoury. The small shack was just how he remembered it on the outside. But, as he discovered, the inside had changed significantly. Gone were the weapons that once lined every shelf. What remained were wooden clubs and broken pieces of armour. Larr, the weapons master was at least still there. The stumpy man sat in the middle of the nearly-empty armoury on a rickety stool, squinting as he smoked a pipe.

"Larr!" Kael exclaimed. "I haven't seen you in a long time!"

As Kael approached him, he was reminded of Larr's most prominent feature. His stench.

Larr gave him a leery look with his good eye. "What? My goodness, you're alive. Well now, you're full of surprises indeed. Last time I saw you was after your silly castle raid. You were running off into the darkness. Then you were banished. Took some time, but I guess you finally came back." He cocked his head. "I heard you were captured."

"Do I look captured?" Kael countered. "I take it my gift from the castle helped you some?"

Larr leaned back with a sly grin, puffing his pipe. "Aye, it did. Bought meself a nice house I did. Very nice house, with a pretty view and everything. Darn thing was destroyed first day of the war. Fancy that, eh?"

Kael scanned the shelves, looking for *anything* that would be useful in combat. "Do you have any weapons left that I can use? Also, a set of armour—and a shield."

Larr shook his head and chortled. "Everything's been used, sonny. Whatever armour we had left was put into protecting that dragon."

"You mean," Kael scoffed, "you made armour for Shatterbreath? I...didn't know that."

"Yep. Well, *I* didn't make it. Not sure who did."

"I think I have an idea."

Larr stood up with a grunt. "Well, don't fret, sonny, I think we can get you a suit of armour yet. Maybe even a weapon too. Come with me."

Larr waddled out of his armoury. Kael kept a reasonable distance away from him, trying to avoid breathing in his stench. Now that he smoked, it was even worse.

They worked their way across the training grounds—towards the hospital. It slowly dawned on Kael what Larr's intention was.

"No, I can't do this. I'm not going to steal an injured person's armour!"

Larr frowned. "Who said they're going to be *alive?*"

"I'm not going to wear a suit of armour someone died in!"

219

Larr stopped and pointed a finger at Kael's chest. He flinched. "Haven't you before?" Larr raised a brow as Kael hesitated. "You need armour. They *don't*. Now come on."

They reached a large tent that was fully enclosed. Larr threw open one of the cloth doors and peeked inside. "Oi," Kael heard him call. "Any deceased in here? We need armour."

"You again?" a woman's voice replied. "Get out of here."

Larr grinned and stepped into the tent. Kael stayed where he was. In the BlackHound camp, he had been right inside their hospital. He didn't want to see the wounded. Hearing their moaning from where he standing was torture enough.

"Aw, why so harsh, sweety?" Kael could hear Larr say. "Aren't you glad to see me?"

"Get out of my face, you pig. When was the last time you bathed?"

Larr only laughed. "Give me a kiss, sweety."

"Don't make me call the guards again. They'll whip you this time. I have better things to do."

Larr laughed some more. Kael was beginning to wonder if he was sober. "Larr?" he called out.

"Who's that?" the woman's voice asked. "Another one of your surly friends?"

"Naw," Larr replied coolly. "His name is Kael Rundown. I'm supposed to be finding him some armour."

Kael heard the woman gasp. "Rundown?"

Kael backed away from the tent door and a moment later, the woman Larr was talking to emerged. Kael didn't recognize her.

"Well, would you look that," she said, sizing up Kael. "I've heard plenty about you, but was beginning to wonder if you were simply a myth. All that you've done...seems like too much to be true. Befriending that dragon, discovering King Murderdale's plot... Rallying together an army." She shook her head. "Truly amazing."

Kael nodded, unsure what to say.

The woman thrust out her hand. Kael considered her. She was tall, though still shorter than Kael, with tanned skin and strong arms. Mid thirties. She must have been a field worker once. Her hair was a rosy brown, almost bordering on red. Her expression and demeanour were friendly enough, so Kael took her hand.

"I'm Cressida, head medic." She gave a sad laugh. "Gods, how did that happen? Mentioned I my mother was a nurse and here I am. Barely knew anything about medicine more than a few months ago."

"Kael Rundown, didn't know much of anything a year ago."

There was a gleam in her eye. "Well met."

Larr exited the tent, wearing a goofy smile. "Larr," he said, "used to own a nice house. Looks like we've all changed. Now, if you're done, sweety, I need to procure a set of armour for sonny boy here."

"I have a name you know," Cressida countered. "Maybe if you actually used it once and a while—"

"Oh, spare me."

Her scowl was toxic. "Come this way, Rundown. We may have something yet." There were about five large hospital tents set up. Cressida started towards the furthest one. "We haven't had any opportunity to recover our dead," she explained, "which means we haven't been able to salvage any armour."

"Don't you ever stop talking?" Larr said with a gasp.

Cressida ignored him. "Fauron wasn't doing too well yesterday. Punctured lung and internal bleeding. There isn't anything we can do."

She stopped in front of the last tent. Kael frowned. "Do you mind...if I stay out here?"

"Of course. Hey, swine, give me a hand."

Larr nodded. "Lead the way, sweety."

"Stop calling me that!"

They disappeared inside the tent, leaving Kael alone. He watched people going about their business in the training grounds, carrying their plates of food or sparring with one another. Even as he waited, the gates opened up, revealing an exasperated group of soldiers, carrying injured men amongst them. They went straight to the hospital tents.

Cressida and Larr exited soon after, carrying various pieces of armour.

221

"Here we are," Larr said with a grunt, throwing the metal to Kael's feet. "I hope you don't mind wearing Arnoth's crest, sonny."

Kael knelt down and rubbed the crest on the breastplate. "This is perfect. Thank you."

"It was my honour, Rundown." Cressida gave him a bow. "Fight well. Now excuse me, I heard more injured come in. I have to attend to them at once."

She handed a pair of pauldrons and grieves to Kael, then hurried away.

"That was fun." Larr scratched his belly. "Come on then, let's get you suited up."

Twenty minutes later, Kael was wearing his new suit of armour. It was a bit tight, but after Larr pounded out the dent in the chest and adjusted some straps, it fit comfortably around his body. He made a fist with his gauntlet, which Larr had also removed a finger from. It felt good to be wearing armour again. It gave him a sense of protection he hadn't felt for what seemed like an eternity. The armour also came with a helmet, which Kael realized he had never worn before. Carefully, he fitted the sallet over his head and turned to the smudgy mirror nearby. The helmet disguised his grin.

"Your shield, sire." Larr handed him a wooden buckler, gouged from where arrows had struck it. It wasn't as sturdy as his last shield, or as beautiful, but any extra protection would still help. Kael figured he could just swipe a BlackHound shield out on the field, anyway.

Korjan entered the armoury right then.

"You're looking like a warrior once again," he commented, sizing Kael top to bottom. Korjan's own set of armour was far more impressive, with intricate carvings covering the chest and pauldrons and an iridescent sheen that Kael had never been able to replicate. Obviously, Korjan had forged his own armour. "Are you ready for this, Kael?"

Kael turned back to the mirror. Hatred burned in his chest towards the BlackHound Empire. "I'm ready," he said with conviction.

"Then come with me."

"Wait, I don't have a sword!" He had forgotten that *Vintrave* was gone.

Korjan unsheathed one of his thinner swords. He inspected the edge before handing it to Kael. The blade was longer than *Vintrave*, not as wide, but just as light. Not nearly as extravagant, but sturdy all the same. It would take some getting used to; still, Kael was thankful to have the blade.

Luckily, it was easier for them to acquire a bow. Kael and Korjan stationed themselves just north of the western gate. It was a popular place for BlackHound soldiers to try and climb the wall, Korjan told Kael. As such, the Allegiance always had dozens of archers lining the wall. The moment they arrived, Kael and Korjan were handed arrows, then directed a further down the wall by a man with large ears.

They day was spent waiting for BlackHound soldiers to make an attempt at the wall. Only twice did Kael actually have to fire his weapon. Both times, the soldiers were killed by different arrows. Hour after hour dragged on and Kael found himself simply watching the war raging out in the fields.

Massive projectiles were flung from one force to the other throughout the day and screams were ever-present. Shatterbreath made a fleeting appearance to try and burn the BlackHound camp. Before she even reached it, Kael was started to see Silverstain swoop out of the clouds. They roared at each other for a long time before Shatterbreath finally retreated. At least, Kael reasoned, Silverstain was making no attempt of his own to burn the Allegiance army.

"It's been feeding them," Korjan told Kael him after Silverstain disappeared back into the clouds. "Shatterbreath brings us deer and likewise, that dragon brings them fish. A lot of fish."

"Has he made any attacks of his own?"

"No. Shatterbreath and our ballistae keep him at bay. Just like how they keep her away."

"Then we're at a stalemate."

Korjan shook his head. "Unfortunately not. It's hard to see it now, but the BlackHound is winning. They've started using…explosives of some kind."

Right then, fire bursted up from the middle of the battlefield. Korjan pointed at it.

"See there? They use small orbs of some kind. Throw it at groups if we're too close together. They're devastating."

Kael pondered. "An unfair advantage," he thought out loud. "That's something we need. We've got a defensive advantage, but we need more than that. We need an *offensive* advantage as well."

"As soon as you come up with one," Korjan grumbled, "you let us know."

Shatterbreath had begun to circle high above Kael. She roared down at him and he waved back. Hearing her voice gave Kael an idea. He didn't like it though so he decided to dismiss it. But as he watched the fierce battle, he found he couldn't forget it.

At noon, Kael and Korjan were relieved by the afternoon battalion. As Korjan explained, the combined forces had been split into two groups. One to fight in the morning, the other to fight until nightfall. The BlackHound Empire was doing something similar.

Although Kael hadn't even fought, the day had taken its toll on him. Being under the sun for so long had made him weak. Shatterbreath must have noticed him, for she came swooping down to land on a smashed-up building. Kael grimaced from the buffet of wind and dust she created.

"How was the fight?" she asked.

Kael studied the armour covering her body. Pieced together by breastplates and pauldrons. Korjan scowled and avoided looking at Shatterbreath. Did he blame her for Tooran's death?

"I'll see you tomorrow, Kael," Korjan said. He pointed a finger at Kael. "Eat lunch and then go to your room. Stay put and recover. You understand, boy?"

"Okay." Kael turned to Shatterbreath. "Fight? What fight? We just sat up on the wall, waiting for soldiers to come. I need a real fight."

Shatterbreath hummed, leaning towards him. Part of the wall crumbled and she found a new place for her paw. "You better learn patience, Tiny. Nobody's expecting you to beat the BlackHound

Empire on your own. Especially under your conditions. Recover first, then fight to your fullest."

Kael walked over and leaned against her tail, which was just touching the ground. "Silverstain is helping them," he stated.

Shatterbreath huffed. Smoke escaped her nostrils. "Indeed."

"I have an idea to turn this fight, Shatterbreath." Kael turned around to watch a catapult launch a boulder over Vallenfend's wall. It soared away and out of sight.

"What is it?"

Kael was considering going to the castle for his lunch. He didn't want to be near people. "Take us to the cave and I'll tell you."

She nodded and stretched her wings. Kael held tight to her tail and she lifted him up to place him on her back. With three mighty flaps, they were well on their way to her cave.

Chapter 21

"No," Shatterbreath snapped. "Never again."

As Kael prepared the coyote Shatterbreath caught him—something he'd never eaten before—he had relayed his plan to her.

"I knew you wouldn't like it." Kael took a bite of coyote. "Hmm. But we're getting killed out there, Shatterbreath. We need something to turn the tides—for good."

Her tail thrashed. "Not an option. Kael, the wyverns are peaceful. I will not allow them to be used for war."

"Not all of them!" Kael countered. "Only a half or a quarter of them. Their species should be fine. They have the Vigilant Five to protect them and there's more than enough to spare."

"They cannot be used for war. Not again."

Kael bent to pick up his spice can, but stopped. "Again?"

Shatterbreath winced. She huffed. "I lied when I said they couldn't support a rider. The empire which the Favoured Ones defeated used them as their mounts. Their war nearly killed them all. What remains of the wyverns is only a fraction of how many there used to be."

"I see." He fell silent for a spell, staring into the visor of his helmet which was lying nearby. "I still think my plan will work."

Shatterbreath slapped the can of spice out of Kael's grip with her paw. The force of her swipe also knocked off his gauntlet, cutting the back of his hand as well. Kael yelped and clutched it. Shatterbreath leaned in close, letting her smoky breath waft over him.

"No," she rumbled.

"Okay, okay. Sorry."

With the sound of scales sliding against stone, Shatterbreath stood up, casting him an acidic look before meandering closer to the entrance of her cave. She stomped on his can of spice, flattening it. Then, slowly, she sat down on her haunches, giving Kael a splendid view of her backside.

Kael turned his attention back to his meal. He could smell the spice wafting through the cave and wished he had some for the meat. Shatterbreath sneezed.

"How would we get them to come with us anyway?" Shatterbreath asked suddenly. She was still turned away.

"I don't know," Kael said between chews. "You can communicate with them, right?"

"I told you, they're more like horses than anything. They understand body language. I don't think I could convince so many to come with me. Flying through their trees is one thing. Fighting a war is another."

Kael frowned. She was right. There was no way to get them to come, even if Shatterbreath did agree with his plan. His heart sank. How were they going to win the war?

Once he was finished, Kael collected his things and stood up.

"Alright. I'm done. Let's head back."

"You don't have to fight any more today," she said longingly. "The rest of the day could be ours."

"I want to fight. I mean *actually* fight. I'm going to the front line, Shatterbreath."

"Very well." There was sadness in her voice, and her tail was dead still. "Let's go."

Bunda stumbled, nearly spilling the extra helping of stew she was bringing Kael. She cursed at the bump in the floor—the same one she always tripped on. Who designed this castle, anyway? Like a maze it was. With bumps and cracks and things sticking out for her to trip on. She cursed again. She missed her meat shop.

And why in the world was Kael's room near the top floor? Did they want her to huff and puff like an old dog? *Gods*, she thought life was difficult before Kael was enlisted.

At last, she reached Kael's room. She knocked three times and called his name. No reply. Odd, Korjan said Kael would be in his room, recuperating. She pushed open the door, peaked inside and swore. He wasn't there.

Of course he isn't there, Bunda thought bitterly. *As if he was going to listen to Korjan. Blasted boy is probably out fighting again.*

"He's going to get captured a second time," Bunda said out loud. She hurled the bowl of stew of the window. "Stubborn boy. Can't you learn the first time?" After a few more swears, she fell silent. The stink of Kael's room—the smell of perspiration and illness—won over and she had to leave.

She closed the door gently behind her, placing a hand against the grainy wood. It reminded her of her husband—he had always wanted to be a carpenter. A noise caught her attention. Blinking back tears, she focussed on the sound. Soft footsteps.

Curious, she followed the sound down the hallway and peaked around a corner. There was a man walking away from her, garbed in black robes. King's Elite? This high up the castle? Kael made it clear that nobody except his friends were allowed to be on that level.

The man rounded the corner. Bunda waited a heartbeat, the followed after him, doing her best to muffle her footsteps. She was impressed with her own stealth. Maybe *she* should have joined the King's Elite instead of being a cook for the war effort.

She peaked around the next corner and gasped. The man was gone! A click told her where he went. Zeptus's room was just right there. She smacked her forehead. He didn't disappear, he went in the room.

She was contemplating returning to her business until she realized she could hear a conversation through the crack in Zeptus's door. Silently, she sidled over until she was a hand's breadth away from the edge of the door.

Her breath caught as she heard the words, "...and the fat butcher?"

Zeptus. She never saw much of him. He usually kept to his quarters, only coming out to get food or relieve himself. Whenever she did see him, shivers still ran down her spine and a bad taste filled her mouth. She same taste made her choke right then.

"Negative." That must have been the King's Elite's voice. "We were lucky with Tooran. Dragons took him out for us."

"Hmm. What are you going to do about the others?"

228

"The boy will be easy to eliminate. Same with the Stockwin girl. We will catch them in battle. The blacksmith as well. The others might pose more trouble. That is, if you still intend it to be *silent.*"

"Yes. The BlackHound Empire is gaining ground. Soon, they may breach the city." Zeptus hesitated. "In the chaos, you and your men should be able to kill the others with ease. Until then, keep me posted, soldier. If any attempt is made, I want to hear about it first."

"What about Rundown?"

Bunda heard Zeptus sniff. "The dragon guards him close. Not much will escape her. Leave him be."

"Aye, sir."

Kill? What was Zeptus planning? And why? She needed to tell somebody...needed to warn...

Without warning, the door swung open towards Bunda, shielding her from the guard's view. She held her breath, frozen to the spot. The assassin seemed to stand there forever until finally, he moved off in the opposite direction. Bunda released her grip on the cleaver which she kept at her hip at all times.

As soon as the soldier rounded the corner, Bunda hurried off in the opposite direction. Her mind was racing. Who could she tell first? Korjan. She needed to find Korjan.

"Good evening," a voice croaked from behind.

Bunda winced. Taking a breath to compose herself, she faced Zeptus. He was standing there, wearing a complacent look, one hand resting against the open door.

Bunda faked a smile, but couldn't stop herself from cringing. "Oh, hello. I was just...bringing some stew to Kael. Got lost I'm afraid."

If Zeptus was angered by her eavesdropping, he did a swell job hiding it. "Better not let that happen again." A touch of spite in his voice betrayed his calm manner. "They'd behead you for being in the wrong part of the castle at the wrong time—under ordinary circumstances."

"When have circumstances *ever* been ordinary?"

Zeptus put his hand to his mouth thoughtfully and narrowed his eyes. "Indeed." He gave a short bow and the clasped his hands behind his back. "Have a good day, miss."

"Th—thank you." Bunda swallowed. "You too."

Bunda could feel Zeptus's purple eyes boring into her as she walked down the hallway. Once she turned the corner, she shivered for a long time, both frightened and disturbed. When she caught her breath at last, she headed down the castle. She needed to warn the others.

Before it was too late.

Kael slew another soldier and pushed the body aside, moving to the next man. He was in the battlefield, fighting with Arnoth's ranks. He was in a fury, slicing down any enemy that got in his way. He channelled the pain and hate from his torture into his weapon. Consequently, he ruined several blades and had to swap out often. There were more than enough lying around.

Friendly soldiers guarded his flanks. They were holding the ground in front of Vallenfend's western gate and right then, it was obvious that the BlackHound Empire's main concern was pushing through to capture the city. If that happened, it would be all over.

The soldiers that surrounded Kael were the best out of all the allies. More than once, Kael had spotted Vert, Clodde or King Henedral. He tried to avoid them. He was worried they'd send him back inside the city to rest. Kael didn't want to rest. He wanted blood.

Kael had to admit, he wasn't in his top fighting shape. He wasn't used to using unfamiliar swords and his body was still weak from his being tortured. As he fought, he discovered that when he used his ability to slow time, he couldn't carry through as well as before. It was as though his body was simply slower. Or was his ability failing? Had the BlackHound tortures suppressed it in a way? The magic inside his chest seemed dormant as well.

Several times, Shatterbreath came swooping down, killing a soldier that would have otherwise struck Kael. It always worried him when she did. For not long after she retreated back into the sky, all sorts of projectiles would whiz past seconds later. Large bolts or more ball-and-chain things. He still didn't know how they launched those. Modified catapults or ballistae probably.

He had lost count of his kills long ago. By the time the sun was preparing to set, he must have killed over a hundred soldiers. His ferocity had made him a target. It wasn't hard to tell. Soldiers would go out of their way to kill him. Luckily, he had chosen powerful allies to fight with. Alek and Morkay—he learned their names quickly. They were actually better fighters than Kael. As soldiers moved in to kill him, Alek and Morkay would cut them down. Kael was serving more of a distraction than anything. Occasionally, an Arnoth general assisted him as well. Kael hadn't learned his name. He had nicknamed him Plate, because his bald head shone like platemail and he refused to wear a helmet.

A smash accompanied by a scream caught Kael's attention. He backed behind Alek and Morkay to catch his breath, peering over their heads at the same time. A shape hulked above the regular soldiers, almost as tall as the few cavalry scattered around. Kael gasped as he realized it was a *person*.

"Champion!" Alek yelled.

The BlackHound Champion swung again, crushing a soldier's head with a hammer the size of a horse's head. Standing a head over Kael, he was almost as large as the masked giant in Wyrmguard and even more-heavily armoured than Nestoff's guards, girded head-to-toe in spiked armour with a helmet shaped like a wolf's open mouth. His armour was like grease, black with an iridescent shine and traced with gold. Kael marvelled at him. Each pauldron must have held enough metal to make a sizeable shield. Aside from his open visor, there wasn't a single spot on his body uncovered.

From in between the open maw of his helmet, Kael could see white teeth flashing through a tight grin as he snapped the back of a soldier over his knee. Besides that, his features were shadowed by his mask and dark skin.

"Stay back, Rundown," Morkay warned, holding his sword in front of Kael's chest. Until then, Kael hadn't realized that Alek and Morkay actually knew who he was.

231

Kael would have obeyed him, if he hadn't spotted the sword in the Champion's other hand. *Vintrave* looked like a dagger in his grip. Holding his current chipped sword high in the air, Kael gave his best war-cry.

The BlackHound Champion smashed through a soldier and ran another through with *Vintrave.* He spotted Kael and stopped to give him a twisted smile. He held up *Vintrave* and licked the blade, which was covered in blood. Kael bent lower, his brow furrowing in a disgusted scowl.

The Champion laughed and rushed at Kael. Alek jumped in the Champion's way, but the man knocked him aside with his hammer. Kael backed up, holding his shield up in front of him. Suddenly, the small piece of metal-studded wood seemed very inadequate.

Kael dove out of the way as the Champion brought down his hammer. The weapon *thudded* solidly against the ground. Coming out of a roll, Kael made an attack of his own. His blade bounced against the Champion's thick armour.

Ducking under a swing from the hammer, Kael made another attempt, sticking his sword into the Champion's armpit—a weak spot for most knights. The blade only hit more metal. This time, the BlackHound Champion's caught Kael in the gut and he was lifted off his feet.

Kael fell heavily to the ground, dazed and breathless. He caught his wits in time to see the blade coming down. He rolled onto his belly to dodge *Vintrave,* and then scrambled to his feet, simultaneously dodging the hammer as well.

Morkay came screaming in from the side and tackled into the Champion. It must have been like running into a wall. Morkay bounced off the side of the man's breastplate, sprawling out. It was enough to make the Champion step back. Kael saw an opportunity. He tackled right into the Champion's chest, shoving as hard as he could. Like Morkay, he too, bounced off.

This time, the Champion stumbled. He tripped on a body and crashed to his back. Kael leapt up to deliver a final strike, but a boot caught him in the chest. The Champion kicked him away, sending him sprawling.

Kael recovered at once. He brandished his weapon as the Champion slowly got back up to his feet. That was the Champion's weakness. It was hard for him to stand back up with all that metal. Kael needed to knock him over again.

A clap of thunder sounded off close overhead. Shatterbreath came roaring in, claws outstretched, teeth bared. The Champion, instead of backing off, only lowered his hammer, seizing the handle with both hands, with *Vintrave* still clutched by two fingers.

It became clear that Shatterbreath's intention was to catch the Champion with her jaws. But as she neared, the Champion brought up his hammer with great force.

And struck her against the side of her muzzle.

Kael could clearly see the surprise in her face, as well as the fragment of tooth that careened out of her mouth like a piece of shrapnel. Knocked askew, she tumbled out of the air, taking out clods of bloodied earth before sliding to a halt.

The Champion raised his hammer and yelled in triumph. Kael charged at him, but he whipped around, swinging his deadly hammer. Kael's shield saved his life. The force of the hammer shattered it to pieces. *Better it than my ribcage,* Kael thought as he reeled backwards. He fell to one knee, unable to breath. The wind had been knocked out of him and he gasped.

Before Kael could stop him, the Champion strode over to Shatterbreath and stabbed *Vintrave* into her shoulder, between her plates of armour. The blade halted only when it struck bone. Shatterbreath roared, blood and spittle flying from her mouth. When the Champion removed the blade, blood gushed out of the wound and flowed down her foreleg, staining her scales crimson.

He laughed maniacally and raised the blade to strike again. Shatterbreath swatted him before he could, receiving a long gauge in her foreleg. She snarled viciously and snapped at him, catching his hammer and part of his arm.

The Champion howled in pain. Before he could retaliate, Shatterbreath tightened her jaws and shook. The thick armour he was wearing didn't help at all as the dragon tore his arm off from the elbow. Casting both the hammer and the Champion's arm aside, Shatterbreath reared and launched herself into the air.

With her gone, the Champion, holding the bloody stump of what used to be his arm, turned back to Kael. Murder burned bright in his eyes. Kael caught his breath at last.

The Champion took a menacing step towards Kael. He didn't get any further as a screaming Morkay leapt onto his back. The Champion failed as Morkay yanked off his thick helmet. Kael watched in bewilderment as Morkay raised a dagger and buried it in the base of the Champion's neck.

The Champion spun around sharply, flinging Morkay from his back. Morkay hit the ground, and a second later was impaled by *Vintrave*. The Champion tried to stand back up to his full height, but faltered. To Kael's astonishment he succeeded the second time.

Once again, he turned back to Kael, blood gushing from the fresh wound. Kael rushed at him, but his sword only created sparks against that thick armour. The Champion was slowing down, but there was still considerable strength behind his attacks. Morkay's knife must have only nicked his jugular vein.

Kael stumbled over a body. It cost him. Time slowed as he realized what happened. In agonizing slow-motion, he registered that the BlackHound Champion had *Vintrave* raised. The sword was then moving towards Kael, and there wasn't anything he could do to stop it. It crawled towards him, relentless, sharp. He struggled to bring up his own blade in time. At the last moment, Kael's blade came between *Vintrave* and himself.

Vintrave cut straight through Kael's sword. The blade missed Kael's face by a finger's breadth, sinking into the dirt behind his head.

Time returned to normal with a flash. The two halves of Kael's sword fell to the ground. The BlackHound Champion laughed throatily, raising *Vintrave* for another attack.

Kael spotted something behind the Champion. Thinking fast, he rocked forwards and dove between the man's legs and snatched at it. His hand wrapped around the handle to a thick mace. Before he even realized what it was, he twisted around and smashed it against the back of the Champion's knee.

The massive soldier fell to that knee, giving Kael a clean shot to his unguarded head. Kael swung the mace. But it missed. The Champion fell to his stomach and the rolled onto his back. Kael fell forward, straight onto the awaiting tip of *Vintrave*.

There was a rush of power from deep within Kael's chest. Then he stopped, with the tip of *Vintrave* centimetres from his chest. Some sort of force held him away from the blade, keeping it from impaling him. At once, Kael understood why.

Vintrave was his sword.

It was meant for him.

Kael planted a foot on the Champion's stomach to regain his balance. He scowled at the man. "You presume to kill me with my own blade?" he snarled.

"Rundown," was the first and only word Kael heard the man say.

"Aye." With that, he caved in the man's skull with the mace. Then, reverently, he removed *Vintrave* from his grasp. Oh, it felt good to have his blade back. It was like regaining a piece of his soul. *It belonged with him.*

Strong arms seized Kael's shoulder. He resisted the urge to fight free himself once he realized it was Alek. "Come, Rundown. The BlackHound Empire advances. You have done enough for today."

Plate was there too. Together, he and Alek half-led half-carried Kael back towards Vallenfend. Through his sudden fatigue, Kael heard people cheering his name, shaking his hands. He tried to put a face to each handshake, but there were just too many people surrounding him. Amid the chaos, he recognized a single person. And his moustache so blonde it seemed white.

The voice he recognized too. How could he forget? It was the Captain's.

"Kael Rundown!" Captain Terra exclaimed. "Our paths meet once again. But I assure you, this time we are friends." He twitched in his certain way. He had given up his cap for a visor-less helmet. Kael shook with anger. "At last, I get to see some real battle! It will be an honour to die in combat."

235

Kael struggled for a long time to find words. How could he sum up his hatred for the Captain? It rivalled with his hate towards the BlackHound Empire. He quickly decided an appropriate response.

With both hands, Kael gripped *Vintrave* tight and ran the Captain through. His armour was useless against the enchanted edge. "Then let me help you," Kael whispered to him.

The Captain's moustache was flecked with blood. His eyes were wide and he started twitching violently—perhaps having a seizure.

Kael removed the blade and watched as the Captain collapsed. Kael was then enveloped by bodies and noise. Armour clanking, feet shuffling, voices swearing. He didn't care. He let himself be carried off, feeling a sense of fulfillment.

It had been a good day. He now had his sword back and the Captain was dead.

Good day indeed.

Chapter 22

"By the gods, what were you thinking, Kael?" Korjan screamed.

Kael was ignoring him, focussing instead on the deep wound in Shatterbreath's shoulder. While he had been fighting the Champion, Shatterbreath had flown to the training grounds where Cressida had sewn the wound shut. They were clean, practised stitches, but the wound was very deep. It would take a long, long time to fully heal. She would probably have muscle damage for the rest of her life. Of course, nobody had mention this to her.

"It's a good thing he didn't stab your wing muscles instead," Kael said, gently touching the swollen area around the wound. "Otherwise, you wouldn't have been able to escape."

Her eyes were dreamy. She had lost a lot of blood. "You better pay attention to your friends," she muttered. Her jaw was swollen too, where the Champion had struck her. The tooth behind her canine had shattered and her lip was cut badly. Kael couldn't imagine how much it hurt.

Kael rolled his eyes and face Korjan. They were in Shatterbreath's cave. Korjan wanted their conversation to be absolutely private. Vert, Sal'braan, Alek and Faerd were also frowning at him.

"What?" Kael said casually.

"Excuse me? 'What?' Aren't you paying attention?" Korjan's face was so red. "You disobeyed me. You nearly got yourself killed. You're clearly not in the right of mind. You're clearly not ready to be out in the battlefield. If you can't take—"

"Killing an ally isn't good for morale," Vert interjected. Korjan inhaled sharply and clenched his jaw. Vert continued. "Do you realize how many people saw you stab him? They are going to question your allegiance."

"Like King Henedral does?" Kael pointed out.

"Well, at least you know." Vert put a finger to his temple. "Right now, that is precisely what you want to avoid. You brought us all together, Kael. Everybody is looking to you right now. And because rumours of your capture spread fast, people are watching you *very* closely."

"If people think you've switched beaks to the BlackHound Empire," Sal'braan added, "this whole operation you have going could very well collapse."

"And everything you've worked for would come crashing in on you," Korjan said ominously. "You are—and always have been—the key to this war."

Vert clasped his hands behind his back and started pacing slowly around Kael. "As well, you should know what the consequences of deliberately slaying an ally are."

Kael caught a hint in his voice. He believed he already knew. Still, he asked, "What?"

"Death." Vert stopped pacing. Shatterbreath tucked her tail defensively around Kael. "Public execution by beheading. Every army enforces the same rule."

"Then here he is," Shatterbreath growled. "Come get him."

Korjan pointed at her. "You stay out of this! You are the *core* to all this. If it wasn't for you, Vallenfend would still have an army to fight with, Kael wouldn't have been tortured and Tooran would still be alive!"

Shatterbreath only hissed.

"Ah, just shut up!"

"Hey," Kael snapped, "don't you talk to her like that! Show some respect. You'd all be dead if it wasn't for her!"

"She's a bloody animal! I'll talk to her how I like."

A fierce argument broke out between Korjan, Kael and Shatterbreath. Somehow, Faerd and Vert were siphoned in as well. It got to the point where Kael just threw curses as loudly as he could. Alek and Sal'braan stood where they were, looking pale and out of place.

It was Korjan who made the first physical gesture. With a zealous curse, he pulled out an axe and hurled it at Shatterbreath. The blade bounced off her armour and fell uselessly to the ground. Kael doubted the attack would have made a mark in her scales anyway.

Shatterbreath rose to her feet and roared, silencing the argument. When she was finished, she snarled and leapt at Korjan. With one swat, she knocked him on his back.

"You have fifteen seconds to get out of my cave," she rumbled. "Leave now."

Korjan picked himself up and scowled at her for a long time, fists clenched. He spat and turned to leave. His gesture only infuriated Shatterbreath further.

She swung her tail at him and he was only just able to duck under it. It smashed against the cave wall, causing rocks to come loose from the ceiling. His expression changed from anger to terror and Korjan sprinted the rest of the distance out of the cave. Shatterbreath would have bounded after him if Kael hadn't called her back. She settled to breathing fire towards him before he slipped out of the cave.

Kael slumped to the ground, holding a hand to his forehead. He had the worst headache.

Shatterbreath lay down beside him, pouting.

"Please, Kael," Vert broke the silence. "Don't go killing any more of our own men. Okay? If you do it again, we will take your life."

Shatterbreath growled. Kael silenced her with a gentle touch. "I won't. Only the Captain, I swear."

"Alright." Vert coughed. "Well, on the plus side, you managed to take out a Champion. That one had been no end of trouble."

"Yes," Sal'braan said, beaming. "Killing a Champion is a very impressive thing, Rundown. Only two others have been slain so far. They will surely feel the loss. In the BlackHound Empire, you earn what you kill. Today, you are our Champion."

"Thanks, I think."

"Championslayer," Faerd said delicately, as if tasting the name. He crouched down close to Kael. "A mouthful, but suiting."

Kael gave him a weak smile. Faerd faltered. "Kael, your back."

Shatterbreath sniffed him. "You smell of blood."

Kael glanced over his shoulder. His tunic was stained red. "Hey, how about that." He tried to take off his breastplate, but couldn't because of the pain. "Could you...?"

Faerd helped Kael removed the breastplate. Vert produced a knife and cut Kael's tunic off, to his displeasure. Vert, Faerd and Shatterbreath all gasped in their own way as they spotted the gauges left on his back from his whippings.

"Feels as good as it looks, believe me," Kael remarked.

"We should get you to Cressida at once," Alek exclaimed. "She can heal your wounds."

Vert placed a hand on Kael's shoulder. Kael bit his tongue. "I hope you know," Vert said, "you won't be battle-worthy for several days because of this. You *have* to heal first. Shatterbreath, make me a promise you won't let him fight until he regains his strength, at least."

"Of course. I'm in no condition right now either. I'll keep him in check."

Kael gritted his teeth. *He was afraid of that.*

Chapter 23

Kael spent most of his time for the next few days in one of the hospital tents. Cressida looked after him, tending to his back and making sure he didn't strain himself. She also cleaned Shatterbreath's wounds too, which Kael found amusing. Shatterbreath terrified Cressida and she wasn't good at hiding it, no matter how hard she tried.

Shatterbreath spent most of her time in the air, watching the war and relaying anything interesting to Kael—though he didn't need her observations to tell that it wasn't going well for the Allegiance. Less and less soldiers showed up for their meals, while more and more filled the hospital tents. It was amazing, really, how Cressida was able to deal with them all and spend so much time with Kael.

Kael liked Cressida. She had spunk, like Bunda, but she was tougher. She was earnest and tried with all her heart to save the people that were regularly brought to her. More than once, Kael caught her crying over a soldier she hadn't been able to save. She talked a lot, but Kael didn't mind. He had a lot of time to listen. She did her best to teach him the ways of the healer's art as well—more than stitching a wound or making a sling, but more advanced things, such as what herbs contained healing properties and how to tell if a bone was either fractured or broken. Kael didn't have a knack for it, but she never lost patience.

Eating meals had become the biggest task for Kael. The first meal, he grabbed his food and simply stood there for a long time, unsure where to go. He scanned the crowds of soldiers, either standing or sitting on the ground as they ate. He felt so out of place.

He would have stood there longer if Alek hadn't come by and invited Kael to sit with him. They strode through the training grounds, weaving in between the soldiers, until they had come to a wide circle of boisterous men. They all bore Arnoth crests. Alek had joined right in, talking and laughing in between bites. Kael didn't feel any more welcomed they he had to start out with. He awkwardly slunk in between two soldiers and tried to avoid attention.

He was thankful Alek didn't make a deal of introducing him. Halfway through his meal, Kael quietly excused himself and found a secluded spot near the schoolroom-like building where he had received instructions from the Captain so long ago. He had eaten lunch in solace.

Three days later, he still ate his meals near the school building, but no longer alone. Faerd and Laura would join him for supper— they were both in the morning garrison—and sometimes Janus Morrindale as well. Kael found Laura's interactions with the princess more interesting than any conversation they shared. Laura didn't seem to know how to handle herself near Janus. She never once looked the princess in the eye. Was she jealous Kael had more interest in the princess than he did in her? Didn't she belong to Faerd now?

During his recovery, Kael only saw Korjan twice. The blacksmith ignored him both times and hurried on his way from one end of the training grounds to the other. He and Kael only exchanged glances once. His expression had been unreadable.

Kael had plenty of time to think throughout the day. He found wyverns taking up the vast majority of his thoughts. He was positive that if they could get the wyverns to help, the Allegiance would certainly win. But the question put up by Shatterbreath remained: how? As he lay in bed one night, a prospect dawned on him. *Zeptus.* With Skullsnout's magic, they had been able to control BlackHound soldiers. Could they do the same thing with the wyverns—but with Shatterbreath acting as the communicator instead of Zeptus?

His mind raced at the possibility. Would it be possible for Shatterbreath to *borrow* Zeptus's power, in a similar way as Kael could borrow her strength or vision? As much as this new revelation excited him, the night was late. He settled that at the crack of dawn, he would find Shatterbreath and relay his thoughts to her. Maybe she would be convinced yet.

Before the morning came, however, Kael was jarred awake by a commotion; a rattling *boom* then *whoosh*. He shot to the window of his room and glanced out. Torches. Many hundreds of them towards the west. Even as he watched, several explosions lit up the night sky

242

for but a fraction of a second. The explosions were focussed around a single building. Even from where he was, Kael could hear wooden beams being wrenched apart and see the haze caused by its destruction. The explosions illuminated suits of armour that shined like iridescent beetle carapaces.

Kael watched as BlackHound soldiers poured into the city. He was as confused as he was horrified. What was happening down below?

He snatched up *Vintrave,* which he kept at his bedside every night, but stopped himself before he reached the door. He couldn't fight. The scabs all over his back were tender, any exertion would split them open and he'd be right back where he was a week ago.

So instead, he leaned out the window again, watching the progress. There was fighting in the street where the Allegiance had engaged the BlackHound Empire. The swiftness of the BlackHound attack, as well as their numbers was winning over. The three catapult stations Kael could see from the castle had already been overrun or destroyed.

Kael whistled as loud as he could. Not three seconds after he finished, Shatterbreath flew in and clung onto the castle's side. Her eyes were wide and her scales bristling. "The BlackHound Empire has broken through the wall!" she exclaimed. "Quickly, Tiny, they are taking the castle this very moment! The order of retreat has already been made."

Shivers ran down Kael's spine. He could hardly believe it. It almost seemed like a dream.

Kael climbed over her shoulder, but not to the middle of her back where he usually went. Clinging tight to her scales, he leaned as far forwards as he dared so he could watch the happenings below.

"Hold on, Tiny!" Shatterbreath warned. She launched off the surface of the castle, pointing straight to her mountain.

"Wait!" Kael shouted. "Lend me your vision. We have to make sure my friends get out too! Find them, get them!"

"It is too dangerous!"

"Just do it! Check the streets first, then head back to the training grounds. Quickly!"

243

Shatterbreath rumbled in annoyance and twisted her body. She dropped down low and swept over Vallenfend, her claws almost grazing the tops of the buildings. Kael was thrust into her vision and she began scanning the crowds at a dizzying rate. Kael sensed her muscles underneath him tighten as she spotted a friend.

"Grab her! Grab her!"

With a roar, Shatterbreath dove into the crowds, knocking most of them over with her wings and body to pluck Laura out of the chaos with her talons. She reached back and placed Laura on her back, still scanning the crowds.

"Kael!" Laura gasped. She threw her arms around him. "What's happening?"

"The BlackHound Empire broke through somehow. They're attacking with everything they've got." He paused. "We're going to lose the city."

"What can we do?"

"Get as many people out as we can. Where's Faerd?"

"I don't know. You haven't seen him?"

She screamed as Shatterbreath lunged to snatch somebody up with her mouth. She craned her neck to flick Korjan onto her back. Kael grabbed him before he slipped of Shatterbreath's breastplate armour. He was unconscious. With Laura's help, Kael placed Korjan in the middle of Shatterbreath's back, nestled between two protruding spines.

A moment after they had finished, Alek joined them, this time caught by Shatterbreath's tail. He screamed as she alighted on a building, dumping him on the roof. She crouched low and Kael caught his hand to pull him too onto her back. His face was white and he was unresponsive to Kael's voice. Shock. Kael placed him behind Korjan.

Without warning, Kael was in Shatterbreath's vision. She focussed on a large group of Allegiance soldiers, fleeing eastward. Then to the castle, where the BlackHound Empire was heading almost unheeded towards.

"Get to the training grounds!" Kael yelled to her. She didn't need to be told.

She soared over the high wall, which seemed to be giving the BlackHound soldiers no end of trouble. Allegiance soldiers were manning the walls, shooting arrows down and dropping pitch. It wouldn't be long until the castle—Vallenfend's last stronghold—would be overrun.

Shatterbreath landed heavily in the middle of the training grounds, spooking several horses. Kael stood up on her back. His heart jumped as he beheld the crowd moving towards them.

Perhaps through instinct, Shatterbreath roared at the incoming crowd. They stopped at once. They were mostly unarmed women. The quarter or so of the cooks and medics who hadn't been able to evacuate before the BlackHound Empire reached the castle. They must have closed the doors once the enemy soldiers got close.

Among them, Kael spotted Cressida. Somehow, she heard her name over the screams and pleas as he called out to her. She pushed her way through the crowd as Kael jumped down from Shatterbreath's back.

"Kael, we're trapped!" she cried, collapsing in his arms. "The doors are locked, we're surrounded. There's no escape!"

"Don't worry," Kael said, "we can get you out. Shatterbreath can carry you."

Shatterbreath nudged Kael from behind. "Not this many," she whispered to him. Her eyes were darting, sizing up the crowd. "I can only take ten, maybe fifteen at a time with all this metal on my back."

"How many people are there?"

Cressida was flustered, but she had regained her balance. She wiped tears from her eyes. "Uh, thirty, forty?"

"Forty-two," Shatterbreath corrected.

Kael held the dragon's muzzle. "Then we'll have to make three trips. The castle's defences should hold up until then." He turned to Cressida and helped her climb onto Shatterbreath. "Take as many as you can safely. Fly as fast as you can. I'll be waiting here for you when you get back."

"No, Tiny. Get on. I'm taking you first."

Kael ushered the people towards her. "No, Shatterbreath. There's somebody I need to find first."

She huffed. "Kael..."

A dozen people had already climbed on. Kael shook his head. "No time to argue. Just go."

She bared her gleaming teeth at him before taking off. "She'll return," Kael assured the rest of the crowd, "stay here and wait for her." He thought for a moment. "Does anybody know where Zeptus is?"

"He was in the castle last, Kael!" Janus squeezed through the crowd. "Nobody has seen him exit yet. He's probably still in there somewhere."

Kael squeezed her hand. "Thanks, Princess. I need to go find him. Stay here."

Leaving them behind, he sprinted to the castle and flung open the doors—and was nearly skewered by an arrow.

"Easy, archers!" Plate yelled. "Rundown, what are you still doing here? You must get out at once."

"I could ask the same question," Kael said, working his way around the line of twenty archers.

"Kill as many as we can," Plate replied, cocking his head. "The city belongs to the BlackHound Empire now. It won't be long until we've lost the castle too. Whatever you forgot better be important up there."

"Believe me, it is." Kael saluted him. "Fight well."

"To you too, Rundown. It was a pleasure."

Those last words echoed through Kael's mind as he made his way deeper into the castle. He would never even know Plate's real name.

He went as fast as his body would allow. The scabs had all but healed, but the scars were still very tender. He did his best to ignore the discomfort. As he passed a window halfway up, he spotted Shatterbreath landing in the middle of the castle grounds. Her second trip. He needed to hurry.

By then, he had learned his way quite well through the castle. In record time, he was nearing the top floor—where he hoped Zeptus would be. He would have headed straight for the man's study if it hadn't been for the splotch of blood he espied on the wall. There was more blood on the floor, tracing a path along the floor. Cursing, he went down that hallway to follow the trail.

"Zeptus?" he called out. "Are you here? Anybody? We need to evacuate at once, the BlackHound Empire is—"

Somebody nearby took a haggard breath and Kael's heart leapt. Clutching his chest, he turned the corner and found the source of the sound. It was Zeptus. Blood utterly lined the hallway, splattered on the walls and flecked across the ceiling. Great pools of it surrounded the former advisor, streaming out a huge gash in his stomach which he held with both hands, struggling to keep his innards inside his body.

Bunda was standing beside him, holding a stained cleaver. There was another man lying off to the side, garbed in black and obviously dead. Bunda had a cut across her forehead, so deep that her eyebrow was almost hanging over her eye. He winced when she spotted Kael and snatched at her loose brow.

"No!" Kael shouted. He rushed over to Zeptus, but his hands stayed away, shaking. "No, no, NO! Bunda, what have you done? Zeptus, stay with me, stay alive. Bunda, what happened here?"

"He was planning on killing me and the others. Kael, you have to believe me!" The cleaver fell from her grip, making a wet *clang* in the fresh blood. "He was going to do it tonight, I heard him talking to that bloke!" She pointed at the body nearby.

"That's absurd! Why would he want to kill us?" Kael reached behind Zeptus's neck and tried to prop him up. Zeptus groaned as he did, heavy lids all but covering his purple eyes. "No, you can't die, Zeptus, we need you more than ever! You are the key to winning this war, you can't die now!"

"He's a traitor, Kael!" Bunda cried. She bent over and picked her cleaver back up. "He's been plotting to kill us all along! He's evil, I always knew it! He used you like he used everybody else! But he wouldn't fool me. I saw through his words. I got him before he got me."

247

The hallway suddenly seemed so tight. So hard to breathe in. Kael held Zeptus closer. His face was paler than it ever had been. He was going to die, and there was nothing Kael could do to stop it.

"For once in your life," Kael growled, "tell me the truth, Zeptus. Is she correct? Were you going to kill my friends?"

Zeptus's eyes found focus on Kael. A grin spread across his lips. When he inhaled, Kael could hear gurgling in his chest. "Never. This was all...for me."

Kael's throat seized. He couldn't find words.

Zeptus actually laughed. It was haunting. "After all these years of convincing people to kill each other, it was easy to convince someone to kill *me*. I shall have my peace."

If Kael clenched his teeth any tighter, they would have shattered. "Why now?"

"If the BlackHound wins, I am a dead man. Allegiance, the same. Why prolong the inevitable?"

Kael rested him back against the wall. Zeptus was still alive, but well on his way out.

"K—Kael?" Bunda muttered. Her voice never sounded so frightened.

"You've killed out last chance." He was helpless as the life slowly drained out of Zeptus. A clap of thunder made Kael perk up. "Hold on, maybe not yet!" He darted to the window and threw it open. Shatterbreath was descending into the castle grounds.

His mind was racing. He whistled. His plan could very well still work. But they needed to work quickly, before Zeptus died. He whistled again. Shatterbreath angled away from the remaining people waiting to be evacuated. They didn't seem too happy about it either. In a few strong wing beats, she was clinging to the side of the castle wall.

"What is it, Tiny?" she asked worriedly. "What is—oh. What happened? Is he still alive?"

"He tricked Bunda into this." Kael placed his hand to Zeptus's neck. His heartbeat was faint. Very faint. "We must hurry, Shatterbreath, before he dies! We have to take his ability!"

Bunda coughed. "Excuse me?"

Shatterbreath shook her head. "Who would take it Kael? It is a curse, not a blessing. You already have an ability of your own—not to mention Skullsnout's magic." Kael looked hopefully to her. "And there is no *way* I'm taking it."

"What are you talking about?" Bunda asked.

Kael ignored her. "Shatterbreath, we *need* his ability to convince the wyverns to help us. It is the only way." She tried to speak, but he interrupted her. "Even if you disagree with that, you *have* to realize the importance of his power. We cannot just let it...let it slip away!" An idea struck Kael and he reached over to seize Bunda's arm. "You earn what you kill. Shatterbreath, put it in her."

Her nostrils flared. She scowled at the dying Zeptus. "I don't know if it can even be done. She is no favoured one. She holds not the connection you and I do. I don't even know where to begin."

Zeptus's body was beginning to relax. "It's now or never, Shatterbreath." Kael ushered her to come closer.

"Bring him to me," the dragon muttered. "We might as well try."

"Bunda, give me a hand."

The butcher gave him a sceptical look. "Why? What are you going to do? Put *what* in me? What are you talking about, 'his ability?' I think I deserve to know."

"Just obey!" Shatterbreath snapped, curling her lips.

Bunda's face turned as white as Shatterbreath's canines. Wordlessly, she bent lower and with a look of disgust overwhelming her face, pressed her hands against his chest, just below either collarbone. Kael in turn squeezed her shoulder and placed a hand against Shatterbreath's snout.

The rush of energy between them was strong.

Zeptus's eyes snapped open. He convulsed and blinked rapidly. Bunda tried to pry her hands away, but a force held her fast. Shatterbreath hummed a tuneless song and closed her eyes. With the rise and fall of her voice, surges of energy flowed between the four bodies. It seemed to work its way through all of them in turn, trying to find what they sought. Zeptus's dying body seized again as the full force of the energy pierced deep into him.

249

Then, from the inside, it tore its way out. White light burst from Zeptus's eyes and mouth. Where Bunda had placed her hands against him shone like intense fire—so bright, Kael had to turn his own eyes away. Kael could hear Bunda scream, but it sounded distant. Then, abruptly, it all stopped, leaving behind a lasting whistle, like the sound of metal striking metal and a strange smell that reminded Kael of freshly chiselled stone.

Bunda collapsed, Kael stumbled and even Shatterbreath almost lost her footing against the wall. Zeptus's body went completely slack and Kael knew at once he was dead.

Curious, Kael leaned over the body. His eyes...they were now blue. Seeing that caused a stirring in his chest Kael couldn't describe. It was as if for the first time ever, he truly knew Zeptus— only through death.

"D—did it work?" Kael found his voice first.

Shatterbreath cocked her head and huffed, sending warm air flooding into the chilly hallway. "I think so. Only time will tell right now. But right now, we don't have *time* to spare. The BlackHound advances."

Bunda lay on her back, twitching slightly. Kael lifted her eyelids, curious, but her pupils were rolled to the back of their sockets. With some difficulty, he hefted her unconscious body onto Shatterbreath, then climbed aboard himself.

Leaving the castle wall, Shatterbreath angled down towards the stragglers. She landed in their midst, knocking a few women over with her wings. She had been more affected than Kael thought.

Kael helped the peopled climb up, scanning their numbers as he did. *Eighteen.* Eighteen was too much. She didn't tell Shatterbreath. From her sour expression, he could tell she knew.

As he pulled up the second to last person, an explosion rocked the gate, sending a fireball pluming high into the night sky. Every face turned towards it. A second after the first fireball, another explosion blew the gate apart, sending foot-long pieces of wood showering.

Kael pulled the last person up roughly and yelled at Shatterbreath to take off. Bobbing her head from the effort, she beat her wings as hard as she could, only rising by a matter of a few feet with each stroke. It wasn't nearly enough.

The BlackHound soldiers shot arrows at them as they lifted off. Most bounced off Shatterbreath's breastplate armour—proving it a good investment after all. A few arrows struck the passengers on Shatterbreath's back and they tumbled off, crashing to the ground below. As terrible as it was, the loss of weight allowed Shatterbreath to fly with greater ease.

Before more than five people were killed, she was out of the archers' range. She started towards the mountain but Kael stopped her.

"Head north first," she shouted to her, pointing to corroborate. "They'll be expecting you to go due east again."

She banked sharply, doing as Kael suggested. As hard as she tried, she couldn't keep her altitude. She slowly dipped downwards until her claws grazed a tall rooftop. At the next roof, she had to rebound off of it, gaining more altitude at the expense of her passengers' comfort. She did this three or four times before they were finally clear of the city.

It was inevitable that she had to land. By then, they were out of ballistae range and well away from any soldiers. Still, Shatterbreath bounded across the land rather stiffly, inhibited by her injured leg. After a few more kilometres of going in a northeast direction, she stopped near the base of the mountain.

Panting heavily, she crouched low to let her passengers climb off. Kael jumped off as well to hold her muzzle in his arms. "You did well," he told her.

Her exhalations ruffled his pant legs. She nodded her head slightly. "As always. We'll have to camp here for the night. I am fatigued."

As the passengers—none of whom Kael knew or recognized—picked clean spots just inside the forest to sleep, Kael and Shatterbreath stayed out in the fields, sheltered by a tall pine tree. She curled up against it while he sat down against her neck.

"I'll keep watch for awhile," he assured her. "Get some rest."

She turned her head to regard him with one emerald eye. "The BlackHound took a large bite today, one that might've mortally wounded us."

Kael clenched his jaw. "Yeah."

"We cannot lose this war, Kael." She lifted her head off the ground. "We have to wound them worse than they've wounded us. We cannot do it alone."

"Are you saying...?"

"To make a bite that lasts, we need the help of the wyverns." There was a pained expression on her muzzle as she considered her own words. "Tomorrow we will check if transferring Zeptus's ability worked, return these people to the camps and then set off to the Grove of the Vigilant Five."

Kael laughed. "Bunda won't be happy about that."

Shatterbreath gave him a strange look then placed her muzzle back on the ground. "For the wyverns' sakes," she muttered, closing her eyes, "I hope this plan of yours works, Tiny."

Kael took a deep breath. A gently breeze carried the comforting smell of the hayfields, which could not be overpowered by Shatterbreath's earthy musk. The wheat rustled in the wind and a shiver ran the length of Kael's spine.

For all their sakes, he hoped his plan worked.

Chapter 24

Kael snapped awake when whatever he was resting against suddenly fell away. Shatterbreath nuzzled him with her snout, humming.

"Great watchman we have," she mused. "Very vigilant."

"Did you sleep well?" he asked.

She stretched her wings and hummed louder. "Very. Your fire-headed friend has awoken as well. See to her and then let's be off."

Kael walked up the grassy slope a short ways to where the group had camped. From their slumping bodies and lack of conversation, Kael guessed none of them slept much. There was one person that was very active however.

Bunda was sitting against a mossy boulder, holding her hands over her face and muttering feverishly. Kael approached her carefully, squatting down nearby.

"Bunda?" The sound of his voice halted her chattering.

"Kael? Kael, is that you? What did you do to me?"

"How are you feeling?" Kael asked, dodging the question.

"My eyes, my eyes..." Bunda squeezed her fingers tight against her scalp. "Purple...purple... They haven't gone purple, have they? My eyes? Oh, Kael, say it isn't so! I don't want purple eyes! I don't want to be like him! Please, take it away!"

"Relax, relax." Kael touched her hand and she winced. "Remove your hands. Let me see."

Shivering, she removed her hands gingerly, but kept her lids shut tight. Somebody had sewn the gash over her eyebrow closed through the night.

"Let me see," Kael coaxed.

She opened her eyelids and stared at Kael, blinking several times. "Well?"

"Still brown," Kael told her. He took note, however, that a foreign colour seemed to be creeping in from the edges of her irises. Would they *turn* purple yet? Even that added smidge of violet made Bunda seem so different.

Of course, he didn't tell her. It would only make her more worried.

Kael instructed the people to pack up their things, which didn't take very long. Only two people had grabbed blankets, the rest slept on the ground. In no time at all, they were all piled on Shatterbreath again.

Their weight was still too much for her to fly with, so she half-flew, half-bounded along the forest's border towards the Allegiance camps. If the city was to be taken, Vert had proposed the armies gather where Arnoth had first made camp, and set strong defences. Kael never thought they'd ever have to follow his advice. When they arrived, he was glad to see that Vert's foresight had paid off.

They had set up many makeshift tents in the short time they had been their already, most of which Kael was guessing housed the injured. There were several dozen ballistae set up, their metal tips gleaming in the morning sun. There were no fires, for they wanted to keep their location hidden as long as they could—which would actually be easy to do. They were deep enough in the forest so that enemy projectiles wouldn't be effective. From the sky, it was nearly impossible to see anything that would reveal the area as the Allegiance camp. If Shatterbreath hadn't have known where it was, they might not have been able to find it.

Shatterbreath swooped in low, landing as quickly as she could to avoid revealing their position to enemy sentries. She just fit through the gap in the trees. As soon as she touched ground, her passengers practically leapt off. Some of them even fell to their hands and knees to kiss the ground. Kael rolled his eyes. They hadn't even been *flying*.

Clodde was the first to greet Kael and Shatterbreath. "Hail!" he cried, waving at them.

"Hail." Kael slipped off Shatterbreath to clasp his hand. "Where's Vert?"

Clodde put a hand to his chest. "Vert...didn't make it, Rundown. His horse was hit in the neck by an arrow as he fled. He stayed with it as it died. The BlackHound soldiers overwhelmed him. There was no escape."

"Oh," was all Kael could manage.

"I'm glad to..." Clodde's voice cracked. "Ahem. I'm glad you all made it out okay. You two saved many lives."

"We may yet save a great many more," Shatterbreath rumbled. Her tail was thrashing and she kneaded the ground underneath her talons. Was she as excited for Kael's plan as he was?

"Assemble the leaders," Kael ordered Clodde. "We have much to discuss. I believe I have a way to turn this battle."

Clodde looked between Kael and Shatterbreath a few times. He nodded. "Aye, I'll send runners at once. Stay here, please."

"Is Kael there?" King Henedral appeared through the trees. King Respu, Sal'braan and Korjan appeared shortly after.

"I guess we don't have to assemble them after all," Clodde chirped.

"I'm glad to see that you're unharmed," King Henedral said calmly, clasping Kael's arm.

"And you as well, mighty Shatterbreath," King Respu added.

Shatterbreath gave him a short bow—more of bob of her head than anything.

"The BlackHound Empire has taken the city," King Henedral said, folding his arms. "They killed many of our men that day as well. We don't have enough troops to take it back."

"With their taking of the city, they may have just won this war," Sal'braan sighed. "There is no way we can take it back—even if your reinforcements arrive."

It took Kael a moment to realize what he was referring too. He had completely forgotten about Nestoff. He didn't even know if they *would* be coming.

"We will take the city back," Shatterbreath declared confidently. "With the help of the wyverns."

King Respu's face lit up. The others frowned. Korjan's expression remained steady, as if they had just suggested something crazy and he was choosing to ignore it.

King Henedral spoke first. "Excuse me? What is a wyvern?"

"A smaller dragon," King Respu told him, corroborating with his hands. "Sharp teeth, sharp claws, but no front legs. They rely most on their wings to hunt and move about."

"As all dragons should," Shatterbreath added.

"We have to leave at once," Kael said firmly, "so you will be without Shatterbreath for a matter of days. Can you last that long?"

Clodde rubbed one of his sideburns. "That depends on so much. Our aim is limited under the trees and right now, the blue dragon is our biggest threat. It could give away our position to the BlackHound or just burn us down. Without her here, there isn't much else we can to do stop it from doing either—or both."

"We will have to be swift then," Shatterbreath exclaimed. The thrill of adventure was thick in her voice. "Besides, I see no other option here."

"Vert told me to think of a way to turn the tides," Kael further explained. "I believe this is exactly it. Unless anybody has...a better idea?"

The men murmured, but nobody said anything coherent.

"I thought not."

Clodde clapped his hands together. "We'll prepare accommodations for your journey," he announced. He then headed off, yelling commands to the bystanders who had collected.

Muttering something intelligible, King Henedral walked off as well.

"Take me with you," Korjan said suddenly. The first words he had spoken to Kael in days.

Shatterbreath growled. Kael folded his arms. "Why?" he asked.

"I'm sorry that I yelled at you. I'm sorry for how callous I've been lately. To you as well...Shatterbreath." He bowed his head. "Tooran's death has weighed heavily down on my shoulders. For a time, I was overwhelmed with grief. It muddled my thoughts and made me angry. I was selfish; I am not the only one who has lost a loved one to this war. Y—you've lost even more than me, Kael. I'm trying to make amends. I want to help. I understand if you don't want me to—"

"We don't," Shatterbreath snapped. Kael tried to protest, but she interrupted him with a snort. "The wyverns can be quite temperamental. They are friendly to dragons, and therefore the Favoured Ones. As you are neither, I cannot predict what their reaction to you would be. It is for your safety."

It took a few seconds for Shatterbreath's words to sink in. Korjan frowned, but nodded. "I understand."

"Wait, what about me? I don't want to get eaten!" Bunda exclaimed. "I'm not a favoured whatever."

"You've been one for about half a day now," Shatterbreath countered.

The blood drained from her face. "How about that then..."

"A safe journey to you three." Sal'braan gave them a strange salute. "The best of luck."

Kael hesitated. "Before we go...I need to know what happened to the others—the ones we didn't save. Is Tomn okay? And Faerd and Helena and Mrs. Stockwin?"

Sal'braan nodded. "They all made it out, Rundown. Your friend, Faerd, was struck by an arrow as he fled. He is in a serious condition, but he will survive."

A rush of air escaped Kael's lungs. He nodded. "Thank you. We go as fast as we can. Stay strong."

Clodde arrived with a large bag. He passed it to Kael, who passed it to Shatterbreath. Gently, she gripped it with her teeth and placed it on her back, behind Bunda. The butcher tied it down to her armour.

Kael said his thanks then climbed aboard Shatterbreath and sat in the crook of her shoulders, just in front of Bunda. The dragon flared her wings and rose up on her hind legs. She was about to roar but stopped herself. Having to do so seemed to upset her and she huffed in a humorous way.

"Alright," Kael said with a laugh, "let's go. You can roar once we're on the *other* side of the mountain."

She sniffed. "It's not the same."

257

With a powerful leap, she was just above the forest canopy. She skimmed the tops of the trees and did a wide loop before rising. Hopefully, that would keep the camp's location safe for the time.

Shatterbreath ascended up the mountain, slowing down when they neared her cave. "Last chance," she yelled behind. "Do you need anything?"

"A bag!" Bunda replied.

"For what?" Kael scoffed.

Bunda's focus was glued to Shatterbreath's wings. "To throw up in! I'm not a flyer, Kael!"

Shatterbreath reached the peak of the mountain just then. The fog was so thick, Kael could barely see Shatterbreath's horns out in front of him. But rather suddenly, it gave away, giving the trio a dazzling view of the backside of the mountain. From their height and angle, it looked far steeper than it actually was.

Letting loose her pent-up roar, Shatterbreath angled her body down the slop and tucked her wings in slightly. They picked up speed swiftly and soon, they were rocketing towards the base of the mountain. The wind screeched like a banshee in Kael's ears and he had to put an arm to his face. He became aware of another sound and glanced back. Bunda had her mouth wide open, screaming. Tears streamed from her face.

Shatterbreath cut her diagonal dive close. Within metres of hitting flat ground, she pulled out. The membrane of her wings rippled, sounding like a flag caught in fierce wind.

Once they levelled out, Shatterbreath roared again.

Kael chuckled. When he spotted Bunda lying flat on her back behind him, he began laughing hysterically. She had fainted! Curious, Shatterbreath glanced back as well. In her own dragon way, she started laughing too.

They caught each other's gaze. Shatterbreath rumbled. "We could just leave it all behind, you know," she said. "Right now."

For a moment, Kael was tempted. She had said something similar to her before, but this time was different. He truly debated his options. Last time, the decision had been quite clear. But this time... Kael frowned. "We could," he muttered. "But...no. We won't." That was his only argument. He couldn't think of anything else.

Shatterbreath nodded. "Then we won't. For now, let us enjoy our temporary freedom. Before we are bound by war once again."

Kael played at a scuff in his breastplate armour. *Bound by war.*

They flew for the rest of the day without stopping. Kael and Bunda even ate the lunch Clodde prepared for them while sitting on her back. It wasn't comfortable by any means sitting on plate mail for hours on end, but they made excellent time. In the week it took Kael and Shatterbreath to reach the Arnoth mountains, they had made it in a mere day.

As the sun began to set, Shatterbreath started looking for a place to stay for the night. Remembering the incident with the Bloodwolves, they decided to just stay in the fields to the west of the mountains.

Kael and Bunda threw down their bedrolls as Shatterbreath curled up nearby. She closed her eyes and after a few minutes, her breathing became heavy and slow. Kael knew better though—she was still awake.

"What exactly did you do back there in the castle, Kael?" Bunda whispered.

"We gave you Zeptus's ability to control people."

"H—how? Isn't that just a...talent? Like being a painter or writer?"

Kael shook his head and repositioned himself so he could see her better. "Not with him, no. It's difficult to explain, but a long time ago, the dragons gave a group of humans wonderful gifts—magical abilities—in order to accomplish a certain...task."

Bunda pulled her bedroll closer, entranced.

Kael continued. "Once they accomplished their task, these people—known as the Favoured Ones—turned on the ones who gave them their power."

"They turned on the dragons?" Bunda asked incredulously.

Shatterbreath huffed, as if there was something caught in her throat. She continued to pretend to be sleeping. Kael understood her message. He was telling Bunda too much.

"Long story short, Zeptus was a descendant of the Favoured Ones. I am as well. We inherited their powers." He left out the fact that Zeptus's ability had been flawed.

Bunda's eyes went wide. "You?" She barely said the word. "B—but you said the Favoured Ones attacked the dragons. How come you and Shatterbreath get along so well?"

Kael studied the butcher for a moment. It suddenly occurred to him how white her orange mop of hair had become. Although she had lost weight, the wrinkles in her face were deeper. She was so much different than the woman he once knew.

"I don't know," he said at last with a shrug. "Call it fate."

"Hmm. So if Zeptus's gift was persuasion...what's yours?"

Kael had never told anybody before. He supposed that Bunda had the right to know. "Time slows in my perspective, giving me a huge advantage in battle."

She whistled. "Wow. I always thought magic was out there somewhere, just...never so close to home."

"We have a long day ahead of us. You better get some sleep, Bunda."

The butcher nodded and slipped deeper into her bedroll. Kael rolled onto his side, trying to get comfortable on the rocky ground. After a few minutes of tossing and turning, Bunda spoke again.

"Kael?"

"Yeah?"

"Do you think this will work? Getting flying lizards to help us..."

Kael grimaced, but Shatterbreath was already asleep. She wouldn't have been happy to hear Bunda call the wyverns that. "Of course."

Or at least, he *hoped* so.

The next day was almost an exact replica of the latter half of the previous. They just flew, for hours on end. Only the landscape changed. Along their way, Shatterbreath descended into a ravine containing several lakes. They had missed this area during their previous flight to the grove; before, they came northeast from

Silverstain's cave. This time they flew southeast from Arnoth's mountains.

"Look at that," Kael exclaimed, pointing towards the water below. An especially large fish cleared the surface, making an impressive splash as it hit the water.

"It just ate a bird."

Kael furrowed his brow. "Really? No way. I don't believe you."

"Are you saying I'm lying? Whose vision is better?"

"Fine, bring us down. I want to see up close."

"How about not?" Bunda piped.

Shatterbreath huffed and banked to the right. Moving in wide circles, she descended until they were only a few metres above the surface of the water. The lakes were far vast than Kael had thought. This one alone was the thrice the size of Vallenfend. The water was a charming turquoise colour and the banks lined with thousands of bulrushes. Herons and kingfishers roamed amongst the plants, snapping up water snakes and frogs. There were no ducks or geese though, Kael noted.

"Over there," Shatterbreath announced, pointing her muzzle to the side. A swallow was skimming the surface. A shadow was forming underneath the water. A massive fish jumped out of the water, mouth wide. The swallow disappeared behind a row of finger-length teeth and the man-sized fish hit the water.

"Now *that* was a terrifying fish," Bunda remarked, dumbfounded. "Did you see those teeth?"

"Yes." Shatterbreath lowered her tail into the water, causing a wake to form.

"What are you doing?" Kael asked her.

The dragon regarded him before craning her neck to watch her tail. "Tonight, we dine on fish."

Bunda scoffed. "You can't be serious."

Kael stood up so he could see her tail. Tentatively, Bunda followed suit. His heart skipped a beat as he spotted a shadow in the water. He frowned. "Uh, Shatterbreath..."

She ignored him. The fish was nearing the surface—Kael could just make out its features. Shatterbreath yanked her tail out of the

261

water just before it bit. A second after, the fish jumped clear out of the water. It was huge! Almost twice the size of the fish they saw before!

Shatterbreath swung her tail in a circle and struck the fish in the head. The force of the blow knocked in completely sideways and it actually skipped across the surface once before stopping in the water, belly up. Shatterbreath looped around and sunk her claws into it, seizing it out of the water.

"Oh, this thing is heavy!" she gasped.

Kael leaned over her side. "It's still alive too."

She found a better grip, placing her claws into its gills, and squeezed. It thrashed a moment longer, shuddered, and then was still.

"What if that thing bit you?" Bunda yelled. "What then?"

"Hmm, indeed. *What* then?" She raised the fish to her mouth and took a gory bite. Brow raised, she glanced back at Bunda, entrails hanging from her teeth. Then, she chewed rigorously before swallowing. "Don't worry, I'll save you some."

After another bite, Shatterbreath resumed her flight, returning to their previous height. "I always wondered why Thicktail used to live near here," she commented through chews. "Now I know. These fish are immaculate. Too dangerous for hatchlings though."

"Was Thicktail a friend of yours?" Kael asked.

The muscles around her eyes tightened. It was almost as if she was blushing. "No," she said quickly. "He was...my mate."

"Oh. Sorry."

"Never mind. We're making good time."

She was right. By the end of the second day, the towering branches of the Vigilant Five could be seen in the distance. The trees themselves were still a ways off, so they decided to stay the night at the edge of the forest bordering the grove. They dined on what remained of Shatterbreath's fish. She had been right, the meat was sweet and filling.

Even though they were still a fair distance away, the shrieking of the wyverns could be heard long into the night. Although she didn't admit it, the noises scared Bunda and it took her several hours to fall asleep. She complained the entire time. Not just about the shrieking, but *everything* else as well. Shatterbreath seemed apt at ignoring her and soon fell asleep. Kael wasn't so lucky.

But he found as the butcher drifted off to sleep, he couldn't do the same. He was concerned whether or not his plan would actually work and if his friends were alright. How Faerd was doing, if the Allegiance camp had been discovered and if so, if Silverstain had attacked them.

When morning rolled by, he had hardly slept an hour. Shatterbreath rolled onto her back and stretched, pointing her four paws high into the air.

"Have a good sleep?" Kael scoffed.

The dragon sniffed. "Adequate. You didn't sleep very well."

"If at all."

She trained those emerald eyes on him. "Relax, all will be well, Tiny." There was great reassurance in her voice, but Kael didn't feel any better.

"Well, enough dawdling," Bunda chimed in, rising to her feet. "Let's get this over with, eh?"

Within minutes, they had packed up their things and were soaring towards the Grove of the Vigilant Five. As before, Kael marvelled at the sheer size of the trees. Each one towered like a mountain, dwarfing the surrounding forest.

Also like before, flying into the canopy was like entering a new world. Inside the canopy was permanent twilight, with beams of light cutting through the air at scatter random. The wyverns didn't make themselves present at once, choosing instead to fly from branch to branch uttering low screeches. Bunda whipped her head to each sound, mouth open and face pale.

Shatterbreath alighted on a tree branch as thick as a house. She glanced around and roared. There must have been a hundred delighted screeches in reply. All at once, wyverns seemed to burst out of from behind every branch, corner and nook. They swarmed around her flying in tight circles around the branch, creating a cyclone of frenzied air around them.

One by one, the wyverns alighted on the branch around Shatterbreath. They nuzzled against her, rubbing their snouts against her body. Many of them seemed disappointed when they touched metal instead of her scales. Shatterbreath positively beamed.

"Hmm, they remember me. I missed you too." She lowered her head into the ground to nuzzle some of them back. This only made them more excited.

It occurred to Kael that Bunda wasn't screaming. He turned back and found her paralyzed, eyes wide and brow furrowed. She just stared at the moving throng of purple bodies, aghast. Kael hesitated, but touched her hand, which was gripping a spine tightly. "It's alright," he goaded, "you're safe. You're okay. They mean us no harm."

Just as he finished his words, a wyvern climbed up the back end of Shatterbreath. Snuffling the whole time, it sidled closer to Bunda, twitching its head like a curious bird. Several more watched it.

It approached Bunda and huffed, ruffling her hair. She grimaced, but remained stiff. The wyvern sniffed her head to toe then reared its head, stunned. For a moment longer, it considered her from a distance. After more contemplation, it threw its head back and screeched. Bunda's trance was broken and she shied behind Kael, wrapping her arms around him as if he would protect her from the creatures.

"Relax," Shatterbreath cooed, "they have accepted you. See? They like you."

Kael reached out and patted one on the head. It bobbed its head like a horse, nudging Kael with its pointed snout. He laughed and rubbed it some more.

Bunda, wearing a sour expression reached out to a nearby wyvern as well. It snorted, startling her, but stayed steady. Her fingertips grazed the tip of its muzzle and she withdrew her arm. Apparently the faint touch wasn't enough for the wyvern and it threw its head onto her lap, making a sound that resembled a purr.

"I'm quite done here," Bunda said, trying to push the creature away. "Can we—" A wyvern shrieked, cutting her off. "Can we get this done and over with?"

Shatterbreath hummed, amused. "Certainly." She stood up, roared, then plunged over the side of the branch. The wyverns followed. For the next hour, she flew through the Grove, weaving between the huge branches. More and more wyverns followed. When she alight on another branch, the wyverns crowded around her, hanging from smaller branches and clinging upside-down to the trunk. The mass of purple was so thick, Kael could barely see daylight, let alone the brown of the tree's bark.

"This should be enough," she said, scanning the wyverns she had gathered. "I believe this is just under half their total amount."

Kael nodded. "Let's do this."

"Butcher, climb over here." Shatterbreath craned her neck. "Right here." Bunda sat down obediently where Shatterbreath's neck met her body. "Hold tight."

Bunda leaned forward and gripped a spine. Kael sensed a surge of energy in Shatterbreath's body. At once, all the wyverns fell silent and still. Every muzzle turned to her. Kael shivered, disturbed by how eerie it was. Bunda was just as still as they were.

Shatterbreath broke the calm by hunching her shoulders and arching her tail. The wyverns perked up. She made a low hiss at the back of her throat and flared her wings. Only a handful of the creatures didn't mimic her.

With a snarl, she sprang to her feet and threw her head back, puffing out her chest. The wyverns began snarling as well, thrashing their limbs. Whatever she was doing, it seemed to be working. They were following what she was doing.

Then, without warning, Shatterbreath leapt off the tree branch. The move startled Kael and he nearly toppled off. She dipped underneath a branch and roared, sending echoes through the trees. She beat her wings fiercer and fiercer as they approached the wall of hanging branches. The wyverns flapped along beside her, drowning out any other noise. Just before they hit the wall, Kael noticed several dozen of the creatures halt in mid-air with worried screeches.

Shatterbreath passed through the branches, scattering them. Seconds later, thousands of wyverns passed through as well, leaving the safety of the Grove of the Vigilant Five.

Once they were gliding over the forest surrounding the Grove, Bunda gasped and sagged. Kael climbed up and pulled the butcher onto Shatterbreath's back. She put a hand to her forehead and gawked at the sky.

"Wow," she grunted, "*that* was different. Hope I never have to do that again."

Shatterbreath snorted. "You will. I only told the wyverns to follow. I will have to tell them to *fight* later."

"How'd you know they would follow?" Kael asked. They had to speak loudly to each other. The wyverns were very noisy.

She rolled her shoulders, nearly pinching Kael with the metal covering her back. "I didn't. I just hoped they would. I guess it worked."

"Mostly. Many of them turned around just before the outside branches."

Shatterbreath nodded. "I noticed as well. I blame the butcher."

"Hey!" Bunda cried.

Several of the wyverns nearby screeched. Their shrieks sounded suspiciously like Bunda's protest.

"Hmm." Shatterbreath rumbled. "I think they're following you, not me. You are the one with the ability. Fascinating."

"Ah! No! I don't want them after me!" Some of the wyverns turned back.

"Uh, I think you do actually." Kael pointed as a dozen more angled away. "Deep down, I'm sure you do want them. For the good of Vallenfend, right?"

Bunda scowled at him before faking a smile. "Of course. Who was I kidding? I love these scaly, overgrown bats. How could you *not?*"

Two wyverns landed on Shatterbreath's back and started a competition to see who could get closer to Bunda. She gasped, as if about to scream. Shatterbreath craned her neck and glowered at her. Bunda stifled her scream and instead scratched one under the chin. It made a purring noise and rubbed its neck against her.

"You know, these things aren't too bad," Bunda stated. "Almost like horses."

Shatterbreath shot Kael a knowing look. He only rolled his eyes.

Suddenly, the wyvern sneezed in Bunda's face. This time, she did scream. Startled, both wyverns leapt off Shatterbreath's back to join the ranks of the others.

"I hate horses," Bunda said bitterly, rubbing her face with her sleeve.

Kael and Shatterbreath both had to turn away to hide their laughter.

Throughout the day, more wyverns left. Only three or four during the whole day, but it was enough to upset Shatterbreath. "They won't make it back," she lamented. "They will surely die."

However, when night fell and they landed to the west of the Arnoth mountain range, Kael was content with their progress. The vast majority of the wyverns were still with them and Bunda was actually warming up to the creatures. A success by his standards. As he fell asleep that night, surrounded by purple bodies, he could feel his heart thrumming in anticipation. With that many wyverns, there was no way the empire could succeed.

His plan would work.

Chapter 25

The rest of the trip back to Vallenfend was uneventful. Despite Shatterbreath's lofty pace, the wyverns kept up with ease. It was somewhat difficult to keep a steady conversation amid the din of the flying creatures. Tiring too. After only a few hours, Kael and Bunda fell silent, content to admire the swarm of wyverns as they pumped their wings. Shatterbreath, whether uncomfortable from the quiet or simply happy, would roar almost hourly, often waking up her passengers. Perhaps *that* was her reason.

By the end of their fourth day of journeying, before the sun had even reached the horizon, the Vallenfend mountain range was looming in view. To Kael's surprise, instead of flying over, she found a glade halfway up the east side of the mountain. A minute or so after she landed, all the wyverns had found somewhere to perch.

Kael was confused why they had landed, but the reason dawned on him. In order for their attack to be most effective, they needed two things: surprise and coordination. The wyverns needed to strike at the same time as the Allegiance army. That brought up a question though.

"Shatterbreath, how are you going to keep the wyverns here?"

The dragon stopped licking a wyvern to raise her brow at him. She shifted her mischievous look to Bunda. "Don't you dare," Bunda warned with a frown.

"We have to leave you here, butcher. That's a statement, not a suggestion."

Bunda crossed her arms. "Sure, why not. Everything's been against my decision so far anyway. Why change things now?"

Shatterbreath hummed and cocked her head. "That's better. At least you know your place now. Humans are *under* dragons." She gave Bunda a gentle shove with her tail. As Bunda climbed off of her back, Shatterbreath leaned in close to Kael. "I like this one. Why aren't you more like her?"

"Why do you say that every time somebody patronizes you?" Kael scoffed.

She yawned. "Patronize? Hardly." She stuck out her jaw, as if deep in thought. "I call it...voicing the truth. Proclaiming the obvious, even."

"Dragons..." Kael rubbed his face. "Listen, Bunda, we'll hurry right back, okay?"

"How soon? You're not going to leave me out here overnight, are you?"

"Scared?" Shatterbreath mocked.

"Certainly." Bunda put her hands to her hips. "Do you have any idea what dangerous creatures are out here? I'm not interested in being breakfast!"

She was in the mood to complain some more, but Kael interrupted her. "Bunda, Bunda! Do you realize what you're surrounded by?" She hesitated and looked around at all the wyverns. They stared expectantly back. "Do you really think a predator would try to attack you?"

Her hands fell limp to her side. "Point taken. Well, go then. What are you waiting for?"

Shatterbreath sighed and shook her head. Without a further word, she took to the sky, leaving Bunda behind with the swarm of wyverns.

"I take it back," she snarled. "I *don't* like that one. Chatty like a squirrel. Smart as a deer."

"And you're perfect I suppose?"

"I *am* a dragon."

"So?"

"That's as close as perfection gets." She coughed, jarring Kael before he could retort. "Glad to see you agree."

Compared to the journey they had just made, the flight over the mountaintop was quick. Within ten minutes, Shatterbreath was landing in the same tight clearing as before. It took a while but this time, it was Tomn who greeted them first.

"Oi, s'bout time you two returned!" he chortled. "Wher you been? Blitty then."

"Tomn!" Kael jumped off Shatterbreath's back. "Oof. Hey, it's good to see you! When was the last time...?"

269

"Before yer capture," the bandit king replied. He scratched at the back of his head. "I was real busy, see? Hope yeh don't mind thert I didn't see yer. Couldn't get around teh it. A—are yeh alright? I heard that they...tortured yer." Tomn moved closer, perhaps to clasp Kael's shoulder to try and comfort him.

"I'm fine. Well, mostly." Kael clenched his jaw and sidled out of Tomn's reach. "There are things here and there, but all in all... Don't worry about me. I'll recover."

"Well then." Tomn smiled at him for an awkward moment. He seemed at a loss for words. Apparently, comforting somebody was beyond a bandit's ability. Kael was fine with that. "Hey listen, ther leaders will be happy to see yeh. They's been wondering 'bout yeh."

"Can you take us to them?"

Tomn shot Shatterbreath an apprehensive look. "Uh, I can take yer, but she's gert to stay. Just a blitty too big."

"I'll wait here," Shatterbreath said with a nod. "Go."

"You ther!" Tomn shouted. A bandit who had been sitting nearby, eating an apple, perked up. "Come here, yeh lerk."

The bandit snorted and threw his apple to the side. "Yeah, boss?"

"Come with us, eh?" Tomn sighed and motioned for Kael to follow. They ventured deeper into the forest, leaving Shatterbreath behind with strangers. Kael hoped she wouldn't so anything rash. "These last few days have been lazy. Ther BlackHound discovered us, but they're only sending half-sized forces. Many of me men have been killed. Ther's not many of us left, so..."

"We're just sittin' around," the other bandit squawked. Kael was startled by high-pitched his voice was. He was a pretty stocky man—not the type with a voice like that.

They climbed over a fallen tree. "You're telling me Silverstain hasn't attacked yet?"

"Ther dragon? Nah. It's like they're only gettin' at us to keep us back. Like they're delaying for sommat. Whate'er it is, it ain't going to be good."

"Delaying," Kael thought out loud. He stumbled on a thick root. "Hmm. Why would they do that? Do they think we'll just fade away in the forest?"

Tomn halted, leaning up against a tree. He raised a brow. "Do yer think I know? You'll have ter ask the others. They're jerst up ahead."

"Thanks, Tomn."

"Hey, listen." Tomn fiddle with his fingers. "I'm serry we can't be more help. Ther won't be none of us left if we keep fighting."

"Don't worry about it. You've done your part—all of you. If it wasn't for your people, we wouldn't have had such great success the first day."

"Heh." He took a deep breath through his teeth. "Well... If there's anything yer need, just lert me or Grubgor here know."

A frown stretched across Grubgor's huge forehead. Kael cringed. "That's quite alright. I think I can handle myself for now. Shatterbreath could use somebody to polish her scales though."

Kael thought for a moment that Gubgor's face would collapse in on itself. Tomn smiled. "I'm sure he'd be happy teh help her. I'll leave him with yer then, eh?" Satisfied, Tomn headed back towards the middle of the camp.

Grubgor raised a finger to protest. Kael beat him to it. "You don't actually have to polish her scales. She wouldn't let you anyway."

"Thank yer sir," the bandit replied. "Ther King of Fallenfeld should be just over there." He pointed through the trees. "They've been holding back ther bad guys at the edge of ther forest. They do all their strategizing just ther." Sure enough, a few soldiers marched by. From their dignified manner and banners, they were generals of Arnoth.

Kael nodded in thanks and followed the generals. After passing by a dozen more trees, a glade opened up to reveal a plateau of sorts, jutting out from the mountainside. Kael could see Vallenfend looming in the distance. How different it seemed, knowing it was the BlackHound Empire's now.

Three loud voices penetrated the air, giving away the presence of King Henedral, Clodde and Sal'braan. Kael hesitated at the edge of the plateau to listen in.

"There is no way we can win this," King Henedral shouted. "What makes you think Kael will even be coming back?"

"He brought you together!" Sal'braan countered. "Don't you trust him?"

"No. Not right now. The BlackHound got to him." King Henedral paused; Kael couldn't see why. "They did something to him. He's all...different. Shifty and twitchy."

"So? He's obviously recovering from a traumatic event." That was Clodde's voice. "You have to give him the benefit of the doubt."

"I have given him that by coming here!" King Henedral slapped his hand down on something. There were trees blocking his way, so Kael couldn't see what. "We're losing this war—not insignificantly either. Vallenfend is lost and if we don't retreat, we'll lose our own lands too. Fallenfeld, Arnoth, Rystville... If we focus our attention on defending our own cities..."

"Then the BlackHound Empire will only grow in strength," Sal'braan stated ominously. "This is exactly what they want. To make landfall. I...hate to say it, but this city is nothing more than an entry point. A base camp. This isn't a year's war. This invasion is *decades* in the making. They will make that city a fortress and with such a strong point of entry, send an innumerable amount of soldiers over to take this continent for good."

"If it'll take so long," King Henedral retorted, "then we will be prepared."

"No you won't!" Sal'braan was yelling now. "You see that out there?" Kael assumed he was pointing out at Vallenfend. "That is the BlackHound Empire *unprepared*. Nothing, *nothing* will be able to stop them if we give up now. Then you, King, will be known as the man who let everybody on this continent perish. Can you live with that?"

Everybody stayed silent for a long time. King Henedral broke the silence first. His voice was low and grave. "What chance do we have anyway? Kael and his imaginary *wyvern* creatures couldn't save us now."

"They're not imaginary," King Respu snapped. "I've seen one myself."

Kael flinched as a sweaty young man jogged past. He furrowed his brow at Kael before running towards the leaders and out of sight.

"What is it?" King Henedral growled.

"Sire, we have just received word that Rundown and the dragon have returned.

Kael shuffled closer to the nearest tree. He wanted to see the king's reaction. He spotted the king's dazed expression through the branches.

"Well," the king wheezed, "where is he, son?"

Kael winced as the messenger pointed directly at him. "Right there, Sire."

Putting on the calmest expression he owned, Kael stepped out from his hiding spot and slowly strutted over to the group. Among the three leaders were several generals. Every Fallenfeld general shifted their weight uneasily. Did the rest of Fallenfeld share their king's concerns?

"Kael, y—you're back." King Henedral folded his arms. One of his eyes twitched and deep lines betrayed his clenching jaw. "Excellent. Success, I take it?"

"My *friends* call me Kael," he hissed in reply. "The wyverns will join us in battle. Clodde, King Respu, King...Henedral, prepare the all the men at once. We're taking the city back." He made a fist. "Now."

"B—but..." Clodde stuttered.

"Just do it! I'll be back in ten minutes." Kael whipped around and placed a hand on the hilt of *Vintrave*. "As soon as everyone is gathered, attack. We'll move in as soon as you engage." There was no room for argument. Kael began climbing the slope back up to where Shatterbreath was waiting.

Before he knew it, he had arrived to the glade. He had been fuming the whole way. It was a miracle he had even gone the right direction.

"What has you so upset, Tiny?" she asked, craning her neck closer.

273

He pushed her snout away and instantly regretted it. "King... It doesn't matter. We're going on the attack. Are you ready?"

"Hmm..." She eyed herself over. "What if I said no?"

"Too bad. We're attacking right now. Let's go get the Bunda and the wyverns."

"The blacksmith was searching for you. He mentioned something about your friend, Gaerb."

Kael frowned. "Do you mean Faerd?"

She nodded. "It sounded important."

Kael's heart clenched. "Do you know if he's still alive?"

"The blacksmith is for certain. I'm pretty sure Gaerb is too."

"Alright," Kael sighed. "It can wait then." She helped him up onto her back. "Yah! Giddy up!"

"I am not a horse." Still, with powerful leap, she was airborne. This time, she didn't stress stealth. The BlackHound Empire knew where they were. Even if they hadn't, it didn't matter anymore.

After a chilly trip over the mountain's top, they found Bunda where they had left her. She smiled as Shatterbreath descended, stirring up the wyverns.

"At last!" she shouted. "I've been waiting here for hours!"

It hadn't even been *one* hour. "A shame," Shatterbreath chirped. "I hope you've gained a stronger stomach from our travels, butcher."

"Why?"

"Because," Kael told her, "we're attacking Vallenfend. You get to lead the charge on Shatterbreath's back with me." He had Shatterbreath had discussed it on their journey back. They had both decided on the same thing. They had also agreed not to give Bunda the decision.

"What?!"

Good thing too.

Chapter 26

The wind whipped fiercely in Kael's face, dappled with moisture. The sea breeze, usually calming and sweet, had brought a storm with it. Far out on the horizon, Kael could see rain sweeping towards Vallenfend as the dark clouds churned overhead. An arc of lightening struck the ground, lighting up the sky. Thunder accompanied it ten seconds later. He welcomed the storm. It would play to their advantage.

Vallenfend fit behind Kael's open hand from up so high. Through the gap where his ring finger used to be, he could see the fuzzy outline of the castle. He focussed on it and took a breath.

Another boom of thunder. Shatterbreath answered it.

"You hear it?" she rumbled. "That is fate calling. She opens her wings to us. Her flame will guide us."

Kael sniffed. "Poetic."

"Dragons serve no deity, Tiny." Shatterbreath swung her head side to side to check the ranks of the wyverns. Their wing beats were quick and they darted their own heads around. Could they sense the battle to ensue? "But fate... Fate is something to believe in. Fate is what brought us together. Fate was with us every flap along the way. Fate will grant us victory."

Kael wasn't sure what to think. Perhaps one day, he would know for sure who or what watched over them all.

Another boom of thunder. Shatterbreath's muscles tensed.

"Hold tight," Shatterbreath hissed. "This—this is it."

Yes. It was. If this attack failed—if they couldn't reclaim the city, the war would be lost.

With a mighty roar, Shatterbreath tucked in her wings and twisted her body so that her head was pointed straight downwards. Utter shrieks of their own, the wyverns followed suit. The screaming of the wind around each body was deafening. They were one great chorus of it, falling in wondrous synchronization.

They rocketed towards the foot of Shatterbreath's mountain. Through the tears streaking in his eyes, Kael could see the whole of the Allegiance army rushing towards Vallenfend's eastern wall. BlackHound archers shot arrows into the crowds mercilessly, but there was nothing that could be done to stop the advance. Inside the walls, out of sight from the Allegiance forces, BlackHound reinforcements awaited to repel the borders. They would never get the chance.

Shatterbreath flared her wings, following the curve of the mountain. With the entirety of the wyverns they had brought, they rushed over the Allegiance army in the blink of an eye. Shatterbreath released a jet of flame that swept over a large portion of the BlackHound forces while the wyverns swarmed into the city.

The next moments turned into a bloodbath as the wyverns tore into the soldiers. The creatures couldn't breathe fire, but their dagger-like teeth and hind claws proved to be just as effective. The archers lining the walls turned their attention away from the Allegiance and instead opened fire on the wyverns. The move proved ineffective. They wyvern's hides were tough and they wove through the air faster than striking snakes. It took more than a single arrow to take one down. Still, many wyverns died from the hail of shafts before Shatterbreath incinerated the top of the wall.

Any arrows that found their way to Shatterbreath only bounced off her armour. It was the larger projectiles which she had to avoid. Reversely, bolts or ball-and-chains launched from ballistae didn't seem to bother the wyverns. They were too quick and would simply dodge them. Soon the arrows and larger projectiles stopped entirely. The ground forces were doing their part.

The Allegiance forces cut through the streets, pushing the BlackHound Empire further back with each building. As they went, they cleared out houses converted into archer-towers and either destroyed or captured ballistae and catapults.

The surprise attack proved very effective—until the BlackHound Empire was able to gather their wits. With little more than half the city under Allegiance control, resistance began to form. The BlackHound forces began launching nets lined with barbs into the swarm of wyverns. The tangle of pointed metal would snag a dozen of the creatures at once, dragging the lot of them to the ground, where most would die from the fall. With even more archers dotted throughout the city at strategic locations, as well as hard-to-reach ballistae stations, the air advance was kept at bay.

With a loud sound that resembled a cough, Shatterbreath called back the wyverns. She crashed through a house to duck behind the safety of a thick structure. The wyverns sheltered themselves amongst buildings as well.

"The air is inhospitable," Shatterbreath declared. "The arrows will have to cease before we can take wing once again."

Kael climbed off her back and peered around the corner at the battle. "I don't think that will be possible anytime soon." An idea struck him. "How well do the wyverns move on ground?"

She shot him a glance. "Just as fast."

"Then continue on the ground." He unsheathed *Vintrave*. "It is the only way to advance."

"What about you? Does your back permit you to fight?"

"I've had plenty of time to heal," Kael lied. He rolled his shoulders in anticipation. "I'll be fine. Go, help the allies."

She nodded, but hesitated to glance skyward. "Where is Silverstain I wonder?"

Kael had been pondering the same thing.

Without another word, Shatterbreath pounced from behind her building with all the wyverns scrambling across the ground behind her. She was right, they were very fast even on the ground. They clambered across the side of the buildings, nimbler than squirrels.

Kael spotted the front line of the battle and sprinted towards it. When he arrived, he was relieved to found Korjan fighting amongst Fallenfeld soldiers. The blacksmith slew two men with his axes and kicked another before taking a step back. It seemed the Allegiance had adopted another one of Vert's tactics. Half the front line would attack, then back up so the other half could strike. Then, they'd repeat the process. It gave the men somewhat of a chance to catch their breath while the enemy soldiers were pounded relentlessly. It seemed to be effective so far.

Once the wave of wyverns hit the BlackHound soldiers, the flow of the Allegiance was interrupted. The allies stood back, confused as purple bodies leapt onto soldiers. Kael took advantage to find Korjan amid the screaming.

"I've got your back!" he said, brandishing *Vintrave.* "Let's go!" Kael jumped into the midst of the enemy ranks before Korjan could give an answer.

With the wyverns now on the ground, the Allegiance was taking ground. The BlackHound soldiers quickly realized this and started their full retreat. As they fled, they set fire to every building they could and soon Kael was surrounded by flames and cinders.

The smoke was choking, but it didn't inhibit him as he continued to strike down more and more soldiers. Korjan was at his back, protecting him as well as slaying those who withstood Kael's attacks. They proved to be an effective duo. Kael was fast and caught the soldiers' attention and Korjan's powerful blows never failed to kill.

A large group of soldiers turned heel and ran from the swarm of wyverns and Allegiance soldiers. Most of the wyverns screeched and chased after them, disappearing into a wide alley. Kael burst out in a sprint after them, with Korjan in tow. Kael spotted an Allegiance soldier cowering up against a wall. The soldier stuck out a hand to them, and yelled, "Wait, stop!"

It was too late. Kael and Korjan sprinted around the corner— only to be met with a hail of arrows. Kael shoved Korjan back behind the corner of the building and then dove to his belly. Whatever arrows didn't miss glanced off his armour. He crawled behind the building before the next hail.

"That's Archer Alley in there," the soldier who had tried to warn them explained. He moaned and grabbed at his shoulder, where a shaft protruded.

Korjan inspected the man's shoulder. "How did this penetrate so deep?"

"Steel shafts," he said through clenched teeth. "Only in Archer Alley. That road is a major chokepoint—many of my comrades were slain in there. There's no way to get through and the nearest door is at least twenty yards away."

Kael stood up and pressed himself against the wall carefully, wary that the majority of the house was on fire. He poked his head out to survey the scene.

Before him was one of Vallenfend's largest markets. It had once been the central hub of the city, with two-story shops looming behind smaller fruit stalls, where people would go about their business buying their week's worth of supplies. Fond memories of strolling through the market marvelling at all the strange things for sale flooded through Kael's mind. He shook his head and the ghosts disappeared, instead replaced by the tips of arrows glinting through every window, refracting the orange glow of the burning stalls.

Countless purple bodies lay at scatter-random. At least a hundred wyverns must have been claimed by the alley. At the far end of the derelict market stood a troupe of BlackHound soldiers, well over fifty strong. Kael was forced back behind the building to dodge an arrow.

"What do we do?" Korjan asked.

"We have to clear out that alley, before..."

The ground rumbled, causing debris to rain down on Kael's head. Kael knew the cause before he heard the roar.

"Shatterbreath," he gasped. He turned to see her come barrelling around a corner. Arrows and some spears covered her body, stuck into her armour and scales. Kael couldn't see her, but he assumed Bunda was safe (they had placed a shield over her back for good measure), for hundreds of wyverns swarmed around the dragon.

Disregarding Archer Alley, Kael threw himself out of his cover with his arms out wide. "Stop!" he screamed. Shatterbreath spotted him and dug her claws into the ground, tearing up the road and stopping only a metre or two away from him. A dozen or so wyverns raced past. Kael heard the whistling of arrows and several of the beasts fell dead.

Shatterbreath snarled and flapped her wings with tremendous force, batting away the streaking arrows. Kael was thrown to the ground and tumbled a few times before coming to a rest. A second later, he was scooped up by Shatterbreath's maw and deposited behind the cover of a building across the street.

He groaned as he picked rocks out of his cheeks and shook out his armour. *Better than being skewered by arrows,* he thought bitterly.

"What were you doing?" Shatterbreath hissed. "I nearly ran you over."

There was a shuffle up on her back and Bunda peeked out from behind the huge shield protecting her. "Kael? What happened, why did we stop?"

"That alley is jammed with archers. They'll kill you both if you go in there."

"We are protected."

There was an arrow lying nearby. Kael snatched it up to show her. "They're using steel arrows in there. Probably shot from longbows too. These *will* penetrate your scales and even your armour. You can't run in there."

"Many weapons lie past this alley," Shatterbreath grumbled. "We must make it through to destroy them so the wyverns and I can take to the skies."

"Can't you go another way?" Kael asked.

"I can. But there are many wyverns that will come this way. They will die if we don't destroy this blockade."

Kael gritted his teeth, at a loss.

Shatterbreath perked up. "Your friend calls you from across the street. The blacksmith."

"Help me up." Shatterbreath hefted him up onto her shoulder and he leaned out, holding onto her neck for support. From there, he could see Korjan, still hiding behind the burning building. "Korjan? What is it?"

"Kael, are you alright?"

"Yeah. Do you have any ideas on how to clear Archer Alley?"

After some thought, the blacksmith shrugged.

Shatterbreath rumbled. "I have an idea." She gestured towards Korjan with her snout. "They burn your buildings; we burn theirs—with them inside."

"Those *are* our buildings. I will not suffer my city to be destroyed."

"I will not suffer the deaths of so many wyverns!" she shot back. "So unless you have a better plan, I am going to burn that alley down. Butcher, stay here to keep the wyverns back."

Bunda obeyed. Kael watched her with clenched his fists, aggravated. But the dragon had a point. "Fine. Destroy the left line of buildings how you wish. I'm going to clear the right with Korjan—they may serve beneficial to us in the future. Wait for my signal."

"Suit yourself," Shatterbreath grumbled. "Go with care."

Kael climbed down without so much as a grunt in reply. He sprinted across the road, using his ability to warp time to slip past streaking arrows. Once on the other side, he noticed that several more soldiers had joined Korjan. At least two dozen crouched there, covered in dust and ash, wearing either thick Fallenfeld or Arnoth armour. Good, his task would be much easier with them helping.

"Listen," Kael said loud enough for them to all hear. "We're taking back Archer Alley, now. Who's with me?" Every soldier nodded, except for the injured man. He could only see their eyes through their sturdy helmets. "Good. Keep to the right. Move swiftly, and make every attack count—we don't know what else could be in those buildings."

"On your lead, Kael," Korjan said resolutely.

Kael took a breath. *On his lead.* Shatterbreath's eyes were trained on him from across the street. He pointed at her and gave a nod. She roared and released a jet of flame into the air. Hopefully, that move had caught the archers' attention. After a slight pause, she scaled the building and promptly ignited the first structure along the left row.

Brandishing *Vintrave,* Kael screamed, "Now!"

He and his small battalion of soldiers sprinted into the alley and into full view. An arrow pierced straight through his wooden shield, passing harmlessly underneath his arm. With a scowl, Kael cast his shield aside. It was slowing him down anyway.

Whatever archers had been distracted by the fire and Shatterbreath must have noticed the group of soldiers advancing, for the hail of arrows doubled. Kael heard the steel shafts *whiz* by, closely followed by cries as their tips found flesh just behind him.

Without hesitation, Kael sprinted to the first building along the row and threw himself sideways at the window. He crashed through the glass, landing on his side and sending tiny fragments scattering into the shop. He picked himself up, and was relieved to find Korjan doing the same beside him. Out of the twenty-or-so men there had been, only five had made it.

A roar echoed from outside and then a brilliant flash of orange from the rooftops across the street as Shatterbreath's flames engulfed another building. He heard her yelp in pain. The archers were shooting at her.

"Upstairs, hurry!" Kael shouted.

He climbed the staircase in three bounding steps and sidestepped an arrow aimed at him. The BlackHound archer yelled an unfamiliar curse and attempted to reload his bow. Kael drove *Vintrave* through his chest before he had the chance. Between him, Korjan and the others, the rest of the archers didn't stand a chance.

Once they were all dead, Kael stooped to pick up one of their bows. "Nice weapon," he remarked, running his fingers over it. The wood was sturdy and smooth, reinforced with flexible metal. The craftsmanship was very impressive indeed, from the rosiness of the wood to the detailed head of a snarling hound designed into the handle, so that its nose pointing in the direction the arrow would fly. "I think I'll keep this." He scooped up a quiver and filled it with steel arrows before slinging it over his shoulder.

"This room's clear," Korjan reported.

"On to the next," Kael ordered. "No, not the stairs. They'll be expecting us that way." He pointed at the wall. "All of these apartments are connected. We need to catch them by surprise. Korjan, could you please...?"

With a smirk, Korjan sheathed his broadsword and pulled out his two axes. He drove them both into the wall, tearing apart the boards separating the houses like they were nothing more than parchment. Kael notched an arrow and aimed it at where Korjan was chopping.

As soon as Kael saw him break through, he yelled, "Stop! Get down!"

Korjan dove out of the way and Kael let his arrow loose. He was unfamiliar with using metal bolts, but his aim was still true. A *thunk* and a pained screamed alerted him his arrow hit a target.

"Go now!" Kael ordered.

Three of the Allegiance soldiers tackled into the wall, knocking what remained of it down. Kael let two more arrows loose into the haze before charging through himself. Those archers, though caught off-guard by them coming through the wall, were better prepared than the others. It took a while longer for the Allegiance soldiers to clear them out.

While his allies searched the rooms of the apartment, Kael turned to the windows and gazed out. Half of the block across the street was on fire, but he couldn't see Shatterbreath. Had she been hit? Was she injured? Or worse, dead?

"All clear!" a soldier declared.

A faint knocking caught Kael's attention, coming from the wall opposite the one they had broke through. Curious, he sidled closer to where the sound originated and placed a hand against the wood.

"Clear here too!"

"Kael!" It was Korjan's voice. "It's—ngh—it's a trap!"

"What?"

There came one last loud knock, then the wall exploded outwards.

Through the debris that scattered everywhere, Kael could see shining black armour and traces of gold. He jumped back to avoid a massive broadaxe. As the heavily-armoured body pushed itself through the new hole in the wall, Kael gasped. A BlackHound Champion.

Through the gaping maw of his hound-faced helmet, the Champion peered around until he spotted Kael. Kael took a step back—into the awaiting chest of somebody behind him.

Before he could react, strong arms seized him around his midsection and the tip of a knife to his neck forced him from squirming. Kael could just barely make out the details of the soldier's pauldron holding him. Distinctly Fallenfeld's. His allies were holding him?

Not his allies, he realized as one of them strolled into view to salute the BlackHound Champion. *But the enemy.* They were BlackHound men in disguise.

From the hole in the wall, four archers piled into the room to aim their bows at him. Well, *them.* Kael noticed Korjan thrashing beside him, also held still by the imposters. The Champion stepped up and backhanded the blacksmith.

"Stop squirming, you," he croaked. He grabbed Kael's chin and turned his face to either side. "Hmm. This is him. We knew you'd come this way. Commander Coar'saliz has you all figured out. We've got you now, Resistance Leader. You though before was bad? The Commander is going to make sure you die slowly by his hand. Not even your dragon can save you this time."

Kael spat in his face.

The Champion struck Kael against his jaw. The force of the blow made him see stars and he tasted copper on his tongue.

Wiping his face, the Champion gestured at Korjan. "Who is this man?"

"No idea," an imposter replied.

The burly man sniffed. "Right. Kill him."

"No!" Kael shouted. The Champion smiled at him.

"Oh? Is this man your friend?" The Champion gripped Kael's hand and squeezed tight. Kael bit back a scream. "But...didn't he torture you? Didn't he *hurt* you? That's not what friends do. Why, he sounds more like an enemy."

The pain was doing strange things to Kael's mind. The room started spinning, painting his reality in a peculiar surrealism. Kael stared at Korjan, unable to tear his eyes away. The Champion's words penetrated deep into him, reactivating the confused feelings he thought he had drowned away. Questions began to arise in his thoughts, echoing what the Champion was telling him. *Why would he hurt you if he was your friend? Doesn't he care for you? But why? Why? Why?!*

Kael began to tremble as an overwhelming rage washed over him. Vaguely, he was aware of a pressure being released from his hand and body. There was a slight reverberating noise, like the echo of a laugh through water. None of that mattered. All he could see was Korjan.

Kael's hand tightened around *Vintrave's* handle. Korjan was no friend. *He* was the enemy. *He* was the cause of Kael's pain. *He*...

But...

Korjan had just been there, fighting alongside him. Protecting him, concerned for him. Unless he too was an imposter. A BlackHound imposter.

Imposter.

Kael put a sweaty palm to his forehead, faltering. What was happening?

A sharp jolt of pain to his lower back caused the rage to flood back. Korjan *was* a BlackHound imposter! All this time! He was the enemy! The entire time... And Kael had trusted him. Kael raised his sword, ready to deliver the killing strike.

BlackHound imposter. BlackHound. The BlackHound Empire was the real enemy. They were the core to all his problems. And Korjan was one of them.

Kael winced. *But BlackHound soldiers have dark skin.*

That revelation rocked him. Stunned, he scanned Korjan's face. His skin was mottled from ash and sweat, but around his neck, where his tunic had slipped slightly, showed his natural skin tone. Fair. He had fair skin. Like Kael did.

Korjan was no enemy.

Kael snapped back into reality. *Vintrave* was still raised, posed to strike. The BlackHound soldiers had let him loose, expecting him to kill Korjan.

He nearly had.

With a cry, Kael spun around, driving the tip of his sword through the soldier's chest behind him. He removed the blade by kicking the man over, then leapt at the soldier holding Korjan. Surprise was in his favour and that soldier too, fell to his blade.

Korjan raised one of his axes to deflect an arrow, then hurled it at the same archer. His other axe found another target and then he unsheathed his broadsword from his back.

Kael locked blades with one of the BlackHound imposters. They held for a time until Kael spotted the Champion rushing at him from the corner of his eye. He ducked just in time as the Champion swung his broadaxe. The soldier he had been fighting only seconds before was less lucky. Kael fell backwards, stunned as the soldier's head rolled to the floor.

The BlackHound Champion raised his axe to strike, but it caught in the ceiling, giving Kael more than enough time to scoot out of its arch. It stuck into the floor, and Korjan moved in to strike. His sword glanced off the Champion's armour uselessly. The Champion let go of his stuck axe altogether and kicked Korjan clean into the next room and out of sight.

Kael had a chance to make a strike of his own. But even *Vintrave's* enchanted edge couldn't penetrate the Champion's thick armour.

The Champion snatched Kael's neck up in his gauntlet and lifted him clear off the ground. "I don't care what Commander Coar'saliz's orders were. You killed my brother. So I'm going to kill you."

"Y—your brother?" Kael wheezed, stalling.

"The Champion you somehow managed to kill," he growled.

A crack of thunder resonated from outside, causing the whole building to shake. Debris rattled on the ground and furniture tipped over and even the glass of the windows cracked. The BlackHound Champion looked outside, startled.

"Then let brother meet brother," Kael spat. He curled up his body and kicked the Champion's head as hard as he could, flinging himself from the man's grip.

In distorted time, Kael witnessed as the building's ceiling caved in. Shatterbreath's storm-blue head, wreathed in debris and rainwater, appeared through the mess, teeth gleaming and muzzle affixed in a snarl. The BlackHound Champion screamed and threw his hands out, as if that would protect him from her. She snapped him up with her jaws and with two violent shakes, he was dead. She flicked her neck, sending the body careening out over Vallenfend.

Placing a paw on the building's haggard structure, she hunted down every remaining soldier until they were all dead.

"Are you alright?" she asked Kael, blood dripping from her jowls.

"Yes, thanks to you. I thought you had been injured. I thought..."

She lifted her hind half up onto the top floor of the building—it was a miracle it supported her—to show Kael her flank. There were arrows lining her entire side, most stuck partway in her armour. On her thigh, however, there were three or four that were stuck in all the way to the feathers.

"They hit me alright," she said tightly, biting back the pain. "When have arrows ever killed a dragon though? Can you still fight? The battle continues."

"Go get Bunda and the wyverns. I'll continue on foot. Good luck."

She nodded. "You too. I'll be nearby if you need me."

She flapped her wings, stirring up all sorts of debris and causing moisture to swirl around the room. Once she was gone, Korjan stumbled through the hole in the wall, holding his head.

"What did I miss?" the blacksmith asked groggily.

Kael chuckled. "Nothing much. Come on, let's clear these buildings."

Together, did a quick sweep of the rest of the buildings if any enemies remained. To Kael's dismay, Shatterbreath had burned every building except for the three Kael had fought in.

After they had cleared every smouldering room, they hit the ground level to find a sizeable Allegiance force waiting for them, soaking wet from the pounding storm. It seemed the wyverns were on the move, heading further into the city.

A soldier, Alek in fact, saluted Kael as he approached. "We are your to command, Championslayer. We have been ordered to assist you in any way possible."

Kael gave him a weary nod. "First things first, I need everybody to take of their helmets."

"Sir?"

"We were tricked by BlackHound imposters." He chuckled. "That's hard to believe, isn't it? Just...do it, please."

Wearing a confused frown, Alek turned to the battalion of soldiers—at least fifty strong. "Hats off, gentlemen."

On his command, they all removed their helmets. Kael quickly scanned the crowd. Not an imposter among them. "Alright, that's good. Alek, how are we doing?"

"We're pushing them back steadily, Rundown," he explained. "The majority of their forces are bunched up near the north-western part of the city."

"And the castle?"

"It is ours once again."

Kael put a hand to his lower back. The adrenaline was running its course and the scars from his whippings were beginning to sting. If he strained them anymore, they could split open again. "Alek, would you escort me there? Korjan, you're in charge of these men."

"Aye, Kael," Korjan said with a nod.

The Vallenfend Kael walked through was a different place. Death was present everywhere, from the drenched bodies lying in the streets to the charred husks of buildings that had finally stopped burning, thanks to the rain. It brought tears to Kael's eyes knowing that Vallenfend would never be the same, that his beloved city was well enough destroyed.

Even the castle, when it came into view, no longer held its immaculate white composure. Ash clung to its walls, giving it a morose gray hue and two of its spires had been knocked down. The walls surrounding the training grounds would serve little protection now, for many areas had been blown open by the BlackHound Empire's mysterious explosives.

Kael and Alek walked through a new opening in the wall and through the training grounds, which Allegiance forces had already retaken. The cooks and medics hurried about, seeing what could be salvaged from what remained of the barracks, kitchen and medical tents.

When they neared the castle, Kael bid Alek farewell. With a nod, the man hurried away. The walk through the castle was brief and sullen. In their short occupation, the BlackHound Empire must have made a goal of wrecking as much as they could. Vert had made a point of doing the same, but not nearly to their degree. Furniture lay flipped over in the halls and stacks of burned books still smouldered in corners. In some places, he had to climb over piles of debris or otherwise pick a new route. Rivers flowed down some stairs, fuelled by either rain pouring from the destroyed spires or from new holes in the walls. Or both.

The castle had seen better days.

But at least, Kael thought as he opened a set of double doors, *the BlackHound Empire isn't interested in gold.* All the crates containing the treasure he had promised Tomn were still there. Satisfied, Kael made his way to his room.

Once there, he found himself staring out the window, watching the battle progress. Alek had been correct. From what he could see through the rain, it seemed most of the BlackHound forces were holding out at the north-western part of the city.

"Now if we could get them *out* of the city," he yawned to himself, "we could win this yet."

Somehow, despite the ponderings that churned in his mind like the storm overhead, he fell asleep, leaning against that window.

Chapter 27

The airspace above Vallenfend was clear enough to take wing. With help from the wyverns, the Allegiance forces on the ground had managed to eliminate most of the ballistae. Those that remained were easy enough for Shatterbreath to avoid in the rain.

She scoured over the city, hunting down packs of soldiers that still posed a threat—a battalion attempting to take the castle from behind, a troupe trying to flee to the main group, a demolition squad just after they destroyed a large building.

She watched as the building crumbled down, standing over the bodies of those she had slain. What was the BlackHound Empire using to create such damage? She sniffed at a corpse, paying close attention to what was gripped in its hand. It was a small green orb, hardly the size of a chipmunk. How could something so small explode with such force?

She prodded the body and the orb fell loose. Gingerly, she picked it up between her claws and gave it a sniff. It reeked of magic.

The human on her back stirred, peeking out from behind her shield. "What? What is it?"

Shatterbreath rumbled in reply, pondering the significance of the tiny sphere. If the BlackHound Empire had the skill and knowledge to make these, what else could they do? She feared to discover the answer.

A trumpet sounded north of her. She perked up, along with the wyverns crowding her.

"Was that from us or them?" the butcher asked.

Shatterbreath studied the echoes. "Them."

"What does it mean?"

Shatterbreath huffed. "Nothing good. Something is amiss. Stay here."

She may have talked too much, but at least the butcher knew how to take orders. With her on the ground and well protected by the wyverns, Shatterbreath scaled the ruins of the structure and peered out over the city, curious.

Hundreds of shimmering lights lifted off from the west, just outside the wall. They soared into the sky, blinking in and out of existence. She cocked her head and squinted, trying to make out what they were. Even with her supreme vision, the rain kept them a secret. Torches maybe?

Heart pounding, she took wing, aiming directly towards the swarm of lights. Halfway between the BlackHound Empire and the rubble, she was able to decipher the marvel. Her spines crawled.

She was right. They were torches. Torches held by humans...riding *Icecrows*.

The very prospect baffled her and she halted. She blinked several times, as if the torches were nothing more than a mirage. But they remained, illuminating those jagged beaks and ice-like feathers. Even from her distance, she could see BlackHound soldiers strapped to the back of the creatures, brandishing long, broad-tipped javelins. The torches were attached to the rear of the saddles, no doubt added for intimidation.

A rumbling detonation shook Shatterbreath of her stupor. One of the Icecrows had dipped out of the sky, into the middle of a group of Allegiance soldiers, and had exploded as soon as it hit the ground. She started forward, urgency clawing at her bones. Had it just been shot out of the sky, or was that intentional?

A second later, she received her answer. She flicked her head to watch an uninjured Icecrow dive towards a crowd of Allegiance soldiers. The rider was leaning forward and the Icecrow had it wings tucked in. Also, she noted, the rider carried neither a weapon nor a torch.

Upon impact, the Icecrow and rider exploded, killing more than a dozen Allegiance men. After a few more Icecrows exploded in the

291

crowds, the entire throng descended down on the Allegiance forces or engaged in air combat with the wyverns.

This is what the BlackHound had been waiting for, she realized. This was their grand counterattack. Perhaps they hadn't been anticipating Kael's plan with the wyverns, but certainly they knew the Allegiance would try to take the city back sooner or later.

Shatterbreath beat her wings fiercely, racing towards where the Icecrows and wyverns had begun fighting. Through the rain and icy bodies, she could spot Silverstain's silhouette as well. Was he behind this move?

By then, the rain had become relentless. It bore down on Shatterbreath, its cold tendrils ignoring her armour and scales, biting down deep into her muscle. Torrents of water streamed down the contours of her face and blinded her. Aggravated, she shook her head, trying to free herself from the water.

When she stopped thrashing, she was pointing in a different direction. She was about to turn her attention to assisting the wyverns she spotted several dark forms speeding out of the areal battle. Six Icecrow riders, without torches or javelins. A quick glance to her right told her where they were going.

The castle.

Kael was in there, Shatterbreath had watched him enter.

Changing direction, she beat her wings are hard as she could. If she went fast enough and at just the right angle, she could intercept them. She *had* to intercept them.

The group of Icecrows didn't notice her until she was almost on top of them. With fell slashes, she killed the first of the group, covering her claws in ice. She had almost forgotten that their blood froze almost instantly. She also almost forgot how much she hated Icecrows.

Three Icecrows swerved to avoid her while another latched onto her flank. Clinging to the arrows protruding from her side, it pecked at her armour, tearing a sizeable hole through the metal until she swatted it with her tail. With it dead, she was able to catch another

292

Icecrow as it attempted to swoop underneath her. With a crippled wing, the Icecrow spiralled earthward, striking a building before bursting into flames.

Shatterbreath snapped at an Icecrow that flew past her muzzle and missed. The rain was inhibiting her, dulling her senses and slowing her reflexes. The same Icecrow snatched onto the hole in her armour and she yelped as its beak dug into her exposed flesh. With a deep breath, she incinerated the creature and its rider. She regretted it instantly. Her fire managed to kill the creature, but it also melted the metal still attached to her thigh. The molten metal burned the raw flesh exposed by the Icecrows as well as stick to her scales, and because of the cold rain, it hardened seconds later, causing her leg to go rigid.

Enraged, she sought after the remaining two Icecrows, which had begun to spiral around her, snapping their beaks and talons at her while their riders attempted to control them. The BlackHound may have discovered how to use them as mounts, but the creatures were far from domesticated. Instinct ruled over the commands of their masters. Right then, their instinctual hate of dragons was keeping them from destroying the castle.

Good thing too.

Shatterbreath twisted in the air, catching an Icecrow in the throat with the tip of her wing, which also threw the rider off. Before he plummeted like his mount, the rider managed to hurl a green orb at Shatterbreath—this one the size of a cougar's head. She dipped and the sphere soared over her to strike the remaining Icecrow rider.

The explosion was immense. It rattled Shatterbreath's teeth in her skull and caused a ringing in her ears. The world swooned and she was just able to keep aloft. After a few seconds, though, she had recovered. She let out a roar of triumph. She had saved the castle—and thereby Kael as well. She was about to perform a back-loop to celebrate when she spotted them—more Icecrows. Heading straight for her.

293

With a gasp, she twisted into a barrel roll to avoid the creatures and their deadly weapons. Nine Icecrows passed her by. One clipped her tail.

And detonated.

Shatterbreath's scales could withstand the hottest of fires. But they were useless against whatever magic the orb carried. She howled in pain as the last foot and a half of her tail was blasted completely off, leaving a bloody stump.

Shocked by the pain, Shatterbreath was helpless as eight Icecrows slammed into the castle. Almost immediately, seven of them exploded, sending huge fragments of stone hurling. The explosions cut deep into the structure, causing floors to collapse and walls to crumble. The explosions were few, but they were powerful and the impact profound.

For a time, it seemed as if the castle would withstand the attack. Despite the gaping holes spread across western face, it remained standing, as if defying what the BlackHound Empire had tried to do to it. It was during that precious moment Shatterbreath spotted Kael, leaning against a windowsill, absolute terror spread across his face.

Then, the castle buckled.

The south-western side went first—where the Icecrows had hit the hardest. As the side of the building crashed down onto the base of the training grounds wall, a spire came loose, slowly listing with a terrible *crunching* sound until it broke free of the rest of the structure.

Shatterbreath didn't wait to watch it to fall.

Without hesitation, she threw herself at the building. By the time she reached the window where Kael had been standing, the rest of the castle was crumbling. Ignoring the instinctual scream in her mind that told her to flee, she forced half of her body into the room. Kael stumbled about the room as pieces of the ceiling hailed down.

"Kael, here! I've got you!"

"Shatterbreath!"

The room listed severely and he half-dove, half-tripped underneath. She curled in her body around him, folding her wings, limbs, tail and neck in tight as the ceiling collapsed on them. It was too late to pull out.

The next moments were nothing but chaos. Debris of all sorts crashed around Shatterbreath with tremendous noise, striking her from all angles and forcing the breath from her lungs. She was aware of a vague sense of falling, though it was impossible to tell in which direction. She tumbled head-over-tail, losing all sense of direction. The agony seemed to last for hours, as if she had become perpetually trapped in a waterfall comprised of stone.

Then, they were no longer falling.

And there was nothing but pressure. An endless weight pressing down on her.

Chapter 28

Soldiers saluted Commander Coar'saliz and he strolled through the camps. He ignored them all and continued on his way. After turning down a few more corridors of soldiers standing at attention, he came upon the blue war tent. Throwing the cloth door aside, he entered.

"Sir!" his general barked in their native language. A short, withdrawn little man with a face slanted in permanent concern. He was not the bravest man the Commander knew, but he was unconditionally faithful. Like a dog that was scared to be beaten if it disobeyed.

"At ease. Give me your report, General." His voice was impatient and stern. The general squirmed under his fierce gaze.

"The last few weeks have not been in our favour, Sir. Ever since the castle came down on top of the hostile dragon, our own refuses to fight, giving the Resistance air superiority. And with the arrival of the Resistance's new reinforcements, they now dominate the ground as well."

Commander Coar'saliz placed his hands down on the lone table occupying the room. Over its surface was a stolen map of Vallenfend, with markers indicating the forces of either side. Currently, the Resistance had both location and numbers working for them.

"The banners they carried," he thought aloud. "Were they...?"

"Nestoff, sir."

"By the Homeland," the Commander muttered. "How did they convince that blasted city to assist? There was no way they would have come if..." His voice trailed off as he fell deep in thought.

"If what, sir?"

"...If Knutton was still a threat to them." He seized the table and hurled it across the tent. It tore a hole through the fabric. "Our backup—our own reinforcements—have been destroyed. Nestoff would have not come otherwise."

The General stayed silent for a long time, avoiding the Commander's eyes. "Sir... If I may suggest..."

Composing himself, the Commander clasped his arms behind his back. "What is it? Speak up, you fool."

"I think... The days are getting shorter and the nights longer. There is a chill in the air that refuses to leave. Winter will be upon us soon enough. We won't survive through the winter. Which is why... Why I think we should consider retreating."

"The BlackHound Empire does not retreat" the Commander snapped. "We can still win this yet. With our reinforcements on this continent eliminated, we will simply have to summon more from the Homeland. It will take some time, but we can hold out until then."

"Commander, the Homeland cannot spare more men—not enough to win us this war. The—the Resistance back home, it has gained momentum. Our Empire is fighting to crush it against all fronts. If we turn back now we can h—"

"If we turn back now..." Commander Coar'saliz pulled a dagger from his pocket and held it to the General's chest. "Then the Resistance will only gain *more* momentum. They will see the failure of our great plan. They will know the Empire can be defeated. What sort of morale do you think that will bring for them—or our own troops for that matter? This battle is for more than just this continent now. This battle is for *both* continents. We lose Vallenfend, we lose the *Homeland.*"

The General licked his lips. There was a bead of sweat rolling down his forehead. Gently, the Commander caught it on the tip of his dagger and then backed away. "But, wise General, you are correct. The Homeland cannot spare us any men."

"What are we going to do, Sir?"

The Commander turned away and strolled across the room. "If only I had that Rundown boy a week longer. I could have broken him." He made a fist. "Broken him like a horse. He would have been *mine* to control. I could have swayed the Resistance and made them crumble. Just a week longer..." He stared out the hole in the tent. Vallenfend's wall was just visible over the stretching expanse of the BlackHound camp. "No matter. We will summon our own reinforcements. Fetch Vallenfend's king."

"Sir, you don't mean... No. That alone can save us now!"

297

"Does it matter?" Commander Coar'saliz whipped around and hurled the dagger at the general. The weapon stuck into his thick breastplate but was stopped by the hauberk underneath. Still, the anxious man whimpered as if it had struck flesh. "Do as I order!" the Commander roared.

"I obey at once!" And the General was gone.

The Commander sighed and crouched in front of a wide chest. Producing a key first, he unlocked it and slowly opened the lid. Inside laid a cane, roughly four feet in length and a rosy brown. The head of a cobra, maw wide open and hood fanned, was carved into one end, and a spiny tail described on the other. The head and tail of a splinter-snake. He inspected the smooth finish on the cane for a long time, brooding. Despite its relative simplicity, the cane held great magical power. It was one of the strongest artifacts in the Empire's possession. It had been given to him personally by the Emperor. As a final precaution.

With reverence, he picked up the cane. It hummed in his hand with pure energy. The Commander was one of the Empire's most powerful magicians, but even he had never experienced such strength. A smile spread across his ordinarily passive face.

"Now," he said, twirling the cane in his grip, "it is my turn to fight."

The General re-entered the room, holding King Morrindale by the scruff of his robe. "Unhand me you swine!" the former king cried. "Commander, what is this all about? You promised me immunity!"

"You've lost weight," Commander Coar'saliz commented. He came up close, putting the head of the sneak to the king's chin. Morrindale stiffened. "Situations have changed, dear king. But I have a better proposition for you. How does incomprehensible power sound to you? How about...*immortality?*"

The last word caught King Morrindale's attention. He licked his greedy lips. "Immortality? You're talking about...cheating death? Living forever? And... And power?"

"Yes. It can all be yours, for a small price."

He pulled his head away from the cane and eyeballed it. "A price? What price?"

"Hmm. Glad to see you agree. General, send messengers to the Resistance and bring King Morrindale to the top of the hill. I have a message to deliver to our enemies. Ready the troops as well."

"Aye sir."

"Wait, what price? What price?" Commander Coar'saliz heard King Morrindale scream those words as he was dragged through the camp. "What price?!"

The Commander returned to inspecting the cane. "Today," he told it, "we make our final stand."

The cane glowed red in reply.

Chapter 29

"Kael!" Kael turned over in his bed, trying to ignore the sound. "Kael!" it came again. "Blast it, where are you?"

"Five more minutes," he mumbled in reply.

"Do you know where K—oh, thank you." Somebody shook him rigorously. "Kael, wake up, wake *up*."

"What, what is it?" he turned over, wiping the sleep from his eyes. "I thought it was a weekend..."

"What? No. Kael, it's the BlackHound Empire... Their leader wishes an audience with you." It was Janus. He thought she was somebody else... "You have to go at once! Hurry, hurry."

Kael blinked, trying to process what she was saying. Altogether, her words struck him and he bolted upright in his bed. He was in the barracks, inside the castle training grounds. They were even stuffier than they had been since his stay when he was recruited, but at least they had been fixed up for the most part. The holes had been plugged and the mould scraped away, making the buildings at least inhabitable. The barracks were always filled with soldiers, most of which were raucous and loud as they tried to tear their thoughts away from the war for a short time. Now, they had fallen silent. All eyes were trained on Kael and Janus.

"Where is he?" Kael asked her.

"Standing on a hill just outside of Vallenfend, with..." Her voice cracked. "With my father."

"Okay." He stood up. "I'll go at once. How's Faerd?"

She flicked the hair out of her eyes. "He's doing much better today. I think his fever has run its course. He'll recover yet—he might even be able to get up today."

Kael slipped on his hauberk. "Good, excellent."

Janus watched him put on his armour. "How is Shatterbreath?"

Kael hesitated. "Doing better. She's more cranky about being cooped up than anything."

When the castle had fallen down on her, more than a month ago, it had broken one of her legs, as well as every single spine along her back. It was miraculous that that was the most damaged she had received. She had been bruised and cut all over her body, especially her wings, but it was nothing Kael couldn't stitch closed. Her tail had been injured the worst, but that had happened *before* they were buried alive in the ruins of the castle.

It was also a miracle Allegiance forces had been able to unearth them from the wreckage so quickly, especially with the rain bogging everything down. Kael and Shatterbreath had almost suffocated.

So much had happened since then...

For a week or so, the BlackHound Empire and the Allegiance had fought inside the city limits. Capturing Archer Alley, it turned out, served a purpose after all, and Allegiance archers were able to ambush many soldiers and Icecrows alike in its tight corridor. Despite their two strongest assets gone—Shatterbreath and the castle—the Allegiance kept the upper hand the duration of the battle. Kael was bedridden until recently, but he heard tales of gruelling battles as Allegiance soldiers moved from building to building, fighting ferociously for each one.

Then, at long last, the Allegiance had been able to push the BlackHound Empire out of the city for good. There had been a week-long truce as both sides recovered until the Allegiance went on the offence.

They had been fighting—mostly in the fields between Vallenfend and the BlackHound camp—since then, with little leeway to either side.

Until Nestoff arrived.

Their numbers were few, but the soldiers Nestoff brought were huge, trunk-like men, garbed in thick armour and carrying broadswords or lances. There were only roughly two-thousand of them, but were as efficient as eight-thousand.

With their powerful new addition, the Allegiance was winning the war. It was no longer about taking the city back or even defending it. Now, it was the BlackHound Empire defending against them. Kael and the Allegiance leaders had been speculating something big from the BlackHound Empire for several days. It seemed their insight was correct.

Kael fitted both hands into gauntlets. "Alright, I'm ready. Thank you for informing me, Princess."

She averted her gaze. "I don't think I'm Princess anymore." Kael studied her. She had changed a lot during the war. Fatherless, homeless and without servants, she seemed to have realized that getting her way every time was no longer an option. She was humbler, less demanding and somewhat shy. In Kael's opinions, the changes were for the better.

"I should be off."

"Can I come with you?" she asked suddenly.

Kael hesitated. "If you really wish. I have no idea what their leader is planning. Whatever it is, I'm sure we won't enjoy it."

"I want to be there."

"Follow me then. We'll go to the wall and speak to him from there." He opened the door to the barracks and shielded his eyes from the sun. Despite it, the day was particularly chilly. If he was correct, Fall was rapidly approaching.

A few soldiers—Alek among them—noticed and approached to escort him through the city. With half of it in shambles, there was no telling whether or not the BlackHound Empire had remaining forces in the city. Kael had heard mention a few days ago of an ambush on a pair of cooks salvaging spices from a merchant's hut.

They made their way through the castle's grounds quickly, pushing out into the streets where men usually crowded open fires or sat against destroyed buildings, sharpening their weapons. Now, there were only a few people roaming around.

"Where is everybody?" Kael asked Alek.

"Most of our forces are at the west end of Vallenfend, ready defend the borders. The BlackHound Empire has collected the entirety of their army just outside our archers' range." He inhaled sharply. "It seems they gather for an attack."

Kael stepped over a burnt body. "Why was I not informed earlier?"

"You fought bravely yesterday, Rundown," Alek replied. "Until their leader demanded your audience, Clodde decided it better for you to rest."

Kael bit back a retort. "Thank you."

Sure enough, as they neared the wall, Allegiance soldiers began to appear. Most of them were archers, either positioned in the taller buildings or along the top of the wall. Kael brushed past them to stand near the western gate, where the wall was the tallest. The Allegiance leaders—Kings Respu, Henedral, Goar—were waiting for him, as well as Korjan, Tomn, Bunda and Laura.

Kael gave them a nod before surveying the scene. Before him stretched the Allegiance, and across the war-scarred earth, the BlackHound Empire. Though their numbers were less than a quarter of what they had once been, they were no less imposing. Icecrows hovered above their troops while wyverns circled above the Allegiance armies.

Directly in the centre of both forces, a hill jutted out, giving either side full view of Commander Coar'saliz. To his left stood another man—his general, Kael presumed—and to his right a man thought to be lost. King Morrindale.

So he did run to the BlackHound Empire, Kael thought. *Little help they were.* Clearly, the whole display was against the former king's liking. He squirmed in the Commander's grasp to no avail, arms bound behind his back.

"He demands speak with you closer," King Goar grunted.

"How close?"

King Henedral leaned against his sword. "Twenty paces before of our front line."

"Well within projectile distance," Korjan added.

"That's not going to happen," Kael scoffed. "That's too obvious of a trap."

"What will you do?" King Nestoff asked. "We're on the edge here, Kael. This could be the final battle—but it won't commence without your say."

Kael heard a familiar *whoosh* and frowned. Moments later, Shatterbreath alighted on the wall, favouring her front right leg which had been encased in a thick, sturdy splint. There were stained bandages all over her body and one of her eyes was nearly forced close by a bruise. She huffed, startling the horses down below.

"What is happening?" she said cheerily, wearing a slight smirk.

"You should be resting, that's what."

She blew warm air in Kael's face. "Quiet you. Nobody orders a dragon around."

"Shh!" Laura hissed. "Their leader is saying something."

They all went silent to listen. The supple wind and the soft din of soldiers shifting their weight muffled his voice so that Kael couldn't understand a word.

"You're not going to do what he says, are you?" Shatterbreath asked after a slight pause.

"You can hear him?" King Henedral asked.

She scoffed. "Of course. You morsels can't?"

They exchanged glances. "What did he say?"

"For you to come closer."

"That's not happening. Shatterbreath, your hearing is better than mine and your voice louder. Could you...?"

"He can hear you just fine from here!" Shatterbreath boomed. "Say what you have to say."

Even from his distance, Kael could see the Commander frown. He waved his hand in a strange way and his palm glowed an unearthly orange for a moment. When he spoke next, his voice was tripled in magnitude, so that Kael could hear him easily. So, having him come closer *had* been a trap. "Do you think deflecting this lunge with stop the sword? Do you think the BlackHound Empire would give up so easily?"

"What do you wish me to say?" Shatterbreath inquired.

"Nothing." Kael squinted, trying to make out his features. The king had stopped squirming by then, probably realizing it was futile. "Let him continue."

"Take a long look, Rundown, at your former king." Commander Coar'saliz shook Morrindale. "Can you see him from there? He is frail, he is frightened. He is the embodiment of your petty Resistance. But unlike all of you, he saw the strength of the BlackHound Empire. He knows what we are and what we're capable of. He chose to deal with us wisely—to join us, to help us conquer this land. He chose life over death, strength over weakness.

"We promised him to make him more like us. We promised him riches, power and youth. But you know this already, don't you? I promise you, all of it is possible. Only through us. But you chose to stand against us and face death than to share the riches. All of you. You would prefer to die by the sword for a futile cause? You choose to be like *him* instead of like *us?*"

Commander Coar'saliz was worked up now. His words were thick with emotion and his voice quavered. The Allegiance soldiers were becoming anxious from his display, shifting their weight with more uncertainty and glancing around at their brethren. Kael could tell many of them were considering the Commander's words—what could have been theirs if they were on the other side of the battlefield.

The Commander stroked Morrindale's matted hair, which made the former king cringe. "Alas, it is a shame this man will never get to see our promises come into fruition." The tempo of Kael's heart picked up. "Believe me, we had all intention of fulfilling our promises." The other man on the hill handed the Commander a strange cane with the head of a snake.

Shatterbreath perked up. The muscles in her neck went taut. "Kael... Can you feel that? Dark magic."

Kael nodded. He *did* feel it. He could see it too. A storm was forming above and mist swirled across the plains, slowly creeping towards the hill where the Commander stood in a twisting spiral.

"You've pushed us, Rundown. Pushed us too far. Now, we are forced to do something drastic. I should have seen it earlier—that we would need more than just the strength of our backs to accomplish the task of taking your city. We needed a weapon. A weapon void of compassion. A weapon that could cut down legions upon legions of men without mercy. A man that would trade thousands of innocent lives in the name of greed. A king that would sacrifice his own people to attain his own selfish needs."

Kael didn't dare look away. "Janus," he whispered. She stirred nearby. "Janus. Leave... Leave right now!"

She didn't budge.

"Someone..." The Commander protruded a dagger from his waist. Lighting crackled overhead—flashing green. He rubbed the blade against the haft of the cane and sparks shot out. Pure darkness congealed around the feet of the three standing on the hill. "Someone like your king here."

With that, he stabbed the dagger into the base of King Morrindale's neck. When he removed it, blood spewed out of the wound in an arch and the king went limp, slumping face-first to the ground.

Janus's scream pierced the air. It was the most haunting thing Kael had ever heard. She buried her face against Kael's shoulder and he held her tight, looking away.

For a long time, every soul remained breathless.

Shatterbreath was the first to break the silence. "Kael..."

"Not now, Shatterbreath."

"Kael." This time more insistent. "Look."

"I—I can't..."

"Look," she hissed. It was not a suggestion. "His body moves."

Kael reluctantly let go of Janus and threw his gaze over the field. An arch of green lightening struck Morrindale's body. "Show me."

As soon as he touched her side, he was thrust into her vision. Shatterbreath was right. The body was moving—not just twitching, but writhing, as if being electrocuted.

Another arch of sinister lightening struck the body, and another, though the body itself remained unharmed. In fact, each strike seemed to give the corpse life. The darkness that had surrounded the Commander crept up the body in tendrils. Morrindale's body raised itself up onto all fours, digging fingers into earth. Blood still streamed from his neck—it was no longer red but pitch-black.

"This can't be happening," Kael gasped. "He can't...he can't still be alive, can he?"

Shatterbreath remained silent.

Still in her vision, Kael witnessed as one last bolt of lightning struck down. A wisp of darkness found its way to his neck and altogether, a stream of it forced its way into his body, halting the flow of blood. Morrindale's body seized and his spine bulged, as if it was trying to tear itself free.

Then, Morrindale's flesh tore.

There was a collective gasp as his back ripped open. Even from where he stood, Kael could distinctly here the *rip*. Kael's stomach lurched as he witnessed bloody tendrils protrude from the open tear. Other areas on his body split as well, revealing more tentacles and painting the hillside in his blood.

Besides the tendrils, Morrindale's body was changing in other ways as well. His neck elongated and when he opened his mouth, a full set of jagged teeth flashed brilliant white. The glimpse of his eyes sent shivers up Kael's spine. It was then Kael realized that body no longer belonged to Morrindale.

The tendrils wrapped themselves around the body in waves, completely enveloping whatever had been left of King Morrindale.

"What's happening? What are those?" Kael dared to ask.

Shatterbreath shuddered as she inhaled. "I think...sinew."

Slowly, the writhing mass of sinew took form as every fibrous tendril settled, interlocking themselves together. The body lifted itself onto four limbs, now completely transformed. Through Shatterbreath's vision, Kael could see its details clearly. It stood like a wolf, with hunched shoulders and a pair of lizard-like tails sprouting from its rear end. It was skinless, so that the still-bloody vines of tendons and muscle were fully exposed over its body. Two pairs of eyes—the larger set milky and the other set cat-like, with vertical pupils and no visible whites—were set deep into its wide, blunt muzzle. It snapped its jaws impatiently, testing its strength and licking obsidian-like teeth that stuck out when it open its mouth. It also had a third set of limbs, smaller and tucked in close to its chest, behind its front legs. Each extra limb was garbed with three dagger-length claws that flared open and closed with each heavy breath it took. With every exhalation, a black liquid dripped from its jaws, only to disappear before touching the ground.

Was it literally breathing out darkness?

The monster reared onto its hind legs, body rippling, and roared. Every single person on the battlefield—BlackHound or Allegiance—

cringed and clutched at their ears. Kael was forced out of Shatterbreath's vision as she cringed. He himself doubled over, slapping his hands over his ears. The wyverns quickly darted into the city, perhaps trying to elude the noise behind the buildings. The Icecrows, however, seemed unaffected.

When the creature stopped, its shriek could be heard echoing across the land. A few seconds passed and it came back again, greatly reduced from rebounding off the surface of Shatterbreath's mountain.

The Commander waited a long time before talking. Kael realized he was just waiting for the ringing in everybody's ears to die down. "With this Kellthuzard under *my* control," he yelled, "the BlackHound Empire will be victorious yet! Soldiers! CHARGE!"

On his command, the entirety of the BlackHound Empire started forwards.

"We must keep them away from the city!" King Henedral cried. "Meet them in the middle. Soldiers, attack!"

Most of the men didn't hear, those who did glanced around in confusion.

Shatterbreath rose up on her hind legs and roared, "Attack!"

There was no confusion there. The Allegiance army moved to intercept the BlackHound Empire's advance. As the two mighty forces moved towards each other, Kael noticed the *Kellthuzard* creature leap off the hillside. He lost it the throng of enemy soldiers.

"Shatterbreath, fly away," Kael ordered. "You're not set to fight."

He could see she wasn't happy about it, but she obeyed him, taking wing and retreating back into the city.

"This is it, friends," Kael declared the Allegiance leaders. They all turned to him and he scanned their faces in turn, lingering on Laura. "We've made a valiant stand. Not by the strength of one, but by the strength of us all. Together, let us fight this last time. This— *this* is the final battle. The end of the war."

"Victory or death," Korjan proclaimed.

"Victory or death," the others echoed.

King Henedral clasped a strong hand down on Kael's shoulder. This time, Kael didn't shy away. "It would be an honour," he said, "to have you fight by my side, Rundown. Will you join me?"

Kael considered him. He had been totally distrusting of Kael for the longest time. What King Henedral was really saying was that he trusted Kael once again. "It would be an honour," Kael told him with a warm smile.

"Fight well," King Goar grunted. With a wild spark in his eyes, he jumped off the wall, landing solidly below. Kael watched him storm off into the throng of the Allegiance soldiers, brandishing his sword like a berserker.

"Good luck," Korjan said next. He chose to run down to the gate, unsheathing his duel axes.

"On your call, Rundown," King Henedral said with a nod.

Kael hesitated and held his breath as the two armies came together. There was audible crash, punctuated by the screams of horses and men alike. Explosions dappled the front lines, drowning out the *whizzing* of soaring arrows. Kael squinted, looking for... There! Commander Coar'saliz was right in the heat of battle, toting a sword in one hand and the snake-head cane in the other. He was tearing pieces out of the Allegiance soldiers, lighting groups of them on fire or hurling men across the battlefield, using an advanced magic Kael had never seen before. The cane must have been his source of power; it flashed with every attack he made.

"See that man?" Kael said, pointing. "I want him dead."

King Henedral nodded. "Consider it done."

Backed by several Fallenfeld soldier—most high-ranking generals—Kael and King Henedral joined the battle. They soon found that unlike the other battles before, the BlackHound soldiers were diffused among the Allegiance soldiers and vice versa. This battle was purely to kill the opposition. There was no set point to attack or defend. The BlackHound Empire was like a cornered dog; with no other option, it was lashing out just to tear flesh.

Kael and King Henedral began carving their way towards where the Commander had been. Luckily, Kael had been able to pick up a BlackHound shield early on in the fight. It felt good holding a proper shield again, as if part of him had been revived. More than once, it also saved his life.

The battle was gruelling. The bodies of slain men lay everywhere and the ground was soaked with blood, making a sturdy footing a difficult thing to get. With every man Kael slew, every image of gore—raw cartilage exposed through a face, limbs hewn off and muscle and bone cleaved—Kael became more and more detached, losing himself to instinct.

The amount of men he killed seemed limitless and the amount yet to be killed even greater. With his ability to slow time and the permanently-sharpened *Vintrave,* Kael was not a force to be trifled with. Especially when he was backed by King Henedral—whose skills with a blade were formidable—as well as Fallenfeld's highest generals.

The wyverns played their part too. Whenever an Icecrow flew low enough to make an attempt to attack, three or four wyverns would strike it down first. Still, several javelins thrown by the birds' riders came terrifyingly close to impaling Kael, only to be pulled back by cords attached to the hafts of the blades. If they weren't taken down by archers or wyverns, the Icecrows would retreat back to the skies.

Kael couldn't say how well the battle was going, or how long he fought for before having to pause to catch his breath. It must have been a matter of hours. Guarded by King Henedral's generals, Kael placed his hands on his knees, sucking air. The chill of the day had long been chased away by the warmth emanating from the fighting bodies and hot blood. Kael felt as though he was suffocating in his suit of armour and despite the risks had removed his helmet.

A commotion caught Kael's attention. Standing up straight, he peered over the generals' shoulders. A knot formed in his stomach as he realized what it was. The monster born of Morrindale. The Kellthuzard. Despite all of the many weapons raised towards it, it tore a bloody path into the Allegiance forces. It barrelled past Kael's line of sight, pouncing on two soldiers. With its razor-filled mouth, it tore the breastplate off of a soldier's chest and bit into his innards. At the same time, it clawed at the throat of the second soldier with the third set of limbs affixed to its chest. Protruding from its skinless body were many weapons—poleaxes, swords and over a dozen arrows. Its own black blood intermingled with the blood of the men it had slain, covering almost every inch of its tawny body.

With every movement it made, its exposed sinews and muscles contorted over its lithe body. At first glance, it seemed built thick and sturdy like a wolf, but it moved more catlike than anything. After swatting away a charging Allegiance soldier with its pair of tails, it lifted and cocked its bulky head, entrails hanging from its jowls, to stare straight at Kael. Its frontal set of eyes darted about, scanning its surrounding, but its milky eyes were distinctly trained on him. He froze under the scrutiny of its feral gaze—it was as though he were staring down death itself.

It opened its maw, letting the meat it was holding fall to the ground. When it inhaled, it sounded as though the arrows stuck had punctured its lungs several times over. It shuddered, muscles seizing and nostrils flaring. When its chest was filled with air, it threw its head back, pointing its blood-encrusted snout to the heavens to let loose another ear-splitting screech, as if it was trying to rupture the sky with the very magnitude of its voice.

Everybody within its near vicinity doubled over, clutching their ears. It was an awful noise. High pitched with a strange low tone at the same time that reverberated through Kael's chest. He couldn't stand it. Composing himself, he seized an axe lying nearby and hurled it at the Kellthuzard.

The axe glanced off the side of the creature's head. Bone flashed white through the gauge before overwhelmed by black blood gushing. The blade punctured one of its eyes and it thrashed its head before charging off into the throng of soldiers. Kael could hear it yowling as it ran away.

"By the gods, what is that creature?" King Henedral asked, rubbing his ears.

Kael put a hand to his temple. "The result of greed and dark magic. The more important question is if it can be killed. Weapons don't seem to be affecting it."

"Maybe we could..." Kael didn't hear the rest of his suggestion for he spotted Commander Coar'saliz behind the king, strolling rather calmly into view a bowshot away. The man, wearing a passive expression, twirled the snake-headed cane in his grasp and then pointed it in the direction of an Allegiance soldier. A prominence of light erupted from the end of the cane. When it subsided the soldier—as well as many behind him—was gone. Only a molten streak in the ground remained.

"There he is!" Kael yelled, waving *Vintrave* at the Commander. A twisted grin spread across the Commander's face as he spun the cane in his grip once again. Time slowed to a crawl as the Commander brought the cane forward, aiming the snake's head on top at King Henedral. Kael jumped forward, placing himself between King Henedral and the Commander.

Wisps of air streaked towards the head of the cane. It must have drawn energy out of the surroundings. The cane released its pent-up energy at Kael, who planted his feet and braced his shield and Vintrave in front of his body. There was nothing else he could do.

Kael closed his eyes as the magic raced towards him. He didn't know what he was expecting—what death would feel like. He was aware when the magic finally reached him; it pushed against his body like a wall of water, threatening to push him over. If it wasn't for King Henedral's body behind him, he probably would have.

But that was it.

Confused, Kael opened his eyes. There was a strange buzzing permeating the space around him, as if the air was charged with static. His hair was pushed back and his shield was partially melted, proving that the Commander had indeed thrown something at him. Aside from that, and the tingly feeling in his gut, Kael was just fine.

King Henedral licked his lips behind Kael. The sound seemed so loud in Kael's ear. "What just happened?" he asked.

"Doesn't matter," Kael replied sharply. He pushed against King Henedral's chest to regain his balance. "There's our man. Let's take him down."

"Aye!" King Henedral, sword raised, charged at the Commander, with Kael close in tow. Commander Coar'saliz quickly shook off his

312

surprise at Kael's unexplained survival. King Henedral's sword clacked against the snake-headed cane and a moment later Kael lunged for the Commander's chest. *Vintrave* was stopped by the sword Commander Coar'saliz held in his other hand. But only barely; Kael's sword had gauged halfway through the blade.

Kael saw a frown on the Commanders face before he zipped to the right—faster than humanly possible. He threw a barrage of attacks that were hard to parry, even with Kael's ability to slow time. The Commander was relentless, lashing out with his sword as well as his cane. The cane gave out a jolt of magic every time it struck, jarring Kael. With every magical attack Kael withstood, he could see the Commander's frustrations rising. Apparently, surviving the blasts wasn't normal.

The flurry of attacks seemed to last forever until King Henedral moved in from the side to intervene. The Commander spotted King Henedral almost too late. King Henedral's sword struck against the same nook left by Kael's.

And sheered the Commander's sword in half.

With a sound that resembled a growl, Commander Coar'saliz shot backwards, stirring up dust. He now stood a bowshot away from Kael and King Henedral again. Throwing his ruined sword to the side, he gave them a mock salute.

"Fight us, you coward" King Henedral shouted at him.

Something roared at them from the side in reply.

A tawny shape soared over Kael, ridged with muscle and armed with sharp claws. There was nothing Kael could do as it slammed into King Henedral. They tumbled over the bloody ground in a flurry.

"King Henedral!" Kael yelled. Heart in his throat, he rushed over to the king and stabbed *Vintrave* down to the hilt into the Kellthuzard's side. The demon turned its bloodied snout away from King Henedral to Kael, blood dripping heavily from its mouth and claws. Ignoring the massive wound in its side, it crouched down low, ready to pounce.

Just as it leapt, Silverstain appeared seemingly out of nowhere, seizing the Kellthuzard with his front paws. He transferred the snarling demon from his front to his back and with a serpentine flick of his body, hurled it far into the distance. It screeched as it soared out of sight, past the battlefield.

With it gone, Kael did a full 360, searching for the Commander. He was gone. Silverstain landed beside Kael as he fell to his knees beside King Henedral, who was bleeding profusely from three massive gauges in his chest that stretched from his hips to partway into his neck. At first glance, anybody could tell he wasn't going to survive.

"King Henedral..." Kael was at a loss for words.

The king swallowed laboriously. "It was an honour...to fight with you, Kael. I...I've made my ancestors proud."

"People will remember you for this." King Henedral raised a hand and Kael gripped it tight. "I cannot thank you enough. Fallenfeld will eternally be in our debt."

A content expression befell King Henedral, despite the way his body shuddered. "I have...one final request, Rundown."

"Anything, brave King."

He fumbled for his blade. Kael helped him unbuckle it from his waist. "Take my ancestral sword, Rundown. Let...let the spirits guide you."

"I..."

"And...one more thing." Meekly, he removed his helmet and thrust it into Kael's hands. "I hereby...hereby give you kingship over Fallenfeld."

The helmet was symbolic of the king's crown on the battlefield. It was a sturdy piece of equipment, matching the design of King Henedral's armour, trimmed with gold and red, bearing the crest of Fallenfeld—the soaring bird of prey. Kael struggled to speak. "King Henedral..."

The king smiled faintly. "On the condition... The condition..." His eyelids fluttered, threatening to close forever. Kael squeezed his hand tighter, which seemed to invigorate him. "On the condition you pass this kingship onto my son."

Kael let out a small sigh of relief. "As soon as the war is over, I promise."

"Thank...you..." His head dropped to the ground and his final breath escaped his lungs. The hand holding Kael's went limp. Holding back tears, Kael folded the king's arms over his belly in a peaceful position. There was nothing else he could do.

"He is dead." Kael twisted his head to come face-to-face with a reflection of himself in the silver patch on Silverstain's chest. Kael had no idea the dragon was even there. He noticed several of King Henedral's generals—*his* generals—watching as well. Many of them had tears in their eyes.

"Hail, King," a general said.

"Your highness," another.

"Hail!"

Kael scanned their faces. "King Henedral was a good man. I cannot hope to do justice to his name by taking this..." Kael weighed the helmet in his hands. "But I will certainly try." He fitted it over his head. "Who among you is chief?"

"I, sire." Kael scrutinized the general—a bold-faced man with sandy-brown hair, stern eyes and a modest beard adorning his chin. "Captain Dukeson."

"You are in command until I return. Alert the soldiers of their king's passing, as well as the fact the green dragon is now our ally."

"Aye, King." Captain Dukeson pointed at a couple of soldiers. "You heard your king! Get to it, boys!"

Kael paused to study Silverstain. "Why did you save me?" he asked the dragon.

Silverstain faltered, although his gaze remained steady. "If Shatterbreath desires you to survive, then so do I. The BlackHound is losing; their promises are empty now. I...am trying to make amends."

Kael nodded. "It's good to have you with us now. Could you take me to the wall?"

Silverstain's jaws went taut and he growled under his breath. "Take you to the wall?" he echoed. "By letting you ride on my back?"

"Whatever works for you."

"Wait," Captain Dukeson interjected. "Where are you going, King?"

Kael pursed his lips. "To find out what that *thing* is that killed King Henedral—and how *we* kill *it*. I will return shortly, I promise."

Silverstain's tail thrashed and huffed out smoke. "I will carry you to the wall." Silverstain rose up on his hind legs. After pausing to consider him, Silverstain snatched up Kael with his front paws and then beat his wings powerfully. Performing an aerial feat that made Kael's stomach churn, Silverstain pointed himself towards Vallenfend. It took a while, but the archers along the wall stopped firing at Silverstain when they saw Kael in the dragon's grasp. In a matter of seconds, Silverstain placed Kael up on the wall and twisted away, flying up high into the sky.

Kael shook his head. The dragon's intentions were well, but he acted squeamishly around Kael, they way somebody would if they were handling a spider. Shatterbreath hadn't been nearly as apprehensive towards him, had she?

Kael studied King Henedral's sword. He squeezed the hilt, missing his friend. Kael could hardly believe he was now king of Fallenfeld. He didn't feel like king. He didn't feel any different at all.

The screech of a wyvern passing close by overhead shot Kael back into reality. *There was a war going on.*

Chapter 30

Since the castle had been destroyed, the Allegiance leaders had found a new spot to convene. It had once been an inn—one of the finest in Vallenfend, as Kael recalled. It was built to the southeast of the castle, rimming one of the seven courtyards. Kael had been told numerous times that one could see the entirety of the courtyard and its blooming flowers if they were lucky to get a certain room. As a youth, this had always entranced him. The courtyards were stunning, but one could only view them piece by piece. To see the courtyard as a whole always seemed so interesting. Faerd had once tried to sneak in with Kael. The innkeepers had shooed them away before they got within fifteen feet.

How long ago that was...

When Kael reached the front door of the inn, the guards stared at his helmet, stunned.

"King Henedral was slain in combat," Kael told them morosely. "He declared me his temporary successor."

"Your Majesty."

"Hail to you too," Kael said in reply. He walked past them and paused in the inn's lobby to readjust Fallenfeld's ancestral sword on his back. It added an extra bit of weight Kael wasn't comfortable with, but with no safe place to hide it, Kael decided carrying on his body would be the best course of action. Perhaps he would find himself in need of a second weapon anyway.

He climbed to the top floor and entered a large room only illuminated by three small oil lamps. All the blinds had been drawn to protect the room's occupant from the wyverns. Shatterbreath had convinced the wyverns to attack humans with dark skin. So naturally, Sal'braan had to keep out of sight from them.

Sal'braan squinted through the darkness, leaning over a map of Vallenfend that had been spread across an ostentatious table. "Who's there?" he asked.

"It's me."

"Ah, Rundown. Wh—what brings you here? How goes the war?"

"Commander Coar'saliz did something to Morrindale, Vallenfend's former king." Kael moved to one of the windows. Small veins of light flooded through the tiny holes along the edge of the blinds. "He turned Morrindale into some kind of monster... Swords and arrows don't seem to have any effect against it. It's slaughtering our men. It killed King Henedral not an hour ago. I need to know how to kill it."

Sal'braan laced his hands together. Despite his calm matter doing so, when he spoke there was a tremor in his voice. "He did *what* to the king?"

"The monster killed King Henedral. It leapt at him and..."

"Not that king," Sal'braan snapped. He stood up sharply. "Kael, this is extremely important. What did the Commander do to your king?"

Kael swallowed, reliving the memory. He described the whole process to Sal'braan.

The dark-skinned man slumped into his seat, putting a hand to his head in exasperation. "He summoned a Kellthuzard? Not good...not good..."

"Tell me how to kill it," Kael demanded.

Sal'braan sighed. "You can't."

Kael winced. "What?"

Sal'braan continued. "Summoning a Kellthuzard is extremely dangerous. There are stories from long ago describing magicians who lost control of their Kellthuzards. The beasts killed people by the hundreds. You can stab them, burn them, drown them, decapitate them... None of it will matter. Their bodies will heal and their bones graft back together. Some rumours state driving a golden sword through their heart will kill them."

"That's impossible." Kael shivered. "Otherwise those creatures would still be on the loose. They must have been killed somehow."

Sal'braan closed his eyes. "There is only one solution: kill Commander Coar'saliz. He controls the beast. Only *he* can stop the Kellthuzard. Kill him and you kill it. It's going to be nearly

318

impossible to do that though... The cane you described is an ancient artifact containing strong magical properties. It gives him power unbridled."

Kael put a hand to his chest. If the cane was all-powerful, why hadn't he been killed by the Commander's attacks? The magic Skullsnout gave him! It must have protected him... With that realization came another.

Sal'braan opened his eyes. "What are you thinking, Rundown?"

"I'm the only one who can do it," Kael muttered. Any other man would meet a quick death against the Commander. "I can't go to him though...no." He waved his hand in front of the window, sending the light sprawling across his hand in stripes. "I need him to come to me."

"What are you talking about? Please explain."

Kael perked up when he heard footsteps. In the time it took the intruder to open the door, Kael had bounded across the room to point *Vintrave* at his chest. He withdrew the blade when he noticed it was only one of the guards from downstairs.

"Whoa... I'm sorry to interrupt, Your Majesty, but there is news I think you should hear..."

"What is it?" Kael demanded.

"The sentries spread news of an army approaching from the west."

Kael's heart skipped a beat. "What?"

"What flag do they bear?" Sal'braan asked from behind.

The guard only frown at the dark-skinned man.

"Answer the question, solder!" Kael snapped. "He's one of us. Don't you know that?"

"Apologies, sir. They bear an unfamiliar crest." He hesitated. "I don't know if this is true, but I hear mention that they carry tridents as weapons. That's silly though."

It took a while for Kael to register the information. Tridents... There was something significant about tridents. They reminded him of... Of... Rooster.

Rooster's city used tridents as weapons.

"Snail-town? No... Farvu? Farthu? Farthu!" Kael gasped and turned to Sal'braan. "It's Farthu! They must have come by ships. I don't know if they are hostile or not. I knew someone who... I must check for myself. Thank you for your time, Sal'braan."

"Be careful, Rundown," Sal'braan warned. "If this new piece on the board is friendly to the Allegiance, Commander Coar'saliz will act rashly. He will try to hurt the Allegiance."

"That solves one problem then," Kael said through mock cheeriness. He rushed past the guard and hit the stairs at full sprint, nearly tripping at the bottom. "I won't have to try very hard to get the Commander after me..."

Chapter 31

"King Rundown!" Kael wouldn't have even seen the mounted knight if the man hadn't yelled out to him. It was Captain Dukeson.

Kael skidded to a halt, stirring up ashes. The captain had a group of cavalry with him. There were five knights in total, riding armoured chargers. Despite the heavy protection, they looked around anxiously, as if archers with steel bows were taking aim at them.

"Hail, Dukeson," Kael announced. "Why are...?"

"King Rundown, you are in grave danger!" the captain cried.

A shiver ran over Kael's skin. "The reinforcements?"

"They are not the issue!" He reached out his hand. "Come with us now, the BlackHound leader—"

"Scraah!" The Kellthuzard came screaming around the corner behind the cavalry, digging up sizable clods of road with its might claws. Teeth gleaming, it coiled and leapt at the first horse, which reared in surprise. With an audible *thud*, the Kellthuzard slammed into the side of the creature and its rider, sending them all tumbling.

The moment slowed to a crawl.

The force of the tackle must have winded the horse, for as it spun through the air, limbs flailing, mouth open, no sound escaped. Its rider, however, was fully vocal and a continual hiss escaped the maw of the Kellthuzard. Kael ducked by folding backwards, cringing as the trio soared over him. The body of the Kellthuzard struck the road mere feet behind Kael.

The horse died on impact, hitting its head against a protruding slab of stone. The Kellthuzard, as Kael witnessed, bounced once, caught hold of the soldier's head with one of its front paws and then slammed it into the awaiting wall.

The world returned its regular pace. What remained of the building crumbled around the monster. With Sal'braan's words ringing clearly in his mind, Kael shuffled away. Sure enough, he saw two tails flail through the haze and a moment later, the demon hopped out of the debris, seemingly unscathed.

'How do you kill it?'

321

'That's the thing. You can't.'

It spotted Kael and hissed.

"Rundown!" Kael glanced sideways to see Captain Dukeson galloping at him with his horse. Kael threw up his hand and the captain hefted him onto the horse without breaking pace.

Kael glanced back. The Kellthuzard made an attempt to pursue, but was knocked off its feet by one of the other cavalry's flail. Not a second later, a fireball incinerated the same man. The horse of another rider was startled by the conflagration. It spun around and reared up, only to have its chest blown open by another fireball. The rider was thrown from its back several metres.

The last thing Kael saw of the man before he, Captain Dukeson and the remaining horseman turned the corner was Commander Coar'saliz decapitating the fallen soldier from the back of his own horse.

Seconds later, the Kellthuzard rounded the corner, skidding into a wall before regaining its pace. They were riding down an alley—it had a straight path to them and it was much faster than Captain Dukeson's horse. Body pumping, it rapidly approached, baring its teeth all the while.

"Captain..." Kael warned.

"Hyah! Faster, you mongrel!" It didn't matter, the Kellthuzard was nearly on them.

"For Fallenfeld," the soldier declared beside them. He saluted and yanked on the reigns, forcing his horse to stop.

"Brother, no!" the captain screamed.

"Keep going," Kael ordered. "He's made his decision."

There was nothing either of them could do at that point.

The Kellthuzard hit the captain's brother at full speed, sinking its teeth and claws into flesh. As Kael watched the gore, a shimmering object caught his attention. It was the snake-headed cane, raised in Commander Coar'saliz's grip. A fireball launched from the cane, arching towards Kael and the captain.

Kael slapped Captain Dukeson's shoulder. "Veer left!" he cried.

Luckily, the alleyway opened onto a road. Dukeson steered his horse left and the fireball missed. Stinging flecks of debris pelted them from behind and Dukeson's horse whinnied in protest.

Uninhibited, Dukeson rode down the street and turned at the next road. Pushing his horse further onward, he turned corners at random, trying to lose both the Commander and the Kellthuzard.

Their flight took them near Saint Briggon's monastery. The spires, depicting angels and demons in eternal conflict, peaked high above the surrounding buildings. Most of all, the bell tower caught Kael's eyes. He had heard rumours a demon had been banished there centuries ago. Apparently, the more superstitious nuns refused to climb up to the top.

Captain Dukeson stopped his horse suddenly. Kael hadn't realized how worn the beast was until that point. Sweat trickled down its sides and foam dripped from its mouth with every haggard breath it took.

Dukeson dismounted his horse and helped Kael down. His horse staggered. Dukeson held its reigns tight. "This horse cannot take us any further." He sighed, patting its exhausted side as it sucked air. "I will hold them off as long as I can. Get somewhere safe."

Kael hesitated. "Captain?"

"I have made my decision." Their eyes met. There was a wild fury in Captain Dukeson's eyes, like a man who saw death's face and laughed. "Go. Find somewhere safe—return to the battlefield if you can. Your subjects will do well to protect you."

"I cannot thank you enough."

"Win us this war, Rundown, and my brother and I well rest in peace."

Kael was in a state of shock. His face felt void of blood and he blinked several times, trying to bring it back. Captain Dukeson drew his sword slowly, still holding on the reigns of his horse. A screech emanated from the end of the street. Dukeson nodded once at Kael, then turned to face the sound.

Broken of the trance, Kael spun on his heel and sprinted into the nearest alley.

At first, he had full intentions of getting back to the battle, but when he heard Dukeson's horse scream, he changed his direction. The battlefield was too far away, there was no way he was going to make it. The decision was made in an instant. Saint Briggon's Monastery. It was his only choice.

Snarls and growls chased Kael through the streets. At first, he thought it was his mind playing tricks on him. After spotting a tawny shape leaping across the rooftops, he knew otherwise. The Kellthuzard was stalking him. *Why won't it pounce?* Kael wondered. He wasn't about to argue its hesitation though.

Kael darted past another corner. His throat tightened as he heard a *thud* behind him. He didn't dare look back—he could hear the heavy breathing of the demon following him. The street opened up to the plaza skirting the front of Saint Briggon's Monastery. There was no cover, nowhere to dive behind—and the monster was directly behind him.

Kael pumped his arms and legs harder, forcing his body to go faster. Faster, faster! He sprinted across the plaza, unsheathing *Vintrave* as he went. The front doors to the Monastery seemed so far away—an unreachable goal. Still he ran and with every footstep, two more reverberated behind him, inching ever closer.

Kael glanced ahead. The doors were open! He could make it, he could make it! Apparently, the Kellthuzard realized the same thing for its footsteps stopped. The only reason that would happen is if it was leaping.

Kael's foot pounded over the first step, triggering time to slow to a crawl. Kael could clearly count all the steps leading up to the door. There were four of them. If he jumped off the second he could make it through the doors. Yes, they were opened just wide enough to allow his body to pass through, even with King Henedral's sword on his back. None of it would matter if the demon grabbed hold of him first though...

With a new plan already formulated, Kael hit the second step and twisted his body. *By the gods,* he managed to think. The Kellthuzard had all its limbs outstretched towards Kael, maw opened as well, showing its array of sharp teeth. Even as Kael witnessed, its smaller set of claws snatched onto his right leg, tearing straight through his armour as if it was parchment. Kael winced as the claws dug deep into his muscle.

Midair, Kael twisted to face the demon, bringing *Vintrave's* edge to its neck with both hands.

Time lurched back to normal.

Kael hit the ground on his side, sliding across the lobby of the monastery. The body of the Kellthuzard slid past him, ramming into the far wall. Less than two seconds later, its decapitated head followed suit.

Wincing, Kael sat up, clutching his leg which had begun to bleed profusely. He quickly removed the mangle plate from his shin. The sight of his own blood and muscle made Kael feel faint. Hiking his chainmail legging up to his thigh, he attempted to stand up. After his third try, he managed to hobble up onto his good leg.

Kael glanced around the lobby for anything that could be used to stop the blood. The curtains would suffice. He made a move towards them, but stopped dead when the body of the Kellthuzard twitched.

Breathless, Kael stared disbelieving at the demon. He had decapitated it—and it moved? Impossible.

Sure enough though, its body distinctly twitched. Its dual tails lifted and slashed threw the air and its long claws scraped against the ground as they pulled its body closer to its severed head. Kael gasped when it blinked its eyes. The milky pair trained on him and it seemed to try and growl at him. Without lungs attached, it only succeeded in working its jaw.

That was all Kael needed to see.

He half-ran, half-hobbled to the curtains and used *Vintrave* to cut a long strip off. As he wrapped the cloth around his wounded leg, he glanced around the room. There were many rooms that branched off from the lobby. It was the staircase that caught his attention, however.

There were two identical doorways leading to stairs, one nearby and another in a symmetrical spot across the room. From the outside view of the structure, Kael had to guess either one led up to the spires and ultimately the bell tower.

Kael shuffled over to the doorway and chanced a look back. The body of the Kellthuzard was more or less standing. Its shoulders were hunched as to touch the blood stump of its neck to the back of its severed head. To Kael's horror, the thick tendons that comprised the beast were *latching onto each other.* Even for the few seconds he was watching, the tendons pulled the head of the demon back into place. It was *healing.* Mortified, he hopped over the small guardrail—used to keep orphans from venturing up the stairs—and proceeded to climb.

He wasn't fast by any means, but fortunately the demon's rate of healing was slower. He passed window after window climbing the wide spiral staircase. With each pass around, he glimpsed a higher view of Vallenfend. The sun was low in the sky.

Kael paused when he came to a door. That high up, it could only be the bell tower's entrance. The staircase continued upwards, but it would only lead into the spires or up on the roof.

He jiggled the door handle. It didn't budge. Kael groaned in frustration. He considered climbing higher, but an ache from his leg made the decision for him. Backing up into the hall, he tackled into the door. It remained secure. Catching his breath, Kael slashed two of the three hinges then tried again. This time, the door crashed down.

A *ping* confused him, until an arrow fell to the ground nearby. He had been hit by an arrow. Nearly. It had glanced off his pauldron. *Archers up here?*

"Hold you fire!" a voice declared. "It's Kael!"

The sunlight pouring through the open end of the bell tower was blinding. Kael couldn't see her, but he knew the voice all too well. "Janus? What are you doing up here?"

She came to his outstretched arms. "We needed a safe place to watch the battle. Once we got up here, we realized there aren't any windows even pointing to the battlefield... Figured we might as well stay up here though... Safest place to hide, right?"

Janus led him out of the blinding light. "Who else is up here?" Kael asked.

Movement caught Kael's attention. He stepped around the massive bell hanging from the domed ceiling to get a full view of them. There were a dozen of them, with at least half that number being nuns. The rest seemed to be former castle attendants. Only one of them actually looked prepare for battle, holding the bow which had nearly killed Kael.

"Listen, Janus, you are all in grave danger," Kael declared. "You have to get out of here at once!"

The princess's face went bright red. "What? Why? What's wrong?"

"The Kellth..." Kael hesitated. He had forgotten who the Kellthuzard used to be. He avoided her eyes. It didn't matter, she knew exactly what he was getting at.

"My father?" she gasped.

Kael nodded. "And the BlackHound Commander. They'll be here any minute. You have to hide. You must leave!"

The group of women stood up. A couple of them had even started crying. Janus strode towards them and tried to comfort them. "What about you?" she asked over her shoulder.

"Just...get out of sight. I'll be fine." Kael put on his sternest expression.

Somehow, Janus read right through him. After all that time, was he still as readable as ever? Or did the princess have a talent for seeing through people? She didn't say anything, but gave him a concerned frown.

"Okay. Come on ladies. There's another way down over here." She ushered them to the far end of the bell tower, to where the door to the other staircase was. Flustered, they filed through the door. Janus turned to Kael. "Good luck, Kael," she said.

A deep rumbling emanated from the doorway Kael knocked down. The Kellthuzard was approaching. Kael nodded to the princess. "Start going down, but stay quiet."

She nodded and slipped into the stairway, shutting the door behind her.

Kael brandished *Vintrave.* "This is it," Kael murmured to himself. The rattling in the stairway grew louder. The Kellthuzard howled, curdling Kael's blood. He took a deep breath and let it linger in his chest. "For the better or the worse, this is the end—at long last."

The Kellthuzard burst out of the doorway, taking a large chunk of the frame with it. It planted all four paws and hissed. Kael stood strong, twisting his sword in his grip. Seconds later, Commander Coar'saliz appeared just outside the bell tower, literally *hovering* in the air. His cane glowed bright with energy; when he stopped into the bell tower, the glow ceased.

Only after glancing between the two—an agitated monster and a powerful wizard—did Kael falter. *How would he survive?*

The Kellthuzard made the first attack. It made a move right, so naturally Kael dove in the opposite direction. To his surprise, it *changed direction* before actually pouncing. It was smarter than he thought.

All Kael could do was put *Vintrave* out in front of him as it raced for his chest. The blade found the Kellthuzard's maw, pieced the back of its throat and protruded out of the back of its neck. Kael had to close his eyes to keep the demon's blood and spittle from going into his eyes. It was just as well. The heavy stench of its breath was stifling and the *snap* of its jaws was all too close to his face. He was only just able to pull his hands away before they were caught in its teeth.

The force of the Kellthuzard's tackled sent Kael skidding across the floor. Bruised but not broken, he scrambled to his feet with some difficulty. The Kellthuzard, with *Vintrave* rammed through its throat was less well-off. It coughed up blood, thrashing it head and workings its jaw, trying to get the blade out.

Kael unsheathed King Henedral's ancestral blade and held it warily with both hands. He wasn't used to using such a long blade. He glanced over at Commander Coar'saliz—just in time to dodge a bolt of lightning directed from his cane.

Meantime, the Kellthuzard grabbed hold of *Vintrave's* hilt with its long claws. It wrenched the blade free, sending a cascade of blood spewing from its haggard maw. Kael and Commander Coar'saliz both hesitated to watch it, either intrigued or repulsed by the act. When the blade was free, it remained clutching the sword. Kael gritted his teeth; there was little chance he was going to get it back any time soon.

Before the healing process was finished, the Kellthuzard snarled at Kael. The sound that escaped was muffled and saturated. It started low and worked its way higher, ending off on a sound that almost sounded like a door creaking.

Kael winced. It *was* a door creaking. Janus Morrindale poked her head out from behind the door at the back. "Kael? What's ha—" Her eyes shot wide when she spotted the Kellthuzard.

"Janus!" Kael's scream only turned the demon's attention towards her. It slapped both tails against the floor and hissed. "Get out of here, run!" Janus retreated back into the stairway.

It was too late. The Kellthuzard bounded twice and crashed through the door, tumbling down and out of sight.

"Janus, no!" Kael made an attempt to save her, but was stopped by an unseen force. It was as though a grown man had shoved him back. Again it came, this time against once shoulder, as to face him towards Commander Coar'saliz. One more invisible shove backed him into the gigantic bell. He hit it with a resounding *gong*.

"Watch her die, Rundown," the Commander spat. "There's nothing you can do about it. My Kellthuzard will skin her alive. A similar fate awaits you and the rest of your *Resistance*."

Kael threw a profane curse at the Commander. One ever Larr would find offensive.

Commander Coar'saliz shrugged it off and laughed. He strolled towards Kael, drawing small circles with the tip of his cane. With every loop, more force pressed against Kael, keeping him tight against the bell.

"I will relish this moment forever, Rundown," the Commander purred. "You will regret barring the progress of the BlackHound Empire. Now, how should I kill you? Slow and painful? Should I make you beg for death?" He raised the tip of his sword. "No. I've already made you do *that*."

Kael hated the sound of his voice. A snake held more charm. He pushed against the invisible restraints again, this time managing to break free. He batted the Commander's sword away and swung his own recklessly. The initial attack caught Commander Coar'saliz by surprise. Kael's sword swept across the man's face, carving into his cheek.

"You insolent!" The snake-headed cane found its way to Kael's face. There was a flash, then the world dipped into darkness for several seconds. When his vision returned, Kael found himself lying on the ground, face first in a puddle of his own blood. When he swallowed, all he could taste was rust.

"That blow would have killed a giant," the Commander exclaimed. He turned Kael over with the foot of his boot. "You have a strong resistance to magic, almost like a dragon. Perhaps this is why I couldn't break you before. I promise you I will discover the source of your resistance, even if I have to tear you apart strip by strip."

Kael clenched his empty hands. King Henedral's sword was lying to his right—too far away. Commander Coar'saliz bent over and hefted Kael by the neck of his breastplate and held him up against the bell so that Kael's feet weren't even touching the ground. Kael couldn't do anything about it; he was still reeling from that strike. The sun was right behind the Commander's head so the man's features were hidden in shadow.

"Any last words, Rundown?" the faceless Commander asked.

Kael looked past Commander Coar'saliz. A new shape was blocking out the sun. Flat except for in the middle. He thought at first it was Shatterbreath. The size gave it away. Silverstain outstretched his claws as he approached the tower.

Commander Coar'saliz cocked his head, obviously confused why Kael wasn't paying attention to him. The man winced and whipped around, discovering the incoming Silverstain at the last moment. He threw Kael to the side and screamed something. A bolt of red lightning erupted from the maw of the staff, lancing out to strike Silverstain in his silvery patch.

The dragon roared. The attack, though failing to kill Silverstain, caused him to miss his attack. Commander Coar'saliz hit the ground, dodging bladelike talons by a matter of a few feet. Silverstain crashed headlong into the bell. His wings tore the walls of the tower, causing the ceiling to buckled and collapse around him. Kael folded himself into a ball, covering his head with his hands. He had been in a building when it collapsed once before and it wasn't an entirely pleasing experience. He had been vainly hoping to never find himself in such a situation again.

As if he was that lucky.

When the immense noise had ceased, Kael dared to unfold himself. A cloudy sky presented itself to him, unhindered by the ceiling of the bell tower. Indeed, the entire mechanism had been wrenched loose. What remained of it—mostly thick ropes and crooked beams—hung over the back end of the tower in shambles. Silverstain—as well as the bell itself—were nowhere to be seen.

Kael stirred, and so did Commander Coar'saliz nearby. They spotted each other at the same time. The Commander glanced at his hand and winced. His cane was gone. He and Kael remained still for a while as the significance of the cane's disappearance sunk in.

Commander Coar'saliz rolled onto his feet, crouching among the debris to search for the cane. Kael picked himself up as well, favouring his injured leg. Luckily, the Commander had thrown Kael towards King Henedral's blade. Holding the sword with both hands, he charged at the Commander.

Kael's sword clashed against the Commander's. They held for a moment, glaring at each other, until they simultaneously broke off. Kael's ability to slow time was infallible, but with his hurt leg, he couldn't use it to his full potential. Without the cane in his grasp, Commander Coar'saliz was considerably slower as well. As such, the battle moved considerably slow, but the blows they exchanged were powerful. More than once, Kael's arms shuddered as if they were liable to give up on him at any moment. With the amount of blood he had lost already, he was surprised he didn't collapse.

They were both panting after a matter of minutes. They locked blades again and held like that for a long time, as if a silent agreement had been made to let them catch their breath. The Commander glanced sideways and did a double take, eyes going wide. When he looked back to Kael, he wore an expression of desperation. Kael didn't have to see what the Commander had espied. It was clearly the cane.

At once, they both made a dash towards the cane. The Commander reached it first. Sliding feet-first, Commander Coar'saliz snatched it up and popped back upright as to face Kael. Undeterred, Kael dove at the man's feet, tripping the man with his body. The Commander jolted forwards, smacking his face against the hard ground.

Kael was the first to rise. He needed to kill him before he had a chance to use the cane! He tried to stab the Commander through the back, but he rolled out of the way of Kael's sword. Before Kael had another chance, he twirled the cane and uttered an incantation. A pulse emanated from Commander Coar'saliz's body, sending Kael reeling.

The Commander stood upright, holding the cane slightly out in front of him. He wiped his nose with his forearm and then spat out blood. From the way his nose stuck out at an angle, Kael was guessing it was broken.

"A thousand curses to you, Rundown," he hissed. He raised the cane and pointed it at Kael. Kael was standing where the bell had once been—right in the middle of the bell tower. There was no cover. "Enough of this." Another pulse from the cane drew Kael back several feet. With one more, Kael was dangerously close to the edge. "You may have skill with a sword and resistance to magic, but gravity rules us all."

"You coward!" Kael screamed. "Fight me! No magic, no tricks! You and me, sword against sword. You honourless cretin!"

Commander Coar'saliz sneered. "Spare me your honour."

Kael glanced behind himself. There had been a wall there before Silverstain had come crashing through. Now only a knee-high pile of bricks remained, and beyond that, what would surely be a fatal drop onto the roof of the monastery. The Commander made a gesture and

Kael winced, ready for the next deadly pulse. Before it came, a *crash* stopped the Commander.

A pile of debris to the left of Kael exploded outwards, releasing the Kellthuzard. It landed on all fours and shook itself, scatting splinters. The Commander's detestable smirk intensified. "You want honour, Rundown? To die by your king's hand will be a grand death. Go, my Kellthuzard, slay him!"

Kael straightened his back. There was nothing else he could do. As the Kellthuzard turned its sinister muzzle towards him, he could feel the energy drain from his body. He had done it. He had survived the first encounter from Shatterbreath. He had discovered King Morrindale's plot. He had rallied together an army powerful enough to defend against the BlackHound Empire's invasion. He had succeeded. Vallenfend was safe. That had been his only goal for so long. Now that it was accomplished, he no longer feared death.

It would be a release.

Kael closed his eyes, waiting for the inevitable. *What will death feel like?* After being exposed to it for so long, he had become numb to death. Would he be numb to this too?

One slow breath. Two slow breaths. Nothing. Eyes still closed, he frowned. *Why hasn't it attacked yet?*

"What are you doing?" Kael heard the Commander yell. "Him, you awful creature, attack *him!*"

Kael opened his eyes, curious.

The Kellthuzard was attacking Commander Coar'saliz! The Commander kept it at bay with his cane, shooting a beam at the demon which created layers of ice across the Kellthuzard's chest and face. The Kellthuzard thrashed in the beam, shattering the ice as soon as it was created.

"Get him, Daddy!" That was Janus's voice! She was peering out of the debris where the Kellthuzard had erupted from, waving her fist through the air.

Daddy?

"Janus?" Kael shouted.

"Kael! You're alright! Thank the gods!"

An explosion turned Kael's attention back to the Commander and the Kellthuzard. Half the demon's muzzle was missing, exposing the gleaming white of its tapered skull. Its right side must have taken the brunt of the attack for its front limb was mangled and the muscle along that side was stripped away, leaving yet more bone exposed.

Despite the damage, it continued to attack the Commander without relent. Whatever wounds Commander Coar'saliz inflicted trying to fend it off would only heal seconds later.

"You idiots!" Commander Coar'saliz hollered. "What have you done to my demon?!"

Truthfully, Kael had no idea.

Then, something seemed to snap within the Commander. He threw his sword to the side and held the cane with both hands. The air around him went all wavy, as if it was a hot summer day. Darkness pooled at his feet the same way it had when he summoned the Kellthuzard with begin with.

The demon leapt at him, but a tendril of darkness lanced out and swatted it away. Commander Coar'saliz let out a feral scream. The very foundation of the bell tower shook and cracks weaved their way across the surface of the floor. The tendrils of darkness spread across and the tower, weaving into the cracks and spreading them wider. Lightning crackled around the Commander and anything flammable near him was instantly set ablaze.

"He's going to take down the tower!" Kael exclaimed. The tower groaned in reply. It was dangerously close to collapsing. A crack split open between Kael's feet, which was quickly filled with darkness and wrenched even further open.

"What do we do?" Janus cried. Kael looked to her, at a loss. He gasped when he saw what she was holding. *Vintrave.* Kael's mind began to race. Silverstain had blessed Kael with his magic—he had also fixed the sword. If Kael's body was resistant to the Commander's magic, wouldn't *Vintrave* be as well?

"Janus, my sword! Pass it to me!"

She nodded and flung the blade towards him. It landed amid the debris several metres away. Kael ran as fast as he could to it, ignoring the searing pain in his leg. Halfway to *Vintrave,* the area before him split in two. Kael couldn't stop in time, so he leapt across. There was no chance he was going to make it. The gap was too far.

A scream worked its way up Kael's throat, but before it could escape his lips, he was jostled by something. He gasped as he realized the Kellthuzard had caught him, mid-air. They twisted so that it landed on its back on the either side of the gap with Kael was nestled in its grasp. Having something save him that had been trying to kill him moments earlier was not an entirely comforting experience. Still, Kael was grateful towards the creature.

He stumbled out of its paws, uttering awkward thanks. It didn't acknowledge him, but instead focussed on Commander Coar'saliz. Perhaps it *was* still King Morrindale after all. It had saved him, but it clearly didn't like him. Janus must have reached her father through its sinewy hide.

Kael picked up *Vintrave*. "Basal," he muttered to the Kellthuzard. It trained a milky eye on him. "Right behind, okay? You have one chance: take it."

It bared its teeth. Kael could only hope it understood what he was asking.

Kael took a deep breath, sizing up Commander Coar'saliz. The man's features were barely visible through the darkness, like the silhouette of a person in fog. *Now or never,* Kael thought. He charged at Commander Coar'saliz, keeping Vintrave down low.

Kael stumbled on the shifting ground, but kept his momentum. Despite the magical attacks that were thrown at him, he charged straight towards the Commander. He was aiming for one thing.

Jumping up, Kael raised *Vintrave* high above his head. With all his strength, he brought it down—straight at the cane in the Commander's grip.

The sword cut the cane in half.

The magic ceased. Stunned, Commander Coar'saliz took a couple steps back, gawking at the two halves on his now-worthless cane. Kael remained where he was, crouching and clutching his injured leg. Not three seconds later, the Kellthuzard soared over Kael.

Kael witnessed as the Kellthuzard slammed into Commander Coar'saliz, throwing them both over the edge of the bell tower.

"Daddy, no!" Janus screamed.

Kael ran over to the edge and peered down. Commander Coar'saliz hit the ground in front of the monastery inaudibly. With its master dead, the Kellthuzard turned to stone. It shattered to pieces the moment it struck the monastery's plaza.

Janus fell to her knees at the towers edge, sobbing. "Daddy!" she wailed.

Kael hesitated. He knelt beside her and wrapped an arm around her. She cried into his shoulder and he held her right. King Morrindale had done the right thing in the end. Did that reconcile the lengths of his greed? What would be the terms of his fate? Only the heavens knew now.

The tower shuddered. Kael and Janus jumped to their feet, exchanging frightened expressions. "Kael?" she whimpered.

He pulled her close. "There's nothing we can do now."

She was reluctant at first, but as she gazed into his eyes, her expression changed. She closed her lips tight and set her brow, giving him a stern yet accepting look. "We did it."

A sense of peace welled in Kael's chest. "We did."

She drew close to him. He drew close to her.

"I have you, humans!"

Kael flinched. Laura blushed and turned away. Silverstain hovered just near them. Kael hadn't even noticed him approach.

The dragon swooped over the top of the tower, picking Laura and Kael up with his paws. As they soared away, Kael watched the bell tower collapse. It fell backwards onto the monastery, caving in the roof.

Then the adrenaline ran its course. Kael blacked out.

Chapter 32

Kael was awoken by growling. He considered falling back asleep again—and would have—he he hadn't realized it was Shatterbreath who was growling.

"Let me see him, you silly morsels. I'll lick off all your faces if you don't!"

"Please, Shatterbreath..."

"Quiet Silverstain. Quiet...you. Who are you? His doctor?" She huffed. "I don't believe you."

Kael heard Cressida let out an exasperated sigh. "Just listen to me. He needs his rest. Please don't..."

"He's rested long enough. Now where is he?"

Things *clanged* nearby. Kael opened his eyes meekly. He was inside a large green tent, lying in a soft bed covered with thick blankets. He didn't know what ached more, his head or his leg. Outside, he could see the silhouettes of many people and two dragons. The larger shape moved about, tail thrashing, searching the camp.

"I'm here, Shatterbreath," Kael called out.

She perked up. "Kael? Kael?" Her snuffling ruffled the cloth of the tent. "Aha! You really thought you could hide him from a dragon?" To their protest, she stuck her head in the tent's door. Her face absolutely lit up when she spotted him.

"Hey, Shatterbreath." Kael smiled.

"Tiny!" She stretched her neck out until her shoulders nudged the edge of the tent. "Are...you...okay?" She paused between words to sniff him head to toe. Her ashy exhalations washed over him in waves, warming his body.

"I'm fine, I'm fine."

"Doctor, is he fine?"

Cressida ducked under Shatterbreath's neck. "He should be." She winked at him, placing a hand on her waist and cocking her hips. "Like I was *trying* to say, the demon's teeth reached down to the bone. He has permanent muscle damage and he'll probably spend the rest of his life with a limp—but at this point, I'm pretty sure he'll survive. How are you, Kael?"

"Groggy," Kael replied. "Glad to know I'll have a limp forever; thank you for that bit of information, Cressida."

She shrugged. "We *were* considering amputation. Would you prefer that?"

Shatterbreath squawked. "What?!" She lifted her head, tearing the ceiling of the tent in away to reveal the blue sky.

Cressida frowned. "While you're awake, Kael, there are some people who'd like to see you. Are you up to it?"

Kael pushed himself up. His leg throbbed, but his elation helped to mask the pain. "Of course!"

Cressida whistled. Moments later, Korjan, Helena, Mrs. Stockwin, Bunda, Laura and Janus and Faerd entered. Then the Allegiance leaders, Kings Respu and Goar. Lastly came Tomn, closely followed by Sal'braan.

After a round of his friends asking how he was, Kael got to the main question. "What happened to the BlackHound Empire?"

"We won," King Goar announced. He held up a flagon, flared his eyebrows and took a swig.

"Farthu arrived as an ally," Korjan explained. "They came in from the back while our forces surrounded the BlackHound army from the front—almost like the first day of the war."

"They were doomed," Sal'braan continued, "and they knew it. Once Commander Coar'saliz was killed, they surrendered. Their losses were still great. Less than a thousand survived."

"What will you do with the survivors?"

"We decided to let them return to the Homeland," Sal'braan replied. "Since they deconstructed their own ships to make weapons of war, Farthu is lending them several vessels. Farthu forces are overseeing their exodus as we speak."

Kael pondered for a moment. "Are you sure that's a wise idea? Won't that be detrimental to your resistance back home, Sal'braan?"

"You've defeated their invasion force, Rundown." Sal'braan's voice quavered. "The Resistance will only grow from this."

"We figure it be better ter show some mercy," Tomn said. "Ter show we're stronger then thems. It was my idear."

Kael grinned. He didn't know if it was really Tomn's idea or not, but he liked the concept all the same.

"Alright," Shatterbreath announced abruptly, "you've all gawked at him long enough. I want to be with him alone."

Laura put up a hand. "But..."

Shatterbreath huffed, sending a wave of thick black smoke over Laura and those unfortunate enough to be standing near her. Kael's friends proceeded to exit the tent, coughing as they did.

When they were all gone, she nuzzled him with her snout, bringing the front half of her body over the tent's wall. "I was worried about you, Tiny. Such a fragile thing you are."

Kael chuckled. "You don't have to worry anymore. It's all over now. We can relax."

Silverstain's finned blue head appeared over the edge of the ripped ceiling. "What will you do two now?" he asked.

"I said I wanted to be alone with Kael," Shatterbreath growled. Silverstain frowned and began to turn away. "I heard Silverstain saved your life, Tiny," Shatterbreath commented. Silverstain stopped.

"More than once, actually."

"I guess there isn't any harm if you stay then," Shatterbreath mused. The blue dragon sat down on his haunches near Shatterbreath—close enough that when she wasn't paying attention, he could sniff her mischievously; far enough that she didn't notice.

"What will you two do?" the blue dragon asked again.

Shatterbreath regarded Kael. "What indeed?"

Kael couldn't come up with an answer. Now that the war was over, he had no drive, no purpose. It had been his sole focus for so long, he almost felt lost without the burning desire to protect his city. It was almost disconcerting. He wanted to be with Shatterbreath, but besides that, he didn't have any other plans.

"I wouldn't mind exploring," Kael said with a shrug. "Most of this continent is unexplored. Who knows what could be out there. If that's alright with you, Shatterbreath."

339

She hummed louder. "That sounds like an excellent idea, Tiny."

"Whatever the future hides for you," Silverstain said tentatively, "I hope your plans may include me someday, Elder."

"You?" Shatterbreath scoffed. "Silly hatchling, you lied to me and fought *against* me—more than once. I should banish you to Icecrow Island and let the detestable creatures devour you. I doubt they would though, seeing as you flew alongside them during the war."

"Shatterbreath..."

"Silverstain." Her scales bristled and they stared each other down for an intense moment. Silverstain looked away first, bowing his head.

Kael beckoned Shatterbreath closer. She leaned in, wearing a scowl across her body. "He has feelings for you," Kael whispered, "can't you see that? He mentioned before he was hoping to have a family with you."

Shatterbreath clenched her jaws and tucked her wings in tighter; the dragon equivalent to blushing. "So?" she countered.

"He's your own kind, you silly lizard." He patted her snout. "Can't you at least give him a second chance?"

Shatterbreath sighed and craned her neck to consider Silverstain. He raised his snout hopefully. "Alright," she purred, "I'll take your offer into...*consideration*." She rubbed the end of her tail against his chin and his scales shivered. When she pulled her tail away, he stretched out, as if trying to keep it there. This amused her and she rumbled, sending deep vibrations through the ground.

Three days later Kael stood on the western wall of Vallenfend, overlooking the Allegiance army. He leaned heavily on a cane, hand-crafted by Korjan, because his leg could no longer support his full weight. Shatterbreath sat beside him, surveying the crowd.

Kael took a deep breath. He had feared this moment, but now that he was actually standing over the crowd, his heart was strangely calm. Everything was right in the world, for that one moment; there wasn't any reason to be anxious.

A few words are all we need, King Respu had told Kael, *just tell the soldiers they did an excellent job. You brought us together, Kael. It is only appropriate you have the final say in all this. Make it last.*

How could he sum up how truly grateful he was? How could he sum up the significance of what those men had accomplished? As he scanned the crowd, thunderous in their applause, tears clouded his vision. When he raised his hand, they all went silent.

It was eerie. Every eye was trained on him. Every face was pointed in his direction—those few from Vallenfend, those from Rystville, Arnoth, Fallenfeld, Nestoff and a great number from Farthu—eagerly waiting to hear what he had to say.

"We came..." Kael stopped at once, realizing his voice wasn't near loud enough. He turned to Shatterbreath. "Do you think..?"

She nudged him and Kael felt a flow of energy. The next time he spoke, his voice was greatly amplified. Shatterbreath must have lent him the strength of her own voice. "We came here as strangers. To some, as enemies. Now, we stand united as the victors. The BlackHound Empire has crushed—not by the strength of one, but by all!"

The crowd cheered wildly. Kael waved his hands and they fell silent, allowing him to continue.

"Thanks to your valiant efforts, we have secured a future for our people. Our ancestors will look back on this day with respect. And now at last, our sons and our daughters may live in peace!"

There was another round of cheering, which Kael had to wave down again. When he spoke again, his voice wavered.

"We have...lost many." The silence was choking. Only the wind stirred. "But we have gained a great power. The very thing the BlackHound Empire could not destroy. Friendship. The bonds we've created are stronger than any blade, sturdier than any shield. Our ties together will not be forgotten. The Allegiance will stand as a beacon of hope. Of freedom." Kael raised his sword and yelled triumphantly, "Freedom!"

"Freedom!" the crowd roared. Kael was overwhelmed by their cheering. The soldiers banged their swords against their shields and stomped their feet. They yelled and cried with one accord. Kael saw

341

many of them crying and hugging the person next to them. It didn't matter where they were from or how they were different, they were all united.

Shatterbreath took back her voice and beat her wings, lifting up onto her hind legs. She roared as loud as she could but for the first time ever, her voice was drowned out by the cheering of the crowd. In a greater moment of euphoria, the sun burst through the gray clouds, washing over the plains in great golden waves.

Kael found the faces of his friends down below. They stopped their dancing and shouting long enough to give him a salute. Those near them noticed and saluted as well. The gestured flowed through the crowd until every man was making his own salute towards Kael and Shatterbreath. Moments later, they broke out cheering again.

Shatterbreath twitched beside Kael and craned her neck down to his level. "Look, Kael," she said, "they cheer for you."

Kael shook his head and shuffled closer to her. "No, Shatterbreath. They cheer for us." He met her gaze and drank in the warmth of her body close to his. "They cheer for us," he repeated.

He felt her hum. Content to remain silent, Kael and Shatterbreath turned back to face the crowd. Kael's spirits had never been higher. *We've done it,* he kept repeating in his mind.

We've done it.

The next few days were tiring. With most of Vallenfend in shambles, the Allegiance had rallied together to help rebuild as much as they could until winter. Men and women alike worked day in and day out to snuff out any remaining fires and fix any patches in what buildings could be salvaged. The bodies were collected, stripped and then burned in the western field. The ashes plumed high into air before dispersed by the wind. Kael spent nearly a day by the fire that burned the bodies, unable to tear himself away. Perhaps there was something symbolic to him seeing the remnants of the BlackHound Empire turned into smouldering embers. Perhaps the fire represented a drastic change in his life—the end of his turmoil and suffering. Either way, only Shatterbreath convinced him to leave the fire, sweeping him up in her wing. Nobody expected anything more from him. He had done his part, time and time again.

By the second day—even with the help of two dragons—it became quite clear that fixing Vallenfend up to its former glory would take months, even years. With what was left of Vallenfend's population diminished from the war, Tomn had proposed the idea that the bandits simply move in. The idea was not accepted at first, but then Tomn made the arrangement of paying for Vallenfend's reconstruction with the treasure Kael had promised to the bandits. In turn, several hundreds of Allegiance soldiers offered to lend their services for wages.

There were still many kinks to straighten in the plan, but Kael was optimistic.

During the repairs, Kael heard several reports of a murderer lurking around Vallenfend. It seemed the person would slit soldiers' throats as they slept. Kael had been relieved to hear the thief had been caught before he had managed to kill more than four men. He had been even more relieved to discover the same person was Rooster.

The body brought up questions Kael demanded to be answered. Namely, why Farthu had charged the young man to follow Kael. He had demanded a meeting with Farthu's generals at once. To his surprise though, none of them recognized Rooster's body—not even the Council's main representative.

"I'm sorry, Rundown," the representative had said with a shrug. "But the Council never ordered anybody to accompany you on your journeys—especially not *this* person. I know every one of the Council's messengers and representatives. *He* is definitely not one of them. He's a hard one to forget."

That declaration only left one conclusion: Rooster had been a BlackHound spy. From the very beginning. It was difficult to digest that; but knowing the influence of the BlackHound Empire, it was certainly feasible. But as upset Kael was about the revelation, he was nowhere as irate as Shatterbreath. For two whole days she nudged him constantly, giving him looks that said *I told you so.*

It was actually Faerd who suggested to the Allegiance leaders that for all the hard work of the soldiers, both in battle and in the cleanup, they had not truly celebrated their epic victory. The very same day, the debris in training grounds was cleared to give room for the greatest celebration Vallenfend had ever seen.

For hours on end, men and women danced to the beat of drums, flutes, harps and horns. The music wasn't especially grand, but it didn't matter. With the amount of wine, mead and ale that was passed around, *anything* would have sounded great. Kael walked around, flustered by the whole event. Everywhere he went, people were shouting and dancing and slapping him on the back. Faces red with alcohol smiled at him and women he didn't even know jumped out of the crowds to kiss him.

He wasn't complaining though.

More than enough drink was offered to him, but in the end, Kael only ended up drinking a single goblet. After all he had done, it didn't seem right to drink. Alcohol dulled the senses and fogged the mind. He couldn't even stand the thought of that—perhaps the warrior inside him refused to let go.

The celebration lasted hours. Even when the sun crept under the tops of the walls, it continued, unhindered. Kael tried to keep near Laura and Faerd as they danced, but also close to Shatterbreath as well. The dragon sat on a collapsed section of the wall, patiently watching the excited throng with a passive expression. Someone had convinced her to drink some ale at some point. She must have thought the same as Kael, for she only drank one goblet and promptly spat it back out. Those who gave it to her howled in laughter. To Kael's surprise, her only reaction was an annoyed raise of her brow.

Keeping close to her meant losing his friends several times in the crowd. This didn't bother Kael. Laura and Faerd were more interested in each either than they were with him. Several times, they embraced each other, pressing their lips so tight together it almost looked as though they were trying to suffocate each other. They did this so long at one time, Kael thought one of them had succeeded.

Laura and Faerd weren't the only ones displaying their affection towards each other. Kael spotted Korjan and Helena embracing one another many times. Once, he even spotted them leaving the training grounds, holding hands.

It wasn't until Silverstain approached to lie down near Shatterbreath did a sense of loneliness overwhelm Kael. Silverstain sidled closer to Shatterbreath. In turn, and to both Kael and Silverstain's surprise, she leaned against him.

Kael rested against a wall, feeling lonelier than he had ever been. He hated himself for it. *This is your time of celebration,* he scolded himself, *why aren't you enjoying it?* He considered visiting the table where the wine was held. They said alcohol was the only thing that could cure loneliness...

Kael was about to get up when a hand touched his shoulder. He craned his neck to see Janus standing beside him, smiling down at him. For the first time, with the moon hanging angelically behind her, she looked truly beautiful.

"May I?" she asked politely.

Wordlessly, Kael nodded. Careful with her dress, she sat down beside him. Kael felt his feelings of forlorn drift away. Just having her there so close to him was comforting. He never wanted her to leave.

Somehow, their hands found each other. Despite how numb Kael's behind got, they remained there for hours. Kael never wanted the celebration to end.

Kael and Shatterbreath left Vallenfend the very next day. They had to return King Henedral's sword to its rightful owner after all. Kael had the strange feeling, however, that they wouldn't be returning to Vallenfend any time soon.

Epilogue

Kael unfolded his map out on a flat boulder and smoothed out the wrinkles with his forearm. He twisted a quill in his hands for several seconds. He glanced up. He was standing on a beach, with the finest sand he had even seen. It was more like dark flower than anything else. It was hard for him to believe the same sand stretched for miles inland before slowly drifting into dense jungles. The meeting of the land and the sea was a delicate one along this coast, as if the two were simply lying atop each other; the ocean wasn't deeper than three feet for at least a mile.

Shatterbreath snorted, creating two plumes of sand that floated slowly at Kael. The sand wrapped around him, sticking to his tunic and working its way under his clothing. When he moved, he could feel the fine graduals chaffing against his skin.

"Oh, you silly lizard," he scoffed, "now it's all over me!"

She huffed, sending another plume of sand over him. "Poor hatchling," she purred. She flipped onto her back to roll in the sand.

"It's going to get all in your scales you know," Kael commented.

"And?"

"Never mind. Look, we've finished the map." Kael took his quill and drew a line on the far right of his map. They had surveyed the coast for a long time before coming down to land; it was impossible to draw while flying on Shatterbreath's back.

They hadn't stayed long in Vallenfend. Something forced Kael away. A strange restlessness in his stomach he couldn't ignore. After so much stress and adventure, he needed to do something more. So he and Shatterbreath had taken on the huge challenge of mapping the land—which until then was largely unexplored.

"Are you sure? That can't be our entire continent."

Kael flattened the map again. Sand was stuck to it as well now. "It certainly is. Look close, here's the Hook and the Bait..."

"Where you were nearly crushed in an avalanche."

Kael retorted, "Only because you roared! I told you to stay quiet."

She snorted out smoke. "Quiet? Like *you* were in Brunburn."

"That wasn't my fault."

"You go on believing that."

"No, really. That was *your* fault again!" He threw a handful of sand at her. "You ate the farmers' sheep. You don't even like sheep!"

She curled her lips. "I hate sheep. Some dragons like them you know. I hate them."

Kael only shook his head and laughed. Shatterbreath could win every argument somehow, even if she *agreed* with whatever Kael came up with.

Shatterbreath rolled onto her belly and took a deep breath, gazing out to sea.

"What do you think lies out there?" Kael asked. "Do you think the world ends? Or would we eventually run into the BlackHound Empire's homeland?"

"The BlackHound Empire," Shatterbreath repeated thoughtfully. "I had almost forgotten..." She craned her neck to nuzzle him. "How long has it been?"

"Three years." Upon uttering those words, memories came flooding back into Kael's mind. Memories of death, destruction and despair. A time of constant worries and endless struggling. Reflecting on the time he and Shatterbreath had shared together since then, it was hard to believe they had even gone through such an ordeal.

It was also hard to believe how he had changed since then. He was now a man by all standards, with stubble lining his chin and shaggy hair he hadn't found time to cut. Though his lifestyle was calmer than it was before, he was still firm with muscle. Cressida was right when she had said Kael would walk with a limp for the rest of his life, but not once did he let that interfere with his adventures. He was just as able-bodied as any other man—he wasn't afraid to fight anybody who said otherwise. In fact, he enjoyed duelling; it was one of the few reasons he would stop by a city. During their travels, Kael had only lost two duels. One of them was against King Goar's champion.

347

Shatterbreath had changed as well. Her bones had mended seamlessly though her body had a fair amount of scars left over from the BlackHound War. The tip of her tail was still missing but Korjan had fashioned a silver cap for it before they had departed—with the words *Noble, Strong and Proud* written on its surface in an elegant manner. She never admitted it, but Kael knew she adored it. The most noticeable change was her scales. Each one shone like a pool of water after rainfall, though quite clear enough to make out a reflection. Sometimes the sun hit her scales at a certain angle and they would send fractures of light splaying in all directions. It was then Kael joked she was at her best.

"So," Shatterbreath ventured, "what do we do now?"

Kael folded the map back up and carefully slipped it into his pack. He strode over and sat against Shatterbreath's foreleg to enjoy the view of the clear ocean. "I suppose we go back home. I wonder how much has changed. I wonder if Vallenfend has been all fixed up."

Shatterbreath flared her wings and roared. The roar echoed across the land until it was nothing but a faint memory. "We'll know soon enough." They sat there for several moments, enjoying each others' company. "Kael..."

"Yes, Shatterbreath?"

She hesitated. "I never...formally thanked you."

Kael frowned and looked up at her. "For what? I have so many reasons to thank you. Sparing me, assisting me on bringing together the Allegiance, fighting in a *human* war..." He chuckled. "And saving my life more times than I can count."

"No, you've done for me something far greater than any of that."

"Saving my life is pretty important," Kael chuckled.

Shatterbreath's scales bristled. "I'm being serious, Kael." Kael pursed his lips. "No matter who won the BlackHound War—them or us—there would still be humans on the earth. Do you understand? What I'm thanking you for is...saving my species."

Kael pushed his hands into the sand, pondering her words. "I don't follow."

"You set a new name for dragons, Kael," she explained. "Before I met you, I was considered nothing more than a savage, mindless beast. But then your humans began to see me differently—because of you. They believed in you, Kael. They trusted me because *you* trusted me." She hummed. "I was even considered a *hero* after the war. Image...a dragon being a *hero* to the humans. Never have humans and dragons coincided together so well. Even Silverstain chose to stay behind until Vallenfend was fully repaired."

"I don't think all of that was because of me," Kael countered.

"Yes, it is. You've set a new name for dragons, Kael. You've made it known that we are merely *misunderstood*—that we are trustworthy."

"If not stubborn," Kael added. She scowled at him.

"I will forever be in your debt, Kael Rundown."

Kael smiled and rubbed her scales. "Stay by my side, and that is payment enough."

She hummed and nuzzled him lovingly. "I can afford that."

Kael stood up and drank in as much of the view as he could to try to lock it into his memory. Then, he climbed up Shatterbreath's shoulder to nestle in his spot between her shoulders.

He pointed to the northwest—their continent was not as horizontal as they once thought—and declared, "Let's go back home."

"Aye, Tiny," Shatterbreath purred in reply.

With four strong wing beats, they were well on their way.

As they travelled, Kael could only wonder...

What adventures waited in Vallenfend?

The End.